PRAISE FOR STRATAGEM

"With *Stratagem*, Caroll has created a tightly twisted plot that will keep the reader guessing from the first chapter. Creative and unique, the book is a winner that will linger with readers."
—Cara Putman, award-winning author of *Delayed Justice* from the Hidden Justice series

"Follow the clues to find the murderer, but you may change your mind before the stunning end."
—Richard L. Mabry, MD, bestselling, award-winning author of medical mysteries with heart

"There's no escaping *Stratagem* once you enter its deadly game! Caroll pens a riveting novel of intrigue and danger that leaves the reader anxious for justice—and escape! This book doesn't disappoint!"
—Ronie Kendig, author of the award-winning, bestselling Tox Files series

"*Stratagem* by Robin Caroll is high-stakes suspense on steroids. The fine writing and atmospheric setting make this outstanding novel a standout. Highly recommended!"
—Colleen Coble, *USA Today* bestselling author of the Hope Beach series and the Lavender Tides series

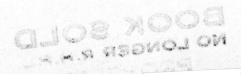

STRATAGEM

ROBIN CAROLL

SHILOH RUN  PRESS

An Imprint of Barbour Publishing, Inc.

Print ISBN 978-1-68322-730-4

eBook Editions:
Adobe Digital Edition (.epub) 978-1-68322-959-9
Kindle and MobiPocket Edition (.prc) 978-1-68322-962-9

Cover Design: Faceout Studio, www.faceoutstudio.com

Published by Shiloh Run Press, an imprint of Barbour Publishing, Inc., 1810 Barbour Drive, Uhrichsville, Ohio 44683, www.shilohrunpress.com

Our mission is to inspire the world with the life-changing message of the Bible.

 Member of the
Evangelical Christian
Publishers Association

Printed in the United States of America.

DEDICATION

For Lisa
My brother blessed us all when he brought you into the family.
Thank you for all your love, support, and encouragement.

ACKNOWLEDGMENTS

I never cease to be amazed by the multitude of talented, hardworking people it takes to produce a book. I'm so grateful to the entire team at Barbour Publishing, but especially Annie Tipton, Jessie Fioritto, Shalyn Sattler, and Liesl Davenport. From acquisitions to contracting to editing to cover design to marketing, this team is awesome, and I'm grateful to work with them.

As always, I'm extremely grateful to my agent, Steve Laube. You, sir, are the best sounding board and tether to reality I could ever ask for. Thank you!

Huge thanks to my beta readers, who have the best eyes to catch inconsistencies and plot problems. I don't know what I'd do without you: Lisa Burroughs, Tracey Justice, and Heather Tipton.

Every writer needs a circle of fellow writers who "get" to celebrate with you, and also hold you up when needed. I'm eternally grateful to my circle: Colleen Coble, Pam Hillman, Ronie Kendig, Dineen Miller, Cara Putman, Cynthia Ruchti, Cheryl Wyatt, and Becky Yauger.

I so appreciate the unwavering love and support of my extended family in my writing endeavors. My heartfelt thanks to Mom, my precious grands—Benton and Zayden, Bubba and Lisa, Brandon and Katie, Rachel and Thomas, Justin and Baby G, Robyn, Rebecca, and Rion.

Enormous love and thanks to the amazing people I share a home with: Casey, Remington, and Isabella. You three have no idea how much it means to have your support, acceptance, and willingness to jump in and help. I can't imagine writing without y'all. I love each of you to the moon and back!

All glory and praise to my Lord and Savior, Jesus Christ. I can do *all* things through *You*, who gives me strength.

PROLOGUE

"According to your estimation, she has eight minutes to figure out she can't open the door unless her employee uses the key he got in the last room." Pam leaned back in the chair and tilted her head toward the live feed. Her brightly dyed hair shimmered with the movement.

The woman on the screen stumbled around in the room. Her breathing came out labored—harsh in contrast to her platinum-blond hair that caught the dim light. She ran to the only visible exit and turned the knob. Her body slumped against the locked door.

"They'll get it." Grayson was rarely off by more than a few minutes at most. His job was to study the financial, medical, background, and psychological reports on each of the game participants to find their weaknesses and strengths, then use it all against them. To break them to the point where they couldn't escape the game—win—unless they worked as a team. That was the whole purpose of the games, and why they signed waivers.

"I think you read her wrong." Pam tapped the monitor and took a sip of her white mocha. "I bet they won't escape according to your time frame."

Grayson grinned at his collaborator. "Wouldn't be the first time I misjudged." He stared at the blond woman, now on her feet again, running her hands over the walls. "But I don't think that's the case with this one."

"Twenty bucks says you're wrong." Pam dug a bill out of the back pocket of her jeans and slapped it on the long desk they shared.

He shook his head. "Why must you bet on every single game we run?"

"Adds to the excitement." Grinning, she shrugged. "Are you going to put your money where your calculations are, hotshot?"

"Of course." He laid a twenty on top of Pam's and stared at the woman on the monitor.

"Six minutes."

The blond woman's hands fisted at her side. Grayson could almost feel her frustration as he gave the computer command that opened the sliding hidden passageway. The woman's employee all but fell into the room. The blond rushed to him.

Grayson smiled as the woman helped the man stand. Just as he'd predicted, her nurturing instincts kicked in. He pressed another button, and a recording of a child crying out for her mother filled the room. One of the woman's greatest fears was being unable to protect her child.

The woman pounded on the door. Her employee eased in front of her and rammed his shoulder against the door. His protective instinct came right on time, as Grayson had estimated.

"Four minutes." Pam leaned forward, closer to the monitor.

It might be close.

The woman sobbed, shoulders shaking as she hung her head.

"She's freaking." Pam rubbed her hands together and pushed the button to increase the volume on the child's wails.

The woman slumped against the wall beside the door—defeated.

"That's almost cheating." Grayson leaned forward, his nose nearly pressing against the monitor.

This was the most intense part of the game, the flipping of personalities. The employee saving the employer served a twofold purpose: the employee built confidence in himself as a vital part of the company team, and the employer learned that the company can accomplish nothing without the input and dedication of its workers.

The woman shook herself and turned to beat on the door, almost in hysterics. She twisted the knob, rattling the lock.

"One minute." Pam rubbed her hands together.

Come on, man. Figure it out. Grayson locked his jaw, concentrating on the monitor.

"Thirty seconds."

The more frantically she turned the knob, the louder the lock rattled. The man hesitated in his ramming.

That's right. The key. It's in your pocket.

"Twenty."

Slowly, the man pulled the key from his jacket pocket and thrust it at his boss.

"No!" Pam glanced at the timer. "Ten seconds."

The woman turned the knob, and she and the man both slipped through the door.

Grayson stared at the timer. "With four seconds to spare." He grabbed both twenties.

Pam shook her head but grinned. "You make me sick, you know that, right?"

He waggled his eyebrows. "When are you going to learn not to bet against me?" Grayson stood as the monitor flipped to the "recovery room" where the man and woman were taking bottles of water from Grayson's congenial business partner, Colton York.

Pam stood as well. "One of these days, Grayson Thibodeaux, you're going to lose."

Some days, it felt like he'd already lost all that he'd held dearest, but he shook his head at his assistant anyway. "I think I'm gonna call it a day."

"Sure, take the money and run." Pam laughed as she shut down the monitors.

"See you tomorrow." Grayson headed down the hall to his office, ready to grab his laptop and head home.

"As usual, my timing is perfect."

Every hair on the back of Grayson's neck stood at attention. No mistaking that voice. He turned. "Hello, Anna Belle."

"Don't 'hello' me." She marched around the receptionist, who threw Grayson an apologetic look. "Did you think I wouldn't find out?"

He sighed. No use trying to shut up his ex-wife or even get her to speak with him privately. Nothing would work until she had her say. He knew. All too well. "Find out what, Anna Belle?"

"About your dad's duck hunting gig in Plaquemines Parish. You failed to mention that in our divorce, and it's worth over one point five million dollars. I was entitled to half that amount in the settlement."

"My father didn't own that. It's a hunting lease. I was accepted as a legacy." He caught a flash of Pam's lavender-pink hair from the corner of his eye. Humiliation would come later.

"Which is still worth a very healthy amount of money and was passed down to you. You didn't declare it, Grayson."

"But I can't sell the land because I don't own it. That's why it wasn't addressed in the divorce settlement, Anna Belle. It's not something I own."

"I'm entitled to half what the lease is worth." She popped her hands on her hips and tightened her lips into a firm line.

At one time, that move would have made him reverse his stance. That was then, this was now. "I don't care what you think you're entitled to, Anna Belle. I suggest you call your lawyer if you have a problem with the divorce settlement because I really don't—"

Her slap brought a stinging to his eyes. He grabbed her wrist. Held it. "How dare you, Anna Belle? To come to my job and assault me?" Grayson ground his teeth so hard it was a wonder he didn't crack a couple.

Pam was beside him in a flash, her hand on his forearm. "Don't bother, Grayson. She isn't worth it."

He let go of his grip on Anna Belle with a jerk.

"You should leave. Now." Pam's voice shook with the hatred she felt for Anna Belle.

"This isn't over, Grayson." Anna Belle spun away from him, her long, blond hair flung over her shoulder as she marched toward the front door, her spike heels tapping angrily against the cool tiles.

"Everything okay out here?" Colton stood in the hallway, his embarrassed-for-someone-else look planted firmly on his face.

"We're fine. Just leaving for the day." Pam took Grayson's arm and turned him toward the back door.

The mortification had already wormed its way into Grayson's chest. No telling how many people just saw the exchange. Pam, Colton, Jackie the receptionist, and possibly clients. He didn't need his assistant or his business partner to take up for him with his ex-wife. Every time he saw Anna Belle, the pang of her betrayal nearly strangled him. He didn't want to hate her, prayed daily that his heart would be softened to forgive her, but she still stopped him cold.

He cleared his throat. "I need my laptop."

"Not tonight, boss. Take the night off. Read a book, watch a game, do whatever you need to do to unwind. You've earned it." Pam had that look in her eye, the one that said it was easier just to do what she wanted because she could be almost as relentless as Anna Belle.

Almost, but in a much better way.

He gave a curt nod and dug his keys from his jeans pocket. "I'll see you in the morning."

She rested her hands on her hips, shifting her weight from one leg to the other.

Grayson had one thought when he headed to his truck. He desperately needed a vacation. Soon.

ONE

Home sweet home.

Long weekends were great for a getaway to think and refocus, but Grayson Thibodeaux itched to get back home. He turned onto his street and let out a sigh—he'd sleep in his own bed tonight. Tomorrow would start a new week, and he could put the last couple of months behind him, especially the past two weeks.

Maybe then he could put the last several years in his rearview mirror.

The drive had been slower than usual, but with Mardi Gras coming next week, New Orleans burst at the city limits with tourists and carnival people. Bright, sparkly greens, purples, and golds lined the French Quarter and beyond. The floats housed in the many warehouses would receive final touches before the upcoming parades.

Tension gripped Grayson as he spied a car parked in the driveway of his home. He didn't get random visitors, and very few people knew he'd even left town, much less when he'd return. He didn't recognize the vehicle.

He eased his truck behind the car, effectively blocking it in. Grayson stepped silently onto the concrete and stared at his front porch. No one there.

Zydeco music blasted from the house next door: an early Mardi Gras celebration in full swing. Smoke from a grill drifted from the couple's backyard, sending a mouth-watering aroma wafting through the garden district neighborhood.

Grayson gently pushed the truck door closed, then headed

down the cobblestone path that ran alongside the old house. Even in the waning light, his steps found the stones with no stumbles. He'd grown up in this house, had helped his father place the very cobblestones he now walked on into the sod.

The light by the kitchen door illuminated a man and woman standing on his back porch, their backs to him. The woman had her hands cupped around her face as she pressed against the kitchen window.

Grayson's muscles flexed. "May I help you?"

The man and woman spun at the same time, both setting their hands on the butts of their respective side arms.

Recognition came instantly. "Brandon?" Grayson asked.

"Hey." Brandon Gibbons, Grayson's old college buddy and currently a detective with the New Orleans Police Department, removed his hand from his sidearm. Grayson had worked with Brandon when he was a consultant for the department.

"You remember my partner, Danielle?" Brandon nodded at the woman beside him.

Black-as-night hair, brown eyes, and a chip on her shoulder bigger than a boulder—yeah, he remembered Danielle Witz all right. "I do. Hello, Danielle."

Her eyes narrowed. "Thibodeaux." Apparently she still hated his guts. It'd been months ago—how could she still carry a grudge for his not calling her sister after their blind date?

"What're you doing back here?" Grayson asked. It wasn't like Brandon to creep around backyards.

Danielle leaned against the porch's support beam. "Where have you been?"

In a split second, Grayson took in their body language and the microexpressions most people didn't even realize they showed. Brandon's lips were thinned, and he wouldn't meet Grayson's stare. Danielle, on the other hand, narrowed her eyes and held eye contact, dropping her chin as she glared.

"Why?" Grayson stood a little straighter.

"Maybe we should go inside?" Brandon asked, looking quickly at Grayson, then darted his gaze to his partner.

Grayson crossed his arms over his chest as little pinpricks of apprehension pimpled his arms. "Why don't you tell me why you're here, peeking in my back windows?"

Brandon met his stare. "I think you'd rather us go inside to talk, Grayson."

This wouldn't be good, but now curiosity nibbled at the edges of his mind. He sighed. "Sure. Come on."

Grayson led the two detectives around to the front door. He unlocked it, then stepped inside and punched in the disarming code on the keypad to his alarm system.

Brandon and Danielle followed him into the cool house. Grayson took a seat in his recliner, leaving the two to sit on his couch. But Danielle didn't sit; she stood behind the couch, facing Grayson. She wore her animosity like a shield.

"So, again, why are you here?" Grayson rested his elbows on his knees and let his hands hang loosely.

"Why—"

"Grayson, I'm sorry," Brandon interrupted his partner.

"For?" His gut twisted.

"It's Anna Belle."

Grayson gripped his hands together and squeezed. "She's hurt? Was she in an accident?" Images of the way his ex-wife drove filled his mind. She often forgot to wear a seat belt. "Is she okay?"

"She's dead." Danielle's words were too flat for the information. She had to be wrong. This was a mistake. Had to be.

"D–dead?" No, Anna Belle was too—well, she was just too alive to be dead.

"I'm sorry, bud. I hate to be the one to tell you, but it's true."

Brandon leaned forward on the couch. Empathy did little to soften the severity of his expression.

Anna Belle—dead. She couldn't be—he couldn't— "What happened?" She was vibrant and always driven. She couldn't be dead. Not Anna Belle.

"She died from anaphylactic shock."

Grayson snapped his attention to Danielle. "That can't be." He shook his head. Sure, Anna Belle would take risks, but not with her allergy. She'd always been extremely careful about that and never went anywhere without her EpiPen.

"It's true. The autopsy confirmed it. I'm sorry." Brandon's words registered with Grayson, but he still couldn't fathom the finality.

Numbness spread out from his chest like icy fingers as images of Anna Belle sped across his mind like a movie.

In college, her hair flowing and eyes flashing against Death Valley stadium lights as the Tigers won the national championship. The warmth of her body against his as she hugged him in her excitement.

Her fingertips grazing his cheek as he cried at his father's funeral. The surprising strength of her small stature as she held him up at the grave.

Her unmistakable beauty in her wedding dress as she said her vows to him in the cathedral.

The hardness of her eyes when she told him she was filing for divorce.

"Grayson?" Brandon's voice cut through the memories.

He looked to his friend. "She's always extremely careful about her allergy. She steered far away from anything that could remotely have cherries or cherry juice or even be cross-contaminated with them. She was almost paranoid about it." Privately of course. Not many outside her tight circle of family and friends knew of the allergy.

Brandon nodded. "So we've been told."

"But either way, she always carries her EpiPen. In her purse. In her car. In her office. Everywhere." The woman nearly mortgaged their house with how many she bought and stowed everywhere.

Brandon nodded again. "We've opened an investigation into the circumstances surrounding her death."

Wait, what? "Do you suspect foul play?" That would be the only thing that made sense. Anna Belle would never be so reckless with her allergy.

Then again, who would want to hurt her?

"Why don't you tell us where you've been the past several days?" Danielle interrupted, crossing her arms.

Ahh. Yes. Reality crashed into his racing mind. An ex-husband would definitely be of interest when his wife died in such an unusual manner. Ex-wife. "I went out of town. To St. Francisville."

"What were you doing there?" Danielle's body stood as rigid as her tone.

"Playing golf."

"Where?" She stared straight at him.

Grayson tightened his jaw. She might just be doing her job, but she didn't have to have such an attitude.

"The Bluffs. And before you ask, I stayed at the lodge there on Thompson Creek."

Brandon sat on the very edge of the couch, writing in a small notebook balanced on his knee. "When did you leave town?"

"Wednesday. About eleven that morning."

"You've been gone, what, five days?" Danielle's eyes were still narrowed. "That's quite a long weekend golf trip."

Grayson didn't reply because there wasn't a question. He knew how this played out. He'd consulted enough.

"Were you playing in a tournament or with a group?" Brandon's pen hovered over the notebook.

"Not a tournament. I played Thursday with some friends of mine from medical school. We had an 8:00 a.m. tee time."

Brandon scribbled. "Their names?"

"Skipper Bertrand, Tom Bridges, Robert Bertram, and Donny Olson."

"What time did you finish up?" Brandon asked.

Grayson lifted a shoulder. "About noon or so."

"And after you finished the round?" Brandon's gaze held an unspoken apology.

"We grabbed lunch at the club."

"All of you?" Danielle interrupted.

"Yes. All of us."

"Then what?" Brandon asked.

Grayson shifted in his recliner. "I went back to my room at the lodge and fell asleep in front of the television." He cut his stare to Danielle. "*Tombstone*, starring Val Kilmer and Kurt Russell, and I don't remember what channel."

Brandon tapped his pen against the notebook. "Do you remember what time you left the club?"

Grayson's mind wouldn't function right. "I'd guess about one or so."

"And you went to your room and watched television? Fell asleep watching a movie, you say?" If Danielle tried to hide her disdain, she failed miserably.

"Yes. I woke up about six and took a shower."

"Why? What did you do that night?" Danielle asked.

Grayson ran a hand down his face. "I met my friends at the Francis Southern Table. Our reservations were for seven."

"How long were you there?" Her tone matched her facial expression.

"I'm not sure. When we finished eating, we left. I got back to the lodge about eight thirtyish."

"Why didn't you answer my calls?" Brandon asked. "I left you a voice mail."

"I lost my cell phone in Thompson Creek." For the first time in a really long time, he wished he'd had his phone.

"When did you lose it?" Brandon asked.

"Thursday morning. First hole." Grayson shook his head "I figured that was a sign of how I'd be playing that day, but I actually shot two under." Seemed lame now, considering Anna Belle was dead.

"So you were *asleep* from about one until six, alone in your hotel room?" Danielle took a step around the couch, still staring him down.

Grayson nodded. "I was dozing in front of the TV. I don't know what else to tell you. That's what I was doing."

Brandon shot his partner a hard stare. "What about Friday? Did you play with your group again?"

Grayson shook his head. "Only Tom and I played."

"All day?" Danielle pressed.

Grayson shrugged. "Basically a repeat of Thursday. I got up and ate breakfast in the club, then met Tom at eight for a round."

"Did you have lunch at the club when you were done?" Brandon asked. "Or go to a restaurant?"

"The club." Now even Brandon was pushing the envelope.

Grayson shook his head. Enough. He'd been a consultant for the police department, had worked with Brandon many times, for pity's sake. "What happened with Anna Belle, Brandon? She'd always been so careful about her allergy. She saw it as a weakness in herself and hated it. She let very few people even know about it."

"We can't really comment on an open investigation—"

"We're still working on gathering all the facts." Brandon cut off his partner.

Grayson's throat tightened as if concrete filled his mouth, and his memory raced through police procedure. Notification. That's what they were doing here, but as an ex, he wasn't legally considered her next of kin.

Anna Belle had alienated her mother, the only living relative she'd had, but Grayson had liked her the few times he met her. She still lived in a double-wide in Breaux Bridge, about two hours away. He looked at Brandon. "Have you called her mom? Do you want me to?"

"Her next of kin has been notified." Danielle shifted her weight from one foot to the other.

"Her mother is staying at the Darkwater Inn," Brandon offered.

Danielle took a couple of steps toward him. "Did anybody see you at all Thursday afternoon in St. Francisville?"

"I don't know."

"What about the rest of the weekend? What did you do?" Danielle pressed.

He opened his mouth to answer that he'd slept in, then went and toured the USS *Kidd*, but clamped his mouth shut in that split second before he spoke. The clouds of shock in his mind cleared just enough. He cut his eyes to Brandon. "When did Anna Belle die?"

Brandon and Danielle looked at one another. A volume of unspoken words passed between them.

Finally, Brandon turned to him. "Thursday afternoon."

Grayson shook his head. "That can't be. She was scheduled to be involved with a corporate game with her company at a rented house all day Thursday, Friday, and Saturday. It was a controlled environment."

Danielle nodded. "She died during the course of the game, Mr. Thibodeaux." She paused, letting her words sink in. "The game *you* custom designed for her to participate in."

Just when he thought it couldn't get any worse.

"You need to come to the station with us and answer some questions." Danielle put her hands on her hips. The leather of her holster creaked. "About that game."

"Have you already spoken to my business partner? Colton York? He handled the contract with Deets PR." Grayson tightened his jaw. He'd told Colton that they shouldn't have taken the job. Even worse, Colton and the Deets PR contract didn't allow for the players to fully know they were involved in a game, so they were playing in the dark.

Brandon gave a little nod. "He gave us some basic information and is going to speak with us again. But he said you were the actual creator of the game."

Grayson paused. While he knew he didn't have to go anywhere to answer any questions, he wanted to help Brandon in the investigation. But not tonight.

"I'm happy to assist you in your investigation, but I think it best I wait to answer any questions until I can adjust from the initial shock." Right now, he needed to process.

Brandon nodded, even though Danielle looked ready to spit nails.

"How about I come in Tuesday morning about nine, and we can talk then?" Grayson stood and led the way to the front door. He needed time to process everything.

"Sure." Brandon hesitated at the door. "I'm sorry, man. See you Tuesday." He headed out, Danielle not saying a word as she followed.

Grayson moved his truck to let them out, then grabbed his duffel and clubs and brought them into the house. He made it as far as the dining room before he dropped them on the floor, the thud of his clubs against the hardwoods echoing in his head. He gripped the back of a chair, steadying himself against actuality.

Anna Belle—dead.

The room seemed to be spinning, but Grayson recognized his mind was trying to accept she was gone while his emotions spun off in varying directions. His psychologist's mind attempted to categorize what he thought. To characterize his emotions. The shock and disbelief, then the uncertainty of what he even felt. All normal reactions but nonetheless destabilizing. He forced himself to head to his bedroom.

He could almost see her here, in the room once called theirs. Her long, blond hair splayed across the pillows as she slept, looking more like a porcelain doll than a young woman. Curled up in the chair in the corner with a book, her feet covered in fuzzy socks on the ottoman. Bouncing on the bed and yelling at the TV as LSU lost against Alabama—again. Running across the room in her fleece pajamas after turning off the light to jump on the bed and under the covers, unnerved from watching a scary movie.

Cherished memories assaulted him. The gentle love they shared early in their marriage. Laughter and midnight picnics in bed. The whispers of encouragement. The tenderness of her fingertips on his cheek. Sharing secrets. Making plans. Holding on to each other through the pounding of multiple hurricanes. The sweet kisses and passionate embraces. The loving until the sun rose over the crescent city.

But it all changed. Oh, did it change.

What was once passion mutated into heated exchanges. His trust lost in her betrayal. His honesty discarded with her lies. Lashes meant to cut. Words used as soul stealers. Accusations. Lies. Her deception challenging the boundaries of his forgiveness.

Now she was gone forever.

TWO

"He's as guilty as Adam and Eve in the garden. I could tell by looking at him." Danielle stomped on the brake at the end of Grayson's subdivision.

Brandon had already heard his partner's ranting about Grayson Thibodeaux and accepted this would be one of the few cases they wouldn't see eye-to-eye on. "Because he didn't break down in tears when we told him she was dead? It was a shock, and you know that's what it was. People react differently to bad news."

"Yeah, but he sure didn't look upset over the information that Anna Belle had been killed." She turned the unmarked cruiser toward the precinct.

"I think he did. He was shocked. That should tell you that he didn't kill her." No way would he believe his friend and former consultant would kill anyone, much less his wife. Okay, ex-wife. Same difference.

"Maybe he didn't mean to kill her so that's why he was shocked."

"So he poisoned her for what reason?"

"You talked to the same witnesses yesterday and today that I did, right? Remember, many people heard him and Anna Belle argue and saw her slap him." She eased up to a traffic light and brought the car to a stop. "She made it clear she intended to take him back to court for omitting a sizable asset from their divorce decree."

"Newly divorced people argue. You know this as well as I do."

The light turned green. Danielle took off a little faster than she'd planned, jerking them. "If he's so innocent, why wouldn't he come down and answer questions tonight?"

"Because he worked as our consultant and knows he doesn't have to." Brandon let out a slow breath. "He has to know that he's the primary suspect because the ex always is. He's a psychologist for pity's sake—he probably knew what we were thinking before we thought it. He's coming on Tuesday."

"Mm hmm. I ain't buying it. That dog don't hunt."

"Look, I know you don't like Grayson because of your sister, but you can't let that jade you against him in this investigation."

"And you're his friend, so you can't let that bias you for him."

"Fair enough. We'll let the facts stand on their own."

She pulled the car into a parking spot behind the precinct. "Deal."

He followed her into the building, the bantering and boisterousness of the station a siren's song of welcome to him.

Detective Brandon Gibbons loved few things, but one of them was being a cop. Proud to be a third-generation New Orleans police officer, Brandon had risen through the ranks as a beat cop, then in Property Crimes, working pawn shops and forgery before earning his shield and moving to homicide. He loved everything about law enforcement, even if that meant putting up with the derelicts and destroyers of his city.

He and Danielle made it to their desks but hadn't yet sat when the commander called them into his office.

"What'd you do now?" Danielle whispered under her breath as they entered the commander's office.

"Nothing. This is all yours," he whispered back as they stood in front of their boss.

"Shut the door, please." Commander Ellender didn't stand, didn't even look up from his notes laid out on the desk in front of him.

Brandon did as asked.

"Take a seat."

Both he and Danielle dropped to the seats.

Commander Ellender tossed off his reading glasses and peered at them. "I understand you're working the Anna Belle Thibodeaux case."

"Yes, sir." Brandon couldn't recall the last time the Commander took an interest in a specific case.

"I also understand the prime suspect is Grayson Thibodeaux, yes?"

"Yes."

"He's one of the suspects."

Commander Ellender tented his weathered hands over his desk. "Well, which is it?"

Brandon cocked his head. "He's the victim's ex-husband, so that automatically makes him a suspect."

"But he also has motive for the murder and has no verifiable alibi," Danielle interjected.

Brandon shot Danielle a hard stare. So much for their truce. "Correct. No *immediately* verifiable alibi."

Commander Ellender lifted his glasses by the earpiece and spun them in slow circles. "Grayson Thibodeaux is a friend of yours, Detective Gibbons?" It was a question but came out more like an accusation.

Facts were facts. "Grayson and I are friends."

"So you understand I'll need to assign this case to another detective."

No. This was important not to let Grayson get railroaded. "With all due respect, sir, Grayson is well acquainted with most every detective and officer in the precinct because he was a consultant for the NOPD for two years."

"I'm well aware, Detective."

"Then I respectfully request you leave me on the case. My record speaks for itself: I've never allowed my personal connections or prejudice to obscure my investigations."

"So I see." Commander Ellender tapped the files with the end of his glasses. "Your employee record is quite impressive, Detective. And we are shorthanded due to the increased populous from Mardi Gras." He tossed the glasses back on his desk and let out a long breath. "What do you think, Detective Witz? Do you believe your partner can be fair and unbiased when it comes to the case of his friend?"

Brandon met Danielle's stare and held it for what felt like minutes.

Finally, she looked back to their boss. "I do."

"You don't seem to share your partner's opinion that Mr. Thibodeaux is only a suspect because he's the ex-husband."

"No, sir. I think there's more."

"Lay out the case for me." Commander Ellender leaned back in his chair. "Just the basics."

Danielle pulled her smartphone from her pocket, opened her notes app, and read. "At approximately 4:18 p.m. on Thursday, 911 answered a call that there was an unconscious woman at a rental property located on Esplanade Avenue. Ambulance arrived at the scene at 4:32 p.m. Unresponsive woman identified as Anna Belle Thibodeaux, age thirty-three, a senior account rep at Deets PR. Divorced from her husband, Grayson Thibodeaux, approximately six months ago. No children from their marriage. Owner and manager of Deets PR, Tim Dubois, was performing CPR on victim upon arrival. EMT took over CPR, and ambulance transported her to University Medical Center, arriving at approximately 4:49 p.m. Victim never regained consciousness despite attempts made in the ER. Victim was declared dead at 5:21 p.m. on Thursday."

Danielle glanced to the commander, who nodded at her. "What were they doing at a rental property?"

"According to the deceased's employer, Tim Dubois, he and his board of directors had hired Game's On You to create a customized game to help them determine which of their four employees under consideration for a big promotion would be most likely to succeed in the position. Mr. Dubois stated that he was aware that the deceased's ex-husband was a partner in the company he hired, but until Mrs. Thibodeaux's death, he was unaware that her ex-husband was the person who actually created the game."

"Interesting." Commander Ellender shifted in his seat. "Continue."

Danielle nodded. "Following Louisiana directives, the hospital ordered an autopsy, which was conducted by Dr. Kelly Shannon, a physician pathologist, at approximately 9:00 a.m. on Friday. Cause of death was determined to be anaphylactic shock. Next of kin, the victim's mother, Monique Fredericks, indicated the victim's extreme allergy to cherry juice. Toxicology confirmed the victim ingested cherry juice that brought on the anaphylactic shock that killed her."

"Homicide by allergy—that's a new one." The commander wore an expression of fascination. "Go on."

"At approximately 10:00 a.m., the case was turned over to field medicolegal death investigators who oversaw the CSI unit at the house on Esplanade Avenue. All evidence was collected and the scene cleared by 1:00 p.m. A shot-sized bottle of an energy drink was open on the desk in the room the victim had been staying in. Tests run on the liquid left inside the bottle detected trace amounts of cherry juice, which the ingredients don't list. We're waiting for the manufacturer to confirm that. The victim's purse was recovered from the scene, and an EpiPen was inside, unused. Tests run on the pen show that it was as dispensed from the pharmacy—untampered with—and would have worked as prescribed. Anna Belle Thibodeaux's death was marked a homicide and turned over to the NOPD. My partner and I were next up on rotation, so we received the case." Danielle paused.

"Please keep going, Detective."

"Yes, sir." Danielle tossed Brandon an apologetic look. "Following initial interviews with all persons at the Esplanade Avenue house, we learned that several people recalled seeing an argument between the deceased and her ex-husband, Grayson Thibodeaux. The incident in question happened approximately two weeks ago at Mr. Thibodeaux's business, Game's On You, during which they not only exchanged harsh words, but the deceased slapped Mr. Thibodeaux. This was witnessed by several people. Many heard the deceased accuse Mr. Thibodeaux of nefarious activity regarding their divorce decree and her declaration that she would take him back to court."

Brandon interrupted. "We've left messages for Anna Belle's attorney to return our calls as soon as he's able, so this isn't confirmed yet. Additionally, several others that were present in the Esplanade Avenue house have been presented as possible suspects in the investigation."

Danielle narrowed her eyes. "Yes, this is true. We will be bringing in those persons for another round of questioning immediately." She turned back to the commander. "When we went to question Mr. York and Mr. Thibodeaux, we learned Mr. Thibodeaux was out of town, having left the day prior to the homicide. No one in his business knew of his whereabouts, nor had he answered or returned his assistant's multiple phone calls."

Again, Brandon interrupted. "He was on vacation, one he had scheduled months ago, according to his assistant and business partner, Colton York. Most people go on vacation to get away from their job and don't check in."

Danielle continued, ignoring him. "We met with Mr. Thibodeaux last evening upon his return into town. He claims his cell phone was lost on Thursday morning in St. Francisville, which is his excuse for why he didn't answer or return calls. While he claims to have been in St. Francisville the entire time, including the time of death of the deceased, it appears he has no verifiable alibi for the hours leading up to her homicide."

"We just received his initial information and haven't had time to check out details yet to see if anything is verified." Brandon glared at Danielle. This went beyond animosity because Grayson hadn't called her sister back after their blind date. How could she throw Grayson to the wolves like this?

"We requested Mr. Thibodeaux come with us to the station to answer some questions, but he refused."

"He declined to come tonight. He'd just learned of his ex-wife's death. He volunteered to come in Tuesday morning." Brandon sat on the edge of the seat. "He worked here as a consultant for a couple of years. He knows he's a suspect. He's coming and speaking to us in two days."

"We've just started to investigate, sir." Danielle closed the app on her phone.

Commander Ellender hesitated as he leaned forward, propping his elbows on his desk. "Well documented, Detective. I'm going to allow you two to stay on the case. With one condition."

Just when Brandon was ready to let the relief wash over him. There was always something. "Sir?"

Commander Ellender met Brandon's even gaze with a steel one of his own. "Despite the seniority order, Detective Witz is lead detective on this case."

THREE

Bam! Bam! Bam!

Grayson tossed the now-empty duffel into the closet and headed to the front door. If it was Brandon and Danielle again. . .

He jerked open the door to find Pam standing on his welcome mat.

"Are you okay?" In typical Pam fashion, she pushed past him into the foyer and faced him with her hands on her hips. "Why haven't you answered your phone? I've been calling practically nonstop all weekend. I was about ready to send a search party out for you."

As much as he would've thought he didn't feel up for company, Grayson was happy to see Pam. Her straightforwardness and inability to gloss things over was just what he needed. "Come on in." He led the way to the kitchen and pulled the coffeemaker from under the cabinet. "I haven't answered my phone because I dropped it into the creek at the golf course on Thursday morning."

"Oh." Pam perched on one of the barstools at the kitchen island. Silence filled the space between them until she cleared her throat. "Are you okay?"

He glanced over his shoulder to make eye contact with his friend. "I'm not sure yet." He finished putting the coffee on to brew and moved to lean on the counter opposite Pam. "The police told me Anna Belle died from anaphylactic shock, but that's pretty much it." Just saying the word *died* in relation to his ex-wife still sounded like a punch line to a very bad joke in extremely poor taste. "Tell me what happened."

Pam shook her head. "I don't understand either. After you left, we finished everything we needed. Everything was set before they arrived on Wednesday afternoon. That evening everything we'd designed went off without a hitch—the cooking mishap, pool scare, roofing—all of it right down to the fire truck response."

Just as he'd predicted. Except he hadn't been able to foresee Anna Belle dying.

A pang tightened in his chest as soon as he finished the thought. It was still hard to accept she was gone.

"Are you sure you want to hear this?" Pam's voice softened, which was unusual for her.

No, he didn't want to hear details of Anna Belle's death, but he needed to hear them. He had to know what happened. "Yeah, I think I need to."

Pam hesitated, then nodded before continuing. "Thursday morning, everything was right on schedule. The props were left as planned while they were having breakfast, and everyone followed instructions. The two teams came up with their campaigns and turned them in to Mr. Dubois before lunch. The group ate together, and as you had predicted in the planning, it was one tense meal." Pam smiled. "It amused me to see everyone forcing themselves to act normal when they were just waiting for Mr. Dubois to judge which team's campaign was better."

Yes, he'd banked on their competitive edge in creating a campaign to spin a politician's potential scandal into a positive light. With limited resources and a short time limit.

Pam kept on as the coffee moved into its final brewing stages. "Both teams reported for the escape room. Anna Belle and Hugh escaped before the two-and-a-half-hour limit, but Georgia and Franklin didn't."

"They didn't?" He hadn't seen that one coming. He'd thought both teams would've made it out. Barely, but successfully. Grayson turned away from Pam and pulled two mugs from the cabinet.

"Nope. They didn't make it, so we had to unlock their door at four."

That was the contingency plan he'd written of course, but he never thought they'd have to implement it. "Vic did the unlocking, right? And no one saw him?" The game would fall apart if anyone realized everything was part of the game. He poured the coffee, took the cups to the island, and set them down before moving the sugar bowl in front of Pam.

"Yes, Vic unlocked the door and no one saw him, just as you'd instructed."

"Good." He opened the refrigerator, pulled out the milk, and set it in front of his assistant. He took a sip of his coffee, nearly scalding his tongue.

Pam dumped one, then two, then three heaping spoons of sugar into her cup. "Everyone was supposed to be in their rooms, freshening up for dinner at four thirty. It was about four fifteen when Georgia Vescot started screaming upstairs. Vic and I checked and saw Georgia standing in the doorway of Anna Belle's room. We all rushed to find out what was going on, and we saw Anna Belle on the floor, unconscious. We called 911, and Mr. Dubois administered CPR until the ambulance arrived."

That didn't make sense. Anna Belle knew her body and knew the symptoms of an immediate onset of her allergic reactions. She knew how to treat herself. She would've reached for her Epi immediately. "How did Anna Belle look to you?"

"Very still." Pam took a sip of her coffee, then added another spoon of sugar.

Grayson just couldn't wrap his mind around what happened to Anna Belle. "Was she flushed? Anything out of the ordinary?"

"She was more pale than flushed, although she had some swollen spots on her neck. Maybe a couple on her face and arms. I don't know really."

"Like welts?"

Pam nodded and poured the milk all the way to the mug's rim. "Kinda. Now that I think about it, she looked like she'd been stung by a couple of bees or something." Finally finished doctoring her coffee, she put the milk back into the refrigerator. "The paramedics said it looked like she had an allergic reaction."

"Was her EpiPen beside her?" Maybe she'd grabbed her shot, but her symptoms had come on too quickly and she hadn't been able to inject herself. That was the only thing that made sense to him.

"No, not that I saw, and I stayed there until they rolled her from the room into the ambulance."

Where was her Epi? It was always in her makeup bag in her purse. Always. No matter what, she always had it on her. Or her backup in her toiletry case? She never traveled overnight without that.

"Hers is a food allergy. Had she eaten or drank anything during the last bit of the game?" Although, her reaction was immediate, so she would've had to have ingested cherries or cherry juice just before her symptoms appeared.

Pam shook her head. "They were getting ready for dinner. They were only gone for about fifteen, twenty minutes, tops." She took another drink of her coffee. "Unless she had something in her room, which I guess she had to have had."

Anna Belle would never knowingly have anything with cherries in her room. Ever. People with serious allergies made sure to keep their allergens at bay if at all possible. Anna Belle was strict about it.

"Was there anything in her room that looked out of the ordinary?"

"Not that I saw, but, Gray, I wasn't looking. I didn't pay attention. I didn't think I needed to." She took another sip, then set her mug on the counter, tracing the rim with her finger. "It's no secret that I didn't like Anna Belle, but I'm sorry for you. I know that despite everything she's done, you probably still have some sort of feelings for her."

If only it were that simple.

Grayson pulled one of the barstools around the island and sat. "It's not that I have feelings for her, exactly." He searched for the words to put to his feelings. "It's more like I miss who she once was—who we both were when we first met and fell in love. I grieve our marriage." He shook his head. "Don't get me wrong, I despise what she did to me, to us, but I know I need to let it all go and forgive her. It's just so hard."

"You're a better person than I am, that's for sure." Pam pushed off the stool and poured herself another cup of coffee, then topped off Grayson's. "Because after all we learned about her. . .well, it's not like we uncovered anything redeeming about her personality. My opinion of her went down further, something I didn't even think possible." She grabbed the milk from the fridge and poured.

He was having a problem with what they'd found out too. Still. Probably always would. He took a sip of coffee and redirected the conversation. "After the ambulance left, what happened?"

Pam stirred her coffee absentmindedly as she sat. "Every-one was upset of course. And nobody really knew what to do. The employees of Deets PR had no idea who we were and why we were in the house. We didn't know what to say either. Tim Dubois mumbled something about we were there with the house or some such lame explanation." She took a drink. "After he did that, he left. The entire mood of the house was very subdued. Some went to the hospital, some didn't say where they were going, just left. You could tell a couple of them were pretty put out that we were there."

Which is what he'd warned his partner about when they were initially contracted for this job. People didn't like being fooled, even if they did sign a waiver. If they didn't even realize they were playing a game, of course they'd be upset to find out they were in the middle of one. "Who all said they were going to the hospital?"

"Tim Dubois and his wife left immediately behind the ambulance. Hugh Istre. Colton."

Interesting. Grayson took a sip of coffee. "You know the police opened an investigation, right?"

She nodded. "They questioned all of us."

At least he hadn't been singled out. "When?"

"Yesterday afternoon. Colton called me yesterday and told me to expect them. As per their request, he'd given them the names and addresses of everyone who'd been there and had been involved with the game."

"They were here tonight."

"I figured. That's why I just kept coming by, driving by your house until I saw your truck. I tried to call you to tell you, to let you know."

"Yeah." He stared into his dark coffee for a moment. "I'm pretty certain they suspect foul play."

"Really?"

"Brandon *is* a homicide detective. He was the one who came today. It could've been just courtesy because I'd worked with him."

She shook her head. "No, it was him and his partner who came to talk to me." She swung her foot slowly, letting it graze the stool's rung with every pass. "I should've picked up on that, considering the questions they asked."

"Like what?"

"How much did I help you create the game? Who at our company had access to the information sent from Deets PR?" She shrugged. "Was there anything unusual about this game from the others we create? Those types of questions."

Grayson's mouth went dry. Those questions definitely suggested the police thought this wasn't just a tragic accident. They also suggested that the police were looking for suspects. And everyone knew the ex was always the primary suspect.

"They really think someone did this to her, don't they?" Pam's question echoed in his mind. "They said they'd be in touch for further questions."

"They must have something they didn't tell me about." He nodded slowly, going over both Brandon and Danielle's mannerisms. Their exact words. "And I think they're considering me their main suspect."

"No way!"

"Think about how it looks to them, Pam. I'm a recent ex-husband. No denying our divorce was messy. I create a game that she died during, while I was conveniently out of town."

Her eyes widened. "But you would never—"

"No, but they have to follow the information." He turned and grabbed the coffeepot, then filled both their mugs. "So now I need to back up and go over everything with a fine-tooth comb."

"I'll help you."

He smiled. Everything about Pam was just so open and honest. And loyal. "I can't ask you to do that."

"You didn't." She took a long drink. "Where do we start?"

No sense arguing—it wouldn't do any good. To be honest, he didn't really want to go this alone. Besides, Pam was a stickler for details, so she'd notice things he might miss. He couldn't afford to miss anything. His mind wrapped around what he knew. "Okay, everyone went to their rooms to get ready for dinner about four fifteen."

"Four fifteen, four twenty."

"You heard the scream. . . ."

Pam nodded. "Georgia screamed like a banshee, so everyone naturally ran to the room. Anna Belle was laid out on the floor."

He could always get the exact time from when 911 was called. "Then what?"

"Tim Dubois pushed Georgia out of the way, felt Anna Belle's neck, hollered for someone to call 911, then began performing CPR."

"Who actually called 911?"

Pam pressed her lips together. "Hmm." A second passed. Then another. And a third. "I think it was Colton."

Grayson nodded. "What was everybody else doing? We need to account for everyone."

"Vic was standing right behind me. When he saw her on the ground, he held my shoulder." Pam closed her eyes. "Colton did call 911—he stepped into the hall to make the call." Pam turned on the stool. "Mrs. Dubois was comforting Georgia, who was sniffling and sobbing."

One of her rivals crying? Interesting.

"Um," Pam continued, "Wynnona and Keely were behind me and Vic, more in the hall than in the room. I just couldn't look away, but I couldn't move either." She opened her eyes and met Grayson's gaze. "I'm sorry I couldn't do anything."

"Sounds like there was nothing that could be done." He forced a smile that he didn't feel. "What about Stratton? Where was he?"

Pam opened her mouth, paused, then shut it for a moment before she spoke. "I don't know. He wasn't there. Well, at least I don't remember seeing him. He might've snuck outside to have a cigarette and not realized what happened." She shook her head. "I don't really know."

"What about anybody else from Deets PR? You said Hugh Istre went to the hospital. Where was he in the house?"

"He and Franklin were in the hallway. I looked out when Colton made the 911 call, and they were standing in front of Colton, listening, right across from Wynnona and Keely."

That was all the people scheduled to be there. "No one but Tim touched Anna Belle?" Grayson tried to ignore the irony. Tim had been touching Anna Belle for quite some time.

Pam shook her head. "No one but Tim until the paramedics got there less than ten minutes or so after Colton called them."

Average response time for the area. "After the ambulance left. . ."

"Tim told everybody he was going to the hospital. He gave a vague mention of us being with the house and that was okay, then marched off. His wife let go of Georgia and followed him out. Colton told our team that he should probably go to the hospital too, so he told us to pack it up, and then he went downstairs, got his stuff, and left. Hugh waited just a minute or two longer and announced he was going as well and headed down the stairs."

"Did Tim grab anything?"

"I don't think so. They walked down the stairs straight from Anna Belle's room and went out the front door. Their room had been on the second floor like Anna Belle's, right of the staircase, and they didn't go that way to get a bag or anything."

"So their stuff was probably left. What about Hugh? Did he stop for a bag or anything?"

Pam nodded. "He went to his room, then came out again with a duffel bag. All the Deets people's rooms were on the second floor, remember? The only ones downstairs were ours: mine, Colton's, Wynonna and Keely's, and the one Vic and Stratton shared."

Grayson nodded. "The fourth downstairs was the control room. The layout really worked well that way."

"It did."

Logical. "So, after they left to go to the hospital, where did the rest of you go?"

"Wynonna and Keely got their stuff and left. Vic and I packed up our stuff, and Stratton helped us load up."

Since it was Grayson's team running the game, Colton's team wouldn't have the responsibility to pack and load the equipment and get it back to the office. They took limited on-site jobs, but when they did, one team was primarily responsible for the equipment.

Pam continued. "Georgia kept sniffling, but Franklin told her they needed to go. He helped her get her stuff, and they left. Maybe twenty or so minutes after the ambulance had left."

"How long after that did it take you, Vic, and Stratton to get finished?"

"We were about two hours after the rest."

"So, about two hours and twenty minutes after the ambulance had gone?"

Pam nodded.

"Y'all were the last ones out?"

"We were. We didn't have a key to lock up, so we just pulled the door closed and left."

"And y'all went straight to the office?"

Again Pam nodded. "We unloaded and put everything up."

"Did you three leave the office together?"

"No. Stratton helped us unload, then said he needed to leave. Vic and I put everything up and left about fifteen minutes or so after he did."

Grayson's mind raced with processing details. "Colton called you yesterday and told you the police would be contacting you. Do you remember about what time Colton called?"

She pulled out her cell and checked her recent call log. "Four oh four, to be exact." She set her phone on the bar. "How's that work for your timeline?"

"Well, let's see, if we estimate the ambulance arrived at the hospital fifteen minutes after it left the house, which we estimate was about five-ish, if she was declared DOA"—Grayson nearly choked as he said it aloud—"then what happened to make the police be called in?"

Pam nodded. "I know when my aunt died in the hospital unexpectedly, we were told that it was standard procedure to have an autopsy performed."

"People die from food allergies every day. There had to be

something that made them think this was more than just an accidental ingestion."

"I don't know."

Neither did Grayson, but he was determined to find out.

Anna Belle
Wednesday

Cook dinner for everyone? Stupid task didn't even relate to her job at all. Why hadn't that been given to Georgia? She posted on social media all the time about meals she made that were so good.

Anna Belle slammed the door of the armoire closed. It was ridiculous she was here to begin with. Tim should've given her the promotion without this asinine event. The only reason he didn't give it to her to begin with was to punish her for breaking up with him.

She glanced out the window of her second-story room into the backyard. The side security lights shone over the space that was quite overrun with weeds. Why did they have to pick such a creepy house? Couldn't Deets have done their testing in someplace like the Hyatt Regency downtown? Or at least someplace that had housekeeping and room service?

She grabbed her makeup bag and took it into the bathroom. It wasn't like she'd been in love with Tim. Truth be told, she didn't really like him all that much. Weak man, but his power in the company was sexy. Not to mention the good clients he kicked her way. Well worth it.

For a while.

If she'd only known that the executive accounts representative position would be coming available, she would have stuck with Tim, despite his vows of undying love and wanting to leave his wife for her.

Please. As if Emmi would ever let him go. Tim might think he could get away from his wife, but Anna Belle knew better. Not that she really cared. Anna Belle had just gotten out of a marriage and had no plans to get back into one again. Ever. The freedom was intoxicating. Going where she wanted when she wanted. Forming habits without having to consider anyone else. Hey, she might even get one of those Maine coon cats now that Grayson wasn't around to complain about cat hair. She wouldn't even have to vacuum up the hair if she didn't want to. Yeah, single life was pretty good.

She hung her robe on the back of the bathroom door. She enjoyed the freedom of single life, but being married had had its advantages too. Like Grayson's back rubs. Man, she missed those. The man missed his calling as a masseuse. He had strong but gentle hands. And he made her coffee. Took care of her when she didn't feel well. He was always willing to go the extra mile to make her happy, putting her happiness over his own 99 percent of the time.

Even though she missed Grayson, she knew letting him go had been the right thing to do, and not just for herself. For him too, even if he didn't understand it. Maybe one day. . .

Anna Belle smiled to herself as she walked back into the bedroom and moved to close the drape in front of the windows. Movement in the yard below caught her attention.

She squinted, then gasped. A man in all black, wearing a shiny purple, green, and gold Mardi Gras mask stood there looking up at her.

Her stomach twisted into a tight knot. Her pulse skyrocketed, pounding, pounding, pounding inside her head.

He was back!

She blinked several times and demanded her breathing regulate.

He lifted a white gloved hand and made a slicing gesture in front of his throat.

Anna Belle backed away, falling against the bed. She clamped her lips together tightly, the scream turning into a whimper in her mouth, unable to escape. Tears burned her eyes.

She inhaled, held it, and then slowly released the breath.

On trembling legs, she inched to the window and peered around the curtain.

Nothing. No one.

She ripped the curtains closed and stumbled back to sit on the edge of the bed. She hadn't imagined him. He'd been there. She wasn't crazy. She wasn't seeing things. He had been there, looking at her. Threatening her. Just like before.

Her stalker was back.

FOUR

"Good morning." Danielle seemed more than chipper for eight thirty on a Monday morning.

"Morning." Brandon pulled out his chair as he simultaneously brought his computer online. "You're in early." He usually beat her into the station by at least half an hour.

"You know what they say: the early bird gets the worm. I wanted to look over the case files with fresh eyes. Get a jump on what I want to do today."

Ahh. There it was. The illusion of power from being named lead detective. Brandon dropped into his chair and checked his email, not rising to take the bait.

Long moments passed.

"I've started making the calls for the more in-depth interviews. Georgia Vescot is up first. She'll be here at nine."

Brandon nodded as he closed his email window.

"Anna Belle's attorney called back. He said that Anna Belle had brought him information regarding something that was omitted from the asset list approximately a month ago. He said his paralegal had researched it, and at this point they weren't going to follow up on any court filings."

Brandon glanced at Danielle, raising his eyebrows.

"Which means there most likely wasn't enough concrete evidence that Anna Belle had any right to additional property."

He nodded and opened the folder, reviewing the original statements given by the people who were at the Esplanade Avenue rental house.

Danielle stood, hovering.

He could feel his partner's stare burning into him as he flipped through the many pages of handwritten notes.

Danielle waited a beat, then two. She sighed, loud and long. "Look, I know you're upset about me being named lead detective, but that's not my fault. It's not like I asked for it. You were there. You know Commander Ellender just made the decision."

He rested his elbows on his desk and slowly raised his gaze to her face. "You should know that wouldn't upset me. We've been partners for three years now, and you know I've never been one to be hung up on stuff like who is lead detective or who has seniority."

She rested a single hand on her hip. "Then what's stuck in your craw? You seem to have an attitude."

Could she really be so clueless? Could she not read him at all? "Danielle, since we were called in to the scene, you had your scope focusing on Grayson, and only Grayson."

"He's the ex, Brandon. You know how this usually goes."

"*Usually* being the operative word. There are plenty of other suspects, and you know it." He dropped the folder on his desk. "That is filled with statements from people, most of whom had a motive to kill Anna Belle." He leaned back in his chair, gripping his hands together over his desk. "I'm just curious why you're so set on proving Grayson guilty. Are you still bitter because he didn't call your little sister after their blind date?"

Her expression turned to one of stone. "Of course not." But her eyes told a different story. "I'm following the evidence where it leads. If he wasn't your friend, you'd be all over him as the main suspect too. I'm not going to let him or anybody pull the wool over my eyes. You wouldn't willingly either."

"I would never accuse anyone without a trail of evidence that led to them. You've worked with me long enough to know that." What was wrong with her? It was like a switch had been flipped and she'd turned into someone he didn't even know. Clearly, the lines were drawn as to which side of the investigation they both fell on, and for the first time in their partnership, they were on opposite sides of the case.

"I guess you'll have to trust that I'll do the same." Danielle stood. "I'll just assume you don't want me to grab you a cup of coffee while I'm up." She turned and marched off before he could respond.

Brandon shook his head before he opened the case file on his desk again. Everything Danielle had told Commander Ellender last night had been accurate. There were holes in Grayson's alibi. He'd have to plug them himself because he certainly couldn't trust Danielle to follow through. So far everything was just circumstantial. But Brandon knew that many times circumstantial evidence was enough to convince a jury.

First things first though—the interviews. Georgia Vescot. Thirty-three. Senior account with Deets PR. She and Anna Belle had been up for the same promotion, which is why they were both involved in the game. She was the one who found Anna Belle. Brandon flipped the page and continued reading. According to her initial statement, she had knocked on Anna Belle's door and it had swung open. She'd seen Anna Belle lying on the floor and screamed. Everyone came running. Tim Dubois started CPR. Colton York, Grayson's business partner, called 911. Emergency dispatch recorded that the call came in at 4:18 p.m. EMTs were dispatched and recorded as arriving on-site at 4:32 p.m. Paramedics took over CPR, but Anna Belle never regained consciousness. She was delivered to University Medical Center New Orleans at 4:49 p.m. The emergency room doctor attempted to revive her, but at 5:21 p.m. Anna Belle Thibodeaux was declared dead.

"Ms. Vescot is in room two." Danielle appeared across from him. "Do you want to take lead in the interview?"

"Sure." Brandon stood and grabbed the file, then followed his partner down the hall of the precinct. He opened the door and let Danielle enter the room before him. She took a seat opposite Georgia, smiling. "Thank you for coming in, Ms. Vescot." His smile was even wider as he sat beside Danielle, directly in front of the woman.

"Of course. Happy to help. And it's Georgia."

He nodded. Already establishing a connection. "May I get you anything? Water? Coffee?"

"No, thank you."

Brandon pulled out the notes with her initial statement and pretended to read when in actuality he was observing the woman.

Georgia Vescot was attractive. Her mocha skin was flawless, as his female friends would say. She didn't need makeup. If she wore any, Brandon couldn't see it. Her naturally curly hair was pulled off her face with a brightly colored band, but little wisps feathered against her cheeks. She was a year older than Brandon's own thirty-two, but she didn't look it. She could easily pass for someone in her midtwenties and was certainly pretty enough to turn many men's heads.

He flipped the page, then closed the folder. Smiling, he addressed her. "Again, we really thank you for coming in."

"Of course. It's just awful what happened." Maybe so, but Georgia Vescot didn't look too broken up over the incident. Not like someone who'd found a body.

"I can only imagine. It must have been awful for you." Brandon avoided looking at his partner. He and Danielle often joked about how sad it was that he could sound so cheesy without much effort.

"It was. I've never seen someone laid out like that."

He nodded. "Maybe you could tell me again what happened." He caught Danielle's glance. She would be taking detailed notes while he kept the connection.

"Sure." Georgia nodded. "I went to her room and knocked, and the door just opened when I touched it. It just pushed open."

"About what time was this?" He knew, but it was important to walk her through it and see where her story changed and where it stayed the same.

"I'd say about four fifteen or so. I don't know the exact time. I'm sorry."

"That's okay." Brandon nodded and gave her a shared smile, building the camaraderie. He asked the next question quickly. "The door just opened when you knocked?"

Georgia nodded. "Yeah. I didn't knock really hard or anything either."

The next question came faster. "What were you going there to see her about?"

"I—I—" She paused.

Ah, the first slip in her exterior. She didn't want to admit why she was there.

"So you went to her room to see her because. . ."

She licked her lips. "I had found a doll in my room, and I thought she'd put it there, so I wanted to ask her about it."

This was new. Brandon glanced at his partner, and she arched a single brow. News to her too. He focused back on Georgia. "A doll?"

Georgia pushed her hands into her lap. "A voodoo doll."

"You found a voodoo doll in your room?"

"Yeah, and it freaked me out." She moved her hands to under her thighs.

No kidding. "I don't blame you. It just showed up?"

Again she nodded. "It wasn't there when I left after breakfast that morning, but it was there that afternoon."

"About what time did you leave when you say it wasn't there?"

"A little before ten."

"And where did you find it when you went back?"

Georgia clasped her hands together in her lap. "Right on my bed. With two pins poking out of it. One out of the torso and one in the head." She started slightly rocking in the seat. "I don't mess around with that stuff. It's real. I know, because my *grandmere* was into hoodoo, and you don't play around with that."

"And you're sure it wasn't in your room before?" He just couldn't wrap his mind around a doll just showing up in a room.

"I'm positive."

"And you thought Anna Belle might've put it in your room?" Brandon had met Anna Belle more than a couple of times, knew her through Grayson of course, but didn't really know her well, yet he couldn't exactly envision her running around with a voodoo doll and putting it in someone's room. To what purpose? To scare her? Well, it had definitely rattled Georgia, that much was pretty clear.

"Maybe." Georgia rubbed her cheek.

Ah. One of those telltale signs. "Why would Anna Belle have put a voodoo doll in your room?"

"She'd do anything to mess with me if it meant that she'd get a leg up on me in any way."

Well, that certainly sounded like the Anna Belle he'd met. "I'm assuming she'd done other things before?"

Georgia nodded. "She stole two of my campaign ideas and passed them off as her own to the clients. I lost the accounts because of that, which meant I also lost the commission money—about five grand."

"Did you tell your boss?"

Georgia snorted. "Of course, but everybody knew Tim was sleeping with her back then. What was he going to do? Confront her? She'd just lie, and he'd believe her." She shook her head. "The first time she pulled a stunt like that, I told him. He didn't do anything, so why bother when she did it again?"

Anna Belle sounded like a real piece of work. "What else did she do to you?" He deliberately lowered his voice and leaned forward, as if they were sharing a private conversation.

His tactic worked. Georgia leaned forward as well. "She sabotaged one of my campaigns for one of our biggest clients. It didn't matter that the company lost the business, she just wanted to make sure I was blamed for the big mess."

"That's awful." And it was. He really felt for his friend now. What had it been like to be married to someone like that?

"She was terrible. She'd run over anyone and anything to get to the top. Sleep with the owner, even though she knew he was married and he and his wife had been trying to get pregnant, sabotage others' campaigns, steal other people's ideas—like I said, anything and everything she could do to stay on top of her career."

Brandon felt Danielle's nudge under the table. Yeah, he knew how to question a suspect/witness. "You know for a fact that Anna Belle did this to other people too?"

Georgia wiped her face again. Ah. Brandon loved those telling signs of deception and discomfort.

"Well, not for positive, not like I know she messed with mine, but I know that Franklin didn't trust her. He told me that much."

Brandon opened the folder and scanned. "Franklin Barron? He was there this weekend too?"

She nodded. "Yeah. All four of us being considered for the promotion to executive accounts director were there. It's a good thing Anna Belle and Tim weren't a thing anymore, otherwise she would've gotten the promotion without question. But since they'd broken up and he'd gone back to his wife. . .well, four of us had a chance. We had no idea this was a game." She snorted. "Some *game.*"

He couldn't wait to get the details of why Grayson's company in particular was hired, but that would come from the owner of Anna Belle's company. He could, however, find out what the unwitting players knew. "What, exactly, were you told about the weekend?"

"Tim had told us—me, Anna Belle, Franklin, and Hugh that we were under consideration for the promotion. He said that a lot would go into the decision, but that he wanted to watch us work, independently and as a team, and we would be tested over a long weekend. To be considered, we had to fill out a stack of paperwork, sign a waiver of release to participate, and authorize the release of our medical records and financials to the company."

"What?" Danielle blurted out.

But Brandon couldn't blame her for breaking their routine. He was just as shocked.

Georgia nodded. "Yeah. I thought it was a little in-depth, but when you think about it, it's not that far-fetched. The executive accounts director would oversee clients that were worth millions. Every aspect of the person who would get the position had to be vetted."

It sounded insane to Brandon, but then again, in his profession he saw the ugliest part of humanity and thus had very little trust in his fellow man.

He resumed his questioning by asking, "So, you went to Anna Belle's room to ask her if she left the doll in yours. You knocked, and the door opened, and. . . ?"

Georgia jumped right back into the retelling. "It just pushed open, and I saw Anna Belle just lying there on the ground. She was just so still and lifeless. I just knew she had to be dying. I screamed my head off."

Overuse of the word *just*. A slight embellishment from her initial statement that she saw Anna Belle on the ground. Her initial statement had nothing about Anna Belle being dead or dying. It never failed—people always deviated in retelling. That's one thing that made their job so difficult: weeding out the fact from fiction.

"Of course you screamed." Building the connection again. "How awful. So then what happened?"

"Everyone came running. Tim started CPR. Another man I'd never seen before called 911. There were several people I have no idea who they were just appeared. Emmi, Tim's wife, hugged me. I was just beside myself."

"I can imagine." Brandon nodded. "So the ambulance came?"

Georgia nodded. "They came and took her out on a stretcher. Tim and Emmi left to go to the hospital." She shook her head. "If I'd been Emmi, I sure wouldn't have been concerned. Anna Belle had had an affair with her husband, after all."

"What about everyone else?"

"Well, we didn't know who all was who. Franklin told me that we needed to go. He waited while I got my stuff and then walked me out to my car."

"Did you take the voodoo doll?"

That threw her off. She gave a little shudder. "Of course not. I dropped it when I found Anna Belle." She crinkled her nose. "I guess it's still there."

It would be in evidence collected by their CSI unit. He'd check if it became an important item. For now he just needed to know what Georgia could tell him. "About what time did you leave?"

"I guess about a quarter till five."

"Did you go to the hospital?"

Her expression showed her disdain. "No." She must have remembered who she was talking to. "I mean, not that I didn't care if someone lived or anything, but Anna Belle wasn't my friend. We didn't like each other. It would've been hypocritical for me to go, right?"

Brandon nodded. "Did you know Anna Belle was allergic to cherries?"

Georgia shook her head. "No. I've never even heard of somebody being allergic to fruit like that."

"Do you happen to know if Anna Belle drank energy drinks often?"

Georgia nodded. "Oh yeah. She drank at least one every afternoon. Called it her *pick-me-up*. Everybody knew. I mean, she kept them on her desk at the office."

"Did you hear from anybody else about the incident after you got home?"

She nodded. "Tim called everybody Friday afternoon and let us know that Anna Belle had died and told us you, the police, would be contacting us. He told us we'd all been in an elaborate game that was created for him and the board to decide who to promote."

Nothing like giving all the suspects a heads-up. "Did you talk to anyone else? Besides Tim and me and my partner here?"

"No."

Brandon slipped on a smile. "Is there anything else you can think of we might need to know?"

Georgia nodded and leaned forward, her eyes widening, and lowered her voice. "The company Tim hired to create the game? The owner is Anna Belle's ex-husband."

FIVE

Monday morning dawned cooler and overcast, as if the weather had been ordered to match Grayson's current state of mind. The night had seemed to stretch on and on with constant tossing and turning. Sleep had evaded him for the four hours he'd actually been in the bed attempting to rest. Most of those dark hours were spent unloading his emotions in prayer. He'd finally gotten about two hours of shut-eye. Not enough, but it was better than nothing.

"Grayson?"

He'd just stepped onto his front porch, about to head into the office, when an elderly woman's voice cut through the February air. Hand still on the knob, he turned to face her coming up his driveway. "Yes?" She looked vaguely familiar.

"It's me. Monique." She strode to the steps.

Anna Belle's mother. His former mother-in-law. "Monique." He held out his hand to assist her up the steps.

The woman had aged rapidly in the years since he'd last seen her. Her gray hair was thinner, her skin more translucent, and if possible, she stood probably an inch or two shorter. Her movements were much slower than he remembered.

She hugged him as she reached him, stretching up on tiptoe, her thin frame feeling very fragile and delicate against his six feet two inches. "I'm very sorry we're having to see each other under these circumstances." She released him. "Do you have a moment?"

"Of course." He pushed open the front door and discreetly checked his watch. Pam would understand if he ran a little late. Or she'd come looking for him. "Come in." He led the way inside, into the living room. "Please, sit down."

She sat on one end of the couch. Grayson slumped to the other and concentrated on Monique Fredericks. If she was here to blame him—

"I don't know the details of yours and Anna Belle's divorce, but I want you to know that I always thought of you as family."

A lump the size of a Mardi Gras float lodged in his throat. All the snide remarks Anna Belle had made about her mother flashed across his mind. Yet Monique had never been anything but cordial to him. "You too, Monique."

She let out a dry, humorless laugh. "I'm not delusional, Grayson. I know exactly how Anna Belle felt about me. She told me every time I saw her that she felt that her poor upbringing had held her back in some way. I can only imagine the tall tales she told you about her childhood."

Anna Belle had been colorful in her description of her mother and her upbringing. According to her, Monique had been lazy and selfish not to provide bigger and better for herself and her daughter. Anna Belle blamed Monique for their situation in life, which may or may not have been true, but Anna Belle could be unforgiving in her assessments. Grayson knew that better than most.

"That's okay. I'm not here to dispute her version of the past. I just wanted to come here to see and talk to you."

For what purpose? Grayson smiled and nodded, letting his mother-in-law get comfortable enough to say what she'd obviously come here to get off her chest.

Monique took a breath, obviously ready to get on with it. "Since you two are divorced, I'm listed as her next of kin to make arrangements." She rubbed her palms against her polyester pants. "I'm ashamed to say that I don't know her preferences. It wasn't anything we discussed before she stopped all contact with me." Her eyes met his. "I'm hoping you'll be willing to help me."

"Of course." But did he really know what Anna Belle would want? They'd never discussed funeral preferences or the like. Sure, he'd been her husband for six years, but in the six months since their divorce, he'd come to realize he didn't know her nearly as well as he'd once thought.

"I don't think she had a will, did she?"

He shook his head. "At our age. . .with no children." The word nearly choked him. "No, she didn't have a will. Not that I'm aware of."

Monique nodded and shifted her weight on the couch. "Did you two own any burial plots?"

"No." If they had, she would've demanded they be cashed in for the divorce settlement.

"I don't think she would want to be cremated though."

Anna Belle would want a grave where people could come and pay their respects to her. She'd want a permanent place to give her a somewhat state of remembrance. "I think she'd want to be buried."

"If you don't mind, I think I'd like her to be buried near my family's plot in Saint Bernard's back in Breaux Bridge. Do you mind?"

"Not at all." He hadn't even considered a final resting place for Anna Belle's body. It seemed right that she be back from the area she came from, even though she'd done everything in her power to get away from there and pretend like it didn't exist.

"Do you have any requests or suggestions for the service?"

His mind drew a complete blank. How would Anna Belle want to be remembered? How could that image correlate with reality? He hadn't a clue, but her mother stared at him with such helplessness. The two people who should have known Anna Belle the best were apparently clueless. Yet he needed to say something. "Roses were her favorite flowers. Pink roses."

Monique smiled. "I remember that. She said they were the prettiest, the most delicate looking and feminine."

As he smiled back at Anna Belle's mother, he took a mental note of the thinning patches of her pants around the knees, the worn places in the elbows of her blouse, and the scuffs on her slip-on shoes. "I'd like to pay for the funeral." He'd blurted the sentence out before he gave it a second thought or considered how to frame his statement.

"That's kind of you, but you were divorced from Anna Belle. You shouldn't pay for your ex-wife's funeral." She shook her head. "It isn't fitting."

Maybe not, but it was clear Monique wasn't in a financial situation to pay for it. "No parent should have to bury their child." The sentence caught in his chest. Oh, the irony. "They certainly shouldn't have to pay."

"Don't you worry about that. I've already spoken to someone who has scheduled my appearance before a probate judge Wednesday. They tell me there should be no problem with me being named executor of her estate unless someone contests it, and the only person who could contest it would be you."

"Of course I'm not going to contest." No way would he do such a thing.

Monique nodded. "There's plenty of money in her account to cover funeral expenses."

Of course there'd be plenty of money in her account. She'd gotten quite the payout in the divorce settlement. Anna Belle never had been good at investing or saving, just dumping all income into a checking account. He suddenly didn't feel like arguing with Monique over who would pay.

"I'll make sure there are plenty of pink roses. What about music? Do you know of any hymns she might have mentioned liking?"

Anna Belle and hymns didn't exactly belong in the same sentence. He couldn't remember the last time she'd gone to church with him. For the last several months of their marriage, she hadn't even wanted to be in the same city as him, much less the same building.

She'd been raised Catholic but hadn't gone to Mass in— Well, he couldn't remember the last time.

Monique interrupted his memories. "I've always thought *Amazing Grace* was a fitting song for a funeral."

"I think that would be nice."

"Can you think of someone I could ask to present her eulogy?"

Oh no. Someone to talk nice about Anna Belle? To say she was a wonderful person? To talk about how much she'll be missed? He couldn't think of a single person.

Monique snapped her fingers. "You know, I ran into an old friend of hers at the hotel. I remembered Anna Belle having mentioned her several times. Laure Comeau. She says they were close. Do you know her?"

Oh yes. He knew her. Laure Comeau couldn't stand him, and the feeling was mutual. "That's her best friend."

Monique nodded. "So I could ask her to write a eulogy."

He nodded. "You saw Laure?" He struggled to keep his voice even.

Monique nodded. "We just passed each other as I was leaving the hotel yesterday. She works there and stopped to offer her condolences and reminded me that she was Anna Belle's friend."

He did his best not to read too much into it. He could only imagine what Laure would say about his and Anna Belle's relationship. She always saw things through Anna Belle's cloudy lenses.

Monique continued. "I'm thinking of having her service on Friday. Would that work for your schedule?"

He hadn't considered all of this yet. Of course he would have to attend her funeral. It would be expected of him. Wouldn't it make him look guilty to miss it? He knew the police usually attended funerals to watch their suspects. Would he provide fodder for the police's suspicion if he skipped the service?

"Would you like to say something at the service?"

"No." The word rushed out in a breath on gut response. No way did he want to speak about Anna Belle, but this was her mother. "I'm sorry."

"No, don't be. I know Anna Belle could be difficult."

That was putting it mildly.

"Loving her could be the hardest thing to do. I know." The older woman let out a heavy sigh.

They were on common and familiar ground together.

"No one will think any less of you for not speaking at her funeral, least of all me." Monique met his stare. "But don't you ever doubt for one moment that she loved you. She did, Grayson, no matter what happened between the two of you. I could tell, and I knew her better than anybody."

His mouth went dry. "I loved her, Monique. You know I did." Even after everything she'd done, the things she'd thrown in his face and the things he'd only recently found out, a part of him still loved her. And would forever love her.

"Like I said, I don't know what happened between you two, and I don't need to know." She plucked imaginary lint from the many snags in her slacks.

"I'm so sorry, Monique."

"For what?"

"For losing your daughter." The knot in his chest tightened. "For not pushing to see you at holidays more often. For not putting my foot down and making Anna Belle act like. . .an adult."

Monique laughed. "Oh honey, I appreciate that. I do, but I know how my daughter was. There wasn't anything you could've done. Anna Belle was always that way. Always going to see and do things exactly her way or no way at all. No one could ever make her see or think differently."

Grayson remained silent. What could he say? That Anna Belle had been self-centered, self-serving, and bordering on downright narcissism? All those were certainly true, but they hadn't made him love her any less. Had Monique felt the same way?

"I can see what you're thinking, son. Anna Belle was who she was. She wouldn't have changed for you, and certainly not for me. I gave her my best efforts until the day she left home. The good Lord knows I tried to get her to act right and be a better person. I tried. And tried. That girl would make the worst decision every single time, even when doing the right thing would've been easier. That just wasn't her way."

That summed up Anna Belle perfectly, but it didn't make accepting it after the fact any easier. Maybe it was even harder now that neither of them could ever help her. He considered her mother. "How did you reconcile yourself to that?" As soon as he asked the question, he regretted it. "I'm sorry. That was out of line." Not to mention rude and thoughtless, considering what brought them together today.

"Oh Grayson. Stop beating yourself up for not being able to change her into a better person. That wasn't your job. Mine either."

"There were things she did. . .things I can't even believe she did, but I know she did." Things he hadn't even known she'd done while they were married. Things that ripped apart his very spirit. Things he knew he'd have to find a way to forgive her for.

"You're a Christian, right?" Monique studied him from over her glasses.

"Yes, ma'am." Which made him want to squirm, considering what he'd just been thinking.

"Then consider this: God is our Father and perfect in every way, right? He loves us and wants the best for us. Always does right by us, yes?"

"Of course." She had his attention.

"Do you blame God for mass murders? Rapists? Child molesters?"

What? "Of course not. Free will gave them the choice to follow God's plan for their lives or to go their own way and sin."

She smiled. "Very true. So if God, the perfect Father, has disobedient children, why are we mere humans so arrogant to think that our children ought to behave as they should?"

Grayson went very still. He'd never considered his marriage to Anna Belle in such a light before. He'd never considered Anna Belle in that way. He'd never thought about Anna Belle being disobedient to God the Father. He'd been too wrapped up in his own emotions to think about the eternal.

Monique inched closer to him on the couch and rested the parchment-paper-thin skin of her hand on his. "I don't mean to pry, Grayson, but did you break your vows to her?"

"No. I wasn't perfect, not by any stretch of the imagination, but I never broke my vows." He'd been so tempted, but the pain she'd inflicted had left him raw. Too raw to reciprocate.

"Did she break hers to you?"

He nodded, slowly, not trusting himself to speak. Even now—especially now—it was hard to admit.

"Then stop berating yourself now that she's dead. Don't turn her into a good person in your mind just because she's no longer living."

The abruptness. . .

She gently squeezed his hand before releasing it. "It's the truth, and we both know it. I'm too old and too tired to pussyfoot around the facts. Or to sugarcoat reality."

He smiled, realizing he missed getting to know a really unique woman whom he would've probably grown to love, had he demanded the chance.

"The hospital said they had clearance from the coroner to release the body. I'll notify the funeral home in Breaux Bridge."

"Coroner's office?"

She nodded. "The hospital said they'd concluded the autopsy, and the coroner's office had received all the reports they needed."

Of course the coroner's office would receive all the autopsy reports, which they would have turned over to the police too. That had to be why they were treating this as a homicide.

"Grayson, I know what the police always think about the ex-spouse."

His gut tightened, and he nodded.

"The police have asked to see me tomorrow. They'll be coming to the hotel at one to talk with me."

"I don't know what to say. I promise you, Monique, I had nothing to do with her death."

She pushed to her feet. "Oh, I know that. Knew it the minute I saw your face. No one fakes the pain they're trying so desperately to hide from everyone."

He stood and faced her.

"And if they ask, I'll tell them just that."

"I appreciate that."

"I'm going to offer you a bit of advice, Grayson. Just an old lady who's been around and seen a lot. Take it for what it's worth." She squeezed his forearm. "Allow yourself to grieve for her. No matter that you're divorced, no matter what she did to you or what you did to her, let yourself grieve the loss of her."

"I. . .ah—"

She tightened her hold on his arm. "You don't have to say anything. Just take a day or two to feel the loss and accept it. You'll need that, and later on you might not have the time or emotional energy. If you don't, you'll regret it. Mark my words."

Maybe she had a point. Grayson nodded.

She smiled. "Look, I'm staying at the Darkwater Inn. Why don't we have lunch on Wednesday before I head back to Breaux Bridge? Maybe there will be information about the case we can discuss."

"I'd like that." He returned the smile as he led her to the front door.

"You take care, Grayson."

"You too. I'll call you tomorrow to set up a time for lunch." He opened the front door.

She smiled as she stepped over the threshold. "I'll go see about the eulogy now."

He held her elbow, helping her down the steps. Better her than him having to call Laure, but he did wonder—what on earth would Laure say about him?

More importantly, would Monique or anyone else believe her?

SIX

"The manufacturer of the energy drink confirmed there is no cherry juice in their mix." Danielle tossed the fax onto Brandon's desk. "Just as our lab reported."

"At least now we know for certain, from the source." He hadn't expected to learn anything different but needed to make sure all the i's were dotted and t's crossed.

Danielle sat at her desk that pushed up against his, facing him. "Look, I might've been overzealous about the case. I want to do a good job, right by the book, play my cards right."

"That's all I ask. I just want Grayson to get a fair shake, that's all."

His partner shook her head. "It has nothing to do with him, and everything to do with working the case, following the trail of evidence."

Brandon crossed his arms over his chest. "Just so long that means not going out of your way to make sure he's incriminated."

She frowned. "I would never go out of my way to incriminate anyone. I'm going to follow the evidence, no matter what rabbit trail I have to hop down."

That's the best he could hope for at this point. "Then we're on the same page."

Danielle hesitated, then handed him a folder. "I've asked Franklin Barron and Hugh Istre to come in. Franklin just arrived, and Hugh will come before lunch."

"Good. Do you want me to take lead on Franklin?" Brandon asked. Danielle had always seemed to prefer to do the observation rather than the actual interviewing.

"Sure."

Interviewing witnesses was one of his specialties. He scanned the file, reading over Franklin Barron's original statement. Seems that he and Anna Belle worked together on a PR campaign the day she died. Could be very interesting.

Brandon stood. "Let's not keep Mr. Barron waiting."

Danielle grinned and followed him down the hall and around the corner to the interrogation room.

It felt right to be back on good terms with his partner. He smiled as he opened the door and extended his hand to the man sitting on the single side of the table. "Mr. Barron, thank you for coming in to speak with us on such short notice. We really appreciate it."

"Yes, sir." Franklin Barron's handshake was surprisingly firm.

Brandon sat opposite Franklin, taking in his initial impression of the younger man, as well as what he already knew. He looked his age, twenty-seven, and while he wore the nerdy look, complete with black-rimmed glasses, that impression was deceptively contrasted by his scraggly and uneven beard and mustache.

Shutting the folder, Brandon smiled at him. "Mr. Barron, why don't you walk us through your Thursday?"

"Sure." Franklin nodded. No offer to call him by his first name. Meeting Brandon's gaze head-on. Nerves weren't bothering this one much at all. "The group all had breakfast in the dining room together at eight sharp."

"The group?" Brandon interrupted. Maybe he could make the man nervous. He liked having his suspects on edge.

"Yes. Tim and his wife. Georgia and Anna Belle. Me and Hugh. We had to report to breakfast at eight on the dot."

"What would happen if you were late?"

Franklin gave him a flat stare. "We would be eliminated from consideration for promotion to executive accounts director. Every instruction was to be followed to the letter."

"Oh. Okay." Brandon leaned back from the table. "Sorry, please continue."

"After breakfast, everyone was dismissed to their rooms. We were told we would receive cards with our next instructions privately. I went to my room."

"Excuse my interruption, but please tell me what you were told about the weekend. What your boss told you in regard to what you were doing."

"Tim told me that there were four of us senior account reps who were up for the promotion to executive accounts director. Everyone wants that job. It's prestigious and it comes with a healthy salary. He said he wanted to watch us work, independently and as a team, and we would be tested over a long weekend."

"I see." Brandon glanced at the notes in the folder from their interview with Georgia. He looked back at Franklin. "What did you have to fill out or agree to before being considered?"

Franklin gave a shrug. "A bunch of paperwork, and we had to sign a waiver of release to participate."

"What about granting access to your medical and financial records."

"Yeah. That was in there too."

"Okay. Sorry for the interruption. Please, continue."

"Anyway, I went to my room and found a card with a Mardi Gras mask. I was told to put on the mask and go to Anna Belle's room and deliver her note to her right at nine forty. So I did."

What? "Wait, you were told to put on a mask and go to Anna Belle's room?" New fact. He glanced over to his partner who raised her brows at him.

"Yeah, and give her note to her."

"What did her note say?"

"I didn't know initially because it was sealed. So I put on the mask and headed to her room, right at nine forty, just like I was instructed."

"You wore the mask to her room?" How did these people just do things so blindly?

"Yeah, that's what my note said, so that's what I did."

Brandon nodded, still flabbergasted that people would act before thinking things through or ask questions. "What happened?"

"She opened the door and freaked out on me. Started hitting and kicking me like a wild woman." Franklin shook his head and gave a little smile. "For such a tiny woman, man, she could throw a serious punch." He pushed up the sleeve to his right arm and pointed to a small bruise. "She got me good there."

"Well, you did show up to her room wearing a mask," Danielle said.

"Yeah, but she went ape-crazy. Started yelling that she'd seen me the night before, sneaking around outside and in the hall outside her room. I reminded her that couldn't be because she knew I was inside because everyone heard me holler when I found the snake in my bed."

"Wait. What?" A snake? Another new fact that was omitted from his initial statement.

Franklin nodded, eyes wide. "Yeah, man. Wednesday night after we finally all went to our rooms, I found a snake in my bed." He shivered. "I'm scared of snakes. Serious scared. Guess because I was bit by one as a kid, and ever since, I can't stand them. Anyway, Hugh said it wasn't poisonous. He grabbed it and took it outside." He wore a sheepish grin and his cheeks tinted pink. "I didn't sleep much that night, to be honest."

"I can imagine." Danielle shook her head. "I'd be rattled for sure, pun intended. I don't like snakes either."

"How did a snake get in your bed?" Brandon couldn't fathom such a thing. He wasn't terrified of them, but that would unnerve him.

Franklin shook his head. "I don't know. I mean, after Tim told us we were all part of this elaborate game that would push our buttons, I guess I figured the snake had been part of that to get to me."

"Did anyone know about your past snakebite?"

"Nah. It was in my medical records though."

If it was part of the game, Grayson's company sure was thorough. And a little twisted. "Okay, sorry about getting you off track. So on Thursday, you told Anna Belle it couldn't have been you she saw in the mask. . . ."

Franklin nodded. "Yeah. Right. She'd accused me of wearing the mask outside and in the hallways on Wednesday night. I reminded her about the snake, so it hadn't been me. She was pretty shaken up about it though."

"Where's the mask now?"

"I left it in her room, now that I think about it." Franklin shook his head. "She was freaked, but then I calmed her down and gave her the note with our task. I guess I forgot about the mask on the desk when we left."

"What did the note say was your next task?"

"For me and Anna Belle to report to the library."

Brandon waited a second, then when Franklin didn't continue, pressed. "So you went to the library?"

"Yeah. There we found out what we had to do. We were told to watch the video set up on the TV. It was about a popular politician and had some photos and information of him about to be caught up in a sexual discrimination scandal."

"Really?" Danielle asked.

Franklin nodded. "Yeah, and I don't think what we saw was man-ufactured in any way to be part of a game. I think it was real, and maybe that's what all this game was really about—to deflect and make us think it was a game."

"What do you mean?" Interesting. Brandon definitely wanted to hear this out.

"This politician is someone who could make a big difference with his plans. Already local supporters are talking about his possible presidential candidacy in coming years. He's got quite a reputation of being honest and a family man, and the conservatives and a good many liberals really like him. But, and isn't there always a *but*? Anyway, from what we saw on that video, there's some compelling evidence of his sexual discrimination as well as lots of innuendo of possible sexual misconduct. If it got out, his political career would be over. No questions asked, he'd be done for."

Franklin stretched his legs out in front of him, clearly relaxed. "Our task was to come up with a spin—a PR campaign to keep the politician in a positive light. To spin what was on the video in a way to minimize reality while keeping him front and center on what his reputation is staked. We had two hours to come up with something. From what the note said, Georgia and Hugh would work together on the same thing, and whichever team produced the better PR campaign would win the contest. It would certainly help us in the consideration for promotion."

Brandon hated to admit that he wished he knew who the politician was. "I'm assuming you and Anna Belle came up with such a campaign?"

Franklin grinned and nodded, straightening in his chair. "We did, and it was kick a—uh, it was amazing, if I do say so myself. No way Georgia and Hugh could even think of coming close to what we came up with. We knocked it out of the park, and I think even Tim was impressed. He sure seemed excited when we pitched him the idea just before lunch. That's kinda why I think this whole game concept was created as a cover for the actual reason we were all there: to come up with a campaign for the politician, but none of us would be aware of it."

"Why would your company do that?" Danielle asked.

Brandon wondered the same thing.

"Containment of course. Because this guy is powerful, and like I said, if this got out, it would wreck his entire career."

"But why go to such extremes?" Brandon asked.

Franklin shook his head. "You guys have no clue how PR works. People will do anything to keep their secrets."

"Even putting snakes in beds?" Danielle seemed to be having as hard a time buying it all as Brandon.

"Yep, even that." Franklin shrugged. "But whatever."

Better just to let that one go. "Okay, so back to Thursday. You were pretty confident in your and Anna Belle's campaign. . . ."

"Yeah. Ours was pretty awesome. I could tell Tim thought so too by the way he nodded all during our presentation."

"So you and Anna Belle won?"

"We don't know for sure. Tim was going to take it to the board of directors to see which campaign they liked better, but I think he was taking it right to the politician. That's what I think."

He thought a little too highly of his capabilities, that's what Brandon thought. "So did you have lunch as a group?"

Franklin nodded. "We all ate, and then, about one, we were given our cards with our next task. We all went to our rooms to open our cards privately, since they didn't seem to be combined. Our next task was to go to a room and it would be like an escape room, and we would have to work together with someone else to figure out the clues of the room and escape."

"So you and Anna Belle had to escape a room?"

Franklin shook his head. "Not this time. I was sent to another room downstairs, and Georgia was there. She was my partner this time around."

"No campaign to create, just a room to escape?" Danielle asked.

"Yeah. You know, like the escape rooms you see around everywhere that you have to solve the clues and riddles to figure out how to get out. But these clues. . .they were personal stuff about me and

Georgia. Stuff we didn't know about each other. Secrets we didn't want to share."

"Like?" Brandon asked.

Franklin's cheeks turned red and he lifted a casual shoulder. "Just personal stuff. Like dating stuff. Embarrassing things, that's all." He cleared his throat and stared at the floor. "We had two and a half hours to escape. We almost got out in time."

"You didn't make it?" Danielle asked.

Franklin shook his head. "The timer went off while we were still working on the last clue."

"So what happened?"

"The timer buzzed, startling the both of us. I thought Georgia was going to cry. To be honest, I had no idea what was gonna happen. We just sat there feeling defeated, and then we heard the dead bolt click. I went over, and sure enough, the door was unlocked. Emmi was in the hallway and told us to go to our rooms and get ready for dinner. We were to be in the dining room at four thirty, and Tim would tell us which PR campaign had won."

"Did Anna Belle and Hugh have an escape room like you and Georgia?"

"I don't really know. Emmi told us to get ready for dinner, so I went to my room. I changed shirts and checked my cell, then Georgia started screaming. I followed the sound, and everyone was almost in Anna Belle's room. Tim was performing CPR, and there were several people I didn't know. Georgia was crying, and Emmi was hugging her. I asked them what happened, and Georgia said she'd found Anna Belle on the floor." Franklin sat a little on the edge of the chair. "The ambulance came and took Anna Belle. It was surreal, you know?"

"Did you know Anna Belle had an allergy to cherries?" Danielle asked.

Franklin shook his head.

"Did you know about Anna Belle's common use of energy drinks?" Brandon asked.

"Yeah. Everybody did. She used to keep them in the break room fridge but got all twisted out of shape one time when one came up missing. She was furious and accused everyone of taking it. From then on, she kept them on her desk."

"What happened after the ambulance left?" Brandon asked. "What did everybody do?"

"Well, Tim started off to follow the ambulance. Emmi let go of Georgia and followed after him. Hugh said he was going to go to the hospital too." Franklin shrugged. "I didn't know the other folks, so I told Georgia we needed to go. We got our stuff, and I walked her out to her car to make sure she was okay, then I went home."

"Why did Hugh go to the hospital?" Brandon asked.

"I don't know. You'd have to ask him." The animosity was almost undetectable.

Almost.

Danielle picked up the questioning, asking the next one quickly. "About what time did you leave?"

"I guess about a quarter till five."

"Did you go to the hospital?"

Franklin paused. "No. I mean, I figured with Tim and Emmi and Hugh there. . .well, somebody would let me know what was going on, you know?"

Brandon nodded. "Did you hear from anybody else about the incident after you got home?"

Franklin nodded. "Tim called Friday afternoon and told me Anna Belle had died. He said the police would probably call me, like you did."

"Anything else?"

"Well, he explained that we'd all been in this game that Tim hired a company to create so the board could decide who to promote."

Franklin sat upright, his chin poking out. "I thought that was a little cheesy, if you ask me."

Interesting that Georgia said the decision was Tim's but Franklin said it was the board's. "Did you talk to anyone else? Besides Tim and me and my partner here?"

"Nope."

Brandon slipped on a smile. "Is there anything else you can think of we might need to know?"

"Well, Tim told me that the company he hired? Anna Belle's ex-husband was one of the owners." Franklin grinned and shook his head. "How messed up is that?"

"What do you mean?" Heat tightened the back of Brandon's neck.

"Well everybody knew Tim and Anna Belle had had a thing. I'm guessing it was over, because Emmi and Tim seemed to have patched things up, and if they hadn't, let's be serious—Anna Belle would've been given the promotion without a game or anything. But then Tim goes and hires Anna Belle's ex-husband's company to create a game that she would play?" Franklin shook his head. "That's like setting Anna Belle up for defeat."

Wasn't that an understatement.

SEVEN

"Where have you been?" Pam jumped out of her SUV outside the cell phone store and popped her hands on her hips. "I was about to come looking for you."

"I had a visit from Anna Belle's mother." Grayson swallowed the smile at Pam's slight self in what he was sure she thought was an intimidating stance. He shut the truck's door and pressed the last two buttons on the keyless entry pad. The doors locked with a click.

"Really?" Pam's dark brown eyes widened. "How'd that go?"

"Pretty good, actually. She's working on making the arrangements and wanted my input." He led the way to the store's glass door, which swung open as soon as they approached.

"Welcome. How may we assist you today?" the young man with an iPad in hand asked, while glancing to Pam's hair, then back to his tablet before sneaking a peek at her hair again.

Grayson took a moment to explain how his cell phone had escaped into a body of water and remained unrecovered, then provided his number and the information needed for the man to pull up his account.

"Would you like to look at the newest version of the phone, sir?" the young man asked, still sneaking sideways glances at Pam.

"I'd really just like the same phone I had. I know how it works."

"Of course, sir. Let me check your account and see if we have that same phone in stock. I'll be right back."

"Okay, spill." Pam tugged Grayson toward one of the tall tables as soon as the salesman left. She hopped up onto the stool and settled on the seat.

Grayson leaned against the table, propping his foot on the other stool's rung and recounted his conversation with Monique, omitting some of the more personal information.

"Wow. She sounds pretty awesome."

He nodded. "She was. Is." He pushed away the regret at never having taken the time to get to know her. He'd listened to Anna Belle's rants about her mother and her horrible childhood, and it had never occurred to him that Anna Belle would have embellished the relationship with her mother. He should have known better. In describing every relationship, Anna Belle twisted facts to make herself the victim.

Grayson knew that better than most.

Pam laid her hand gently on his arm. "Hey, you okay?"

He nodded but knew he wasn't really. So many regrets. So much history. "Just wishing I'd gotten to know her better before now."

"You're in luck, sir, we still had your model in stock." The young man had the box already open as he sat it on the table. "Would you like a new number with your new phone?"

"No. The same, please." He'd had the same number for almost two decades and had no intention of dealing with the hassle of changing it.

Pam rolled her eyes at Grayson.

"Easy peasy then, sir." The young man pulled out the phone and began setting it up. "Do you back up online with your phone?"

Grayson nodded.

"Good. Then you'll be able to pull all your apps and contacts and important stuff." He handed the phone to Grayson. "If you'll just type in your information, we'll get you up and running in a jiffy."

Grayson did, then handed the phone back to the salesman.

"It'll take a few minutes to update. I'll go check on removing your old phone from your account. Let me write down your account information again." He did, then disappeared across the store.

"So, you still want to run out to the rental house as soon as we're done here?" Pam twisted on the stool.

"I do. But if you don't want—"

"Don't you dare finish that statement if it ends with you telling me I don't have to come with you." She gave him a hard stare. "I'm in all the way, so you can stop with all that."

He smiled, hoping it would disarm her frustration with him. He knew she meant what she said, but he didn't want her to feel obligated in any way. Still, he wasn't going to argue anymore. "Then, yes, I want to go there as soon as we leave here. What did Colton say when you called in today?"

"Said he understood and asked how you were. Has he called you?"

"No." Which now that he thought about it, seemed odd. "Has he said anything to you about me?"

Before she could reply, the salesman returned and checked the phone. "Looks like it's done." He handed it to Grayson. "If you'll look it over and make sure all your important information is there."

Grayson scrolled through the apps and his contacts list. "It looks like everything's here."

"Good. Your most recent voice mails and text messages will come through over the next several minutes."

Grayson nodded even as the phone vibrated the alert of such notices.

The salesman continued. "Now, you can either pay here for the replacement, Mr. Thibodeaux, or you can just put it on your account and make a monthly payment. There's no interest, and you can pay it off at any time you'd like."

"Just put it on my account." It'd be quicker, and he itched to get over to the rental house to check it out.

"Yes, sir, of course. Which account would you like the charges put on?"

Grayson slipped the new phone into his jacket pocket. "What do you mean *which account*? I only have one."

"No, sir." The young salesman tapped the screen of his iPad. "I show your current account that has that phone number on it, but I also show a joint account with an active number as well." He ran his finger up the screen. "The account is in your name and that of one Anna Belle Thibodeaux. Different mailing address though." He frowned. "Is this not your account? I can get my manager to look into this."

Grayson's mind raced. "No. I just forgot about that account." He shot Pam a warning glance.

"Oh-kay." The salesman wore a skeptical look.

"Actually, is there a way I could get a record of the calls made to and from the phone number on our joint account?" If he could get access before the police did, he might be able to spot something that seemed off in Anna Belle's call logs. "Say for the past two weeks?"

"You can go online and print it off."

"But can you do that for me? Now? Since I'm already here." He smiled. "Please."

"Let me see what I can do. It'll take a minute."

"Thank you."

Pam waited until the salesman had left before turning on Grayson. "You're still on Anna Belle's account?"

"I didn't know. She must've just changed the address for the bill." Typical of her. She would make sure the billing address was changed and figured that would be enough.

"What do you think is on the call log?"

"I don't know, but I want to see if there's anything out of the ordinary on there. The police will get around to it eventually, and I'd rather beat them to the punch if there's anything that will help us figure out what happened."

"Smart."

"Every now and then it happens." He grinned and winked at her.

"Rarely." But she smiled back.

"Here you go, sir. It's the last ten days." The salesman thrust a small stack of papers at Grayson. "That's all I can pull here, but again, you can access all the information online."

"Thanks." Grayson took the papers from the young man before he could change his mind. "I appreciate all your help today. Thank you."

With Pam on his heels, Grayson made his way to his truck. Pam jumped into the passenger's side as soon as he unlocked the doors. He split the stack in half and handed Pam the bottom half before starting to go through the line items.

He discounted the calls to and from Laure Comeau, her best friend. He recognized her number because it had always been on his and Anna Belle's home phone caller ID before they canceled the landline entirely.

There were many calls to her office, ranging from two minutes to forty-eight. Legitimate work stuff.

Several calls from the same number, always late at night, called her. None were over five minutes, some barely one. Not a single time did she call the number back. Grayson grabbed the pen always tucked under the sun visor and circled that number.

"You found something?" Pam marked her spot with her finger.

"Just a number I don't know that called several times at night—" Wait a minute. He *did* know that number. It was familiar. He'd seen it many times before.

The muscles across the back of his shoulders tightened. "Never mind. It's Dubois's number." Her boss. The man she'd been having an affair with.

Pam didn't say a word, just gave a nod and went back to looking at her stack.

What did she think of him? Really? Pam had been his assistant at Game's On You since the day he hired her three years ago. He and Colton had just opened the business and had signed two large local firms to create and run games for them. He'd needed to hire someone good, who could start immediately, and whom he could trust. Pam had walked in for her interview sporting her purple-pink hair, which matched her lipstick perfectly, and wearing black jeans with combat boots and a worn bomber jacket. Before Grayson could dismiss her on looks alone, she'd wowed him with her knowledge and personality. Going with his gut instinct, he'd hired her on the spot and not once regretted it. They were now so much more than coworkers. They were friends.

Yet she hadn't said what she really thought about his marriage dissolving. Sure, she'd been outraged on behalf of him as the truth—and all the layers of the truth that he hadn't even had an idea had been going on—came out, but in the recessed corners of her mind, did she think he was partially to blame?

How many times had he asked himself that over the last several months? Had he not given Anna Belle enough attention? Had he not cared enough for what mattered to her?

"Grayson?"

He focused back on Pam, in the present. "Yeah?"

"Why did you call Anna Belle Tuesday afternoon?"

"I didn't."

Pam tapped the paper in her hand. "It shows our office number called her at four twenty-eight. The call lasted until five eleven."

He took the paper from her and stared at the log. Sure enough, there was the call. But he didn't talk to her. He hadn't talked to her in two weeks.

"Are you sure you didn't call her for something to do with the divorce or something and just forgot?"

"Talk for almost an hour? Not hardly. I had no reason to talk to her, much less call her."

"Well, I sure didn't call her either, but there's the call from our office, right there on the log."

This didn't make sense. He didn't call her. Their last contact had been brutal to his ego, and his emotions.

Call her? No way. "This has to be a mistake."

"With your work number and for that length of time?" Pam shook her head. "There has to be a logical explanation for this."

"I'd love to hear it." He handed her back the paper. "I'm all ears."

"I don't know, but we'll figure it out." She went back to studying the paper. "Um, Grayson?"

He glanced up. "Yeah?" What else?

"Anna Belle called your cell at 10:12 Wednesday night."

"Yeah, I thought she wanted to yell at me about money or something she didn't like in the final divorce decree. She didn't leave a voice mail or anything."

"Okay. She called you again at 9:12 on Thursday morning."

The day she died.

Grayson grabbed the phone log from his assistant, even though he knew it would reflect exactly what Pam had said. The call on Thursday was only a little over a minute. Long enough to hear his outgoing message and leave one. He pulled his new cell phone out of his jacket pocket. Forty-four missed calls and three voice mails.

He scrolled through the missed calls that recorded from Wednesday night until the present—forty of the forty-four were from Pam. One from Colton—hey, at least he had called. One from Brandon's cell phone. Two from Anna Belle, same times as her call log.

Hesitantly, he accessed the voice mails and played Pam's first, putting it on speaker.

"Hey, Grayson, it's Pam. Where are you? I've been trying to reach you and have called like a gazillion times. Call me when you get this."

Pam shrugged. "Told you I'd tried to call."

He grinned. "Yeah, fortysomething times."

"Barely forty."

He moved to play the next voice mail.

Anna Belle's voice cut through the speaker. "Grayson, it's me. We need to talk."

The hairs on the back of his neck stood at full attention. He felt like a goose had walked over his grave, hearing the voice of the dead. A contrite-sounding Anna Belle was definitely something out of the ordinary.

He played the last voice mail recording. "Grayson, it's Brandon. You need to call me."

Silence filled the cabin of the truck.

"I didn't know her well, but she sounded different than usual on that recording," Pam offered.

He nodded. "She sounded remorseful almost, which we both know is unlike her." He saved all the voice mails and studied the data. "Nine twelve. That would've been after breakfast, right?" He ran a hand over his face, trying to remember the details of the game he'd created that he'd tried to forget this past weekend.

Pam nodded. "Everyone was dismissed after breakfast, about nine, to go back to their rooms before the next stage of their tasks would begin."

"So she would've gone back to her room. I wonder what made her call me then."

"I don't know, but it had to have been something important for her to have called you and sounded so. . .different."

What would have been the trigger that sparked her to call him? What could she say? The more he considered it, the more it didn't make sense.

So many unanswered questions, and to the outsider, he had to look guiltier with every twist and turn.

Why had Emmi Dubois even come?

Well, Anna Belle knew why. Because Emmi knew deep down that Tim was still in love with Anna Belle. It was tragically sad for the woman, but if Anna Belle had to watch her drape herself over her husband much more, she was going to be sick.

She made her way up the stairs beside Hugh, who was telling her some stupid story about a client of his, but Anna Belle stayed in her own mind, mulling things over.

Emmi was so obvious too. Like kissing Tim as soon as Anna Belle walked into the room. Practically lying in his lap when they sat down as a group to eat. So low class.

Pathetic, really.

As if Anna Belle wanted Tim back. She didn't, but if she did, she'd only have to wag her little finger and he'd be at her side so fast it'd make Emmi's head spin around.

If the woman kept on trying to mark her territory in such a fashion, Anna Belle might be tempted to call Tim, just to put Emmi in her place and stop the nauseating public display of affection.

Anna Belle giggled at something Hugh said, not that she was listening as they reached the top of the stairs, but she didn't want Hugh to lose interest in her. He was interesting enough, usually, and certainly attentive to her. Normally, she would show more personal attention to the beautiful man. It was just that she was bone tired, her sleep last night broken by images of Mardi Gras masks and white gloves.

At least in the light of day this morning, she hadn't been scared of seeing her stalker, although she'd caught herself looking out every time she passed a window. How he found her, she would never know. It'd been years, but when he'd been convicted and sentenced to jail time, he'd swore he'd find her and come after her.

He'd obviously succeeded.

She was supposed to have been notified if and when he was released, but after a couple of years, and getting married and moving, she had considered his threat an unimportant thing of her past.

Except now it wasn't.

She missed Grayson terribly right now. He had been her defender back when she was going through the trial. No denying her ex-husband was a strong man. Worked out. Lifted weights every morning at home. Ran when he could. She'd always felt safe with him, knowing he'd protect her until his dying breath if need be.

Anna Belle certainly didn't feel safe right now. Who would protect her here? Tim? She snorted. That was a joke. Franklin Barron? Please, he'd hide behind anybody. Hugh Istre would. He could. She nodded. He was strong like Grayson. Virile. Definitely manly and sexy.

No, she needed to concentrate on whatever Tim had for her to complete today. Hopefully it wouldn't be such a setup for failure like cooking.

She said goodbye to Hugh in the hall, unlocked her bedroom door, and stepped inside. Tim had said they'd get instructions for their next assignment soon. She shook her head. That next assignment had better be more job related than cooking dinner or she was out of here, promotion or not.

Grabbing her lipstick, she headed to the bathroom. There was something on the desk. Who had been in her room? There hadn't been anything on the desk when she'd left for breakfast. She moved to yank it up. Just who thought they could march into her room—

All the air left her lungs. Her hands trembled as she couldn't stop staring at the foreign, yet familiar, pamphlet. She gripped it tighter in her hand, crinkling the glossy paper.

Oh no. No, no, no, no.

EIGHT

"Thank you for coming in, Mr. Istre." Brandon sat across the table from the younger African American man. While his multiple long braids were pulled back away from his face, his suit clung to his squared frame.

Hugh didn't reply, just gave a half smile and a quick jerk of his head. Apparently not a man of many words. Everything about his appearance and demeanor gave the impression of reservation and professionalism.

"We just need to go back over everything to get a full picture of events leading up to Anna Belle Thibodeaux's death."

"So you'd like me to start with Wednesday?" The man's voice was richer than Brandon would have imagined. Deeper than a baritone, more like a bass.

"Please." They could always fast-forward if the details weren't applicable, but it might be nice to have more of an overview. However. . . "Actually, could you provide us details of what you were told about the events that were to take place at the rental house and what you were expected to submit?"

Hugh's forehead crinkled. "We were told that there were four of us employees who were under consideration for promotion to executive accounts director. The company planned a long weekend of events that would challenge us four candidates, individually and as a team, to give the board an encompassing report of our strengths and weaknesses so they could make an informed decision on who to promote."

It sounded logical when put like that, however, that they weren't told they would be involved in a game seemed shady. "What information did you have to provide?"

"A full dossier, basically, complete with access to our financial and medical information. We had to sign a nonliability waiver, which at the time I thought was a little over the top, but now I understand more fully."

Oh, the irony. Brandon nodded. "Okay. So now start me on Wednesday, if you will."

"We—Anna Belle, Franklin, Georgia, and myself—were all instructed to arrive at a house on Esplanade Avenue that the company had rented for a long weekend, and to arrive promptly at one. We were told to leave our laptops and tablets at home, and we could only use our cells in our assigned rooms. To violate this basic rule would remove our name from consideration of the promotion."

Harsh. Brandon nodded, making a mental note that Hugh alphabetized their names as he spoke. Telling of his personality type.

"We all arrived on time and were assigned rooms. All of our rooms were located upstairs in the old house, which looked creepy enough but was actually quite comfortable."

Brandon thought it was something straight out of a horror movie himself. When they'd run the check on the house, they'd learned that the owner often rented it out to groups who used it as a haunted house. The lot's upkeep was abysmal, to put it mildly, and added to the isolation, despite it being in a neighborhood, which played up the eeriness of the complete picture.

"I'd barely gotten settled in my room when a card was slipped under my bedroom door. The card instructed me to go to the house's turret where I was tasked with sweeping off the widow's walk." Hugh shifted his weight in the chair.

Brandon didn't miss the slight fracture in his facade. "Sweeping? How did that tell the directors anything about you?"

"The sweeping part didn't. The location and condition did."

"I don't understand."

Hugh's head tilted ever so slightly to the left. "The widow's walk had a rickety rail, if you could even call it a rail. It was broken in several places."

Brandon still didn't follow.

Hugh let out a slow, even breath. "I'm not too fond of high places. Have felt like that ever since I fell out of a tree house as a young tween and broke my leg in four places."

"That's rough."

Hugh nodded. "Tell me about it. Eight miserable weeks of my childhood."

"So you were told to go up there and sweep?"

"That's what my card said, so that's what I did."

Seemed easy enough, even if it was nerve-wracking for someone afraid of heights.

"Until the fire alarm went off."

This was new. "Fire alarm?"

Hugh shifted again, more than a little visibly distressed. "I heard the alarm go off and turned to the turret. I could see smoke in the hallway beyond the room. I tried to open the door, but it was locked. I yanked and tugged, but it wouldn't budge."

A line of sweat beaded on Hugh's upper lip.

"When I was nineteen, my mother died in a house fire because she couldn't get out of the house."

An ache knotted in Brandon's chest. Suddenly the game had become very personal. More personal for Hugh than it seemed to be for everyone else. Brandon cleared his throat. "How did you get in?"

"I didn't. I didn't know what everyone else was doing, but I could hear a couple of doors opening and closing, so I yelled out for help. No one came initially, so I kept hollering every minute or so." Hugh ran a hand down his face. "Finally, Franklin showed up. I told him I needed help. He left and came back a few seconds later with a ladder. I was climbing down when I heard one of the girls scream, then the fire truck pulled up."

Why was this the first they were hearing about a fire? Neither Georgia nor Franklin had mentioned it at all.

"As soon as I got to the ground, I ran toward the screaming. It was Georgia, but one of the firemen already had her moving toward the street. They led all of us to the end of the driveway. Georgia was there. Anna Belle was already there. Franklin was right behind me. Within minutes, Tim and Emmi joined us in the yard, telling us everything was all cleared. The firemen got in their truck and left."

Brandon couldn't believe no one had reported any of this. He'd pull the report from the firemen and see who had called 911. "Then what happened?"

"We went back into the house, into the dining room where a sandwich and salad buffet was set up. Tim told us that I was the only one of the four who succeeded in our assigned tasks." Hugh smiled. "The others didn't seem too happy about that, but I was relieved, I'll tell you that much."

"I bet." Brandon shifted in his chair. Sounded like it'd been an eventful evening.

"After we ate, we were told to get a good night's sleep because we were expected to meet for breakfast at eight in the morning and not to be late. We all said our good-nights and left. I had time to take a shower, return a few messages and emails, and was getting ready for bed when Franklin started screaming like a girl."

Ah. "The snake in his bed?"

Hugh grinned. "He told you? I didn't think he'd 'fess up to being such a wimp about it."

"He said you got it out for him."

Hugh nodded. "It was just a king snake. On the big side, but still. I let him loose in the backyard where it backed up to the greenbelt."

"You didn't see signs of any other snakes or anything?"

Hugh shook his head. "Nothing. I figured someone put the snake in there, just like they messed with me."

"With the catwalk and being trapped there?"

"Yeah." The wideness of his eyes said there might've been more, but he quickly moved on. "So we finally were able to get back to our respective rooms after ten."

"You didn't see or talk to anybody there after that?"

"No. It actually quieted down rather quickly after the snake. I don't know if people were dealing with their own fear or worrying about it. Either way, I went on to bed by ten thirty and stayed there until I went down to breakfast at eight the next morning."

Thursday. The day Anna Belle Thibodeaux died.

Hugh needed no prompting. "Breakfast was a nonevent. Georgia and Anna Belle weren't speaking, but that just made the meal quieter and quicker."

"Why weren't they speaking?" Another new tidbit they hadn't heard before.

"Something about Anna Belle not helping Georgia yesterday during the fire scare. But really, they'd never been friends anyway, and now they were competing for the promotion." Hugh shrugged. "We finished by nine and were told to go to our rooms to get instructions. When I got to my room, there was this handmade, ugly doll with a couple of stick pins in it in a bag, with a note to me to wait until exactly ten, then to sneak into Georgia's room and put the doll on her bed, but not to tell anyone, especially not Georgia, even if she asked, and return quickly to my room. That's what I did."

So Hugh was instructed to put the voodoo doll in Georgia's room. Had someone else been told to put the tainted energy drink in Anna Belle's?

"As soon as I got back from Georgia's, there was a note to go to the sitting room where I would be partnered with Georgia to come up with a PR campaign for a potential client."

"The politician?"

Hugh's eyes narrowed. "I guess Franklin probably told you about that. He felt pretty confident that he and Anna Belle had come up with a winner." He let out a slow breath and straightened in the chair. "They probably did come up with a better campaign, because Georgia wasn't really any help. She was distracted and couldn't come up with any ideas."

"Maybe because of the voodoo doll you put in her room?" Danielle asked.

"Voodoo doll, huh? Yeah. That makes sense." Hugh gave a little nod. "I thought maybe she was rattled about the doll, and I almost said something, but then I remembered my instructions and wondered if it was all about testing me. What if she had been told not to be helpful and see if I broke the rules and told her I was the one who put the doll in her room? That would hurt my chances of promotion if I couldn't follow orders. And I was personally in the lead, since Tim said I was the only one who met my challenge the night before."

"Right." Logical, but Brandon was having a hard time keeping up with all the mind games. Was everything coordinated to pit one against another, or was someone else using the corporate game to further their own personal agenda?

"Tim didn't say which campaign he preferred. He told us at lunch that he would take both campaigns to the board, and we were given notes on where we were supposed to go next." Hugh stiffened in his seat. "This time I was told to report to one of the rooms downstairs. Anna Belle was there just a minute after me. We went into the room that had two desks, two filing cabinets, two floor-to-ceiling bookcases, and two high-back chairs. There was a note on one of the desks that said we were now locked in the room and had two and a half hours to solve the riddles and escape. So we did."

"You figured it out and escaped?"

Hugh nodded. "The riddles weren't all that hard, to be honest. A little uncomfortable to figure out with Anna Belle there since they were about my past or hers, but we figured it out and found the key in a little over two hours."

"You two were able to work together even if the clues were embarrassing?" Brandon asked. Franklin had made it seem like the extreme personal information couldn't be shared.

Hugh shrugged. "I mean, it's not a big secret that Anna Belle was hot and she and Tim had been a thing for some time. I figured she'd done enough on her own that nothing I said would shock her, so I just didn't hold anything back. Besides, we'd gone out the weekend before."

Interesting. "Oh?" Another new layer of information they didn't have.

"It was nothing serious. She had broken things off with Tim and just wanted to have some fun, that's all. Nothing serious or anything."

"She's the one who ended things with Tim?"

"Yeah. I mean, if they were still going at it, the whole weekend would've been unnecessary because she would've just been given the promotion. But she broke it off with him, which I bet she regretted doing once she found out the position was available." Hugh shrugged. "And his wife stuck to him like crazy, so she took him back, apparently."

"Apparently." Danielle's tone had hardened.

"I'm betting Emmi fought like everything not to have Anna Belle under consideration for the promotion."

"But she was." Brandon studied Hugh's reaction.

Hugh's expression was as neutral as if they were discussing the weather. "She was good at her job, no doubt about that. She might've been a bit sharp and driven, but if she'd been a man, nobody would've thought twice about her attitude."

Danielle's harrumph was so low that Brandon almost missed it, but her disdain showed in the beginning lines around her eyes.

"Anyway," Hugh continued, "since we'd just gone out and it wasn't serious, we were able to solve the riddle and get the key and get out of the room."

This wasn't going to be glossed over. Brandon glanced at Danielle before asking Hugh. "You two went out to eat or to a movie, or what?"

For the first time all day, Hugh looked uncomfortable. "We just hung out together."

"Hung out? At a bar? Restaurant?"

"At my place." Hugh's face darkened. "We hooked up, if you get my drift."

Oh, Brandon got the drift. He resisted the urge to flash a smile at his partner. Hugh had been with the victim the weekend before she died, and he was one of the last people to see her alive? "I get it. But it was just that once?"

"The Friday and Saturday nights, but we weren't dating or anything."

"Just hooked up. For fun."

"Right." Hugh pushed onward. "Anyway, we unlocked the door, and Emmi was in the hall. She told us to go to our rooms and get ready to meet in the dining room for dinner at four thirty. I had some emails and calls to return, then checked my cell just before I heard screaming. I ran toward the sound, and it was Georgia, outside Anna Belle's room. There were people I'd never seen before in the hall, and Tim was performing CPR on Anna Belle. I asked Emmi what happened, and she told me Georgia had just found Anna Belle like that."

Hugh's words seemed to spill out. "It felt like forever until the ambulance got there. The whole time, Tim kept doing CPR. The paramedics got there and took over doing CPR. They wheeled Anna

Belle out on a stretcher. She looked so still."

"Did you know Anna Belle had an allergy to cherries?" Danielle asked.

Hugh shook his head. "We never talked about allergies or anything."

"But you knew she drank those energy drinks almost daily, right?"

Hugh nodded. "Everybody knew that."

"What happened after the ambulance left?" Brandon asked.

"Well, Tim and Emmi headed out to the hospital." Hugh shrugged. "I felt bad. I mean, I liked Anna Belle and knew many people didn't. I went to the hospital behind Tim and Emmi."

Brandon wasn't about to let that one slip by. "What do you mean you know that many people didn't like Anna Belle?"

Hugh lifted one shoulder, almost too casually. "Of course Emmi hated her, but who could blame her? I'm betting Tim was hurt she'd broken up with him. She was ambitious and wouldn't let anyone get in her way. Sometimes how she acted on that ambition hurt people and they took it personally." He shook his head. "With Anna Belle, it wasn't personal. It was all business. It didn't matter who it was, she was going to do whatever she could to get ahead. You had to respect that."

No, not really. Brandon had seen many detectives earn their shield by playing dirty and using the backs of their fellow officers to climb up the ladder, and he never respected them. Actions did, in most cases, speak louder than words.

Danielle picked up the questioning, flipping the question back around to Thursday afternoon. "What happened at the hospital?"

"I found Tim and Emmi in the waiting room, so I hung out with them. One of the guys from the house, his name was Cole or something, was waiting there for word too. He was with the game company. Well, I know that now. I didn't that night." Hugh let out a slow breath, his shoulders sagging just a little. "Anyway, a doctor finally came out and asked if we were with Anna Belle. We said we were, and the doctor said he was sorry, but that she hadn't made it." Hugh shook his head. "I was in shock. Guess Tim was too, because Emmi had to lead him out. That other guy just left, didn't say anything. It was so unreal."

Brandon nodded. "When did Tim tell you everything had been a game?"

"Tim called Friday afternoon and told me. He also said he'd given all the information to the police to help with the investigation."

"Did you talk to anyone else? Besides Tim and me and my partner here?"

"Nope."

Brandon slipped on a smile. "Is there anything else you can think of that we might need to know?"

Hugh opened his mouth, then clamped it shut.

"Anything at all?" Brandon pressed.

"It's probably nothing."

"What?"

"When we were in the waiting room at the hospital, Emmi had gone across the room to get coffee. Tim sat there, hanging his head, and he was mumbling under his breath. It took several minutes of me listening really hard to understand what he said."

"Which was?" Danielle asked.

"He said, *It's all my fault. It's all my fault.* Like, over and over again."

"Do you have any idea what he could've meant?" Brandon asked, even as excitement built inside him.

"I don't know. I wondered if maybe he meant because he did something to make her break things off with him. Or if he meant that he had us all there under false pretenses. I just don't know, man. You'd have to ask him."

Oh, Brandon intended to ask him when they interviewed Tim Dubois later that afternoon.

Hugh stood. "Can I go now? I have some things I need to take care of."

Brandon and Danielle stood. Brandon extended his hand. "Thank you again for coming in. We really appreciate it."

"Sure. Anna Belle might've had issues with some people, but she didn't deserve to die." Without any further explanation, Hugh passed through the door Danielle held open.

"Well, that one was different." Danielle led the way back to their desks.

"You'd think we'd be used to getting new information out of every witness by now, but this one. . ."

"Yeah, this one seems to take the cake."

"I want to go over the inventory from the CSI unit again and see what jumps out as not belonging. Voodoo dolls, Mardi Gras masks. . . . I can't believe we didn't question those items to begin with."

"Me too." Danielle quickened her stride and reached their desks first. She grabbed the folder from CSI and flipped pages. "Toxicology reports on every item found in the victim's room. Autopsy report. Here we go, inventory report of the actual crime scene room." She ran her finger down the page. "We didn't question the items because there's no mention of any doll or Mardi Gras mask." She handed the folder to him.

Brandon quickly scanned the page, then flipped it over. Danielle was right—no mention of either item. Plenty of other items: list of articles of clothing, eye mask, suitcase, purse, energy drink, toiletries with items like moisturizer, makeup, perfume, and the like, but no mention of a doll or mask. He handed the file back to her, his gut tightening. "This is crazy. How could such items be missed? Who went from CSI to the house?" Brandon's irritation blossomed into full-fledged anger. Cases were thrown out of court because of mishandling of evidence, and it sure looked like there'd been some mishandling on this case already.

"Kara Cobb signed the sheets." Danielle shook her head. "There has to be something else going on."

Brandon nodded. "Kara's the best we have." There was no way she would've missed not one, but two critical items.

"Let me check in with her." Danielle moved to sit in her chair.

While his partner made the call, Brandon went through the file again.

Anna Belle's body had been released to a funeral home in Breaux Bridge, where Anna Belle had been from and where her mother still resided. He and Danielle were scheduled to visit Mrs. Fredericks tomorrow afternoon at her hotel. The mother had already explained that she and Anna Belle were almost estranged, so she didn't know how helpful she would be to the investigation. In his experience, Brandon found that those were usually the interviews that garnered the most truth about the key players.

He glanced over the rest of their notes. They were scheduled to talk with Tim and Emmi Dubois, separately, this afternoon. Tim at Deets PR and Emmi at her home. Considering what they'd learned, they would most likely be very interesting conversations.

No mention of firemen being dispatched to the house on Wednesday evening. Another piece of the puzzle missing? This case was turning into a colossal mess. Commander Ellender would have his and Danielle's heads rolling down the hall. He quickly fired off an inquiry to see why and what time the firemen were dispatched. Hopefully, the report had just gotten put in the wrong place or something and he'd get a copy ASAP for the file.

Danielle replaced the headset to its cradle. "Kara says she's positive there were no dolls or masks at the house."

"Could they have been missed? Maybe pushed under a bed or

something by the paramedics?"

Danielle shrugged. "Guess there's only one way to tell for sure." She stood.

Brandon pushed to his feet as well. "Now that we've heard three accountings, it'll give us a better feel to see the scene again anyway."

And maybe they'd find some answers.

NINE

"What exactly, are we looking for"—Pam stared at the rental house on Esplande Avenue through the front windshield of Grayson's truck—"if we can even get in?"

"I don't know. Something that might explain why Anna Belle didn't use her Epi. It just doesn't make sense that she didn't even go for it. That wasn't like her. I'm trying to understand exactly what happened." He eased the truck into the driveway and turned off the engine.

"You might need to start concentrating on finding evidence to clear your name, Grayson. No offense, but it seems as if the police are focusing on you."

"I'm the ex-husband, so it's natural they'd look hard at me." He wasn't ready to admit just yet how badly it stung.

"No offense, but let's be honest. Anna Belle had a lot of enemies. A lot of people who would like her out of the way. Even permanently. You aren't even the top tier of suspects." Pam flipped down the sun visor and opened the mirror. She used the tip of her ring finger to dab at her lipstick.

"How do you figure?"

She snapped the mirror shut. "Sure you're the ex-husband, but the emphasis is on *ex*. You'd already discovered her affair and didn't kill her. You didn't commit a crime of passion, instead opting to divorce her. You took the higher road. Even during the divorce proceedings, which she wanted to get dirty, you didn't lower yourself to play dirty. So, if I'm a cop, a good one, I'd be asking myself why on earth you would all of a sudden break and kill her."

Grayson's heart raced. If the police knew what was in Anna Belle's files, they'd have the answer to that question. Movement on the front porch caught his attention. "Hey, that's the owner. Let's go." He got out of the truck, heard Pam shut the passenger door behind him, and made his way up the overgrown walkway.

The concrete and brick of the front porch pillars were dirty and covered in kudzu vines. The whole front of the white and redbrick house needed a serious pressure washing. The old house looked as weathered as the many storms it had withstood.

"Can I help you?" The older man wearing overalls as worn as the house tucked a screwdriver into his front pocket.

"I don't know if you remember me, sir. Grayson with Game's On You?"

The man squinted. "Yeah, I remember you." He nodded at Pam. "And you. Because of that loud hair of yours."

Pam giggled. "Yes, sir. I do like to stand out." Grayson's assistant might be a little on the weird side, but she had a way with clients, especially men. Didn't matter if they were young, middle-aged, or old, she managed to handle them all with ease. Grayson had never appreciated that particular gift more than at that moment.

"We were just wondering if we could have a quick look around."

The man stared at Grayson through eyes squinted by many years of long hours in the sun.

"We'll only be a few minutes." Pam smiled, her pinkish-purplish hair seeming to brighten in the sun that was peeking through the gray clouds.

"You know one of those girls died here, right? I mean, she actually died at the hospital, but she was one of the people here." He hardened his stare at Grayson. "You know anything about that?"

Pam looped her arm through Grayson's. "We're as shocked as you are. We're trying to figure out what happened."

Grayson checked that there wasn't any yellow sealing tape on the door. "I assume the police have already cleared your property?"

"They told me they were done and I could have my cleaning crew come in. I'm waiting on them to get here now."

"I promise we'll be as quick as we can." Pam widened her smile. "If you'll just let us in for a few moments. Please."

He hesitated only a minute before he gave a curt nod. "I guess that'd be okay."

"Oh, thank you so much," Pam gushed as Grayson tugged her toward the door.

"You're incorrigible," he whispered as they entered.

"Hey, we're in, aren't we?" Pam grinned. "So, what do you want to check out first?"

"Let's go to Anna Belle's room." The man could change his mind any minute now, and Grayson wanted to at least check for himself that Anna Belle's Epi hadn't just been missed.

Pam led the way up the stairs. The wood creaked under their weight. "A little creepy when there's not a lot of people." Her tone was hushed in the house as empty as a crypt.

Grayson's senses were assaulted as soon as Pam opened the door to the room Anna Belle had stayed in. The lingering tendrils of her signature perfume, Chanel No. 5, drifted over him, wrapping him in a cloak of memories. He swallowed. Hard.

"Are you all right?" Pam's concerned expression nearly choked him as much as Anna Belle's presence.

"Yeah. Let's see if anything was missed." He dropped to his knees by the bed and peered beneath the bed skirt. Dust bunnies greeted him, but no Epi. Not even a track of where one might've skidded under the bed if dropped during a panicked haste.

"I'll check the bathroom." Pam's footfalls were soft on the old hardwood floors that popped as she went into the adjoining room.

Grayson pulled open the desk drawers, hoping to find—just

what, he didn't really know. Something that would help make sense of what had happened to Anna Belle. Anything. He was desperate for answers because right now nothing made sense.

Cabinets scraped open and popped shut in the bathroom as Pam went through the bathroom.

He shut the last desk drawer and glanced around the room. Now what? He pulled back the curtains covering the balcony door. It was locked with a dead bolt. No sign of anything out of the ordinary.

"Didn't see anything odd in the bathroom. I'm going to move on to some of the common areas we know she was in. I'll start in the kitchen." Pam waited for him to nod before she headed toward the stairs.

He moved beside the bed and halted. The fragrance of Anna Belle's perfume was strongest here. No surprise since she'd always used the Chanel No. 5 bath oils to help her relax. She said the smell calmed her. He sat on the edge of the mattress, letting the grief grip him. How had everything gotten so messed up?

Grayson opened the bedside table drawer, then reached to turn on the lamp. He pressed the button on the lamp's base, but nothing happened except that the button shifted. He looked again and realized it wasn't the lamp's button at all. He pulled the white, black, and gold magnetic circle off the metal lamp base. His heart and gut flipped places.

It was his St. Andrews golf course ball marker. Or one just like his, not that he had any monopoly on the item sold in the pro shop at the course. He and Colton had gone two years ago and gotten them as souvenirs, and there had been more than plenty for sale there.

Why did Anna Belle have his? It was usually kept in his display box in his office. Why would she bring it here, to this place, at this time? He ran his thumb over the raised design. Had she kept it as a token to remind her of him?

That didn't make sense, but then again, nothing seemed to make sense and hadn't for some time. It made no sense that their love hadn't been as deep and strong as he'd thought. It made no sense that she'd had an affair. It made no sense that she'd—well, that she'd done some of the horrible things she'd done. He wasn't perfect, not by any stretch of the imagination, but he'd loved Anna Belle with the most consuming love he'd ever felt.

"Grayson." Pam's voice drifted up the stairs. Maybe she'd found something.

"Coming." Grayson stood and pocketed the ball marker. He'd figure this one out later.

Pam met him at the bottom of the steps, Brandon and Danielle hunkering behind her.

Perfect. Just perfect.

"Brandon." He nodded at the cops. "Danielle."

"What are you doing at the crime scene?" Danielle's eyes were harder than the chip on her shoulder.

"I'm guessing the same thing you are—looking for answers." He had permission to be on the premises from the owner, but he had to admit, to the police it would shine a very unflattering light on him.

"This is our job, Grayson. Not yours." Brandon's words were delivered without attitude.

Which made Grayson feel all the worse. "I'm just trying to figure out what happened to her."

"Or maybe you're here to make sure you covered your tracks and didn't leave anything incriminating behind?" Danielle's hands were fisted on her hips.

Grayson opted to keep his mouth shut and just stared at Danielle.

"We just came by to look for her EpiPen," Pam told Danielle in her matter-of-fact way. "Grayson is convinced that as soon as she had symptoms of having ingested her allergen, she would've gone for her Epi. Since she didn't use it in time, obviously, we just wondered if maybe she got to it too late."

Grayson nodded. "If the symptoms came on too fast, maybe by the time she got it out, she couldn't function and she dropped it and it rolled under some furniture or something."

Brandon slowly nodded. "Did you find one?"

"No. Not even a trail of it in the dust under the bed." Grayson's disappointment was as tangible as the tension in the room.

"The one recovered in her purse hadn't been used." Brandon shrugged. "It hadn't been tampered with either, for what it's worth."

Grayson nodded. "But she always carried a backup pen in her toiletry case. Was that one recovered?"

Brandon shook his head, but his partner interrupted.

"We could arrest you now." Danielle propped a foot on the bottom stair. "For interfering in a criminal investigation."

Brandon glared at his partner for a nanosecond before looking back to Grayson. "It was a bad idea to come here, whatever your reasons. You should know better."

He did, but. . . "I'm just trying to figure out what happened. None of this makes sense." He really needed it to make sense.

"I understand, but you have to stay out of our way." Brandon shifted his weight from one leg to the other. "Let us do our job."

He hated to admit it, but he was in way over his head. "I'm sorry. We'll leave now." He motioned for Pam to follow him as he strode for the door.

"Just a moment, Ms. Huron," Danielle called out after them.

Pam turned to face the police. "Yes?"

"Could you be so kind as to come to the station for further questions? Say tomorrow afternoon around three?"

"Sure."

Danielle smiled, but anybody could tell it was fake. "Thank you. See you then."

Pam held her tongue until they were outside. "Grayson, that

woman's got it in for you. I don't know what the deal is, but trust me on this, that woman is determined to see you're blamed for Anna Belle's death."

He couldn't argue the point because now, more than ever, he knew how guilty he looked.

TEN

"Thank you for making time for us, Mrs. Dubois." Brandon took in the home of the owner and CEO of Deets PR.

The house itself sat in the Lakeview neighborhood, considered to be a very successful line between suburbia and the big city life of New Orleans. With its great schools and easy access to City Park, the neighborhood was a popular choice for young families. Numerous neighborhood coffee shops, stores, and restaurants fed the sense of community.

"Of course. I'm happy to help in any way I can." Emiline "Emmi" Dubois set the coffeepot on the tray and handed Brandon his cup before doing the same for Danielle.

"Thank you." Brandon studied the woman over the rim of the china cup. He knew from the case file that she was thirty-eight years old and had been married to Tim Dubois for eight years. She was an LPN who worked at a nearby nursing home. They were a comfortable, middle-class, working couple by all observations. Yet they had secrets in their marriage. Could they be hiding other secrets? He intended to find out.

Setting down his cup, Brandon pulled out his Field Notes notebook and pen. "Can you tell me what happened, as far as you know, about Anna Belle Thibodeaux's death?"

She rattled her cup in its saucer. Brandon had opted to jump right into the death questions to knock the woman off balance. By the flush of her face, he'd made the right decision.

"Well, we were all getting ready to meet for dinner when Georgia began screaming. Naturally, we all ran to see what was wrong."

Brandon wouldn't let this questioning go so easily for someone he considered a prime suspect. One of the reasons he was glad her interview was in her home—it gave her a false sense of security. "But hadn't there already been things that caused screams and shock, events orchestrated by your own husband to cause fear and surprise? Wasn't that the whole purpose of the *game*?"

Emmi's face turned a brighter pink. "Yes, but we knew what those were. And we knew when they would happen. Nothing was supposed to happen before dinner on Thursday."

"Unless it was part of the game that you weren't aware of perhaps? Maybe something your husband had set up without you knowing?"

She shook her head. "Tim wouldn't have kept something from me."

"But hadn't he kept his affair with Anna Belle from you for some time?"

Emmi gasped, then covered her mouth with her hand. Her swallowing seemed to echo off the wallpaper-covered walls of the living room. "That's really none of your business, Detective."

"This is a murder investigation, Mrs. Dubois, so it is my business. Please answer the question. Isn't it possible that your husband might have added in something in the course of the game and not told you?"

"Of course it's possible, but that isn't what happened in this case."

"Please, continue telling us what happened." Danielle's voice sounded soothing, but Brandon could tell she was furious with him despite her tone.

Too bad. After not finding the doll nor the mask at the rental house, Danielle was convinced Grayson had taken them before they got there. He needed to offer another, more viable suspect, and Emmi Dubois was his best candidate. Poison was, after all, the most common type of murder committed by women.

Emmi turned slightly in her seat so she was facing Danielle

more than Brandon. "Georgia had found her on the floor, unconscious. Tim immediately began CPR, and Mr. York called for an ambulance. Everyone else tried to stay out of the way."

Brandon didn't miss how she didn't even say Anna Belle's name.

"I can imagine," Danielle said. "What were you doing while Tim performed CPR?"

"I comforted Georgia, who was crying. It was a most somber mood of course. We were all very shocked." Emmi reached for her cup and took a sip of her coffee.

"Understandable. What happened once the ambulance arrived?" Danielle asked.

"Well, they took over performing CPR, put her on a stretcher, and left. They were very quick and efficient."

"What did you do?" Brandon interrupted.

Emmi set her cup back on its saucer. "Tim thought we should go to the hospital, so we did."

"Just like that?" he pushed.

She nodded. "He is the CEO, and she was one of the company's employees."

"One he'd had a long-term affair with."

"Yes." Emmi's stare was harder than Danielle's. "You already know that Tim had an affair with her. You know that I know. I don't know why you must keep bringing it up and throwing it in my face."

"We don't mean to hurt you, Mrs. Dubois," Danielle started.

"But we're conducting a murder investigation," Brandon finished. "So please accept our apologies if we might hurt your feelings a little as we work to bring out the truth." He sat up straight in the most uncomfortable chair, not enjoying that he had to keep Emmi Dubois off balance. "So, yes, we know about Tim and Anna Belle's affair, and it seemed most everyone in the company knew as well."

"Yes, most people did know, but I don't see how that matters now. The affair ended a few months ago, and Tim and I are in marital counseling, not that it's any of your business."

"We understand that Anna Belle ended the affair." Brandon paused, waiting for her reaction.

Her jaw tightened, the muscles jumping as she ground her teeth. "That's correct, and I'm sure you'll read something more into it. The truth is, it had run its course and they both were over it. She just said it first."

"Did Tim ever ask you for a divorce?" Brandon remembered that the affair was what Anna Belle used to get Grayson to agree to the divorce.

Her face paled. "We discussed all our options, including divorce, but since we love each other, we decided to make our marriage work."

Not "try to make," but "make."

"So, you went to the hospital?" Danielle asked, cutting her eyes at Brandon. They'd definitely have an intense conversation, but he didn't care. Something told him Emmi Dubois was hiding something about Anna Belle's death.

Emmi nodded. "We got there and were told to have a seat in the waiting room, which we did. Colton York from Game's On You came in next and sat in the waiting room, but not really with us. Hugh arrived about fifteen or twenty minutes after us and waited with us. It felt like hours, but I guess it was really less than an hour before a doctor came out and told us she had never regained consciousness and had died."

Brandon studied her face, her mannerisms, for even a microexpression of grief or sadness. Nothing.

"Tim was naturally upset. I took him to the car and drove him home."

"Did you know she had a cherry allergy?" Danielle asked.

Emmi put on a smile that was clearly just for appearances. "I'm sure you can understand that I didn't know much about her, nor did I want to."

"When did you get your belongings from the rental house?" Brandon asked.

"Excuse me?" Emmi's eyes went wide.

"You said you drove home from the hospital. When did you get your clothes and things from the rental house? I'm assuming you didn't grab them when you left to follow the ambulance to the hospital."

"No, of course not." She crossed and uncrossed her legs. "After we got home, Tim needed to call the board members of the company, so I went to the rented house and collected our things."

"Alone?" Brandon asked.

Emmi nodded. "I just said Tim was making calls, so of course I went alone."

"Did you see anyone there? Anyone see you?" he asked.

"No. I got our stuff and shoved it into the duffel, then locked up and came back home. That place was even creepier at night."

Danielle nodded. "I bet. Well—"

"What did you think of it all?" Brandon interrupted.

Emmi's proper posture snapped back into place. "What do you mean?"

"That your husband hired a company to create such an elaborate game to decide who would get a promotion?" Brandon grinned and shook his head. "I might be just a simple cop, but I've never heard of something so complicated. To me, whoever does the best job gets the promotion."

Emmi visibly relaxed a little. "It is odd, but after the position became available, the board decided it should be a group decision as to who would be promoted. Since most of the board members don't know the employees personally, they wanted to see how those employees would react under stress. Many of the larger companies are doing similar things. It's the newest fad, if you will."

Just as his initial research had shown. But Brandon still had a hard time understanding the complexities. Guess it went over his head.

Danielle stood. "Well, thank you for your time, Mrs. Dubois."

"Of course." Emmi stood and opened the front door for them.

Brandon had no choice but to follow them. "We'll be in touch if we have any follow-up questions."

"You do that." Emmi smiled that fake smile again.

Brandon had barely latched his seat belt and started the cruiser's engine when Danielle jumped in on him.

"I can't believe you were so hard on her. That poor woman."

"Poor woman?" Brandon backed the car out of the driveway and steered it down the road. "She's a murder suspect, not some sad victim."

"I don't think she's a suspect."

"Because she's a woman whose husband cheated on her? That makes her a victim, right?" Brandon snorted as he eased to a stop sign. He glanced over at his partner. "Think about it for a minute, Dani. She couldn't even say Anna Belle's name."

"I can't blame her for that. I wouldn't either."

Some of Danielle's personal feelings were overflowing into the investigation, but Brandon didn't think it wise to bring it up at the moment. He pulled in a calming breath. "Look, I agree that Emmi Dubois got the short end of the stick when it comes to husbands, but that just gives her all the more motive to get Anna Belle out of the way."

Danielle shook her head and gripped the armrest. "Then give me your theory. Go."

"Okay. We all know that poison is usually a woman's method of murder."

"Too coincidental, my friend."

"Wait. Hear me out."

Danielle threw her hands up in the air. "Okay."

He expertly changed lanes as he headed toward the offices of Deets PR. "All right. We know that Tim and Anna Belle were having an affair. Since everyone seems to have known it, I'm guessing they weren't too discreet. Anyway, they were having an affair. Anna Belle used the affair to get Grayson to agree to the divorce. By Emmi's reaction when I mentioned if they'd ever discussed divorcing, I'm going to guess that Tim did, in fact, ask for a divorce."

"You don't know that," Danielle interrupted.

"No, I don't, but I do plan to ask Tim in a few minutes when we talk to him."

She made an *mm-hmm* noise but didn't say anything else.

Brandon figured that was his cue to continue. "So, let's say, for the sake of argument, that Tim does ask Emmi for a divorce because he's in love with Anna Belle, and now that she's getting a divorce, he thinks they can live happily ever after."

"For the sake of argument, okay, I can see how that gives Emmi motive. But the timing doesn't work. Anna Belle called it off with Tim at least a month or more ago. She was no longer a threat to Emmi's marriage."

"Ah, but you don't know that. See, if Tim was really in love with Anna Belle, and she was now divorced, maybe he had hopes of rekindling their romance."

"I'm not buying it. From everything we know about Anna Belle, she was the type to do whatever it took to get ahead. If she thought she could, she would've rekindled things with Tim when she found out about the promotion."

She had him there. Unless. . . "Or maybe Tim wanted to test her and see if she was playing him or if she really loved him. I can see him demanding she win the promotion on her own."

"But they didn't know they were in a game, right?"

Right. He let out a soft sigh. "Unless Tim told her to give her a heads-up."

"Which doesn't make Emmi any more of a suspect than anyone else. Yes, poison is usually a woman's method of murder, but Georgia was in the house, is a woman, and didn't like Anna Belle."

"But Emmi is in the medical field. As a LPN, she'd know how fast an allergy like Anna Belle's could kill her. She'd know to keep the EpiPens out of reach."

Danielle laid her head back on the headrest. "So your theory is that Emmi was jealous and wanted to save her marriage, so she finds out about Anna Belle's allergy, gets cherry juice, taints an energy drink, and gets it into Anna Belle's room without anybody seeing her? Just so her husband won't divorce her?" She shook her head. "Seems a little too complicated to me."

"It's not. Come on, Dani, think about it. You're Emmi. This woman, who is beautiful and successful, has been having an affair with your husband for months. She suddenly becomes divorced. Your husband asks you for a divorce, and you know why. Deep in your heart, you know. But you love him and aren't ready to let him go. You beg, you plead. . .you do whatever you can to make him stay. When he does, you think you've gotten him back. That he'll fall back in love with you again and you'll live happily ever after. Then you learn that the only reason you haven't been served papers is because she broke it off with him. You know, somewhere in the darkest part of your heart, that he loves her and if she'd have him, he'd be gone in a minute."

Danielle didn't say anything, just stared straight out the front windshield.

Brandon kept on. "Your life hangs in the balance based on what this woman wants because it's a daily fear that she'll decide she wants your husband and will call him to her, and then you'll be left. Cold and alone." He checked for cars, then turned onto the road where Deets PR sat. "Then an opportunity falls in your lap. You can take her out of the picture, save your marriage and your love. All you have to do is put a little cherry juice into one of the drinks that everyone knew she drank like crazy. Just sneak it in there, and it's not like you really killed her. It's not like you shot her or stabbed her or even put toxicity in her body. Cherries are, after all, fruit. It's her body's fault that it causes a reaction."

His partner's silence told him she couldn't discount his theory. Even so, it didn't make him happy. A woman was still dead. It was up to him to speak up for her.

"Emmi could've taken the mask and doll out of the house when she went back to get her and Tim's things."

"Whatever for?"

"Killers keep trophies, right?" He turned into the parking lot and inched into a space. "Emmi would have it made. Her competition is gone, she's a hero for staying with her husband during what had to be the most traumatic time of her life, and she's just a little happier knowing she took control of the situation."

"Control?"

He nodded. "Hell hath no fury like a woman scorned, as they say, right?"

"Well, it's an interesting theory and one I can't destroy. Let's go see what her husband has to say. He'll either strengthen your theory or rip it to shreds."

"Then let's go find out." Brandon led the way into the building and to the receptionist's desk. "We're here to see Tim Dubois. He's expecting us."

"One moment."

Brandon glanced around the office space. It was in a prime downtown location and, by the looks of the front room, recently renovated. Lots of glass and mirrors. Water treatment right inside the frosted glass doors. He moved to the group portraits hanging on the wall. One of them had a large group of people, but prominently smiling in the front were Tim, Anna Belle, Franklin, Hugh, and

Georgia. The next portrait was one of five people, and Brandon only recognized Tim. This was probably the board. He made a mental note to make sure to review the board members.

"He'll be right with you," the receptionist said.

"Thank you." Brandon glanced at his partner. "Nice digs," he whispered.

"Being successful isn't a crime, remember," she whispered back.

"But murder is."

ELEVEN

"I can't believe I didn't immediately think of bringing this over." Pam shook her head as she made her way into Grayson's living room and plopped down on the couch. She set her laptop on the coffee table and opened the lid to the Mac.

"Me too." Grayson moved to the kitchen to put on a pot of coffee. It might be afternoon, but he and Pam drank java all day every day. "If it hadn't hit me immediately, I should've picked up on it last night when you told me about taking the equipment back."

"Ditto that." Tapping echoed as her fingers flew over the computer keys. "I'm connected to the office server. Let me access the saved video feeds."

Grayson pulled mugs from the cabinet and set them on the counter, then hesitated. He wasn't sure how he was going to feel about actually seeing Anna Belle again. It was one thing to see her picture but something totally different to see her moving and talking, alive and vibrant. He needed to steel his emotions.

"Hmm. This is odd."

"What?" He joined Pam in the living room.

"Someone accessed the file through the server this weekend."

It was so encrypted, no outside entity could get in, so that wasn't a worry. "The police?" But they would have the means. "Did they serve a warrant on the business?" As co-owner, he should have been informed if that was the case.

"I don't think so." Pam continued to click the keys. "It looks like someone accessed on-site."

"At the office?"

She nodded, staring up at him. "Who would do that, and why?"

"I don't know." No one should've been in those files. "What did they do in there?" He sat on the arm of the couch.

Pam typed again, her eyes squinting at the screen. "Nothing was uploaded. Doesn't look like anything was deleted."

Then what was someone doing in the files? Just seeing what was on them?

"I can't find a log where anything was messed with." Pam readjusted herself, bringing her legs up on the couch and crossing them.

"Maybe it's a glitch giving you the indicators that someone accessed it?"

"Maybe. Let me take it off the server in case there's a glitch there. I'll upload it back again tomorrow morning when I get to the office." She typed as fast as usual. "There, it's now off the server. I sent a copy to you too just in case the file is corrupted on my system. Now, let's check out the video feed."

He moved to sit beside her on the couch. The scent of her musky-smelling shampoo was such a contrast to the sweetness of Anna Belle's perfume.

"Okay. Let me focus on just the camera in the hall outside of Anna Belle's room." She brought up a file folder and scrolled through the contents faster than Grayson could even read a line or two. "Now let's center on Thursday only." She clicked keys, and the screen filled with the image of the hallway.

Game's On You used motion-activated cameras to send live feeds, with backup recordings, to the company's server.

The monitor filled with the image of Georgia Vescot walking down the hall. She paused outside Anna Belle's room for a moment, then moved on to the stairs. The screen froze for a moment as the motion activation ceased.

"That was seven forty on Thursday morning. Breakfast was at

eight." Pam adjusted the laptop to remove the glare.

Movement on the screen. Franklin Barron strode down the hall, his head down. Screen freeze again.

"Seven fifty-one."

Hugh Istre came down the hall. He stopped and knocked on Anna Belle's door. His lips moved, then he walked toward the stairs. Screen froze.

"Man, I wish we had sound. That was at seven fifty-six."

Grayson nodded. He'd love to know what Hugh had said to Anna Belle. Probably just a reminder not to be late for breakfast, but interesting that he would take the time. Especially since they were competing for the same promotion.

Anna Belle filled the screen, wearing a pair of jeans and a light sweater, both of which clung to her every curve. She made a straight line for the stairs. The computer screen froze.

Pam cleared her throat. "That was at seven fifty-eight."

Grayson stood, needing some space and a moment to himself. "I'll grab our coffees." He went into the kitchen and poured the fresh brew into the cups. He dumped three spoons of sugar into Pam's, then added a splash of milk before stirring.

Seeing her—he couldn't put a label on what he felt. He had already gone through the phase of missing her so much that he felt like he couldn't breathe. Divorce did that. He'd walked through the house for days—even weeks, sensing her everywhere and missing her so much that he didn't know if he could live without her. He survived and managed to start acknowledging the hurts she'd caused and he'd endured.

Those feelings of void were nothing like knowing she was dead. Gone. As much as he had adjusted to missing her, it was no comparison to knowing she was dead, then seeing her. He felt like he'd been gut punched.

"Grayson?"

"Coming." He carried the coffee into the living room, setting both cups on the coffee table as he sat back down beside Pam. "What's up?"

"Nothing but Nora putting the mask in Franklin's room and Vic putting the doll in Hugh's, just as planned." She pointed to the computer. "But watch. This is at eight-fifty, just before Tim dismissed them to their rooms for their cards. Look." She started the video.

Emmi Dubois moved down the hall, glancing over her shoulder. She had what looked like a pamphlet in her hand. She paused outside of Anna Belle's room, glanced toward the stairs, then used a key and opened Anna Belle's door. She disappeared into the room. The screen froze.

Pam met his gaze. "What was she doing there?"

"And what was in her hand?" Grayson asked.

Before Pam could answer, the screen filled with Emmi peeking out of Anna Belle's door, then stepping into the hall and shutting the door behind her. She rushed to the stairs. The screen froze.

"That was just four minutes after she went in."

"She didn't have anything in her hand when she came out. She left whatever it was in Anna Belle's room." Excitement, with some dread, lanced Grayson.

"Let me see if I can blow it up enough to see what it is." Pam pulled the Mac into her lap and ran her fingers over the built-in mouse pad. "Ugh. It's not going to be easy. I can tell it's a brochure of sorts, but that's about it." She set the laptop back on the coffee table. "I'll come back and try to clean it up, but let's finish going through the day first, okay?"

He took a sip of coffee and nodded. What had Emmi Dubois put in Anna Belle's room?

The action moved on the screen as Pam restarted the feedback. Georgia and Franklin walked together down the hall to their respective rooms. Hugh and Anna Belle followed. All seemed to be talking with someone.

Man, he really wished they had sound.

Anna Belle stopped at her door. Hugh said something to her, and she smiled. One of her genuine, 1,000-watt smiles that could send Grayson to his knees at one time. He sucked in air, unable to stop himself. Even on camera, Anna Belle's beauty was breathtaking.

Hugh nodded and headed to his room. The computer screen stopped.

"That was six after nine." Pam's voice came out soft, the tone she used when she was being nice to Grayson.

He nodded, struggling to stamp down the emotions clogging his throat. "Wait a minute." He jumped up and pulled his phone out of his pocket. He scrolled through the voice mail receipts. "She called me at nine twelve."

"Any idea what prompted the call?"

Grayson shook his head. She'd looked so beautiful. Almost . . .happy? And that's when she'd decided to call him? He played the voice mail recording again, on speaker.

Anna Belle's voice shattered the silence. "Grayson, it's me. We need to talk."

She didn't sound happy there. So what changed in the space of six minutes?

"I have no idea why she called right then." He wished he did. He wished he hadn't lost his phone in the creek. He wished a lot of things.

"Me either." She took a swig of coffee, then unpaused the feedback. "This is nine forty."

A man, wearing an ornate Mardi Gras mask with elaborate purple and gold and green feathers exited Franklin's room. He walked cautiously down the hall to Anna Belle's. Even on video, his hesitation was noticeable. A pause. Then two. Finally, he knocked on Anna Belle's door.

She opened it, then immediately began hitting him, kicking him.

He basically pushed her into her room, and the camera couldn't pick up any other details.

Seeing his plan play out and knowing how fearful she must have been in that exact moment, even if it was just for a few minutes—well, Grayson wondered again if maybe he shouldn't have stayed as a police consultant instead of joining Colton in the business. But Anna Belle had encouraged him to try it. Do something different. Make more money. Be his own boss.

The irony of her dying during the course of one of his games wasn't lost on him. Apparently it wasn't on the police either.

"This is nine forty-four."

Franklin and Anna Belle walked out of her room. She shut the door behind them, and they rushed to the stairs.

"Nine fifty."

Georgia walked out of her room, down the hall, and to the stairs. She didn't meet anyone, nor did she stop or pause.

Vic snuck out of the hall closet and unlocked Georgia's room, then disappeared through the back stairs.

"And at ten on the dot, just as you planned."

Hugh headed out of his room with the voodoo doll in hand. He opened Georgia's room and disappeared, then reappeared, shut the door, and headed back to his room. A moment later, he emerged again and headed down the stairs.

"And that's all from the morning. They had lunch right after their campaign creation, then the video starts again at five after one."

The four candidates again came up the stairs. Franklin and Anna Belle both wore smiles. Hugh and Georgia wore unreadable expressions. Disappointment? Anger? Frustration? Any or all could apply.

"Now check this out. This is at one fifteen." Pam took another sip of coffee as Georgia left her room and marched to Anna Belle's. Her stance and steps screamed anger. She paused outside the room, appearing to take in several deep breaths, when Emmi Dubois appeared at the top of the stairs. She said something to Georgia, who turned from Anna Belle's door and went to Emmi. Together the two women descended the stairs and were out of the camera's range.

"That is interesting. Tim and Emmi were instructed to follow the plan exactly."

Pam nodded. "Nowhere does it say Emmi was supposed to lurk at the top of the stairs."

"It was almost as if she knew Georgia would go to Anna Belle's room for some reason." But that didn't make sense. None of them could know how each person would react. Not for sure. Grayson used his training and experience and usually made a very good outcome guess, but nothing was set in stone when it came to human behavior.

"Georgia would've found the doll in her room. Maybe she wanted to talk to Anna Belle about it?" Pam asked.

"Maybe." He shook his head. "They didn't like each other very much. I doubt Georgia would confide something in Anna Belle." He considered what he remembered about Georgia's psychological profile. "Accuse her, maybe."

"Probably. So why would Emmi stop her?"

"That's a very good question." He lifted his cup and motioned toward the screen with it.

Pam restarted the playback. "This is nineteen after one."

Franklin walked down the hall, directly to the stairs.

"And this is one twenty-three."

Hugh strode down the hall. Anna Belle's door opened just before he reached that part of the hallway. He turned to her, took a moment to look back down the hall and then to the stairs, then in a rush, pushed her up against her doorway.

Pam gasped as Hugh grabbed Anna Belle's chin and held her head steady as he dipped his head to hers, capturing her into a kiss.

Grayson tensed. Every muscle in his gut clenched as Anna Belle's hands grabbed Hugh's long dreadlocks and pulled. His head jerked back. Anna Belle smiled, then stood on tiptoe to kiss him.

Something must have sounded, because they both lurched away from one another. Anna Belle rushed toward the stairs. Hugh grabbed her door and pulled it closed, then followed her.

Tim Dubois stood at the end of the hall, his hands balled into fists at his side. He backed into his room and shut the door. The computer screen went blank.

"I–I'm sorry, Gray." Remorse filled Pam's voice.

He shook his head. "No, it's okay." But it wasn't. He knew Anna Belle had had an affair with Tim Dubois. She had thrown that fact in his face so many times he had stripes of scars from it. That was quite different than seeing her with Hugh. She'd always been aggressive, he knew that well, but. . . "We're divorced, right?"

"Doesn't mean it makes it any easier."

He stood, grabbing both their cups. "Time for refills." In the kitchen, he gripped the side of the island and ground his teeth. *God, why? I can't take much more.* If only any of it made sense. Her cheating. The divorce. The ab—

"Grayson, we have a problem."

"What?" He left the mugs and returned to the living room. What could be more of a problem than what he'd already seen?

"That accessing of the files I mentioned?"

"Yeah?" He sat beside Pam again.

"Look." She tapped a line in a code. "I noticed a blip in the playback, so I tried to look at the code and found this."

"I have no idea what that is." He could use his computer, but that was the extent of his knowledge base about them.

But Pam was brilliant. "It's a break in the recording."

"What do you mean?"

"It means that the camera was activated and started recording again at two forty-one, stopping to record at two fifty-nine."

"Okay, let's see it."

Pam nodded. "That's just it. Those eighteen minutes are gone."

"Gone?" That didn't make sense. "I don't understand."

"I didn't either until I looked at the logs. Whoever accessed the files removed that part."

"I thought you said nothing had been deleted."

Pam shook her head. "The files aren't deleted, but they've been tampered with. Someone went in and deleted those eighteen minutes, and that's all."

"Wait, out of the entire time at the house, only those eighteen minutes are gone?"

Pam nodded.

"Are you sure?" Grayson forced himself to concentrate.

"Positive. I checked twice. The recording picks back up at three fifty-five when Anna Belle and Hugh return to their rooms and again at five after four when Georgia and Franklin do the same. There's nothing in the system that shows anything is missing on the entire recording except that eighteen minutes."

Grayson's mind raced. "Eighteen minutes is plenty of time to sneak up to Anna Belle's room and put the energy drink with the cherry juice in it on her desk."

Pam nodded. "Plenty of time. Anna Belle and Hugh were in one escape room and Georgia and Franklin were in the other."

Grayson nodded. "Where were Tim and Emmi?"

Pam shrugged. "I don't know. I was in the control room monitoring the escape rooms. Vic was with me until I sent him to go unlock Georgia and Franklin's room. Wynnona and Keely were in the room with us, watching the monitor observing Anna Belle and Hugh's room. Stratton was off helping Colton with the next setup, I think." She shook her head slowly. "I can't say where Tim and Emmi were."

Grayson couldn't help but recognize the expression Tim had worn as he'd seen Anna Belle and Hugh. Grayson recognized it because it had stared back at him in the mirror.

"It's back on track here at four fifteen." Pam started the playback again.

Georgia, carrying the voodoo doll, marched to Anna Belle's room. She lifted her hand and hit the door with the side of her fist. The door eased open. On the screen, Georgia stepped across the threshold.

"And this is at four seventeen."

People ran toward Anna Belle's room. Tim and Emmi from their room. Hugh and Franklin from down the hall. Vic and Pam rushed into view followed by Colton, Keely, and Wynnona. They crowded into the doorway and spilled into the hall. Colton pulled out his phone and stabbed the screen. Emmi pulled Georgia out into the hall.

"This is at four thirty-two."

Stratton led two uniformed EMTs with a stretcher up the stairs. They rushed into Anna Belle's room. Tim stepped into the hall and spoke with Colton.

Grayson found himself holding his breath. He knew what was happening in the room, that the paramedics were desperately trying to find a pulse and perform CPR.

They burst out of the room, pushing Anna Belle on the stretcher down the hall. They each took an end and disappeared down the stairs.

Grayson let out the breath he'd been holding.

It looked like Tim said something, and then he took off toward the stairs. Emmi almost had to run to catch up to him. Everyone stood still for a moment, as if dazed, then Colton turned and spoke to Pam and Vic.

"He told us that he was going to the hospital and to clear out," Pam volunteered.

The Game's On You teams all scattered, leaving the Deets PR

employees stunned. Finally, Hugh said something and headed to his room. Franklin turned and said something to Georgia, then they headed to their rooms.

"This is at four forty."

Hugh, pushing an elite-style carry-on bag, walked down the hall and disappeared down the stairs.

"And at four fifty-three."

Franklin knocked on Georgia's door. She opened it, and together they descended the stairs.

"The rest is just us taking everything down. Like I said, Keely and Wynnona had already left. Stratton helped me and Vic, then we all went back to the office to unload."

Grayson thought out loud. "So there's really nothing unexpected or unplanned except Emmi putting something in Anna Belle's room, Tim seeing Hugh and Anna Belle kiss, Emmi stopping Georgia from knocking on Anna Belle's door, and those missing eighteen minutes."

"Right. Let me work on that part of the video and see if I can make out what Emmi put in her room."

Grayson nodded, but his mind was already racing ahead. As much as he'd like to blame one of Anna Belle's competitors, the video didn't show them putting anything in her room. Of course they hadn't watched Wednesday's video yet, which might very well have been when the tainted energy drink was put in there. Or maybe he was totally off in his assessment.

Either way, it was time to uncover the truth.

Anna Belle
Thursday afternoon

Her hands trembled as she dialed the phone. "He knows," she whispered as soon as the call was answered.

"What? Wait a minute, Anna Belle."

"Yes. He knows. I tried to call him, but he wouldn't answer my call."

"Who knows? What are you talking about?"

Tears burned her eyes. Maybe the stalker wasn't back. Maybe it was Grayson. If he knew, and he clearly did. . .

"Anna Belle, who knows? Knows what?"

"My stalker. . .from college. I thought he was back, but he's not. It's not him. It's Grayson. It has to be."

"Honey, you aren't making any sense. Calm down."

"I saw him outside my room last night. And then he was in the hall, but I couldn't be sure, but now I am."

"Who was outside your room last night?"

"I thought it was my stalker, but it's not. It has to be Grayson."

"Grayson was outside your room last night?"

"It has to be him."

"You don't know? Anna Belle, I'm trying to follow you, hon, but I'm confused. Was Grayson outside your room last night?"

"I think so."

"Did you recognize him?"

Anna Belle shook her head, even though she was on the phone. "No, he had the mask on."

"The mask? What mask?"

"The Mardi Gras mask, just like the one my stalker wore, which is why I thought it was him, but it's not, and Grayson knows what the mask looks like."

"Slow down. So that's what Grayson knows—what the mask looked like?"

"No. Yes, he does, but that's not important. He knows. He left the brochure here with the right date and everything. Why would he do that?" Her mind raced. "Oh, oh, oh. I'm in a game. That's what this all is. It's a game. And he knows and is using it to let me know he knows what I did."

"Anna Belle, you're losing me again. Slow down and explain it to me."

Bam! Bam!

"I have to go. Someone's knocking on my door. I can't. Just. . . I've got to go." She disconnected the call.

This couldn't be happening. No, no. A game. Why hadn't she figured it out last night? The dinner. All of them. The fire. The snake.

Bam! Bam! Bam!

Probably the next phase of the game. No, she could do this. She'd beat Grayson at his own game. She knew how he played. Knew how he operated.

She shoved the pamphlet into her purse. Oh, he thought he'd use this to mess with her mind. She'd show him. How dare he?

Squaring her shoulders, she jerked open the door.

The man in the Mardi Gras mask loomed in the doorway.

Her heart clenched.

TWELVE

"We certainly appreciate you seeing us." Brandon nodded at Tim Dubois as he took a seat across the desk from the man. Brandon knew from the file that Tim was forty, but his face was lined with wrinkles that added years to his appearance.

"Of course." He sat back in his executive leather chair and rested his hands on his desk. A rather large and ornate mahogany desk. Was the company really so successful, or was the elaborateness of the office for show? "We're all just devastated by Anna Belle's death."

Brandon took in the man's gaunt expression and hooded eyes with streaks of bloodshot. "I understand how hard this must be. Losing a valuable employee is always hard."

Tim sat back in his chair, its worn leather creaking familiarly. His Adam's apple bobbed. "I'm sure you're well aware, Detective, that Anna Belle was more than just an employee to me."

Well, well, well. It wasn't very often that people were so forthcoming. It was. . .refreshing. "Yes, Mr. Dubois, so we've been told."

"Please, call me Tim. Since we're discussing my personal life, I believe that's more appropriate."

Brandon nodded his head. "So, why don't you tell us about your relationship with Anna Belle?" He pulled out his Field Notes notebook and flipped the page from his notes of their interview with Emmi Dubois.

"Anna Belle started working for the company about six—no, seven, years ago. She started at an entry-level position, working under account representatives." Tim let out a slow breath. "Not only was she beautiful, but she was brilliant. I'm sure you know she graduated at the top of her class from LSU, but she had a natural way with PR. She could come up with slogans and ideas that would really speak to the customer base. It was amazing."

Brandon let the moment linger because clearly Tim needed to retell at his own pace. After another beat, he tapped his notebook with his pen. "I've heard she was very good at her job."

"She was." Tim nodded. "Soon she was promoted to account rep. Not a single complaint from any client. Every client she handled loved her. She produced quality work, and they were satisfied."

"When did you start the affair?" Danielle interrupted.

Brandon shot her a look, but she just rolled her eyes.

Tim blinked at Danielle. "Um, I guess it was a year or so ago. It was around the holidays. We had been working on seasonal campaigns, and the hours were long and tedious. By this time, Anna Belle had a lot of accounts as a junior rep and was still knocking it out of the park with every campaign she put together."

"So you were working late. Alone?" Danielle pushed him back on track.

"Not at first, but soon, yes." He licked his lips and looked at Brandon. "Soon, one thing led to another and. . .well, we were attracted to each other. She was beautiful, but it wasn't just her looks. Her mind and the way she thought were completely sexy. She was brilliant."

Brandon nodded, all the while feeling ill at ease.

"But you both were married, right?" Danielle asked.

Tim looked at Brandon's partner. "We knew it was wrong, Detective, but it felt right. And then we fell in love. The heart can't be denied, no matter who you're married to."

Except Anna Belle had been married to Brandon's friend. "So what was the plan after you fell in love?"

"Well, at first we fought it. Of course. But once Anna Belle was promoted to senior account rep, we were together a lot more often. On trips to pitch to clients. Hotels. Restaurants."

Brandon didn't even bother mentioning that her promotion sure made it easy for them to be alone together in those hotels and restaurants.

"Who made the promotion decisions, Mr. Dubois?" Danielle asked.

"I did." Tim shook his head. "I know what you're thinking, and I didn't give her any promotions. She was brilliant and earned them. You can ask anyone."

Somehow, Brandon didn't think others would see it that way. "Did you two discuss divorcing your spouses and getting together?"

Tim shook his head again. "We didn't plan that, not exactly, but soon she told me she had asked her husband for a divorce."

"I bet that made you happy." Danielle stared at him.

"It did, but I was sad. I knew it would be hard to lose a woman like Anna Belle, so naturally, I felt sorry for her husband."

"Not your wife?" Danielle blurted out.

"Of course, my wife. I love Emmi. We had just. . .well, I guess we had just grown apart. Drifted from where we had once been. Anna Belle was everything Emmi wasn't. Emmi was wanting to start a family, and I just wasn't at that part in my life. I'm still not. I don't know if I'll ever want a family."

Brandon bit his tongue to keep his opinion to himself: that most people had such an important discussion before they got married.

Danielle didn't. "You and your wife didn't discuss a family prior to getting married?"

"We did, but we didn't." Tim ran a finger along the side of his nose. Brandon didn't miss it and recognized the meaning of the gesture. "We had talked about having kids, but I wanted to wait until we were settled, financially most importantly. Emmi was ready as soon as she got her LPN license. Either way, she became focused solely on getting pregnant. It began to. . .well, it just took the excitement out of the bedroom, if you catch my drift."

"We do. So you were having problems and Anna Belle was getting a divorce?"

Tim nodded, back on track. "Yes. I thought things were going well until Anna Belle told me it was over between us."

"When was this?" Brandon asked.

"Right before her divorce. I assumed her attorney had advised her not to be with me for the sake of her settlement. I know she was worried about her infidelity working against her in court."

Well, duh.

"Anyway, I tried to get on with my life, but I'll be honest—I was miserable. Emmi was begging me to stay and see a marriage counselor. I didn't really want to, but she begged. The attorney I spoke to said I should."

Of course he did.

"So we started counseling, but my heart wasn't in it then. I'll be honest, I'd planned to be with Anna Belle as soon as her divorce was done and we could be together."

"But that didn't happen?" Brandon asked. Twice the man had used the same phrase, *I'll be honest*, which usually meant deception.

Tim shook his head. "No, it didn't. After her divorce was final, I went to her, excited that we could be together, but she told me she wasn't interested. She said she wanted to be alone, to just be free. She said she'd been under constraints for long enough and wanted to be herself." He shrugged. "What do you do when someone you love wants to go?"

Maybe he should've asked Grayson that. But Brandon didn't say that. Instead, he smiled. "You let them go."

Tim nodded. "I did. It hurt to see her going out and doing things, but it made me take a good, hard look at my life and what was important. And that's when I began to throw my whole heart into the counseling. To restoring my marriage. To loving Emmi the way I'd loved her once." He smiled. "It wasn't easy, and it wasn't quick, but together, and with the help of a great therapist, we managed to get back to that love that consumed us. I'm so happy now." He frowned. "But not about what happened to Anna Belle. I never wanted anything bad to happen to her. Especially not like this. Not dying."

"Why don't you tell us about your hiring Game's On You?" Danielle prompted.

Tim nodded and the hardness of his jaw softened. Much more comfortable with this line of questioning. "When the position of executive account rep came up, I'll be honest, my first instinct was to give it to Anna Belle. Then, after discussing it with my wife and the board, we decided that a much fairer way would be to take all the senior account reps who qualified and were interested, and evaluate them."

Brandon could imagine how that conversation had gone.

Tim smiled. "But after we narrowed it to the top four, we realized that it would be almost impossible to choose since their records were impressive and very balanced."

Brandon shot Danielle a look that clearly meant to keep her mouth shut. This line of questioning was critical to the case, and he didn't want Danielle's attitude to affect Tim's statement.

"We—the board, began discussing ways to make a determination. We talked about asking them to submit a campaign for a brand-new potential client, but then we realized that would be just a one-time instance. We needed to see who would consistently deliver the best results." Tim leaned back in his chair and let his hands assist in the talking.

"Everybody's seen the reality TV shows about which person performs the best under extreme circumstances and ends up being hired or being promoted or given a big bonus. It seems to really work, and we were tossing around ideas like that. Then one of the board members mentioned a recommendation for Game's On You. I knew what it was because we'd gotten a flyer for the business about a month before. So, I set up an initial meeting to discuss what we wanted, what we needed, and what it would cost us."

Brandon flipped the page in his field notes. These were the types of details they didn't have yet.

"I met with Colton York, the owner, in his office. I explained what we were looking for: a way to determine which of the four employees would be the best suited for the position. He asked a lot of the questions, which I thought was thorough, then explained that their games weren't just templated, but were custom created for each client. That his partner was a psychologist and did a complete profile on every person in the game: emotional, psychological, financial, medical—everything. His pitch really blew me away, to be honest."

Tim lifted his pen from his desk and began to twirl it between his fingers as he spoke. "We explained that those participating would need to be kept from knowing they were in a game. Colton said they'd have to have their legal team adjust their standard waiver to cover the company against liability claims. Our board understood that, and I guess I do now." He dropped the pen to the desk.

Brandon could almost touch Tim's grief hanging in the office. The man might have had to let Anna Belle go and return to his wife, but it was obvious his heart was broken. By her leaving him, or her death?

Or was it guilt?

"Anyway," Tim continued, "we worked out the details and set up the game. Our part was easy—rent a house that could accommodate our players as well as what Game's On You required. We hired a Realtor to find one with the specs Game's On You sent over, and within a day or so, she found the perfect house that was available."

"What did you tell your employees?" Danielle kept her tone conversational.

"The board and I decided to tell them enough to get them to play but not realize they were playing."

"I don't follow," Danielle said.

Tim nodded. "We told them that they were up for promotion, but we wanted to see how they worked under pressure, alone, and as a team. If they wanted to be promoted, they had to sign the waiver, fill out the in-depth questionnaire—both of which were provided by Colton, and submit the requested documents and forms."

"What, exactly, were the requested documents and forms?" Brandon asked.

"Access to their medical files—releases because of HIPAA laws and such, financial statements, psychological forms—those types of things."

"Did Game's On You provide all of these forms for you?" Danielle asked.

Tim nodded. "Colton delivered a large packet and said he needed all forms and documents completed for every person participating, so we got information from all four of them."

"But not you or your wife?" Brandon asked.

Tim stiffened. "No. Of course not. Why would we? We weren't playing. We were just there to observe and be the liaison between Game's staff and our players."

Brandon raised his brows at the man behind the desk.

"Well, to be honest, Emmi didn't need to be there, but you can understand why she wanted to be with me. And I wanted her there too."

"Of course." Oh, Brandon knew exactly why Emmi Dubois was there, but did she have more than one reason to demand to be there?

"So you compiled all the information on the four of them and turned them in to Game's On You?" Brandon moved Tim back to focus.

Tim nodded. "We gave the employees three days to turn everything in to be eligible. All four of them had everything in on time."

"I'm assuming you looked over the information they filled out?" Brandon noticed Tim's rapid blinking. "To make sure everything was complete before you sent it to Game's On You?"

Tim let out a low breath. "Yes. Of course. I took them home and read over them the night before I turned them over to Colton." He smiled, but he wasn't fooling anyone with the lack of sincerity. "To be honest, I couldn't tell you much of what was in them. I basically just made sure all the blanks had something filled in."

Right, and Brandon was just promoted to detective this morning. "How long after you turned in the packets to Game's On You did they have the game ready?"

"It felt like a really long time, but in reality, it was only a couple of weeks before Colton called and told me they were ready. I called the Realtor, and that afternoon we had a lease on the place and we were all set."

Now was a good time to knock Tim Dubois off his balance. Brandon leaned forward to the edge of his chair. "When did you know that Anna Belle's ex-husband was one of the owners of Game's On You?"

"Ah." Tim sat up straight in his chair, stiffening. He blinked. Again. And again. His Adam's apple bobbed rapidly. "Well, I knew what he did of course. From Anna Belle." He licked his lips.

Brandon stared at him, not blinking, not looking away.

Tim shifted in his chair. "I mean, I guess I knew from the beginning, but to be honest, I really didn't think about it until I saw him at the rental house."

Ah, that one sentence was so much more telling when combined with his manner.

"You saw him at the rental house?" Danielle asked.

Tim nodded. "He arrived with Colton and the rest of their team." He licked his lips again. "I don't mind telling you, I was a little nervous when I saw him." He stared at Danielle as if she was his lifeline in the room. "I mean, he's a pretty muscular man. I knew he worked out, and he's a little scary intense, if you know what I mean."

Brandon did. He'd worked out with Grayson many times, and the man was one strong guy.

"Did he say anything to you? Threaten you in any way?" Danielle asked.

Mentally, Brandon rolled his eyes, but he waited on Tim's response.

"No. He didn't say a word to me. Actually, he acted like he didn't know who I was and basically ignored me."

"Actually. . .basically. . ."

"He and his assistant, Pam, oversaw the rest of the team setting up things while Colton met with me and gave me a layout of what they planned and how they had worked in the campaign request the board needed in the game."

"Did Emmi sit through that with you?" Brandon asked.

"Of course." Tim turned back to Danielle. "They told us who all would be staying, and I'll admit, I was relieved that Anna Belle's ex-husband wasn't one of them."

"But he didn't say anything to you, right?" Brandon wanted to make sure Danielle got that loud and clear.

"Right, but he was still intimidating."

Maybe he wouldn't have been if you hadn't been having an affair with his wife. Brandon bit back the retort.

"Their team decided who would be in what bedroom upstairs and where everything would be located. We walked through the entire house, and they pointed out where props were, where the cameras were, and where their staff would be at certain times."

"Wait—cameras?"

Tim nodded. "Yes, they installed cameras in the halls and common areas. It was one of the ways they monitored the game."

Brandon stared at his partner. Why were they just now learning there were cameras in place? He turned back to Tim. "And the cameras were running all the time?"

"I guess. I mean, they told me and Emmi that they would monitor the game with the cameras. We were able to watch on Wednesday afternoon, so I guess they ran the rest of the time too."

"Were the cameras recording video or just set to watch live?"

Tim shrugged. "I don't know. You'd have to ask them."

Oh, they would. That was a certainty.

THIRTEEN

"Grayson." Pam stood in the doorway.

He closed his Bible and motioned her out onto the back deck. "What's up?"

She sat in one of the patio chairs and set her laptop on the table. "I finally got the video cleaned up enough to get a still shot of what Emmi put in Anna Belle's room."

"Good." But Pam's expression said otherwise. "Okay, not good?"

Pam shook her head.

Grayson sighed. "Just show me then." How much worse could it be than it already was?

She opened the laptop and turned it to him.

He leaned forward and stared at the image. His blood chilled as he realized what he looked at. Oh, it could get so much worse.

Even though Emmi's hand clutched the brochure and curved it, Pam had enhanced the photo enough that it was plain to see it was a Scheduled Maternity pamphlet she held. An appointment card was paper-clipped to the top, with a date written in. The date Grayson had learned the importance of when he reviewed Anna Belle's medical records. The date just months before she'd filed for divorce.

The day she'd aborted their baby and Grayson hadn't even known she was pregnant.

Yes, it was so much worse than he could have imagined. Immediately, all those emotions he'd never gotten to release came back. Back with a vengeance that nearly choked him.

"Grayson, I'm so sorry." Pam's soft tone nearly ripped the rest of his emotions bare. Her sympathy. . .pity. . .

"Well, that explains why she called me."

"Why?"

"She would've assumed I knew and I put it there."

Pam shook her head. "But you weren't there. She didn't know it was a game."

Yet Grayson knew. In the deep pit of his gut, he knew that Anna Belle knew he'd learned about the abortion. "Pam, Anna Belle might've been many things, but stupid wasn't one of them. She was actually very smart. Almost scary smart, considering. After Wednesday night's episodes, then Thursday morning's. . . I'm betting when she saw the pamphlet, she figured out it was a game."

Pam frowned.

He didn't let her speak. "Come on, Pam. Anna Belle knew what I do for a living. She knew I used psychological profiling to push people to their limits, exposing their weaknesses and using them against them. It wouldn't be hard for her to figure out that the weekend was one big game." He shook his head. "I should've thought of that and adjusted. I told Colton it was a bad idea to accept the job."

"You and me both, but he was determined." Pam let out a sigh. "Okay, so she figured it out. Now what?"

"Going back to the video. How did Emmi Dubois know?" None of this made sense. Then again, it hadn't made sense for Anna Belle to have had an abortion. It was the regret that he would forever have to live with: he hadn't confronted her when he found out. He hadn't for a multitude of reasons, the primary one being he was raw at knowing, but also because he was bound by the ethical parameters of his job's confidentiality clause. Nothing about the situation was easy.

"I don't know how she knew."

Neither did he. "What was the point of putting it in Anna Belle's room? To torment her?" He ran a hand through his hair. None of this made sense.

Pam shrugged, but Grayson didn't miss the look in her eyes. "Tell me you've got a theory or something."

"More like jumbled ideas, really."

"Let me hear them, because right now, I've got nothing." Nothing but raw emotions that wouldn't do him a bit of good at the moment.

She hesitated, then nodded. "Okay. First theory is that Emmi knew what Anna Belle had done because her husband told her."

Grayson opened his mouth, but Pam held up her hand. "No, you asked to hear my theories and ideas, so you need to just listen."

She was right. He nodded.

"As I was saying, Emmi and Tim really had reconciled, and he confessed everything. For argument's sake, let's say that he knew about the abortion and was bitter, but when he and Emmi reconciled, he told her."

"Why on earth would he be bitter about it?" Grayson couldn't stop from blurting out the question.

Pam's stare leveled him. "Because maybe the baby was his."

That stole the breath from his lungs. Of course over the last several weeks he'd considered every possible reason for Anna Belle to have done something so awful, and sure, he'd briefly entertained the thought that the baby wasn't his, but to just say it out loud. . . . Wow, the pain scratched open all the new scabs.

"I'm sorry, Grayson, but it *is* a possibility."

"I know." He knew all too well, but that didn't make the news any easier to accept. "If it was, that might make sense, at least to Anna Belle, why she didn't tell me she was pregnant."

Pam nodded. "And it would have made Tim angry. I mean, I assume, but on the other hand, what if he didn't want children?" She caught her bottom lip between her teeth and studied Grayson for a long moment. "What about Anna Belle? Did she want children?"

He considered his answer. "I would have initially said yes, but now, knowing what I know, I don't think so. I think she would have thought a baby would be more of a hindrance to her career." Saying that aloud really clawed at the ache in his chest. How had he not seen what was plain before him? Had he ignored everything that put Anna Belle in a negative light? Had he been that naive?

Well, he'd not known his wife was having an ongoing affair for months until she told him, so yeah, he must've been that naive. Gullible.

"Hey, stop." Pam laid her hand on his. "I can see the wheels turning. You can't take the blame for any of this."

"She was my wife, Pam. My *wife*. How did I not know she was having an affair? How did I miss the signs of pregnancy? And the abortion? Despite my feelings of it in and of itself, that's a medical procedure complete with anesthesia and recovery. I was home that night, and I can remember nothing that stands out about it. How does that happen?"

She squeezed his hand. "I don't know, I really don't, but what I do know is that you loved your wife. Every day countless people are fooled by their spouses cheating on them. I'm sure you're not the first man not to notice every little thing with his wife." She released his hand and sat back in the patio chair. "You need to stop beating yourself up over this, Grayson. Had you known, maybe you could've stopped the abortion. Maybe." She pointed at him. "Either way, Anna Belle made her decision, which included not telling you. What she did and why, that's on her, not you, and I won't sit here and let you beat yourself up over something you have no control over."

Maybe. "I didn't even know our marriage was in trouble, Pam. I mean, Anna Belle was irritated with me for not staying in private practice, but I just couldn't. After that kid I was treating killed himself, I just couldn't."

"Of course not. That's completely understandable."

"Anna Belle knew how much time I spent in prayer over that. How I wrestled with what I should do. She hated me working as a consultant with the police department. I mean, hated it, thought being a civil servant was beneath me. But I enjoyed the work. I liked helping the police by creating profiles."

"I know, and you did great work. I've heard."

Grayson shook his head. "Anna Belle said it was an embarrassment for me to work there. I think she was more in love with the *doctor* title than with me."

Pam's silence spoke loudly.

"Even so, I didn't notice how her unhappiness in my career choices were affecting our marriage." He shook his head, remembering all the arguments they'd had. "She hated that I wasn't bringing in my normal income. Anna Belle wasn't one to accept cutting back graciously."

"Do you hear yourself, Grayson?"

He stared at Pam. "What?"

"You're making excuses for her behavior. I'm sorry, but it's making me sick to my stomach." She bolted upright in the chair. "It's self-centered women like that who give the rest of us females a bad name. You're a good man, Grayson Thibodeaux, and Anna Belle was an idiot. I don't know why she was such a ladder climber, and I really don't care. There's no acceptable excuse for cheating on your spouse. None. Plain and simple, it's wrong. She was wrong." Pam narrowed her eyes and pointed at him again. "Anna Belle was wrong. She did you wrong."

"Yes, but—"

Pam shook her head. "No. There's no *buts* or anything. She was wrong. She mistreated you." She crossed her arms over her chest. "I realize you loved her and she was your wife, but honestly, Grayson, for the life of me, I can't figure out why. Every single thing I know about her and that I learned during the creation of the game, she was one of the most unlikable people I've ever come across. She was a liar, a cheater. . . . She stole clients from coworkers and took credit for work that was theirs. And the worst of it? She didn't care. Not one thing I heard said about her or learned or saw ever indicated she gave two cents about anything that didn't benefit her directly." Pam leaned back in the chair again. "That includes her marriage and her husband, and if you believe otherwise, you're only deluding yourself and aren't the brilliant man I know you to be. So snap out of it."

He wanted to argue, should argue. But he knew everything Pam had said was the truth. A little harsh in the delivery, but the truth.

Grayson closed his eyes and lifted his face toward the sky, letting the late-afternoon sun warm him. He sent up a silent prayer of gratitude for his friend who spoke the truth to him in love, but also for strength to carry him in his weakness and doubt sure to come over the course of the next several days. . .weeks.

He let out his breath in a huff and focused on Pam. "So, in your theory, if the baby was Tim's, and Anna Belle didn't want a baby. . ."

Pam smiled and gave a little nod. "Maybe she told him, thinking he'd be on board with the abortion, but he wasn't. He was angry but realized he couldn't stop her. Maybe that was part of what broke them up. Then, when he and his wife reconciled, he admitted that Anna Belle had gotten pregnant and had an abortion. That would be how she knew."

Logical. "So why put the pamphlet in her room?"

"There's no way Emmi Dubois wanted Anna Belle to be promoted. I'm surprised she didn't throw a fit to have her fired, but that could've caused trouble for her husband. The next best thing would be to set Anna Belle up to fail. Putting that in there would be one way to really rattle her. Get her off her game."

Grayson nodded. "That's psychologically accurate."

"Don't forget Emmi Dubois is in the medical field. She would know about behavior and such."

True.

"Want to hear my other possible scenario?"

He smiled. "Of course."

Pam smiled back. "Maybe Tim *didn't* tell Emmi. Let's say Tim didn't even know Anna Belle was pregnant."

Grayson nodded. Seemed to be Anna Belle's method. Typical Anna Belle—she'd avoid a situation if she couldn't be sure of the outcome being in her favor.

"So when they got the medical records, Tim found out. Just like you did." Pam crossed her legs in the chair, looking more like a teen than the late-twenties that she was. "He was, as you were, devastated."

"I'm not sure I like being lumped in together with him."

Pam wagged her finger. "For whatever reason, you and he both loved Anna Belle. You both were intimate with her. Who's to say that he wouldn't have been as happy with a child with her as you would've been?"

Ouch. The reality hurt, even though it was right on target. Grayson nodded. "Touché."

"Let's say he confronted her, demanded to know if the baby was his, blah blah blah. Emmi would be furious over all of this when she found out. Maybe in pillow talk he accidentally let it slip out because he was so hurt over what she did."

That, Grayson could totally understand.

"Either way, Emmi would be furious and terrified she was going to lose her hold on her husband again."

"So why put the pamphlet in her room then?"

"Because she hoped Anna Belle would think that it was Tim. If Tim and Anna Belle had an argument about it and it was over, putting that in her room would set Anna Belle off again. She would hate that Tim would bring it up again. Now, during the game she wasn't aware she was playing but knew she was in a competition for a promotion. And you and I both know that Anna Belle took her career more seriously than she took anything else."

So true.

"Grayson, I've looked at the scenarios and timelines until I'm blue in the face—"

"Which clashes with your hair, by the way." He smiled, trying to relax the tension that suddenly felt suffocating, even though they were outside with the cool breeze circling the patio.

Pam snorted. "I'm sure. As I was saying, the one person in that house when Anna Belle died who had the most reason to want her out of the way was Emmi Dubois."

"Or Tim."

Pam nodded. "Or Tim. Both probably had access to Anna Belle's medical records about her allergy. Everyone knew about her addiction to those energy drinks." She waved her hand toward the computer. "We have proof that Emmi, for whatever reason, was trying to sabotage Anna Belle one way or another. How much further would she go, knowing what she knew and feeling as betrayed by Anna Belle as she did?"

"Enough to put cherry juice in her energy drink? I don't know if she would've gone that far." Grayson stared at the still shot on the computer screen again. "I don't have a psych profile on her, which doesn't help with this line of thinking."

"No, but that image says she was desperate. Just how desperate is what we don't know." Pam uncrossed her legs and sat up. "There might be a way to find out."

Now he was intrigued. "What?"

"You could talk to her."

Grayson blew out a burst of air and shook his head. "Are you serious?"

"Hear me out."

"This better be good." Only because it was Pam was he even willing to listen to the nonsense.

"You can get anybody talking, but you're in a unique position to get Emmi to open up to you."

"How's that?"

"Come on, Gray, don't play dumb. Your wife was having an affair with her husband. You can play up how you both were so wronged. Even better, you can let her think she has a leg up on you because she managed to keep her husband while Anna Belle divorced you."

He wanted to discount what she said, but his training and experience wouldn't let him.

Pam nodded. "You could probably pull a lot of information out of her without her even realizing it."

"I just don't know if I want to go down this road. Brandon and his partner might see it as me interfering in their investigation."

"Oh, I'm sure his partner would, but you know she's ready to slap the cuffs on you for Anna Belle's murder. You are in the unique position to get information to help yourself, and I think you'd be stupid if you don't use that."

He wrapped his mind around all of that. "I can't just call her out of the blue. She'd be suspicious. I'm sure she's pretty smart in her own right." He pointed at the computer screen. "She did figure that out and use it."

"Good point." Pam pinched her bottom lip between her thumb and forefinger, a true sign her mind was running overtime.

"And, if what we're saying without saying is true and she's involved with Anna Belle's death, there's no telling what lengths she'll go to in order to protect herself."

Pam let out a sigh and shut the laptop. "Maybe we just wait and see what the police investigation comes up with. Any chance you think Brandon might tell you where they are in the investigation?"

"I don't know. I detected he felt really uncomfortable with Danielle's going right at me, but I don't know what evidence they're looking at."

"Well, we know it doesn't lead to you, because you're innocent."

"I am, and surely appreciate your loyalty, but we know that innocent people can be, and many are, arrested and even found guilty for crimes they're later exonerated for."

"I know, and that's what scares me about this. Especially with that cop gunning for you. Excuse the pun."

Grayson didn't say anything because he couldn't. He sent up another silent prayer. This time for the truth to be revealed.

FOURTEEN

"So after you walked through the house on Wednesday, then what happened?" Danielle eased Tim Dubois back to his statement.

"I signed the paperwork Colton gave me stating we had gone over the plan. Anna Belle's ex-husband left, and we got ready for our employees to arrive."

"About what time did Mr. Thibodeaux leave?" Danielle asked.

"I didn't really look at my watch, but it was before noon because Emmi and I had sandwiches delivered since we couldn't leave the house while we were waiting on the deliveries."

"Deliveries of what?" Brandon asked.

"The food. One of the tasks the game had that night was for Anna Belle to have to cook dinner for everyone." Tim smiled, almost to himself. "Anna Belle didn't know how to make a peanut butter and jelly sandwich, much less the crawfish *étouffée* she was scheduled to make."

"One of the tasks for her possible promotion in your PR firm was to cook?" Danielle's expression showed her emotions very clearly, even more than her pointed question served with a side of sarcasm.

"She had to make the dinner for all of us." Tim nodded. "Oh, you'd think that the tasks would be all focused on work stuff, right?" He shook his head. "That's what made the game so amazing. They took all the data we'd supplied them and uncovered all the weak spots of everyone, then set up tasks that would expose that weakness. Brilliant, really."

"Of course, since Mr. Thibodeaux had been married to Anna

Belle, it's not a far reach to think he'd know whether she could cook or not, right?" Danielle asked.

Tim frowned. "I suppose that's true." He lifted his chin. "But he wasn't married to the other three, and he exposed their weak spots just as effectively."

"Why don't you tell us what their tasks were?" Brandon prodded.

"Of course. Let's see, let me start with Wednesday night, the first ones. As Colton explained, these were to really knock the competitors off balance, take them off their game, so to speak." Tim smiled, a genuine smile.

He really enjoyed pitting them against each other and airing their weakest moments. Brandon thought that said a lot about him as a person.

"As I said, Anna Belle had to cook for the whole group. Crawfish étouffée, and she doesn't know how to cook. Then there was Georgia's task. She was supposed to change the oil in the car in the garage." He chuckled. "Georgia hates being dirty. Is almost crazy about getting anything under her nails. I'd bet that woman spends half her paycheck at the nail place."

Both of those sounded pretty harmless and almost like juvenile sorority pranks.

"Now Franklin was tasked with cleaning out the indoor fish pool that was in a room on the back of the house that looked almost like a conservatory."

Brandon remembered. It looked creepy to him.

"Franklin can't stand anything slimy and really doesn't tolerate anything with seaweed or algae that can touch him." Tim snickered. "Finally, there was Hugh, who had to go up on the widow's walk to sweep. He's scared of heights."

Nothing really harmful, but some fears were so intense that people became physically ill as a result.

"So everyone went to do their tasks?" Brandon asked.

Tim nodded. "Everyone was sent to do their thing at two on the dot, and they had time limits. Anna Belle had to have dinner ready by five. The rest of them were supposed to be done before then and in the dining room no later than five fifteen for dinner." He chuckled. "They were all working, not doing so well, when the fire alarm sounded at four forty."

"What happened?" Danielle asked. "Did Anna Belle catch the kitchen on fire?"

"No, there was no fire. See, that's part of the beauty. It was all planned to make them all *think* there was a fire, and to assume it was Anna Belle's fault."

Confused, Brandon asked. "There wasn't a fire?"

Tim shook his head. "No, it was part of the game." He leaned forward, resting his arms on his desk. "They arranged for a fire truck to come, firemen to rush into the house and everything. It was great."

"All so everyone would blame Anna Belle?" Danielle asked.

"You're missing the point. They were finishing up their tasks, and this really threw them off. The alarm shocked them all, and their reactions? Well, that was one of the points."

"Explain, please." Brandon couldn't grasp the importance, but then again, he was a much simpler man than those in the PR field apparently were.

"When the alarm went off, naturally Anna Belle thought it was her fault. She looked around the kitchen, but there was nothing burning or spilling over or anything. So she was confused."

"You were in the kitchen with her?" Brandon asked.

Tim shook his head. "That's when we were in the room with the game people watching the monitors. We were told to be there at four thirty-five, so we were."

"So you were watching her on the monitor?" Danielle prompted.

Tim nodded. "Right. Anna Belle was moving around all frantically. I'd never seen her look so panicked as she checked the oven, the stove, then the oven again." He grinned. "She really freaked when they turned on the smoke."

"Turned on the smoke?" Danielle glanced at Brandon, her incredulous expression matching what had to be his.

"Yeah, they had some cool smoke machines they'd set up in certain places, and at four forty-three they all went on and smoke started filling certain areas of the house. Like the kitchen, the con- servatory room, the room you use to go out to the widow's walk, and the garage."

"All rooms where the four were." Brandon made notes, as did his partner.

"Right." Tim continued. "So naturally they all thought the house was on fire and started to try and get out. That's where it got really interesting."

"How's that?" Danielle asked.

"Well, Anna Belle turned and ran to the front door, but it was dead-bolted and she didn't have a key. It was one of those that had a keyhole on either side. She tried several times to open it, even though she had to have realized it was locked the first time she tried it, but she tried again and again. Panicking."

Tim sure seemed to enjoy others' fear.

"She finally turned and ran to the back door on the other side of the house. At the same time, Georgia tried to get out of the garage, but that door was locked too. She beat on it and kicked it." Tim shook his head but smiled. "Her determination or fear, either-or, had her pick up the metal trash can and break through the only window to get out. It was resourceful of her, but as soon as she stepped out, she started sinking."

"Sinking?" Danielle asked.

Tim nodded, still grinning. "The game people had put some- thing outside the door and the window that imitated quicksand or something. You really didn't sink more than six or seven inches, but if you're already scared, that would freak you out. It did Georgia, that's for sure. She started hollering like crazy."

"I can imagine." Danielle's tone clearly stated she was not amused by the tactics, nor by his obvious amusement at his employees' fear and trials.

"Meanwhile, Hugh was hollering from the widow's walk because that turret room was really filled with smoke and it was locked from the hallway, and there were no stairs down from the widow's walk."

Brandon could only imagine how he'd feel in a situation like that—trapped, with no obvious way out. He resisted the urge to shudder.

"Franklin was trapped in the conservatory," Tim continued, "and I thought for sure he'd just pass out. He beat on the door going out, like, for a good couple of minutes. Then he surprised me. He turned back to the house and tried that door. It was unlocked of course, so he ran into the house and to the closest door outside, the back door that Anna Belle had left standing wide open."

"So Anna Belle and Franklin were outside, right?" Danielle asked.

Tim nodded. "So was Georgia, but she was stuck in the quicksand stuff. Franklin heard Hugh hollering, so he ran that way, saw the ladder that had been leaning against the garage, grabbed it, and put it up so Hugh could get down. I was really impressed with his resourcefulness."

"What about Georgia and Anna Belle?" Brandon asked.

"Well, Anna Belle saw Georgia, who hollered at Anna Belle to come help her, but Anna Belle just headed toward the fire truck that had just arrived."

"Anna Belle didn't help Georgia?" Danielle asked.

Tim shook his head. "No. I mean, she was still upset and everything herself and was probably confused with all the activity and alarms."

Still making excuses for her behavior. Yeah, the guy was still in love with her. Brandon made a note while Tim continued.

"So, Hugh and Franklin turned back and went around the house toward Georgia, I'm assuming to go help her, but the fake fireman already had pulled her out and had her in the street with Anna Belle. Once Hugh and Franklin joined them, and the game people had turned off the smoke machines and sucked up the smoke with fans, we were told it was okay to go tell them that the house was cleared. The fake firemen left, and everyone went back into the house." He grinned. "Georgia was mad at Anna Belle, but everyone really was annoyed with her because they all thought she'd caused a fire while cooking. And whatever she'd left on the stove when she ran out had scorched to the bottom of the pan and filled the downstairs with that burning-food smell, so even though she denied causing a fire, no one believed her."

Wow. This game stuff was more complicated than Brandon would've ever imagined.

"But what they didn't know is the fake firemen had brought in a setup from the local deli, so we were able to eat. At the meal, I told the four of them that only Hugh had been successful in his task because he'd actually finished cleaning off the widow's walk. That made the other three more than a little annoyed at him, to be sure. They didn't show it much in front of me though."

"But you all had dinner together?" Danielle asked.

Tim sat back in his chair. "We did. It wasn't étouffée, but the sandwiches and potato salad were pretty tasty. We had cookies for dessert."

Brandon could really care less what they ate.

"We were done by six, and I told everyone to go to their rooms to be ready for the next day's tasks, which they would receive at breakfast at eight. They were reminded again about no technology except in their rooms and told not to be late. Everyone left to go to their own rooms."

"And you?" Brandon asked.

"Emmi and I cleaned up the kitchen, then we went to our suite. We took showers, then watched a little TV before going to bed around ten or so."

"Nothing else happened that night?" Danielle asked.

"Well, yeah. The snake."

Ah, yes. The snake. Brandon tapped his pen against the notebook. "Tell me about the snake."

"Well, the game people knew Franklin was terrified of snakes, from the forms that everybody submitted. So one of those employees snuck in while Franklin was in the shower and put a snake in his bed." Tim laughed, even slapping the desk. "That guy screamed louder than a girl when he found it."

"I would imagine finding a snake in your bed would make just about anybody scream," Danielle said.

"I don't know about that, but he screamed and got us all there. Hugh got the snake and took it outside and let it loose."

"And after that?" Danielle asked.

Tim shrugged. "It was going to be an early morning, so we all went back to our rooms after Hugh came back inside."

"Nothing else for the rest of the night? Or was there something else planned?" Brandon asked.

Tim shook his head. "If anything happened, I wasn't aware of it. I don't remember if anything was planned or not. You'd have to ask the game company."

There were so many questions Brandon planned to ask Colton and especially Grayson. So many.

Grayson welcomed the silence of his house now that Pam had gone to pick up dinner for them. Not that he didn't appreciate her help and support—he just needed a few minutes with himself. His emotions were so raw that he wasn't sure what he felt. On one hand, he felt the loss of Anna Belle so deeply, more than when she'd left him. The finality of her being gone scraped against his very spirit. Yet, on the other hand, his feelings over her affair and abortion were stronger than he'd realized. He'd compartmentalized—he could recognize that—and put away the enormous rage and pain over the betrayals. Now it was as if they were slapped back in his face.

He had to deal with them. Had to process his emotions. As a psychologist, he knew this. He had to forgive Anna Belle for her betrayals. Had to accept what she'd done. As a Christian, he knew this. As a man, he wanted none of it.

The doorbell disturbed the argument he was having with himself.

Jerking the door open, Grayson expected Pam. It wasn't. Monique Fredericks stood on his doorstep with a roll-on suitcase.

"I'm sorry to bother you twice in one day," Monique apologized.

"You're no bother." Grayson pushed the door open wider. "Come in." He reached for the suitcase and pulled it inside after her. "Can I get you a cup of coffee?" He led her into the kitchen where he'd been sitting. . .thinking. . .praying.

"Oh no. Not this late in the day. I'd be awake all night." Monique took a seat atop one of the barstools.

"Water? Tea?"

"No, honey, I'm fine. I don't plan to stay long."

Grayson stood on the other side of the island, facing her, and leaned to be more at her eye level. He refrained from saying anything, knowing the woman would speak her mind without request.

"That was left for me at my hotel today." She nodded at the suitcase. "I just got back in, and it was delivered up to my room. It's Anna Belle's."

He nodded. "I know. I bought it for her as a gift when she was promoted to senior account rep." He'd taken her out to eat, then dancing to celebrate. When they'd returned home, he'd given her the suitcase, and they'd slow danced barefoot and barely dressed in the kitchen by candlelight.

"I thought maybe the police had sent it over, then realized that couldn't be. I'm meeting with them tomorrow morning, and they would just bring it with them."

Grayson nodded. The police didn't make it a habit to just send over personal items like that. At least none of the officers he'd worked with.

"Then I thought maybe the hospital had forgotten to give it to me when I went to identify the body, but I didn't think so. They gave me the jewelry and clothes she'd been wearing when she was brought in by ambulance and had me sign some papers to take them."

Grayson nodded again. This wasn't making sense.

"So I called the front desk and asked who'd left it, and nobody seems to know. Just that it was there with my name on it."

"What's in it?" Grayson stared at the suitcase. Who would send it to Monique without letting her know who it was from? Who knew who she was and where she was staying?

"I don't know. I was a little apprehensive about opening it."

"You haven't looked inside?"

"No. I brought it here. I thought you and I could open it together." The hope in her voice was unmistakable.

"Of course." He reached for the handle and lifted it onto the island. Slowly, he unzipped the front pocket. Clothes spilled out. Anna Belle's clothes. Underwear, T-shirt, bra, tank top. All with the scent of Chanel No. 5.

Grayson let out a slow breath and steadied himself. He could almost hear Anna Belle's laughter as a memory accosted him. It was right after they'd married, and they were in one of many department stores in the mall, taking back one of the duplicate wedding gifts they'd received.

"What about this one?" Anna Belle sprayed the tester perfume in the

air in front of his face.

The smell stung his nostrils. He wrinkled his nose and waved his hand in front of him to get rid of the stench. "Not that one. It's way too strong."

"Perfume's supposed to be strong. The good ones anyway. So they'll last." Anna Belle lifted another bottle and sprayed in the air. She sniffed. "Not bad. What do you think?"

It wasn't too overpowering. Not like the other one. He reached for the box and took in the price and really almost gagged. "I think for that price it ought to cook dinner for us too."

Anna Belle laughed, that free-spirited giggle that was uniquely hers. "Don't look at the price, Grayson. Smell. Feel. Perfume's all about the floral notes and how they make you feel." She grabbed another bottle and sprayed, then sniffed. "Ooh, I like this one."

Despite the prices, he couldn't deny her. Not when she was so happy. He sniffed and appreciated the scent. Vanilla. Jasmine. Musk. And amber? It was intoxicating. He closed his eyes and inhaled again.

Anna Belle's tinkling laugh opened his eyes. "Oh, you like this one, huh?"

"It does smell nice." Alluring. Enticing. Sexy.

"Then this shall be my signature perfume. I shall only wear this." She lifted the bottle and read. "Chanel No. 5."

"How much is it?"

Anna Belle pressed her finger against his lips. "Shh. Don't be so crude as to ask the price of my appeal."

He chuckled but still tried to reach for the bottle's box. "Anna Belle."

"No. This is for me. Something that's all mine. Whenever you smell it, you'll think of me and only me." She smiled that smile that almost always made his knees go weak. "Forever and ever."

Grayson swallowed back the memory. *Forever and ever* was the truth. Even now, after all she'd done, the scent lingered in her clothes and made him think of her. His heart ached.

"What's in the small pocket?" Monique snapped him back to the task at hand.

He unzipped the small front pocket of the suitcase. He pulled out Anna Belle's makeup case with its familiar ninja cartoon character. He had made such fun of her buying that, but she said it made her feel like a woman ninja, capable of anything.

Grayson unzipped it and dumped the contents onto the island. Amid brushes and cosmetics was a bottle of Benadryl and her EpiPen. He lifted the Epi, realizing that what he held in his hand could have saved Anna Belle's life had she been able to get to it in time. Why hadn't she?

"Was that missing?" Monique asked.

"I don't know. She always knew the early symptoms and would've gone immediately for this. I don't know why she didn't this time. There wasn't one found in her room, and she clearly didn't inject herself." Questions and more questions, that's all he seemed to get.

He scooped up all the makeup and the Epi and put it back in the ninja bag and closed it. He reached for the main zipper.

Bam! Bam! Bam!

"Hurry up, Grayson," Pam hollered from the other side of the door.

She always did have uncanny timing.

"Excuse me. It's my assistant," Grayson told Monique as he went to the front door and swung it open.

Arms filled with boxes, Pam marched inside. "I got two pizzas and cheese sticks and breadsticks too because I didn't know how long we'd be working." She froze as she walked into the kitchen and spied Monique.

Grayson took the boxes from her and set them on the stovetop. "Pam Huron, this is Anna Belle's mother, Monique Fredericks. Monique, this is my assistant and friend, Pam Huron. Pam's been helping me try to piece together what happened."

Pam wiped her hands on her jeans before extending one. "It's nice to meet you, and I'm sorry for your loss."

Monique shook her hand and nodded, but her gaze remained fixed on Pam's hair. It usually did get the most attention.

After a moment passed, Monique withdrew her hand. "Thank you. Nice to meet you too."

Pam nodded at the suitcase on the island. "What's this?" she asked Grayson.

"It's Anna Belle's. Someone left it at the hotel for Monique."

"Who?"

"We don't know," Monique answered. "It was just left for me. Grayson's kind enough to open it with me."

"Oh." Pam looked from Monique to Grayson. "Um, do you want me to leave?"

Grayson shook his head. "Of course not." He realized that the choice wasn't just his. He looked at Monique. "Unless you'd prefer. . ."

"No. I'm fine." Monique nodded at the suitcase. "Let's go ahead and see what else is in there."

He unzipped the case and flipped the lid back.

Monique gasped while Pam let out a low whistle. Grayson could only stare, speechless.

"What in mercy's name is going on? What is that, and why are these things in Anna Belle's suitcase?" Monique asked.

FIFTEEN

"Thursday morning, what was the plan?" Brandon asked Tim Dubois.

"The caterer showed up at seven thirty and set up the buffet in the dining room, and gave us the takeout boxes for the game people. They took the boxes to the game room, set up the buffet, then left in under fifteen minutes. Everyone from Deets was supposed to be there at eight sharp." Tim shook his head. "I have to tell you, Game's On You had the timing down pat. When you look at the overview, with all the moving parts, well, it's nothing short of pretty amazing how they planned it all."

Danielle didn't look impressed. "You let the caterer in, I assume?"

Tim nodded. "Colton had told me to meet them at the back door right at seven thirty. They were there waiting."

"What about Emmi? Where was she? With you?" Brandon asked.

"She was finishing getting her makeup on." He grinned at Brandon as if they shared some inside joke. "You know how women are in taking forever to get ready."

No, he didn't know. "So what time did she join you in the dining room?"

"About five minutes or so before eight, I guess." Tim said. "Everyone else got there right after her."

"What was everyone's moods?" Danielle asked. "How did they seem?"

"Well, Franklin had dark circles under his eyes, like he hadn't gotten much sleep. He probably thought snakes were coming to get him." Tim snickered.

"What about the others?" Danielle pressed.

"Hugh looked like he always does. It's hard to tell about him one way or another. He's pretty even stephen all the time. It's part of what makes him a good account rep. He doesn't get flustered if a client doesn't like a pitch. He's quick on his feet."

"Like getting the snake out of Franklin's bed?" Brandon offered.

"Right. Like that."

"What about Anna Belle?" Danielle asked.

"She looked beautiful as usual but seemed a little jumpy. I remember she kept looking out the window, and then I remembered that the game people were supposed to appear outside her room the day before in a Mardi Gras mask to scare her. They planned for her to catch glimpses of that in the hall and outside in the yard, looking up to her window."

"Why?" Danielle asked.

"It was part of the game." Tim looked like he was tired of explaining complex ideas to small children. "Anna Belle had been stalked in college, during Mardi Gras, by a guy in a mask. So the game duplicated that to scare her and knock her off her game. Like with Franklin and snakes."

Brandon wasn't sure he could reconcile his friend and former consult Grayson with this game creator who seemed to play on people's worst fears. Especially when he considered what Franklin, Hugh, and Georgia had told them in their interviews.

"Anyway, Anna Belle acted a little jumpy, but she was in it to win, just like she always was. Anna Belle was all about succeeding."

That point had been hammered home well, many times over, during the course of the initial investigation.

"And Georgia?" Danielle prompted.

Tim nodded. "Yeah, Georgia seemed more irritated at Anna Belle than jumpy or anything. Probably from Anna Belle not helping her the day before. But the game hadn't focused on Georgia's fears yet. She got a voodoo doll on her bed later that day."

Put there by Hugh. Brandon nodded. "So you ate breakfast as a group?"

"Yeah. It was a little tense, but Colton had warned us about that. Anyway, at nine we'd all finished eating, so I told them to go to their rooms to get their next task delivered to them, just as Colton had said."

"And they did?" Brandon was still more than a little shocked that grown adults would just blindly do as told, ignoring their common sense, which had to be screaming at them not to.

Tim nodded. "They were behind their closed doors in less than ten minutes."

"What about you and Emmi?" Danielle asked.

"We let the caterer's crew in to remove all the stuff from the buffet, then checked in with Colton."

"Oh?" Brandon raised his brows.

"Yeah. He said everything was going exactly as planned, so we could go set up the videos in the two rooms for the team PR campaign creations. So we did. Colton came by after nine thirty and told us we needed to go to our room while the teams got in place."

"You went to your room for how long?" Danielle asked.

"About thirty or so minutes, I guess. I don't really know. Colton knocked on our door and told me that the teams were working on their campaigns, and that we could do what we wanted for an hour or so until the caterers came back with lunch."

"This campaign. . ." Brandon remembered what Hugh and Franklin had said. "Was it real or created?"

Tim's face turned red. "I'm not at liberty to discuss that with you."

"You realize we're New Orleans detectives conducting a murder investigation that occurred during an event you planned, right?" No mistaking Danielle's mood.

"I do, but for reasons I'm sure you understand, I can neither deny nor confirm if the circumstances around the campaign were accurate or made up."

Wasn't hard for Brandon to read between the lines on that one. Tim's lack of denial or even the possibility of such meant it was real. "What happened next?"

"Well, the caterers showed up with lunch and set up in the dining room, as was the norm."

"What catering company?" Brandon didn't have that information. Someone on the crew might've seen or heard something.

"Lagniappe Eats." Tim smiled. "I highly recommend them. Great food. Fast service."

Brandon made a note in his notebook and circled it. "When the time was up for the teams to have completed their campaigns, what happened then?"

"Everyone came into the dining room to eat. I took each team into the library separately to hear their pitch. I gave each team ten minutes."

"While you listened to pitches in the library, the other team and Emmi stayed in the dining room?" Danielle asked.

"Yes, that's right." Tim nodded. "Once I'd heard both pitches and lunch was concluded, I sent the teams back to their respective rooms."

"What time was this?" Danielle asked.

"They all left about one. Emmi went on up to our room behind them while I let the crew from the caterers back in to clean up, then I went up as well since I needed to make some calls."

Or call a certain politician and give him some pitches that would offset the upcoming scandal he was sure to face. "About what time was that? That you went upstairs to your room?" Brandon asked.

"One fifteen or so."

Brandon nodded, writing down the timeline, which seemed to get more and more complicated. All the moving parts of the game—well, he had to respect what Grayson did, even if he didn't understand it. "What was next on the schedule?"

"The four would be put in teams again, this time Anna Belle and Hugh against Georgia and Franklin. They would have to figure out the clues to find the key in a room to open the door in under two and a half hours."

"Like an escape room." Danielle knew from others' interviews, but it was always the plan to get multiple witnesses to collaborate if possible.

"Exactly like an escape room." Tim smiled. "I don't know all the details of the clues, but it had to have been pretty tough because Georgia and Franklin didn't make it out in time."

"Do you know the basics of the clues?" Danielle asked.

Tim stopped smiling and shook his head. "I don't. I was told that some of their most personal information would have to be confessed in order to find the key, but I wasn't privy to that information. You'd have to ask the game company."

"You said Georgia and Franklin didn't make it out in time?" Brandon asked.

"Right. Since they didn't, one of the game people unlocked the door. Either way, the plan was always for us to be in the hall, whether they escaped or not, and direct everyone back to their rooms to prepare for dinner right at four thirty."

Interesting he used *us* instead of his name or Emmi's. Was he supposed to have been in the hall? If so, and Emmi clearly was, then where was he? Brandon leaned forward in the chair. "So you told everyone to go to their rooms?"

Tim's face reddened. "Well, actually, Emmi did that."

"What were you doing?" Danielle asked.

"I let the caterers in to set up for dinner."

Brandon let a pause fall. A second passed. Two. Tim remained silent but fidgeted in his chair. Brandon didn't miss his signs of discomfort. "What time did the teams go into the escape rooms?"

"The doors were locked at one thirty."

Brandon nodded. "And you said they had two and a half hours to get out, so that would run until four?"

Tim nodded. "Except Anna Belle and Hugh got out five minutes early, but Emmi was already waiting in the hall to tell them to go to their rooms."

"You said that during those few moments, Emmi was in the hall and you were letting the caterers in," Brandon started.

"Right." Tim nodded emphatically.

Brandon flipped back through his notes. "You said you and Emmi went to your room for you to make calls and such, between one and one fifteenish?"

"Yes, that's correct."

"And what time did Emmi go wait in the hall outside the escape rooms?" Brandon caught Danielle's gaze and let a volume pass between them without saying a word.

"She had to be there at three forty-five per Colton's instructions. Just in case they got out early, which Anna Belle and Hugh did."

"And at that time, you went to let the caterers in?" Danielle gave a slight tilt of her head, just enough to let Brandon know she understood where he was going.

"Right."

"So what were you and Emmi doing for those two and a half hours, between one fifteen and three forty-five?" Brandon pierced Tim with his stare.

"Well, um, like I said. I, uh, had some calls to make. I do run a business."

His hemming and hawing made him a caricature. "I had to call and update the board too. You know, with the status of what was happening. Frankly, I suspect they were a little anxious to see the outcome on the game. I was too, to be honest."

"Frankly. . . to be honest." Brandon slid to the edge of his chair. "You were making business calls for two and a half hours?"

Tim's entire face was the color of the middle of a rare steak. "I don't know. I don't make a habit of logging my time on calls."

"It's okay, Mr. Dubois, we can just get a copy of your cell phone records." Danielle straightened her posture.

"Um, and I. . .that's right. . .I took a walk. To clear my head. Some of the business stuff was really intense and I needed to just relax a few minutes. Sorry, I forgot about that."

Right. Funny how the mention of cell phone records can prompt a memory of doing something instead of being on the phone. "So you made some business calls and took a. . .walk in those two and a half hours?" Brandon didn't bother to push aside the sarcasm sneaking into his voice.

"Yes." The tips of Tim's ears were bright red.

"Did your wife go on this walk with you?" Danielle asked.

"No. She was reading a book."

Reading. Going for a walk. Brandon didn't think so.

Danielle wasn't buying it either. "Oh, I love to read. What book?"

"I don't know." Tim's Adam's apple bobbed as if it were Halloween night. "Does it matter?"

"No, I was just curious." Danielle tapped her pen against her knee.

Tim made a point of glancing at his watch. "If we could wrap this up, I have an appointment in fifteen minutes."

Sure he did. Brandon nodded. "Where did you go on this little walk of yours?"

Tim's eyes narrowed. "I went into the backyard and just walked around. Look, I can tell you don't believe me, but that's where I was."

Brandon would neither deny nor confirm. He swallowed the

snicker. "Your wife stayed in your room while you went on your walk? Reading?"

"Yes." Tim ground out the word from behind clenched teeth.

"But Emmi was in the hall at three forty-five, and you were letting the caterers in?"

"Yes."

"What happened next?" Danielle asked.

"Emmi and I were talking with Colton in the kitchen, going over the plan for dinner, when Georgia started screaming. And I mean, screaming. Of course, we all ran up the stairs to see what was wrong."

"There was nothing planned to happen then, right? No snakes in beds or anything like that?" Danielle asked.

Tim shook his head. "No. There was nothing scheduled until after dinner."

"You hear the screams and run up the stairs and what?" Brandon hovered his pen over his field notes.

"Anna Belle was lying on the floor. Unconscious. I pushed Georgia, who was just standing there screaming, out of the way and felt for a pulse. I could barely feel one." Tim's hands trembled slightly. "I told Colton to call 911, and I started CPR."

"What was everybody else doing?" Danielle asked.

Tim frowned. "I have no idea. I was concentrating on trying to save Anna Belle's life."

Brandon nodded. "The paramedics came and took over CPR. What did you do?"

"Everyone was there, all our employees and the game people. Our employees didn't have a clue who the game people were. I think I told them they were with the house or something. I told everyone I was going to the hospital. Emmi and I left immediately."

Danielle softened her tone. "We understand Anna Belle never regained consciousness. What happened at the hospital?"

"We sat in the waiting room. Colton came, I guess because he wanted to make sure his company had no liability. At least that's what our corporate attorney said."

So lawyers had already been called. Of course.

Tim continued without prompting. "Hugh came a little bit later and sat with us. None of us really talked, except for mentioning how bad the coffee was."

Brandon remembered Hugh's statement about Tim's mumblings. "Someone overheard you saying it was all your fault. Can you tell me what you meant by that?"

Tim's face went slack. "I don't recall saying that. Who told you I said that? Colton? He was probably trying to cover his own responsibility."

"So, you're saying that someone was mistaken and you didn't say that?" Brandon pried.

"That's what I'm saying." Tim crossed his arms over his chest.

"Okay, so the doctor came out and informed you that Anna Belle had passed. What happened then?" Danielle asked.

"There was nothing left to do. Nothing left to say. Emmi and I left and went home. We were in shock of course."

"What did you do when you got home?" Brandon asked.

"I called the board to tell them." He shrugged. "I don't remember everything exactly. Like I said, I was in shock."

Brandon nodded. "Emmi says she went and picked up yours and her belongings from the house and brought them home?"

Tim nodded but was clearly distracted as grief marched over his expression.

"Anything else?" Danielle asked.

"Nothing until the police contacted me and started asking questions." He stood. "I'm sorry, but I need to end this now. I have an appointment." He moved toward his office door. "I'm sure you understand what a trying time this is for our company."

Just like that, they'd been dismissed. Brandon stood and winked at Danielle. They'd gotten enough. For now.

"Thank you again for your time, Mr. Dubois." Brandon shook his hand, holding the tight grip long enough to add, "I'm sure we'll be in touch again real soon."

Maybe sooner than they all thought.

Anna Belle
Thursday 4:00 p.m.

That should show them all. Not only had her and Franklin's campaign rocked, but she and Hugh made it out of the escape room with time to spare.

Take *that*, Grayson Thibodeaux.

Kicking off her shoes, Anna Belle grabbed her energy drink, twisted off the lid, and gulped it down in one swig. Dinner would be a fun one tonight. Gloating was always so entertaining. And every time she did something awesome, the look on Emmi's face was priceless.

Anna Belle set the drink on the desk. Now, what should she wear to—

Her lips tingled and the roof of her mouth itched.

No! This couldn't be.

She ran her tongue over the top of her mouth. Her tongue swelled, taking all available space in her mouth.

No, no, no, no!

Tightness wrapped around her throat. Constricted her chest. Her arms felt like a million little bitty wasps were stinging her in rapid succession.

Oh, but it couldn't be. This was a full-fledged allergic reaction.

Anna Belle looked for her purse. It wasn't hanging on the chair. Wasn't on the desk.

Where was it? Not where she'd left it. Oh no. No. No. No.

She flung open the armoire, inhaling through her nose. Sweat beaded on her forehead, upper lip, center of her chest, and small of her back. Her eyes watered.

Couldn't take a deep breath.

There it was. She fumbled as she unzipped the makeup bag. Her fingers and wrists vibrated. Heat shot up from her stomach and spread like a wildfire. So hot.

Where was her Epi? She dumped the contents of the makeup bag in her purse. Where was it? It wasn't here.

Anna Belle's hands trembled as her throat closed. She ran to the bathroom, slipping as her sense of balance shifted. Dizziness. Just moving made her feel like she was going to pass out. Her backup was there.

Where was her toiletry case? It wasn't on the counter where she'd left it.

What was going on?

No, this couldn't be happening.

Her eyes filled with moisture. She clawed at her throat.

Couldn't get air.

She struggled to focus. Her purse. Her makeup bag. Her Epi—

Could. Not. Breathe.

Her knees hit the floor. She knew she would lose consciousness in seconds. Her racing heartbeat thudded in her head, pounding in her ears.

Oh God, I'm sorry. I'm so, so sorry.

SIXTEEN

"Grayson, do you know what those things are?" Monique stared at Anna Belle's open suitcase on his kitchen island.

"Yes, ma'am, I do."

Monique reached for the mask, but Pam reached out and stopped her. "I'm sorry. Excuse me." She looked at Grayson. "Since we don't know who packed them up from the house, put them in Anna Belle's suitcase, and sent them to her mother, there's a chance the police might want to look at these items."

She had a point. At least it would show the police that there was another suspect besides him. "I'll call Brandon later and tell him. He'll probably want to swing by and pick everything up." Hopefully his friend would see it as an act of goodwill. He knew Danielle wouldn't for sure.

But at the moment, he owed Anna Belle's mother some explanation. "Monique, did Anna Belle ever tell you exactly what I do now?"

She nodded slowly. "You make those elaborate corporate team building games, right? Escape rooms and stuff like that?"

Pretty accurate. He didn't want to be condescending to Monique but knew that the complexities of what Game's On You did was lost on many people. Better to keep it as simple as possible. "That's pretty much it. My company had been hired by Anna Belle's to create a game for them as part of their process in determining an upcoming promotion. She was part of the game, and these are props that were used in that game."

Monique pointed at the Mardi Gras mask. "Anna Belle hated

those things, you know."

"I do." He nodded.

"Do you know why?"

He nodded. "I remember. She had a stalker on campus at college. He would wear a Mardi Gras mask like that. Left her doubloons everywhere, just so she'd know he'd been there. . .watching. It freaked her out until he was caught by campus police. We started dating soon after, so she was still really leery."

Monique nodded but kept staring at the mask. "This was a prop in your game, you say?"

"Yes." He knew what was coming and braced himself. She could say nothing that he hadn't already said himself.

"You used what she went through against her?"

"We do the job our client hires us to do," Pam interjected.

Grayson smiled at Pam. So like her to jump to his defense. "Why don't we move to the table and have some pizza? I can explain it all to you, Monique, and I'll be happy to answer any questions you might have."

"I don't want pizza. I realize I'm old, and probably simpleminded when compared to you all of today, but it seems like I asked a simple question. Did you use what Anna Belle went through in part of your little game?"

Pam's eyes brightened.

Grayson held up a single finger to Pam but focused on Monique. "I don't think you're simpleminded, and I did not mean to insult you. To answer you, yes, ma'am, I did. Each participant filled out a questionnaire, and that information was used in creating a custom game."

"She included about this?"

Grayson nodded. "I was surprised too because I had nearly forgotten about it. The incident happened so many years ago, and she'd never mentioned it after we were married. I was shocked to see it on her questionnaire."

Monique pointed to the voodoo doll. "And that thing?"

Grayson looked at Pam, who jumped in. "It's a voodoo doll."

Monique's eyes widened. "Anna Belle had something to do with voodoo?"

"Oh no, ma'am." Pam shook her head. "This prop was used for someone else in the company." She looked at Grayson. "Georgia had this when she found Anna Belle. She probably dropped it in the room."

He shook his head. "The crime unit would have taken and bagged everything in Anna Belle's room."

"This obviously was removed before then." Pam tapped her chin. "I don't remember seeing it at all, Grayson, but we know Georgia took it into the room."

"But it wasn't there when the crime unit went, or they would have taken it." None of this made sense.

"So the question is who took it and why?"

He didn't have any answers, only more questions. "And why deliver it with Anna Belle's things to Monique?"

"Was that a prop for someone else too?" Monique pointed at the Scheduled Maternity pamphlet lying by the doll. "That appointment card has Anna Belle's name on it."

Grayson's gut tightened. Pam walked behind him and patted his back. "I think I'm going to go to the table." She lifted the boxes from the stove top and carried them into the dining room, careful to swing the connecting door shut behind her.

"No, Monique. It's Anna Belle's." His mouth was drier than dry.

"But that's. . .that's where they do abortions."

He nodded slowly.

Monique's eyes went wide. "Are you telling me that my daughter had an abortion?"

He nodded.

"No. How could you let her do such a thing?"

"I didn't know. I didn't even know she was pregnant." His voice sounded foreign to his own ears.

"Oh, merciful heavens." Monique clamped a hand over her mouth, her eyes filling with tears. "I'm so sorry, Grayson."

His own vision blurred. "Me too."

Monique was off the barstool and around the island in a flash, hugging him. The warmth of her touch and depth of her emotion nearly broke him. He hugged her back. "She never told me. Ever."

"Then how do you know for sure?" Monique dabbed at her eyes with the edge of her sleeve. "If she never told you. . ."

He handed her a napkin. "It was in her medical records. She authorized the release of them for the game."

Monique balled the napkin in her fist. "She was raised knowing that abortion is murder. A sin." She shook her head. "I just can't believe. . ." She met Grayson's gaze. "Was it yours?"

He lifted his shoulders, letting them ease back down into place. "I don't know. Like I said, she never told me she was pregnant. We were still married at the time, but that doesn't mean the baby was mine."

She grabbed his hand. "Oh Grayson. I'm so sorry."

"Me too. Me too." More than he could ever tell her. He was sorry that things had gotten so sideways between him and Anna Belle. Sorry that he had missed so many warning signs. Sorry he hadn't fought harder for his marriage.

There was the root of his problem: guilt over his failed marriage.

He'd been raised by two parents who loved one another. They'd stuck together even through the hard times, and there were many. They'd raised their son in a loving family. Like Anna Belle, he'd been raised with the knowledge of God's love and mercy and grace. He and Anna Belle might've grown up on opposite sides of the family financial tracks, but they were on common ground when it came to loving Christ. That was part of why he struggled so hard with what she'd done. Not just that she'd done it, but that she'd been willing and able to turn away from the spiritual truths she'd known. How? How could someone just go totally out of character?

"Wait a minute." Monique took a step backward. "You still used this? In a *game*?" Her tear-filled eyes were wide.

"No. I didn't. I wouldn't." He nearly choked. "I couldn't."

"But. . ." She pointed at the pamphlet.

No sense in dragging Monique into all the details. Especially when she was scheduled to meet Brandon tomorrow. "Someone else put it in her room."

"Whoever put the cherry juice in her drink?"

"Maybe. We don't know."

"Well, there seems to be a lot we don't know." Monique smiled at him, tucking the wadded napkin into her pants pocket. "But I'm glad to know I wasn't wrong about you, Grayson. That you wouldn't use something so painfully personal against her, even though you were divorced."

He hadn't even been tempted. Maybe if he'd known sooner, the instinct to exact revenge would have kicked in, but all he'd felt when he found out was immeasurable grief.

"Now, maybe I would like a piece of pizza. If the offer still stands."

"I apologize for showing up unannounced." Brandon stood in front of Colton York's desk in the offices of Game's On You.

The setting sun peeked in through the window of the co-owner's corner office.

"Not a problem at all. You're lucky you caught me. We usually shut down around four thirty, but since Grayson's out, my assistant and I had some things to finish up." He waved Brandon and Danielle to the couch across from the ceiling-to-floor bookcases. "Have a seat." He sat on the matching love seat diagonal from the couch, facing his desk.

Brandon sat down beside his partner and glanced around. "Nice office." He stared at the books, photos, and knickknacks on the bookcase. Golf balls, tees, Vegas dice, and such littered the space. "You're a golfer?"

"I've been called worse." Colton laughed. "I play a little. Do you play?"

"Not me." Brandon shook his head. "Too slow for me."

Colton narrowed his eyes, studying him. "Baseball?"

Brandon grinned. "Basketball."

"Ah. Who do you like?"

Danielle lifted her hands. "Why must men always resort to discussion of sports?"

Colton grinned. "My partner would say it's in our genetic makeup, so we're predisposed to discuss such things."

"Speaking of Grayson. . . ," Brandon began.

"I wondered when you'd show up to ask these questions."

"What questions?" Danielle asked.

Colton smiled and wagged his finger. "Oh, come on. We both know that an ex-husband is always a suspect when you suspect foul play in a death."

"Make no mistake, Mr. York, we don't just suspect foul play. Anna Belle Thibodeaux's death wasn't an accident. It was murder." Danielle's tone leveled Colton.

"I didn't realize it was positive. I thought you were still investigating." He sat back against the plush fabric of the love seat.

"We are, but that's to get to what happened. We know it was murder." Danielle pulled out her notebook and glanced at Brandon.

He already had his field notes out and open. "Tell us about Deets PR hiring your company."

Colton nodded. "We get inquiries every day. Most are just

curious and want to know what we do exactly. Out of every twenty calls, only one usually proves to be a legitimate lead."

Brandon nodded.

"When our receptionist determines that a call is legitimate, they usually are sent to Pam Huron, Grayson's assistant, or Keely Masterson, my assistant."

"Keely was one of the people at the rental house on Esplanade Avenue, correct?" Danielle asked.

"Yes. Let me explain a little of how we're set up here." Colton crossed his ankle over his knee. "We have two teams here—Grayson's and mine. Grayson has a degree in psychology and I have one in sociology, so we both work on every case to some extent. However, the bulk of game creation and implementation is usually handled by one team. Grayson and I, because of our fields and experience, are usually the only ones who work every game. Usually, once a game is given to a team, it's their job from start to finish. Creation, implementation, conclusion."

"Who are on each team?" Brandon held his pen at the ready.

"My team consists of me, Keely Masterson, Stratton Reeves, and Wynnona Juneau. Grayson's team is Grayson, Pam Huron, Nora Savant, and Vic Abshire. Keely and Pam are like mine and Grayson's right arms—they're assistants, but they are very good at their jobs and could easily take over for either of us." He lowered his voice and smiled. "But don't let them know I admitted that."

"So your team ran the game for Deets PR?" Danielle asked.

"Let me back up. When the call from Tim Dubois came in and Jackie, our receptionist, determined it was a real call, she transferred it to me. Tim and I talked, and we set up an initial consultation. Usually Grayson and I are both involved in those."

"But not this time?" Danielle asked.

"Well, of course I recognized the company name as where Grayson's ex worked. I didn't know if maybe this was some sort of. . .

I don't know, but I thought it best to check it out without Grayson being brought in yet."

Brandon could see that. "So you met with Mr. Dubois alone?"

Colton nodded. "I did. I was leery of course and very guarded, but once Tim began explaining what he needed, I knew we could provide that."

"Did either of you discuss the fact that you had ex-spouses working for your respective companies?" Could neither of them see the potential this situation had to blow up in their faces? Brandon couldn't believe these businesses were thriving.

"We both mentioned it, so we were both aware."

"And you didn't see this as a big red flag?" Danielle was as appalled as he was.

"No, because at first glance, I knew it could be done. The fee was agreed upon, and it was one of our higher brackets." Colton smiled. "Grayson would have to do the game creation because of the complexities of what Tim wanted. His expertise would be required on every aspect of the game, but both Grayson and Anna Belle are professionals." Colton cocked his head to the side. "Or so we believed."

"But didn't you say that you witnessed an altercation between Grayson and Anna Belle just a couple of months before the game? Right here in your offices?" Brandon asked. "An altercation that became physical when she slapped him?"

Colton nodded. "That's true, but they were arguing over an aspect of the divorce settlement. Things like that are to be expected."

"Even after that, you didn't see a possible problem in working for her company when she was directly involved in the game?"

"Not really."

Brandon shook his head as he silently made notes. And this guy had a degree in sociology? No wonder the world was such a scary place.

"So, after the initial consultation, you decided that Grayson would need to create the game?" Danielle asked.

Colton nodded. "So that would put the game to Grayson's team. I knew he wouldn't want to be around for the implementation of the game and conclusion, so I would step in for that part. Of course."

"I can't believe Grayson would agree." Brandon said the words aloud, but they'd escaped before he'd considered his statement. Still, it was one of the truest statements about this investigation.

"He didn't at first." Colton grinned and stretched his legs out in front of him. "Oh, he fought accepting. Came up with every reason under the sun not to take the job. Real and far-fetched reasons." He chuckled. "Some were downright ludicrous."

"Yet he finally agreed?" Danielle wasn't amused.

"It took some real work on my part, including bringing up our annual profit-and-loss statement and showing him how this one job could put us in the black for not only this year, but give us a huge head start for next."

"He agreed?" Danielle asked again.

Colton nodded. "Yes. He finally agreed."

"So what was the process after that?" Brandon asked.

"Because of the specifics of what Tim needed in this particular game, we had to have our lawyer draw up a type of ambiguous liability waiver."

"I'm not following." Danielle crossed her legs.

"Because Tim didn't want the four game participants to know they were in a game, the waiver couldn't name Game's On You on the release of liability. The legalese ended up being changed a couple of times by our lawyer, then Deets PR's lawyer until they agreed. Once that was settled, it was smooth sailing." Colton rested his hands in his lap. "After we got the waivers back, we requested the information we'd need to complete a full dossier on each of the four participants. No aspect of their lives up until this point was discounted."

Knowing what he knew, Brandon didn't doubt it. Most everything in their lives was acknowledged and used against them. Or, at least used to torment them.

Colton continued. "Once everything was compiled, Grayson and his team began pulling out aspects of their lives that would show their predisposed behavior in a given situation. And that's where the magic happens—the game creation."

"I don't think I understand fully how that works," Danielle said.

"There's no exact science, but Grayson's got an uncanny ability to read a person, see what their fears are, put them in situations to face those fears, and give them the opportunity to come out victorious." Colton smiled. "You know that. He consulted for the police for a couple of years. You had to see him work his magic before."

Brandon nodded, recalling one time in particular when Grayson's input had made the hairs on Brandon's neck stand up. A suspect denied being involved in his girlfriend's disappearance and later murder. Even though every single piece of evidence, circumstantial though it was, pointed to him being involved, the man swore he wasn't. Grayson had been called in, and after reviewing the man's testimony and speaking to him, he agreed the man wasn't involved. It had been one of the first times that Grayson sided with a suspect over the detectives, but he held his ground.

A week later, a man confessed to murdering the woman. DNA confirmed his claims, and their original suspect was cleared.

Brandon had a hard time doubting Grayson from then on.

"So Grayson created the game for Deets PR by himself?" Danielle asked.

Colton shook his head. "Grayson's team. Mainly Grayson and Pam. I gave input based on my knowledge base of course, but overall it was Grayson and Pam. Primarily, Grayson."

Not what Brandon wanted to hear.

Danielle, on the other hand, sounded sweet as sugar. "How long did it take Grayson to create this particular game?"

Colton shrugged. "After we received all the data, about a month. That's about the usual time it takes for either of us to create a game of that level of complexity."

Brandon still couldn't believe his friend would agree to this. Not only personally, but professionally it was a bad call. "You never questioned giving Grayson access to Anna Belle in a game whose results affected her career? Never had some thought bump you with a *Hey, this might not be the brightest idea*?"

"I told you, the money was good and it was just a business contract, just like the many we do every year."

"Yet Anna Belle Thibodeaux is dead now. That's not just a business contract." Brandon gripped his pen a little tighter.

"No, it isn't." Colton sat up straight in the love seat and met Brandon's stare. "But our business agreement can't dictate what some people decide to do themselves. That's on them personally, and they have to face the consequences of their actions."

"Are you saying you think Grayson Thibodeaux was involved in Anna Belle's murder?" Danielle pushed.

Colton shook his head. "No, of course not, but someone did. Their decision has no bearing on the business contract between Game's On You and Deets PR."

"Maybe not," Brandon said, "but now both companies are involved and everybody's a suspect. Speaking of, I understand that your company runs video cameras during the course of your games?"

Colton nodded. "We do. That's how we monitor each game's progress to make sure it's running as planned."

"Are they just live feeds or recordings?"

"Recordings." He jumped to his feet. "I don't know why I didn't think about it. We can watch the video and see if there's any evidence on it."

Brandon resisted the urge to groan. "Actually, Mr. York, if you'll just give us the recordings, we'll have our team review and analyze them." He crossed his fingers that the man wouldn't demand a warrant. They could get one of course, but—

"Of course. They're backed up on our servers so all our employees can access them." He sat behind his desk and logged on to his computer. "I'll make you a DVD you can take with you."

Brandon stood and looked over the bookcase as he waited. Several pictures in brass frames of Colton and Grayson, golfing and fishing. More of Colton with local celebrities. Mardi Gras group photos.

The odd sound Colton made pulled Brandon back to the desk.

The man typed, hitting the keys with more force than necessary. He frowned at the monitor. More typing. "That's odd."

"What?" Danielle stood and joined Brandon.

"It says the file isn't here."

"What?" Brandon and Danielle spoke in unison.

"I can't find the file." Colton typed more. "Hang on." He reached for the phone on the corner of his desk.

A phone rang somewhere outside the office.

Brandon looked at his partner. This could be a problem. A very, very big problem.

"I'm having trouble accessing the Deets PR video file on my system. Can you see if you can get into it?"

Brandon slipped his notebook back into his pocket. His gut told him this wasn't going to end the way he'd hoped.

"I tried that." Colton typed again. "Yeah, I'm getting the same thing. Okay, thanks." He hung up the phone and stood. "I don't know what to tell you. As best as I can tell, and my assistant said the same thing, it looks like the file was offloaded from our server today."

"Today?" Danielle glanced at her watch.

Brandon glanced at the clock on the bookcase—5:47 p.m. "How can someone just offload the file?" Brandon asked.

Colton sat on the edge of his desk. "All of our employees have full access to all the files. We've never had any reason to limit the access."

"So, an employee took the entire file?"

Colton nodded. "Just took it off the server."

"Why would someone do that?" Brandon hoped there was a legitimate reason for doing so.

"There could be many reasons." But his face clearly said he was at a loss as well.

"Such as?" Danielle asked.

"Well, if the server kept timing out, or there was an error code, we would offload it, then run a scan on the file before uploading it back to the server." Colton nodded. "I've had that happen before and had to do that. It wasn't a virus or anything, just some strange little quirk in the data or something."

"Can you tell who took it off the server?" Danielle asked. "And when?"

"Let me check." Colton went back to his computer and typed away.

Brandon could only hope it wasn't Grayson. He could understand Grayson wanting answers and looking at the video file to see if he saw anything amiss. That was one thing, but if he removed the file—well, that said something else altogether.

"Let's see. Um, looks like it was pulled off around one or so this afternoon by. . ."

Click. Click. Click.

"Pam."

"That's Grayson's assistant, right?" Danielle asked.

"Yes." Colton straightened. "It's odd, because she wasn't in today."

Brandon glanced at his partner. They knew where Pam Huron had been. And who she'd been with.

SEVENTEEN

Crash!

Grayson and Pam both jumped out of the dining room chairs and made toward the sound.

"What was that?" Pam looked up and down the hallway to the side of Grayson's foyer. "Sounded like glass breaking."

"I know." Grayson rushed down the hall, glancing into each darkened room as he did, looking for any sign of something amiss. "Check the back of the house."

"Okay, but it sounded like it came from the front."

He moved to the other side of the front entrance, to his bedroom. The security light from across the street shot through the hole in the window. Lying on the floor was an object. He flipped on the light. "In here."

Grayson bent and picked up what he now recognized as a rock with a paper wrapped around it, held in place with a rubber band.

"What's that?" Pam walked into his bedroom and spotted the broken window. "Oh my. Kids?" She glanced over his shoulder as he removed the rubber band.

He unwrapped the paper and read the bold, black, computer printout message:

> KEEP TRYING TO HIDE BEHIND YOUR
> GAMES, BUT I KNOW WHAT YOU DID.
> EVERYONE ELSE WILL TOO. SOON.

"Oh. Not kids." Pam moved to the window and peered through the hole. "If anyone was out here, they're long gone now."

Of course they were. Grayson slumped onto the bed, not able to look away from the message. At least Monique had already left before this came flying through the window.

"We need to get this taped up or something. I think I have some cardboard from a shipping box in my car. Do you have duct tape?" She turned away from the window and stopped. "Grayson?"

"What does it mean? Hiding behind my games. Does that mean literally like when we sit in control rooms and monitor activity? Or is it meant figuratively like someone implying whatever they think I did to Anna Belle?" It could easily be either.

"Maybe it's both." Pam stood over him, her hands fisted on her hips.

"Both?"

She nodded. "Anna Belle died during the course of a game in which she didn't know she was even playing. Now that it's come to light, you know people are thinking how awful it was." She pushed a lock of her pink hair behind her ear. "You know this. People don't understand that what we do often helps people by getting them to recognize things about themselves and deal with issues. From the outside looking in, it seems like we're mean." She shook her head. "You know all this."

"I do, but this." He held up the paper. "And throwing it through my window. Someone knows where I live."

Pam shivered. "Yeah. We need to call the cops."

Grayson snorted. "Just what I need."

"You brush it off, but you need to call the police."

He could just hear Danielle now. "I don't think so." He stood, still holding the paper and rock.

"Grayson, you have to file a report."

"I'm not. This is just someone messing with me."

She crossed her arms over her chest and widened her stance. "Exactly. Who? And if someone's willing to type and print a message, wrap it around a rock, drive over here, and throw it through your window, what will they be willing to do next?"

He hated when she used logic like that, but he didn't have to be logical at the moment. "I should, I know, but I'm not." He held up a hand. "I'm not, Pam."

"You'll need a police report for your homeowners insurance. To replace the window." She jabbed her thumb in the direction of the broken glass.

He smiled. "My deductible is more than that window will cost to replace. I won't file a claim."

Pam stared at him through narrowed eyes, then let out a weary-sounding sigh. "Fine. Have it your way, stubborn goat. I'll go grab the cardboard from my car. You have duct tape, right?"

"I do. I'll get it." He led the way down the hall. Pam grabbed her keys. He flipped on the front outdoor light for her, and while she headed out to her car, he headed to the garage.

Even though Anna Belle had been gone for months, the emptiness of the garage hit him. She had always parked her car in the garage, the small sedan taking up most all of the limited space. His truck was too large for the garage that was added on many years ago, and to modify now would mess with the design of the house, and the neighborhood, and he didn't want that.

His old family house was built back in the mid-1800s, originally part of the Livaudais plantation. The land of the plantation was sold off in parcels to wealthy people who didn't want to live with the Creoles in the French Quarter. Most of the homes on Prytania Street boasted the original design for the neighborhood: only a couple of houses on each block of the street, but each one maintaining a lovely garden, thus the neighborhood's name. Although, in the nineteenth century, several of the neighborhood's lots were subdivided and late

Victorian style houses were built. Now the garden district was more known for its architecture than the gardens.

Grayson crossed the empty space to his tool chest standing against the other wall. He lifted the lid and grabbed the roll of duct tape. He'd just closed the garage door behind him when Pam slammed the front door.

"Well, you're going to have to call and file a police report anyway." She set a flat packing box on the kitchen island.

"Why's that?" He'd have to call a glass company tomorrow and see if they could install a replacement window in the morning. Hopefully they would have his particular size in stock.

"Because all four of your truck tires are slashed."

"What?" He headed to the front door.

Pam followed. "I'm guessing they were slashed before the rock was thrown."

He stared at his truck sitting in the driveway. Not that he had doubted Pam, but all four tires? It was unbelievable yet true.

"And, uh, there's that."

He looked at her. Pam nodded toward the house. On the exterior walls, highlighted by the security light across the street and the front porch light, eggs stuck in the screens dripped.

Who would do such a thing? Who hated him so much to do this? Or who loved Anna Belle that much?

"Fine. I'll call." He dialed the nonemergency reporting number he knew by heart. He quickly gave his information to the dispatcher, then disconnected the call.

"Now what?" Pam asked.

"It usually takes the nonemergency calls quite a bit of time to get answered. I don't want the eggs to dry and damage anything, so I'm going to go ahead and wash them off."

"Sounds like a plan. Just don't spray in the broken window."

He nodded. "I'm going to take some pictures so I have a record."

Grayson took several with his iPhone, as did Pam. "That should be enough. Let me get the hose." He stuck his phone in his pocket and grabbed the hose from behind the hedges in front of the house. The hedges his mother had loved, so he'd never let Anna Belle replace, even though she had complained many times over how ugly she thought they were.

As he reached the spigot and turned on the water, something shining in the light caught his peripheral vision. It was trapped in the box hedge's grip, almost directly in front of his broken bedroom window. He stretched to snag it between his fingers.

A little metal pendant-type thing. Silver, but one side was blue with a design. A coat of arms. A fish around an anchor? He didn't recognize it and certainly had no idea how it got stuck in his box hedge.

"What's taking you so long?" Pam came up behind him.

He held it out to her. "It was caught in the bushes."

She turned it over in her palm. "It's from a charm bracelet. Looks like the connector ring came loose. It was stuck in the hedge?"

He nodded. "I've never seen it before."

"Odd. You know, maybe I can figure out what coat of arms this is on the internet. I'll go look and see what I can find out."

Grayson chuckled. "You just don't want to help me wash off the house."

"You got me there. I'll see if I can find something before you finish here. How's that?"

"The race is on." He started spraying before she'd even gotten into the house. It didn't take long because the eggs hadn't had a chance to dry, thank goodness. The whites of the eggs could degrade the paint on the house.

And Grayson hated painting.

Approaching headlights illuminated the side of the house.

Grayson hurried and finished winding up the hose, then

straightened as a car pulled into his driveway behind his truck. His heart sank as the car pulled into the light spilling from the porch and he recognized it.

Brandon stepped out from behind the wheel, Danielle from the passenger's side.

"That was quick." He didn't think the dispatcher would have thought to alert the detectives about his call. Guess he was wrong.

"What do you mean?" Brandon walked around the front of the car toward the house.

"My call? Report? Slashed tires and rock through my window?" Maybe dispatch hadn't given them any details.

"Wait, what?" Brandon spun to face the truck. "Your tires are slashed."

"Yeah. That's why I called and asked to file a report." Had his friend gone dense all of a sudden? Wait a minute. . . "You guys aren't here to file the report, are you?"

"What happened there?" Danielle nodded at his broken bedroom window.

"That's the other part of why I called. Someone threw a rock through my window. There was a message wrapped around the rock." Grayson switched his gaze back to Brandon. "Why did you come here?"

Pam opened the front door. "Oh. It's them."

Danielle and Brandon locked stares. "We came to see her," Brandon said.

"Me?" Pam practically squeaked.

"Yeah. About an offloaded video file."

"And the eighteen minutes that are missing were deleted before you opened the file?" Brandon sat at Grayson's dining room table and stared at Pam. The lingering aroma of pizza filled the house.

"Right." Pam sat with her arms crossed over her chest and let out a breath in a puff. "Just like I told you. Twice now."

"We just have to verify every detail." Brandon smiled. "To make sure we're accurate in what you've told us."

"Because giving false statements to the police is a chargeable offense." Danielle smiled from across the table, but Brandon knew it was fake.

So, apparently, did Pam Huron. "And both times, I've told you the same answer. It's accurate." Unlike Danielle, Pam didn't bother to try to hide her irritation.

"Other than those eighteen minutes you've mentioned, the file is complete?" Brandon asked.

"To the best of my knowledge, yes."

"I know how it looks and what you're thinking," Grayson started.

"You have no idea what we're thinking," Danielle interrupted him. "We are simply following the evidence we uncover during the course of our thorough investigation."

Grayson made direct eye contact with Brandon. "It might appear that I tampered with the video. I can understand how that might seem, but I assure you, I didn't."

"Or someone else could've done it at your request or on your behalf. Even without your knowledge," Danielle said.

Pam pushed the chair back so hard it scraped against the tile floor. "I'm sure that someone you're referring to is me. Well, I didn't."

"No one is accusing you." But Brandon knew the implication from his partner was nothing more than a loosely veiled accusation.

"Are you sure about that?" Pam stood, her hands going to her little hips.

Grayson reached out and touched Pam's arm. "Would you mind putting a pot of coffee on, please? I could sure use a cup."

She hesitated. "Sure." She moved into the connecting kitchen.

Cabinets were shut with a lot more force than necessary.

Brandon chose to concentrate on Grayson. "Forensics will go over the file. If there's any way to recover those eighteen minutes, you can bet that Kara's team will."

Grayson nodded. "Good, because I want to know what was deleted. I need to know."

"You know." Danielle jerked her head toward the kitchen. "She was with you at the scene of the crime this morning. She's the one who offloaded the video file from the office server, and she sure seems to know her way around your kitchen." She lifted her brows as she looked at Grayson, cocking her head as she did.

Grayson shook his head. "I see where you're going. Pam and I have never dated, aren't dating, and have no intention of doing so." He held up his hand, palm facing Danielle. "And before you go further, let me assure you that Pam and I have never been intimate, nor do we plan to be. We are friends, and she is my assistant at work. That's it."

"Yet she's here at nearly eight on a Monday night, the night after you found out your wife had been murdered." Danielle crossed her arms over her chest.

Grayson clamped his mouth shut tight and looked at Brandon, silently pleading with him to intercede.

He couldn't. Danielle was just doing her job. Despite Brandon's own beliefs about the case, his partner was following up within the boundaries of department policy. He didn't like it, knew—*knew*—Grayson had nothing to do with Anna Belle's murder, but Danielle could follow her leads.

"Coffee's ready." Pam spoke loudly from the kitchen.

Grayson stood. "If y'all would like a cup. . ." He turned and left the room.

Brandon stood and started to follow.

Danielle grabbed his arm. "Even you have to admit how

convenient it is that there is time missing from the video file," she whispered.

It did look suspicious, but Brandon believed Grayson and Pam's explanation. "And they told us about it, which they didn't have to volunteer."

Danielle frowned. "Are you kidding me? Grayson knows that Kara's team is a beast and forensics would have detected the deletion from the get-go. Volunteer, my foot. They're covering their rears."

"I don't think so." Yet there was no way to prove it. Unless forensics could recover the missing time. "We'll see once the team has time to review it."

"Oh, I'm sure that'll be interesting." Danielle headed into the kitchen.

Brandon pocketed his field notes and joined the rest of them.

Grayson handed him a mug. "One sugar, right?" He smiled.

"Yep. Thanks." Brandon took a sip and then gestured toward the bag he'd put the rock and paper in to take for testing. "I'll put a rush on those results. Maybe it'll give us a lead as to who vandalized your truck and house."

"You really have no clue what that message means, exactly?" Danielle dug her hip into the side of the counter. She'd refused coffee, as if a cup were a peace offering.

Grayson shook his head. "I'm assuming it has to do with Anna Belle's death, but I really don't know."

"Make a lot of enemies during the course of your job, do you?" Danielle asked. "I mean, after interviewing all the employees of Deets PR, I certainly can understand animosity toward you." She ran a finger along her bottom lip, studying him. "Against your company, I mean."

"From the outside, I bet we do look cruel, but there are redeeming results in most all of the games we create. Often people can't see the forest for the trees, to simplify."

"You point out the tree, I'm guessing?"

Pam nodded. "As shocking as that sounds, yes. We help them not only to see the tree but to know what type of tree it is and how to care for it."

"Most people tell us later," Grayson continued, "how much we helped them face a fear or a stumbling block, whatever the case may be. Through recognizing what was holding them back, they were able to make adjustments and work through it."

"So you help them is what you're telling me." Danielle still held the disbelief in her voice.

"Yes. Most people do come back after a game and thank us. They tell us that the game helped them improve their life."

Danielle shook her head. "See, I'm not seeing how putting someone's weakness out there for everyone to see is helping them. Or taking their fear and using it against them."

"It can be confusing," Pam said. "That's why Grayson is a licensed psychologist and we aren't." The sarcasm all but dripped off of her tongue.

Before his partner could explode, Brandon turned to Grayson. "You mentioned there was something else you wanted to show me?"

Grayson met Pam's gaze. A whole conversation transpired between the two of them without either of them saying a word.

The ticking of the grandfather clock in the living room echoed in the stifling silence.

Finally Grayson cleared his throat. "Hang on. Let me get it."

He headed down the hall, his footsteps thudding.

"What else have y'all been up to today, besides creeping around our crime scene and tampering with evidence?" Danielle asked Pam.

Pam might have been a good two or so inches shorter than Danielle, and at least thirty pounds lighter, but when she narrowed her eyes and fisted her hands on her hips, she was just as intimidating. "Well, wouldn't you just like to know?"

Oil and water mixed better than these two women.

Grayson returned holding a rolling carry-on suitcase. He sat it on the end of the kitchen bar. "This was left for Anna Belle's mother at her hotel."

Danielle straightened immediately. "We're supposed to meet with her tomorrow."

Grayson nodded. "She mentioned that."

"What's this?" Brandon asked.

Grayson let out a low breath. "It's Anna Belle's. From the house."

"What?" Danielle's eyes bugged. "How did you get this? What did you take out of it?"

"Nothing." He held both hands up in mock surrender. "Nothing. Monique brought it over here, and we opened it together." Quickly he showed the front pockets' contents of clothes and her makeup bag. "And here's her backup EpiPen. She carried the other in the makeup bag in her purse."

"This is evidence in an investigation." Danielle was already pulling her gloves on. "You should know better than to touch this."

"Yeah, well, I did." Grayson ran a hand over his hair. "I wasn't thinking. Monique came here and wanted to know what was in the suitcase but didn't want to open it herself."

Brandon donned his gloves as well. "What else?"

"Look in the main area." Grayson's voice cracked.

Danielle unzipped the main compartment and opened the flap. She let out a little gasp and flashed a little smile at Brandon. "The missing mask and doll."

Grayson nodded. "They were props in—"

"In the game," Danielle finished. "Yes, we know." Her eyes were cold as she stared at Grayson. "I'm sure these props *helped* the recipients, right?"

Grayson didn't take the bait. "Monique said the hotel couldn't say who left the suitcase for her. Perhaps you might get a better answer."

"I'm sure we will." Danielle put the mask back in and reached for the voodoo doll.

It was creepy. No wonder Georgia had freaked out. Even without having any personal experience with voodoo, that doll alone gave Brandon the heebie-jeebies.

She lifted the doll, and a trifold pamphlet moved. "What's this?"

Grayson's quick intake had Brandon studying his friend's face for microexpressions. He didn't miss the split second of tightness around his mouth and eyes. Nor the little beads of moisture that dotted just above his upper lip.

Without knowing exactly why, Brandon knew this brochure meant a lot to Grayson Thibodeaux. He reached for it, snatching it out of the suitcase before Danielle could.

It was a brochure from Scheduled Maternity that listed their services. An appointment card was attached to it, listing Anna Belle's name and a date of approximately eight months ago.

Brandon wasn't married nor was he seriously involved with anyone, but he knew what this clinic was and what it did. He slowly tore his gaze from the brochure to his friend's face.

Grayson's face was ashen, and the muscles taut, but it was the immense agony in his eyes that told Brandon everything he needed to know about what he held in his hand.

And while he empathized for the obvious pain his friend was in, as a cop, he also knew that what he held offered even more motive for Grayson to have murdered Anna Belle.

EIGHTEEN

"Has forensics been able to recover those deleted minutes from the video file?" Grayson blurted out as soon as Brandon and Danielle walked into the interrogation room of the police station Tuesday morning.

"You don't get to ask questions here, Mr. Thibodeaux." Danielle scraped the metal chair against the floor. She sat diagonally from him, opened her notebook over the closed file folder, and tapped her pen against the table. "You're here to answer our questions."

He looked at Brandon, but his friend diverted his gaze as he took his seat beside Danielle, directly across from Grayson.

Guess that told him loud and clear where he stood this morning. And what a morning he'd already had at the service center. Thank goodness they opened at seven on weekdays so he could buy four new tires and have them mounted before his nine o'clock appointment with the police. He had a really strong feeling Danielle wouldn't have been understanding if he'd been late.

"We've gotten a lot of your preliminary statement at your house on Sunday evening and then again last night." Brandon flipped through pages in the folder he held.

Grayson recognized it for what it was—a stalling tactic to make him feel like he was being judged (which he was) and make him wonder what all information they had in their file (which he did) and generally make him uncomfortable (which he most definitely was). He squared his shoulders and sat up straight in his chair. Let them see he wasn't intimidated. He had done nothing wrong.

Brandon continued flipping pages for another minute or so, then closed the folder and set it on the table. He pulled out a notebook and smoothed it open before clicking his pen. "Let's start with the game you created for Deets PR."

Grayson nodded. He'd talked with his attorney, Ian Lancaster, this morning, who had strenuously advised not to meet with the police without him present. Grayson knew, however, how the police interpreted someone lawyering up and didn't want to give them more fuel for their witch hunt. While he'd declined having Ian present—for the time being—he did take all Ian's other advice seriously, which meant, in this case, waiting until an actual question was asked.

Brandon paused for a moment, then realized Grayson wasn't going to volunteer information. "Colton brought you this particular contract?"

"Yes." He stared directly at Brandon. He could play this game too. In fact, he could play it better. He was the one in the room with a degree in psychology.

"What was your initial reaction?"

"I thought it was a bad idea of course." Oops, Ian told him not to throw in "of course" or "naturally" or similar phrases. Stick to answering the direct questions, preferably with a yes or no if at all possible.

A pause.

"Why is that?" Danielle jabbed her pen into the table. Ah, her frustration was showing.

This might be more entertaining than he'd thought. He widened his eyes and stared straight at her. "Because my ex-wife worked for Deets PR." He might not be able to add on a duh, but he could definitely look it.

Then he remembered the camera in the corner of the room and relaxed his expression. He'd never before realized how much like a fish in a fishbowl people in the hot box felt.

"Care to elaborate?" Danielle's expression said everything her tone might have mistakenly implied.

Ian would have to forgive him. "I thought it was a bad idea for my company to create the type of game they requested for a company my ex-wife worked for when she'd be participating." He included Brandon in his stare. "Additionally, I'm opposed to creating a game for participants who don't realize they're actually playing in a game, despite whatever legal waiver they sign."

"Yet you did create it?" Danielle pressed.

He should've listened to Ian. Grayson sighed. "I did."

"Why? If it went against your better judgment on multiple levels, why did you do it?" Brandon asked.

He'd walked right into those questions, the same questions that he asked himself over and over. "My partner brought the deal to me. I opposed it, but we are a partnership, so just one of us doesn't make decisions alone."

Grayson remembered the heated discussion with Colton and repeated his partner's arguments now. "As the game was for a PR firm, we could most likely count on good future business exposure by their recommendation not only to their clients but also to other companies looking for innovative ways to determine promotions, bonuses, or any type of reward program. Also to other PR firms, who would then recommend us to their clients and contacts. Etcetera, etcetera, etcetera. The possibilities could be endless. Not to mention that the fee that Deets PR had agreed to was one of biggest, because it would be on location, meaning we'd have to provide staff around the clock and the particular details of the custom creation."

When he said it aloud, Grayson understood why he'd eventually agreed with Colton. "In the end, the long-term benefits would outweigh my personal misgivings, so I agreed with my business partner that it would be best for the company."

Danielle and Brandon both made notes. Grayson sat still,

refusing to look at the camera. Everyone would go back and review his expressions and mannerisms. Pretty much like he analyzed people on the monitors during a game. The irony gut-punched him.

"You agreed, knowing you would be the one creating the game. The"—Danielle flipped through pages in her notebook—"team leader, right?"

"Yes." He should stick with Ian's advice.

She flipped through more pages. "Okay, I'm going to need a little help here. You get all this information from those people—who don't know they're playing a game, by the way—and what do you do with it? The financial statements, medical records, extensive questionnaire. I don't follow."

He hated to go against Ian's instructions, but explaining exactly what he did was complicated and couldn't be answered with a few words. Grayson nodded. "Deets had requested that we create events that would help them determine how their four employees worked under pressure, worked individually, worked as a team, and dealt with conflict. The strongest triggers for the human psyche are finances, health, and emotional issues."

Both Brandon and Danielle were listening carefully, so he continued. "By compiling the data from the individuals, we can find the pressure points in each of those key areas and push them. When people's buttons are pushed, so to speak, they react in a manner that is truly reflective of who they are at their core. You can see examples of heroism and integrity, as well as some of the more unflattering traits, such as selfishness and cruelty."

"Some might say that what you do is cruel," Danielle said, but the edge wasn't in her voice. At least it wasn't as obvious to Grayson as before.

"True, and to some degree, it is, but in the fields of psychiatry and psychology and even basic medicine, exposing the hurt, the wound, the tumor, if you will, makes the person aware of it. No one can get better without treatment, and if you don't know what's wrong, you can't treat it."

"Are you comparing people's fears and insecurities to cancer?" And the hardness was back in her tone.

"In a way, yes. Anything in a person that has the capability to harm or destroy them. A tumor is a good comparison because it's an abnormality, but you don't know on first inspection if it's malignant or benign. Tests have to be run to determine that. Just like tests have to be run on people to see if their fears and insecurities will be a detriment to them or not."

Both detectives were silent. Grayson could only hope they absorbed the truth in what he explained. In what he did. That was the main reason he'd left the consulting job and gone into business with his old college friend. Despite Anna Belle's constant bemoaning of how a doctor should make more money than a civil servant, Grayson needed to feel like, in his own way, he helped people improve their lives.

"In this particular case, what did you use for each of the four employees?" Brandon broke the silence. "And before you ask, I checked with the DA's office, and the waiver the four of them signed covers your explanation of game details to us."

Check mark by one of Ian's warnings. "Well, Wednesday night was all about knocking each of them off center. To get them off their game by having them deal with something that was one of their pressure points." The hardness of the metal chair made him want to adjust his weight, but he knew how they'd read that on the video playback. "With Anna Belle, it was cooking, which she hated and didn't know how to do. With Georgia, it was changing the oil in a car, because she hated to get dirty, and getting on a floor under a car and changing the oil is one of the dirtiest jobs there is. With Hugh, it was getting him up on the widow's walk because he had an intense fear of heights. And with Franklin, it was having him clean the fish pond because he detested slimy things."

"Seems like Anna Belle's, Georgia's, and Franklin's"—Danielle used two fingers on both hands to make invisible quotation marks—"pressure points"—she dropped her hands back to the table—"were about things they just didn't like, but Hugh's was about a fear. A real fear from his fall as a young man."

Grayson couldn't help but be impressed that she caught that. He nodded. "Hugh's profile didn't indicate any specific dislikes, so we needed to go with a fear to knock him off balance. Everyone else had a fear addressed that evening."

"You made the decision to put a snake in Franklin's bed." Danielle gave a teeny shudder at the word *snake*.

Grayson nodded.

"You made the decision to have someone put on the Mardi Gras mask to scare Anna Belle," Brandon continued.

Again Grayson nodded.

"Who? Who actually put on the mask and tried to scare her?" Brandon held his pen poised over his notebook.

"Vic Abshire, one of my team members who was at the house. He wore it and made a point to let Anna Belle catch glimpses of him in the hall. Then, while everyone was distracted by Franklin's snake, he wore the mask outside in the backyard, looking up at her window. He made sure she saw him."

"And Georgia? What fear did she face that evening?" Danielle asked.

Grayson resisted the urge to ask for a bottle of water, even though his mouth was as dry as if he'd chewed a wad of cotton. "Her email inbox was filled with images of a *veve* and other symbols of voodoo, and while Vic wore the mask outside Anna Belle's room, Stratton Reeves, one of the guys on Colton's team, had taken white shoe polish and drawn a pentagram on her bedroom window." He caught the look between the two detectives. "He washed it off later that night of course so it wouldn't be detected the next morning."

"And Hugh?" Brandon asked.

"He received several notices via calls, texts, emails, and updates of certified letters that his house was being foreclosed on, creditors were calling." Grayson saw their bewildered looks. *Hmm. Interesting.* Hugh apparently didn't mention any of this in his statement. "Hugh had been a victim of identity theft not too long ago, and he'd just gotten his credit rating and record fixed."

"But a bigger fear of his was addressed with the fake fire, wasn't it?" Danielle asked.

Ah, yes. The fake fire.

"I mean, having lost his mother in a fire, the fake fire was a lot more personal to Hugh than the others." The disapproval lined every inch of Danielle's face.

He'd debated on using a perceived fire. He and Pam had gone over it and over it so many times, but finally he'd decided to go for it. "Every indication I had, and my gut instinct, told me that using this would allow Hugh Istre to showcase his heroic tendency."

"You knew he was heroic?" Danielle asked.

"I didn't know for certain, but his profile put heroism in a high probability." Grayson shrugged. "My gut instinct confirmed it."

"You brought a man's emotional scars to the surface based on your gut instinct?" Danielle's brows were so far up they could've reached into her hairline.

Grayson held up his hand. "That wasn't the best choice of words. Based on my education, training, and experience, I concurred with the markers from Hugh's profile results."

She made a tsking sound but scribbled in her notebook.

"Are you usually right with your gut instinct"—Brandon caught himself and rephrased—"your opinion based on your education, training, and experience?"

Grayson couldn't stop the little grin. "Ninety-nine percent of the time, yes. It's very infuriating to my assistant." He wouldn't use Pam's name to bespeak of familiarity. Not after Danielle's implication last night.

"I would imagine." Danielle clearly related to the emotion. "This fake fire crew—we'll need their names and numbers."

"Actually, we rented the fire truck, which really isn't a fire truck. It's used a lot in parades and private functions. The firemen were actually from the catering company we contracted with."

Brandon flipped pages in the folder. "Lagniappe Eats?"

Grayson nodded. "Our contact there is Xavier Newsom."

"Back to Hugh Istre." Danielle opened her folder. "His mother had died in a fire when he was a teenager because she couldn't get out of the building." She shut the folder. "How could you be sure that putting him in the situation you did wouldn't result in a tragedy?"

"There is no guarantee, not when dealing with people's responses to any given circumstance. Doctors face this all the time."

"But you aren't a real doctor," she blurted out.

Grayson smiled. "Actually, Danielle, I *am* a real doctor. Not only do I have a degree, but I am also state certified."

She clenched her mouth shut.

Brandon set down his pen. "It appears you were correct in your assessment. Hugh did move to assist Georgia, although the caterers had already helped her?"

Grayson nodded. "They knew the props we used and were given the baking soda to throw into the pit to dry it up almost instantly. The point is that Hugh, despite being forced to recall what was probably one of the worst times of his life, and being in a similar situation, was able to rise above it and react positively to someone in need. That's a sign of a good leader."

"He's the one who got the snake out for Franklin as well, right?" Brandon asked.

"Yes."

"It would appear, by the events we've discussed thus far, that Hugh was in the lead for the promotion, wouldn't you say?" Brandon asked. "He said in his statement that Tim Dubois had announced that Hugh was the only one to complete his given task on Wednesday evening. Considering these other aspects, surely that would put Hugh ahead of the rest, right?"

Grayson couldn't get the image of Hugh Istre and Anna Belle kissing out of his mind.

Yes, they were divorced. Yes, she'd already been involved with someone else. It didn't help the knot in his stomach whenever he thought of them together.

Grayson shoved the image away. "That would be my assessment, yes."

"So, at this point, it seems like Tim Dubois would be promoting Hugh. Just based on Wednesday night's results?" Danielle asked.

"I really can't say." Grayson swallowed against his dry mouth as another image filled his mind. Not of Anna Belle and Hugh kissing, but of Tim seeing them. The look on the man's face was a mixture of shock—he didn't know the two were intimate—and rage.

Pure, unadulterated rage.

Had Tim Dubois been so angry that he was no longer in control of his emotions? Grayson could understand how devastating betrayal by the woman you loved felt. He knew how raw and desperate being left without the ability to do anything felt.

Had those feelings been enough to push Tim Dubois to kill Anna Belle?

NINETEEN

Here was what Brandon knew for fact: Grayson Thibodeaux was thirty-four years old, was a licensed psychologist, and was co-owner of Game's On You. Brandon also knew that Grayson had consulted for the New Orleans Police Department for two years following his departure from his private practice with three other head doctors. He knew Grayson had left private practice following a tragedy in which a teen Grayson treated while his partner was away had committed suicide.

Brandon also knew Grayson Thibodeaux wasn't a killer. No way had he killed his wife. It wasn't in his makeup.

Proving that, however, was more trying that he'd initially thought. Especially when Grayson seemed to butt against Danielle at every given opportunity.

"Tell us again about the Scheduled Maternity pamphlet you say Emmi put in Anna Belle's room." Danielle popped her knuckles, then picked up her pen again.

"I didn't know a thing about it until I saw it on the video." Grayson's expression was unreadable, like a mask had slipped into place.

"But you knew about the abortion Anna Belle had eight months ago?" Danielle wasn't going to let up.

Even though it had to be killing Grayson inside, Brandon couldn't say anything. She was doing her job. Exposing Grayson's own tumor. Oh, the irony.

"Yes, I learned about that a few weeks ago when I received

Anna Belle's medical records."

"You didn't know about it when your wife scheduled, had, and recovered from an abortion?" It seemed Danielle would do her best to yank the scab off the wound. Then pour salt into it.

"No." Even Grayson's eyes were guarded.

"But you knew she was pregnant, right?" Danielle asked.

Grayson licked his lips, the first sign of emotion. "No."

"What?" Danielle opened the file and pretended to read. "Her medical records indicate she was thirteen weeks pregnant at the time of the abortion. That's entering the second trimester. Surely you, as her husband, had to have noticed symptoms. Morning sickness. Weight gain. Tenderness in certain areas."

"No. I didn't notice anything."

"Hmm." She closed the file. "According to the clinic files, she was there for six hours, then had to have someone pick her up from the clinic. That wasn't you?"

"No."

"Who do you think it was?"

"I don't know." Little chips in his stone expression pinged out with her every digging question.

She tapped her finger against her chin. "Do you know if the baby she aborted was yours?"

Grayson's eyes widened and the muscles in his jaw flicked. "I. Don't. Know."

But he was about to lose it.

"We watched the video this morning and saw Emmi take the appointment card and pamphlet into Anna Belle's room. Do you have any idea how Emmi would have known about the appointment?"

Grayson shot him a quick look of appreciation. "I don't. I assume either from her husband or she had access to the packet sent over to us."

"Why would he tell his wife?" Danielle asked.

Grayson shrugged. "I don't know. I was asked if I had any ideas. Those are the only two I thought of how she would know." If stares were lethal, Danielle would be obliterated right then and there.

"Anna Belle never said anything, absolutely nothing?" Brandon still couldn't believe that a woman would be so cold and callous to have done such a thing without a word.

Grayson shook his head, but Brandon caught the lightning tic in his right eye.

"Nothing? No matter how vague or minuscule?"

"She called me a little after nine on Thursday morning." Grayson licked his lips again. "That would've been right after she got back in her room after breakfast and found the pamphlet."

"What did she say?" Brandon asked.

Grayson shrugged. "I had already lost my phone, so I didn't know she'd called."

Brandon worked to contain his anticipation. "But you've gotten a new one, with the same number, right, so you could check your voice mail?"

Grayson nodded. "She didn't leave a message that time. But she called me later that afternoon, a little after one, and she left a voice message then that said we needed to talk."

"You need to talk? That's it?" Danielle asked.

"I'm betting she figured out that she was in a game."

"How would she do that?" Danielle asked.

"She was my wife. She knew what I did, knew how our games worked. She'd sat with me and Colton when we first started the company and heard details. She wasn't stupid." Grayson ran a hand over his hair. "I warned Colton that she might figure it out."

Brandon nodded. He'd wondered that himself. "So, let's say she figured out it was a game. Why would she call you? To tell you she knew?"

"If she figured out it was a game and then saw the pamphlet, it's not too far of a reach that she would think I knew what she'd done."

"Still, why would she call?" Danielle asked. "To apologize?"

Grayson gave a wry smile. "It wasn't Anna Belle's nature to apologize. I would guess if she figured out it was a game, and finding that in her room, she'd assume I knew and used her procedure to let her know I knew."

"That's a mind boggle in the worst way." Brandon shook his head.

"I know. It is confusing."

"She would naturally assume, I'm guessing, that you would use this against her in a game. The abortion." Danielle tapped her pen against her hand.

"That's the only reason I can think of why she would call me and leave me a message." Grayson didn't volunteer anything further.

"Let's move on." Brandon silenced his partner with a quick look as he opened his folder and flipped through it, not really having anything else to ask that they hadn't already covered. He closed the folder and his notebook. Time to change modes. "About last night's call. Forensics didn't find any fingerprints on the rock or paper, except yours and Pam's."

Grayson nodded. "I didn't expect much."

"After sleeping on it, did you think of anyone who could have done this?"

"My only guess would be someone who cared for Anna Belle and thinks I had something to do with her death."

"That would be a good guess," Danielle offered, but there was no denying she wasn't a fan of Grayson's and everyone knew it.

"Do you have any leads?" Grayson snapped at her.

Her sarcasm flared. "Not yet. Although, you know, sometimes murderers will do bad things to themselves to garner sympathy and try to throw off suspicion."

Grayson narrowed his eyes and tilted his head. "Are you suggesting that I slashed all four of my tires and threw a rock through my own window to—what did you say?—garner sympathy and throw off suspicion?"

"No one suggested you did anything like that." Brandon shot Danielle a hard look. Wasn't she reading the suspect and the situation?

"Oh, I think your partner was making that very suggestion." Grayson stood. "And I think I'm done."

Danielle shot to her feet. "I'm not finished with your interview yet."

Brandon stood as the two of them squared off. He'd had many criminals in the hot box over the last several years, but never was the tension as taut as right in that moment.

Grayson's stare was pure steel. "Then you'll need to contact my lawyer to set up another interview because—this one?—it's over." He nodded at Brandon, then opened the door and walked out.

"What was that?" Brandon asked his partner.

"What?" She grabbed her stuff and slammed the chair back under the table. "He's sure touchy. Acting like a man with a guilty conscience if you ask me."

"I didn't." He grabbed his own stuff.

Danielle blocked the door. "Look, I know he's your friend, but he's a murder suspect. My top one."

"We have differing opinions. Emmi Dubois is top on my list."

She shrugged. "They both had motive, means, and opportunity, but he's her ex." She relaxed her bulldog look. "Come on, Brando, she aborted his baby and didn't tell him. He might not have planned to kill her before, but after finding out that little bit of info? You know that could've pushed him to it. You saw his reaction. Every time I said the word *abortion*, he about puked."

"Sure, he was upset. That's a lot for a man to take. Especially a man of faith." He'd gone to church with Grayson a couple of times when his church's preacher was out. The man's faith wasn't just a card he carried—it was the life he lived. Another reason he wouldn't have killed Anna Belle, no matter what he'd found out. "But being upset doesn't mean he killed her. Besides, at least my suspect was at the scene. Not a single person saw Grayson at that house after he left town on Wednesday. There is not a single shred of evidence that he came back before Sunday night."

Danielle sighed and started down the hall toward their desks. "Not that it really matters, considering he set up the game and could've put the poisoned energy drink in her room before she even got there, but regardless of that, he can't account for his whereabouts for about six hours. Watching TV and dozing. Really? Those six hours give him plenty of time to drive back to New Orleans, put the energy drink in her room, and get back to St. Francisville in plenty of time to meet up with his friends for dinner."

He matched his partner step for step. "But during that time frame, there's not one piece of evidence that he wasn't in his room at the lodge doing just what he said he was doing."

She shook her head. "Yeah, it's very fortuitous that he lost his phone in the creek so his location couldn't be determined by pinging the cell phone towers."

"People lose cell phones all the time."

"But in this case, it seems to be mighty convenient, now doesn't it?" Danielle wore her smirk like a badge of courage as she pulled out her chair.

But she'd just made him realize something. Brandon dumped his stuff on the desk and opened his notebook. "You do realize what the video also shows, right?" He didn't wait for an answer. "Grayson's statement is that he left the clubhouse on Thursday at one ten. We confirmed it with the clubhouse and his friends. And we know he did go into his room at the lodge, according to the electronic key register, at one twenty-four."

"Right."

"It takes an hour and fifty-five minutes or so to get from the lodge back to New Orleans." He used the calculator on his smartphone and turned it so she could see. "If he left immediately after he went back to his room at one twenty-four, that doesn't give him the time to get back to the house on Esplanade Avenue and be in the hall between two forty-one and two fifty-nine, which has been deleted off the video. He wouldn't have had to get there until after three. It just doesn't add up."

She shrugged and tilted back in her chair. "If someone could delete images off the video, don't you think it isn't too far-fetched that someone could've manipulated the time stamp of the video too? And maybe that's what it is, not just deleted screen images, but time stamp altering as well."

"I think you're reaching."

"And I think you're letting the wool be pulled over your eyes because he's your friend. Besides, he's used to playing mind games. He's smart, right? Like I said, he could've gotten that tampered energy drink into her room at various times we haven't even considered yet. Remember, he helped set everything up on Wednesday morning. So the timing of the missing video minutes doesn't prove his innocence."

She just wasn't going to give up.

"It sure isn't going to prove his guilt though. Not by a long shot." Brandon sat on the edge of her desk and looked down at her. "I don't get what your beef is with him, Dani. You've had him in the crosshairs since we got the case. I thought maybe it was because he never called your sister back after their date, but your attitude is beyond that. . . . I don't know. It's not like you. This feels like it's more personal. What's going on?"

A hardness he'd never seen in her before settled over her face. "I'm doing my job, that's all. I'm sorry if you don't agree with my gut instincts, but you aren't the only one allowed to have them in this department, you know. I know you want him to be innocent. Me? I don't really care. I just want to have justice for Anna Belle, no matter who's guilty. I get that many people didn't like her because they thought she was ruthless to rise up the ladder in her business, but so what? That doesn't mean she deserved to die."

She stood suddenly, almost ramming her chair into his shin. "If a man had acted the exact same way as she did, probably no one would think twice. But because she was a woman, and beautiful, she's being ostracized."

Whoa, where was this all coming from? He pushed off the edge of her desk and straightened, holding his hands up in mock surrender. "Wait a minute, that's not what I'm saying at all."

"Aren't you? You're acting like her having an abortion without telling him was like the most unforgivable thing ever, but you know what? It was her body and her decision. It was her legal right to make that decision."

Brandon took a step backward, ramming into the filing cabinet. "Dani, you were the one pushing him about the abortion during the interview, not me."

"Only because that was an interrogation. I was doing my job, Brandon. Removing my personal feelings from the issue. Did I think she was awful for having an abortion? Nope. Do I think she should've told him? No, because I think their marriage had already deteriorated at that time, and if I had been her, I wouldn't have wanted to have a baby that would forever tie me to him." She snatched up the file and her notebook and clutched them to her chest.

Brandon's jaw went slack.

"See, you're a little shocked. I'm sorry if I've offended your sensibilities. I don't think Anna Belle was this horrible person and Grayson this sad victim. She had an affair. Who's to say that he didn't neglect her or whatever? We don't know what happened in their marriage. We only have his statements, not hers."

"Nobody's saying Grayson is a victim."

"Oh, it's on your face every time you mention Tim Dubois.

Maybe she fell in love with Tim. People do that all the time, you know, fall in love with someone while they're married to someone else. It happens. That's a reason for divorce. And yes, Anna Belle divorced Grayson, how sad for him."

She grimaced. "He's a grown man. He can deal with some disappointment. What is it everyone always tells a woman? Oh, right. Pull on your big-girl panties. Well, Grayson can pull on his Batman undies for all I care. I don't see him as a victim in any aspect. I see him as a man who was humiliated and angry and hurt, and all three of those emotions can make people do the unthinkable."

Danielle slammed her chair back under her desk. "Now, if you'll excuse me, I need to update the commander before we head over to the Darkwater Inn to talk with Monique Fredericks."

Brandon could only stare at her retreating back. What in the world was all *that*? He'd never seen his partner so riled up like this. Over what? Nothing really. They'd debated other suspects before, but nothing like this. He couldn't figure out if it was Grayson she had a thing against or, considering the arguments she'd made just a few minutes ago, she felt more like a defender of Anna Belle's person.

He slumped into his desk. Anna Belle Thibodeaux needed many things, but he'd never considered a defender of her methods and personality to be one of them. She'd seemed quite capable of taking care of that herself, certainly where her career was concerned.

Anna Belle's affair with Tim and her abortion seemed to be hot spots for his partner, and he had no idea why. Had she been involved with a married man before? Had an abortion? So many things he really didn't know about Danielle Witz, even though they'd been partners for three years. He knew she wasn't involved with anyone at the moment, as the guy she'd been seeing for over a year had called it off several months ago, but she was thirty-eight, so maybe she felt like she was getting old and past her prime.

The phone on his desk demanded his attention. "Detective Gibbons."

"Hey, Brandon, it's Kara."

Maybe there'd be some good news on the case. "Whatcha got for me?" He lifted his pen and pulled up a piece of scrap paper.

"No prints recovered on the paper or rock; however, there was a bit of DNA on the paper."

"And?" He crossed his fingers there'd been a match, even though it was really fast to have a result.

"The sample was too poor quality to run the sequence."

His hopes smashed to the ground. "Well, thanks for—"

"Wait, all is not lost."

He held his breath.

"While I can't run a full sequence, I can tell you one big determination from the sample."

"What's that?"

"It's DNA from a woman."

TWENTY

Grayson had told Pam and Colton he'd be in this afternoon before Pam had to go give a statement at the police station at three, but sitting in his truck, staring at the building, he wasn't sure it was such a good idea. The last thing he felt like doing right now was creating a game, talking about a game, or analyzing anything.

The wind kicked litter across the parking lot. Little tumbleweeds skipping along the asphalt looking out of place in the Big Easy.

He couldn't avoid the office forever. There'd be whispers, he knew. He had prepared for them as carefully as he had his interview with the police, and look how that had turned out.

Tap! Tap!

Grayson almost jumped at the knock against the passenger window. Pam smiled. He pressed the button to unlock the door. "What're you doing out here?" he asked as soon as she opened the door and hopped into the cab.

"Going to lunch, but then I saw your truck. How'd your interview go?"

He gripped the bottom of the steering wheel. "About like I thought. Danielle Witz would have the lynch mob after me about now if it wasn't for Brandon."

"I'm not gonna lie—that woman rubs me wrong."

Grayson grinned. "Hadn't noticed."

Pam shoved him. "I'm more than a little nervous about going in myself." She shook her head. "It doesn't matter that nobody did anything wrong. That woman twists it and makes it sound like you're

Jack the Ripper and I'm your assistant."

"I guess she's just doing her job."

"Doing her job would be finding out who really killed Anna Belle, not looking for reasons to blame you."

He smiled. There was never any doubt as to what Pam was thinking, because she usually let it out. Often bluntly.

"In other news, I'm not having a lot of luck on that coat of arms."

"Really?" He'd hoped something would connect with that. "I guess it doesn't matter, really. No telling how long it was in the hedges."

Pam shook her head. "I'm not an expert, but I can almost guarantee it wasn't long. There's no sign of rust or corrosion on it, no tarnishing. With the rains we had over the last couple of weeks and all the flooding, I'm pretty certain it would've been washed out. I'm thinking it's recent. Like night-your-tires-were-slashed recent."

As usual, he couldn't argue with her logic. "But in the bushes? I doubt anyone would get close enough to drop a pendant like that."

"It's a charm from a charm bracelet."

"Okay, but I still don't think someone would get that close for fear of being caught. I mean, obviously I was home since they knew my truck was there."

"Watch this." Pam made a motion like throwing a baseball. "If someone was throwing an egg, or say a rock through a window, this is how they would move, right?"

He nodded.

"If I'm wearing a charm bracelet and a charm is loose that I don't know about, and the connector ring turns with me doing this"—she threw invisible balls again—"then the charm could have followed the trajectory of my arm and whatever I was throwing."

"Good point. So you think whoever threw the rock through my window was wearing a charm bracelet." He tapped the steering wheel. "That would mean it was a woman."

"Or she was throwing eggs just before the guy she was with threw the rock through your window."

"Great, so now there are two people mad at me."

She laughed. "I'm just saying a woman, or women, or a woman and a man." She pulled down the sun visor and opened the mirror, running her finger along the edge of her lipstick. "Maybe a man and woman like Tim and Emmi Dubois."

"Back to them, are you?"

"I'm just saying. We already know Emmi knew secrets about Anna Belle and used them to torment her. Or maybe blackmail her." Pam snapped the mirror shut and popped the visor back in place. "Ooh, I never thought about that. What if Emmi was blackmailing Anna Belle? What if she was threatening to tell Tim and/or you about the abortion if Anna Belle didn't pay her?"

Blackmail—interesting concept.

"I mean, we know Anna Belle had recently really been coming after you about the divorce settlement. Maybe that was because she was being blackmailed."

Maybe. . . "But what would it matter if Tim or I knew? Nothing we could do about it after the fact." Grayson knew that all too well. He'd spent many nights wondering if he'd missed the signs, just like Danielle had grilled him about.

Pam shrugged. "I don't know. Maybe she was ashamed. There was a reason she didn't tell you, even after the divorce. Maybe she thought Tim would fire her if he knew. I don't know."

It wasn't too far out in left field. No more than the police trying to make everything fit him being the guilty party.

"If that's true, then why would Emmi and Tim throw a rock with a message through my window and slash my tires?"

"I don't know. I don't have all the answers. I just thought of the blackmail possibility."

Grayson chuckled. Pam was an original, and not just with her loud hair and makeup and clothes choices. He was lucky to have her as his friend.

"I'm glad you can laugh, buddy. This is your life we're talking about here."

"I know, but if I don't laugh, I might go insane."

"Anyway, back to the coat of arms on the charm. I haven't found out anything. I can't even really tell what kind of fish it is. I thought maybe a marlin or a tuna, but that doesn't match any graphic I've seen. Not having a motto doesn't make it any easier."

"Motto?"

She nodded. "A coat of arms is actually a heraldic design on a shield. It contains four elements: the shield it sits on, the supporters, which are on either side of the shield, the crest itself, and the motto on a scroll thing on the bottom."

"The charm has no motto?"

"No motto, no supports, nor the crest. All I have is the design on the shield."

"I'm guessing that makes it harder, right?" Less design available, less available to look up.

"To say the least." She smiled. "But don't worry. I took a picture of it and sent it to some sources I have to see if they can recognize the fish or anchor. Maybe it'll lead to something."

"Thanks, Pam."

"Of course."

Rare emotions filled his chest. "Not just for this, but for everything."

In a rarer still show of affection, she leaned over and hugged him, squeezing him, then immediately retreated back to the passenger's side. "You're going to get through this. It'll be tough, but you got this."

He smiled and nodded, not trusting himself to speak.

"Well, I'm going to grab a taco. You want anything?"

"No, thanks." He stared at the office. "Guess I'd better get inside."

"Hey." She grabbed his arm. "It's okay. Everyone in there is on your side. Vic has asked me a thousand times how you're doing, and Colton has come into the office like every thirty minutes or so to see if you're there yet."

So maybe the whispering wouldn't be so bad after all.

No time like the present to find out. "Go get your taco. I'm going to work."

After Pam scooted into her own car, Grayson locked his truck and headed into the office. He felt out of place but couldn't explain why. Like a stranger walking into someone else's life. He shouldn't feel out of place. He and Colton had started Game's On You together about three years ago. He could still remember Colton calling from out of the blue and asking him to meet for dinner. Grayson had been curious, so he and Anna Belle had met.

The proposal Colton had presented was simple. At the time, escape rooms were storming the market and were huge hits with individuals, families, and groups, but they were limited. All were the same, and once the room had been played, the players were done with it whether they successfully escaped or not. What Colton proposed was to take the experience and enhance it, based on his and Grayson's degrees and experience. Custom design not just an escape room, although that would always be a part of the game, but really give the players a one-of-a-kind experience. They would market it to the upper-end crowds and businesses. Team building in organizations and groups.

When Grayson had hesitated, Anna Belle had pushed. She agreed with the potential that Colton had projected. She was, after all, in the PR world and could see how such a service could be marketed successfully. When Colton laid out his business prospective, Anna Belle jumped on board. Colton had the resources to provide the start-up capital. Grayson had balked at using Colton's personal money, but he said he'd won it in Vegas and wanted to invest. That still hadn't swayed Grayson, so the two of them each put in a base amount and started smaller than initially projected, but the business had taken off.

Taken off very well. In fact, they'd raised their fees each year yet continued to gain new clients and increase their income. Just when Grayson was getting back in the "doctor income" bracket Anna Belle had so missed, they divorced.

Grayson took a deep breath and opened the front door. Maybe once he was inside, he wouldn't feel so discombobulated.

Jackie Pitre, receptionist, was on her feet and around her desk before the front door even shut behind him. The older woman, short as she was, pulled him into a bear hug. "I'm so sorry, Grayson. So sorry for your loss."

"Thank you." He did appreciate Jackie's unapologetic empathy for his loss. Anna Belle had been his ex-wife, certainly, but she was now gone, and that was a loss Grayson would forever feel.

The phone rang.

"Just know if there's anything I can do for you, honey, you just holler at me." She patted his hand, then moved back to her desk and lifted the receiver. "Game's On You. How may I assist you today?"

He headed down the hall to his office. Each team was housed on their own side of the office space, Grayson's on the right, Colton's on the left. The wings were mirror images of each other: a general conference room to meet and talk with clients, followed by a big office with four cubicles for the team, then the computer room, and finally, Grayson's and Colton's offices. The back of the offices, behind the front facade and Jackie's desk, was the on-site escape rooms setup.

As he passed the conference room with its lights out, he wondered if he would ever create a game again that didn't remind him of this one.

"Hey, you." Nora jumped up from her cubicle as Grayson made

his way down the hall. "Are you okay?" She stopped a couple of feet in front of him, unsure how to act.

He smiled. "I'm going to be okay." She'd been at the house, been there when Anna Belle had died. "How're you?"

She nodded, her midlength curly hair brushing against her collarbone. "I'm okay. Colton had told us all to take off yesterday, so I did. I'm good though. Good." She smiled, her face unmarred with makeup. One of the things he truly admired about Nora was her inability to put on airs to try and impress anyone. She was who she was, without excuse. Maybe that was one of the reasons she and Pam got along so well. She accepted Pam's quirkiness as easily as Grayson did.

"Hey, boss." Vic met him in the hall. "Glad you're back." He slapped Grayson's shoulder as Nora retreated to her cubicle.

"Thanks." Grayson fell into step beside the younger man. He'd hired Vic Abshire and hadn't regretted it once, despite Vic's background. He'd had a stint in a federal prison camp for drugs and came out with a chip on his shoulder and a cry of racial inequality in sentencing guidelines. His involvement as a black man who had been a victim of just that helped change policies in Louisiana. He had emerged a stronger man, and Grayson respected him as a man and as a friend.

"I'm sorry, man. I know you were divorced, but that was still your wife. A piece of paper doesn't cut out what you've felt for someone."

Exactly. "Yeah. I appreciate that."

"I hope you know that if there had been anything I could've done. . ."

"No, I've heard what happened. You couldn't have done anything without her EpiPen." Which was mysteriously unused, unopened, and stored as usual in her makeup bag, which was in the suitcase delivered to Monique's hotel.

"All the same, I'm really sorry."

"Thanks." They reached his office. "I'm going to check my email and messages and such."

"Sure. If you need anything, shout." Vic turned and headed back down the hall toward his cubicle.

Grayson stepped inside his office and shut the glass door. He should've come in the back door, but it was so far in the back of the building that he rarely used it. He dropped onto the couch, staring at the bookcase. There hadn't been whispers that he'd heard, but the sympathy and inquiries were just as draining. Or maybe it was his earlier visit with Brandon and Danielle. Which reminded him, he needed to call Ian and fill him in on that interrogation.

He stood, then stopped and stared at his display case on the bookcase. Sitting there with the scorecard from St. Andrews golf course was his mark repairer and ball marker.

Hmm. If his ball marker was still here in the office, why had Anna Belle had one in the bedroom where she'd stayed?

Where she'd died?

TWENTY-ONE

"Female DNA, huh?" Danielle slipped into the passenger's seat of their cruiser.

"I'm not gonna doubt Kara." Brandon got behind the steering wheel and latched the seat belt. "So there's definitely a woman out there who has some serious beef with Grayson."

"But he's such a charmer."

Brandon started the car but left it in PARK. He couldn't take being at odds with his partner much longer. "Danielle. . ."

She shook her head, clicking her seat belt. "Look, about earlier. I'm sorry. I shouldn't have bit your head off like that."

"It's okay." He softened his tone to match hers. "I'm not just your partner, you know. I'm also your friend. What's the deal?"

She shrugged. "My sister."

Her little sister, the one they'd set up on the blind date with Grayson, was quite a beautiful girl. She seemed a little immature to Brandon, but that wasn't such a big deal. "Yeah? What about her?"

"I feel silly reacting the way I did over this."

Brandon gave her shoulder a gentle shove. "C'mon, partner, you can tell me anything."

She looked at him, her eyes shimmering with moisture. "Krissy's had a rough go lately. After her date with Grayson, she really thought he liked her. When he didn't call her, she was pretty devastated."

"You know that really had nothing to do with her. He wasn't ready to date yet. We kinda bullied him into taking her out." He'd regretted it as soon as Grayson had called him the next morning.

"I do know that. On some level." She shook her head and stared at the dashboard. "I told Krissy that, but I'm not sure she accepted it. She started dating this real lowlife." She locked gazes with Brandon. "And I mean *lowlife*—like the kind we deal with."

"I'm sorry."

"Well, she didn't just date him, she started talking about how much he loved her and so on." Danielle shook her head again, gripping the armrest. "It drove me insane to see how stupid she was over this scum."

Brandon couldn't think of any words of comfort because he couldn't relate. He was an only child and still had his parents. When Danielle's mom died two years ago, Danielle took it upon herself to try and parent her little sister. While Krissy was only five or so years younger, she had been sheltered more in life. Danielle was a cop, had been in the reserves, and definitely was worldlier.

"Anyway, next thing I know, she tells me she's pregnant with the scum's baby. I wanted to scream. Cry. Hit something. Hit someone—a particular someone. But I knew I couldn't." She leaned back against the headrest. "Icing on the cake was when she told him she was pregnant, he called her names and left her."

"Dani, why didn't you say something to me?" Had he given her any indication that he wouldn't be there for her if she needed him?

She gave a fleeting but sincere smile and shrugged. "Embarrassment, to some degree."

"Why be embarrassed? I mean, it's your sister. You love her, but her actions aren't yours. Neither was the scum's."

Danielle swiped at the tears and stared out the front windshield. "Not action, but nonaction. You see, I'd always been anti-abortion. Pro-life all the way with me." She looked at Brandon. "You know how I've reacted to the clinics when we had to go break up a picket."

He did, which was why her defending Anna Belle so staunchly had confused him. He nodded. "I remember."

"But when Krissy told me she'd decided to have an abortion, I didn't open my mouth to stop her. I didn't argue that I thought it was morally wrong. I didn't tell her I thought it was murder." Tears trickled down Danielle's cheek. "I didn't even tell her to think about it a little longer. All I could see was my sister and her life if she had that baby." She wiped the tears away with the back of her hand. "I even paid for the procedure." Danielle sniffed. "Me, the pro-lifer, paying for my sister's abortion. How's that for irony?"

Now it all made sense. Her reaction to Grayson. Her defense of Anna Belle. Everything. Brandon reached over and took Danielle's hand. "I'm so sorry you went through that. Even sorrier that you went through it all alone." He squeezed her hand. "I wouldn't have known then anything more to do for you than I do right now, but I would have been there for you. Always. Regardless." He released her hand and loosely held the steering wheel. "I'm not one to judge, Dani. Not when it comes to matters like this. I've not walked in your shoes. I don't have a sister, so don't know what I would've done in your position."

"Probably not paid for an abortion." She sniffed again.

"I don't honestly know, but what I do know is that I make mistakes every single day. I don't have the answers to most complex situations. All I can do is pray for wisdom, do my level best, send up prayers of thanks if things go well, and ask for forgiveness if I messed up. I think that's all any of us can do."

"But I knew it was wrong before. Doesn't that make me horrible?" Her eyes pleaded with him for something he couldn't give.

"Danielle, I'm not a priest or a rabbi or a preacher. I'm just a man who loves God. What I do know is that God forgives. I know that if you confess your sins and ask for forgiveness, He will forgive you. That's one thing I do know."

"I just feel so guilty, and that's why I lashed out at you." She wiped her face again. "And if I'm being honest, why I've been so hostile toward Grayson. It wasn't his fault what happened to Krissy, but he gave me somebody to blame besides myself."

"You have to forgive yourself, Dani. If you've asked God for forgiveness, He's forgiven you already, but you have to let it go. You have to put it aside."

"I know, I know." She grinned. "Thanks, partner."

Brandon smiled and nodded. "But next time, talk to me." He put the car in gear and steered onto the road toward the Darkwater Inn.

Danielle pulled down the visor, wiped her face as she looked in the mirror, then closed it. "So, who do you like for suspects in the vandalism against Grayson?"

"Female DNA. Initially I thought of Emmi Dubois, but then I started asking what would she have to gain? She clearly didn't like Anna Belle, so the message wouldn't make sense." He took a sharp turn at a red light.

"Unless she was trying to throw him and us off."

"I thought of that, but if she killed Anna Belle, she wouldn't want to throw the scent off another prime suspect." He took another turn, then eased the car into the parking lot of the Darkwater Inn.

Danielle nodded. "It hasn't been in the press, so we have a smallish circle. Considering the message, the woman would be someone who is upset that Anna Belle is dead, and wants Grayson to pay for her murder."

"By that right, the only female I can think of would be Anna Belle's mother." He pulled the car into an empty space and parked. "And how convenient that we're here to speak with her right now. Do you want to take lead or want me to?"

They got out of the car, and he locked it before striding to the front doors of the hotel.

"You, if you don't mind." Danielle pulled out her notebook. "Says she's in room two twelve."

"Lead the way."

They entered the massive hotel that had a history almost as old and rich as the Crescent City itself. The Darkwater homed several original structures that had survived the ravages of time and hurricanes, such as the Isle Dernières in 1856, Audrey in 1957, Camille in 1969, and most recently, Katrina in 2005. It was a landmark of Bourbon Street.

They crossed the lobby to the elevators, smiling at the elevator attendant who took them to the second floor and sent them on their way with a "Have a nice day." They paused only a moment outside Monique's room before Danielle nodded, and Brandon gave the door a sharp rap.

She opened it almost immediately and welcomed them into her hotel room. They took the two chairs while Monique settled herself on the cushioned ottoman pushed up against the wall. "This is where I've spent most of the time reading over the papers from the clerk of court and such."

"Again, Mrs. Fredericks, we're so sorry for your loss." Brandon found that most grieving parents of adult children appreciated the acknowledgment of their loss. Often when younger adults died suddenly, the focus of sympathy was on their children or spouse, which was understandable, but the surviving parents were often left out.

"Thank you. Losing a child is always difficult."

"We hope to solve the case soon so that you'll at least have some comfort in knowing that she's gotten justice." Danielle nodded, not a single trace of her earlier emotional outburst visible. She truly could be a consummate detective. He was proud she was his partner.

"I'd appreciate that, dear. How can I help?"

Brandon figured they might as well just throw the door open wide. He leaned forward in his chair and smiled. "Tell us about Anna Belle, your daughter. We've heard from her employer and coworkers and her ex-husband. Tell us what we don't already know."

Monique didn't smile back. "I loved my daughter very much,

please understand that. I don't want you to think I'm some horrible mother. I loved Anna Belle and gave her everything I possibly could. Maybe I gave her too much, I don't know, but Anna Belle could be difficult."

Brandon eased open his Field Notes notebook and pen. He didn't know what he'd been expecting, but it wasn't this.

"Difficult?" Danielle probed.

Monique gave a little smile. "Even as a child, Anna Belle was demanding. Of mine and her daddy's attention. . .of everything she saw that she wanted. She was a determined little thing too. She could worm her way around just about anything to get what she wanted."

Sounded like most kids he'd known as toddlers.

"After her daddy was gone, Anna Belle changed. She seemed angry all the time, which at first I understood. I was angry he was gone too. But then I realized she was angry at me and at every person who disagreed with her. I tried talking to her, but that did no good. She resented that I had to work to cover our bills. She always wanted more, and when I couldn't give it, she got angry. And stayed that way. Most all of her teenage years she was angry all the time. At the teachers. At her friends who didn't bow to her wishes. At every poor guy she dated who didn't give her everything she wanted and let her have her way all the time." Monique shook her head. "Those were some turbulent times in our household, that's for sure."

Brandon could only imagine.

"Oh, but when she was happy. . ." Monique's eyes took on a far-away look, and she smiled, appearing more like her age of sixty-eight than she usually appeared to be. "When everything was right in Anna Belle's world, it was like the sun lived in that girl. She'd flit around, sending out rays of pure joy and wonderfulness. When she was named prom queen her senior year, you'd have thought the heavens had opened and you were seeing bursts straight from there."

Brandon had seen Anna Belle smile at Grayson before. Not all the time, but once, it'd been a look that he'd remembered. "So after graduation, she attended LSU in Baton Rouge, right?"

Monique seemed to snap out of her waltz down memory lane and nodded. "She received several scholarships, hating every time she filled out an application that I couldn't pay for her education. She went from being furious at me to being angry with whoever created the application and all its questions, and with the group offering the scholarship because of all the questions they asked. But in the end, she got enough to go where she wanted."

Brandon knew that's where she and Grayson had met. But he also knew that she didn't have the easiest time at college. "I understand she had a stalker."

Monique nodded. "It was a very difficult time for her. She was in her senior year and had taken a full load so she could graduate that May. She was also sending out applications for jobs because she refused to leave college and not have a plan in place. College seemed to have brought her focus. She had to plan. Everything was a calculated move with her once she got settled in there, so a stalker threw her for a loop." She let out a sigh. "She didn't tell me about it until he'd been arrested and she was going to testify against him. By then she was dating Grayson. I went for the trial, and that was the first time I met Grayson. I approved of him immediately."

"Why's that?" Danielle interrupted. "What made you immediately approved of him as your daughter's boyfriend?"

Monique smiled. "I saw the way he looked at her. That kind of look, the kind that has all the love in the world in it, can't be faked. I knew he would love her and take care of her. He was very attentive to her, seeing to her before she even asked. Little things like wrapping his jacket around her before she could shiver. Getting her a soft drink before she realized she was thirsty. It was like he could anticipate what she was thinking before she even realized what she wanted."

Brandon knew that to be true, not only because it was Grayson's personality and his profession, but also because he'd seen how the two of them were. Well, at least how Grayson was toward Anna Belle. "That must have made you relieved, as a mother, that your daughter had found someone who loved her?"

"It did. Very much." Monique looked right at Brandon. "I still think he was the best thing for Anna Belle, even though things went so south."

"Oh?" Danielle straightened in her seat and glanced at Brandon.

Monique nodded. "It saddens me and embarrasses me that my daughter did Grayson so wrong. She wasn't raised that way, I'll tell you that. After she and Grayson married and she moved into his house in the upper class, where she always wanted to be, she started taking my calls less and less. Had more excuses not to come visit for holidays. Always said it was work, but I knew the truth—she wanted to forget where she came from. Forget that she'd been raised by a working mother whose husband had gone off and left her for a younger woman."

Brandon didn't know how to respond, so he focused on his notes.

"I knew that. I didn't like it, but I knew how she felt about where she'd come from and who I was. It hurt, sure, but that was who she'd become. So focused on money and position and standing."

"You said you were saddened. . ." Brandon eased her back on subject.

"Yes. She embarrassed me by committing adultery, and considering that's what her father did, it shocked me a little that she would dare such a thing, knowing how it hurt us. I know now why she did it, and it had nothing to do with Grayson and everything to do with Anna Belle. She had an affair with her boss to further her career, but that actually makes it worse."

"She told you this?" Danielle asked.

Monique grimaced, making her ample wrinkles more

pronounced. "Of course not, but as soon as I realized who she'd cheated with, and knowing how she'd turned out, I figured it out. Not hard to do." She shook her head. "So disappointing."

"What about Grayson? Did you ever see the two of them argue or anything? Even the spats we know all married couples have?" Brandon wouldn't let Danielle call him biased, although he doubted she would now.

"No, but to be fair, I wasn't around them together except maybe once or twice a year." She straightened and met Brandon's gaze. "Having said that, however, I will tell you that I never saw Grayson treat Anna Belle with anything other than the utmost respect. I did, however, see my daughter treat him rudely and sometimes just downright mean. And that's not easy for a mother to say about her own child."

Brandon glanced at Danielle, then back at Monique. "Do you have any reason to think that Grayson had anything to do with your daughter's death?"

"Absolutely not. He loved her even though they were divorced. You can see how hard her death is on him even now. Even after everything she did, everything she hid from him—even all the things we didn't know about until after the fact—he still has a soft place for her." Monique shook her head. "Grayson Thibodeaux's a good man, and I'm proud to call him my son-in-law. I'd stake my life on the fact that he had nothing to do with Anna Belle's death."

"We're going to speak to the hotel staff about the suitcase that was left here for you with some of Anna Belle's things. Have you received anything else?" Danielle asked.

"Nothing. Just that suitcase, which Grayson said he'd give to you police."

Brandon nodded. "But if you get anything else, Mrs. Fredericks, you need to call us. Don't touch anything, don't give it to anyone else, just call us."

She nodded. "I know I should've called you when I got the suitcase. Grayson and his little bright-haired friend told me I should have, but it was such a shock. Seeing it. Knowing it was hers and that someone left it here for me."

"We'll do our best to figure out who left it, Mrs. Fredericks."

"I appreciate that. By the way, I've set the service for Anna Belle for Friday at ten. Back home in Breaux Bridge."

"I'm sure it will be lovely." Brandon stood and slipped his notebook back into his pocket. "When will you head back home?"

"I plan on leaving early Thursday morning. I have to go to court in the morning to be named administrator of Anna Belle's estate."

Ah, yes. The details around an unexpected death.

"We'll keep you updated as we get new information about the case." Danielle stood and shook Monique's hand.

"I appreciate that." She extended her hand to Brandon, holding his tight in hers. "Just to be clear, I know the ex is always the main suspect, but that's not so in this case. I know in my heart that Grayson isn't responsible for Anna Belle's death."

Brandon caught Danielle's eye. She gave a brief nod, and he resisted letting out a long breath. Finally, they could work together instead of against each other and find out who really killed Anna Belle Thibodeaux.

TWENTY-TWO

"Hey." Colton stuck his head into Grayson's office.

"Hey. Come on in." Grayson stood and moved around the desk. "Sorry I didn't come see you earlier when I got in, but I've been trying to get all my emails answered and calls returned."

Colton clapped his shoulder, then plopped down on the couch. "How're you doing, buddy? You okay?"

Grayson shrugged. Out of everyone else in the office and Grayson's close circle of friends, Colton knew his and Anna Belle's relationship best. "Not gonna lie. It's been rough."

"I know. I mean, I can only imagine." Colton set up and looked him in the eye. "It was pretty awful. I tried to call you, but then I didn't want to leave a voice mail message."

"Yeah, I saw where you called on my recent calls. Thanks for that." He ran a hand over his face. Shouldn't this be getting easier? "Thanks for everything you did. Tried to do. Calling 911, going to the hospital." Grayson shook his head. "I appreciate it."

"Of course. Of course. I'm just so sorry for you." Colton gave a wobbly smile. "Is there anything I can do for you? You know I'm here for you no matter what."

"I appreciate that." It was during trying times like these that people found out who their real friends were.

"If you need to take time to plan her funeral or anything. . ." At least his business partner understood he'd probably need to take time off in the future. Especially if the police kept coming after him like they were.

"Her mom's here in town for the time being. She's going to have the service on Friday back in Breaux Bridge."

"You're going, I assume?"

Grayson nodded. "You're welcome to go as well. Anna Belle always liked you. Said you had grit." He smiled. "She was the one who encouraged me to accept your offer to go into business together when we met that night for dinner."

"I always figured it was her." Colton smiled back. "I liked her too. I mean, I hate what she did to you, but as a person, I thought she was okay."

Which was more than most people would say, if they were being honest.

Silence filled the space, and for the first time since Grayson could remember, it felt awkward. Odd. Must just be the tension of not really knowing what to say to someone who lost an ex.

"How's the investigation going?" Colton asked. "Those two cops. . .I thought one of them was your friend, man."

"Brandon's my friend." Or he'd thought.

Colton cocked his head. "They sure seemed to focus on you a lot in their questioning. To be honest, I think they're centering their investigation on you."

"I know." Sadly, he knew all too well. "I guess they grilled you pretty hard, huh?"

"Yeah. I mean, first because we even took the job, and then because I was there and all."

Grayson nodded. "I'm sure. They keep asking me the same questions over and over. Like I'm going to change my answer?"

"I hear you." Colton stood and moved to peer absently at Grayson's bookcase. "Oh hey, it's that time to renew our corporate liability insurance. I'll get the stack of papers ready and mark them so all you'll have to do is sign by the red arrows, okay?"

"Thanks. I'd appreciate it."

Colton turned. "Well, I'll let you get back to it." He motioned toward the hall. "Pam already left?"

Grayson nodded. "Her interview was set for three." He glanced at his watch. "Which is about now."

"Good deal. Let me know if you need anything, okay?"

"Thanks, Colton."

Grayson watched his partner leave. There was something he'd meant to ask Colton, but he couldn't remember what now. He shook his head. Not surprising his mind was all over the place, considering the circumstances.

He glanced at his bookcase. The pictures he once had there of himself and Anna Belle were in a box in the garage at home. Most of Anna Belle's things or things that reminded Grayson of her he'd stuck in the garage after the divorce was final. Maybe he should do something to preserve them. For what, he hadn't a clue. It just seemed wrong to throw them away or leave them in the garage.

Vvvvvvv!

His cell phone vibrated on the desk. "Hello."

"Hi, Grayson. It's Monique. Anna Belle's mother."

He grinned into the phone. "Yes, ma'am, how're you?"

"Okay. Those police detectives just left. Don't you worry none. I told them I knew you had nothing to do with Anna Belle's death."

"I appreciate that." He remembered he had told her he would call her today and set up lunch tomorrow. He'd forgotten. "Are you still interested in lunch tomorrow? After court?"

"Yes, I am. I'd like to see you again before I head back. I mean, I know I'll see you Friday at the service, but we won't get to visit much then with everybody there."

His gut tightened thinking about the service—all the stares he'd have to endure. Skipping the service wouldn't be that big of a deal because ex-spouses weren't required to attend funerals of former spouses, but it meant a lot to Monique for him to be there, so be there he would. "Yes, ma'am. How about I come to your hotel, say at one? We can go somewhere if you like, but I happen to know the hotel chef is brilliant."

"Yes, the food here at the hotel is wonderful. One is fine. I'll see you then, Grayson."

He disconnected the call and leaned back in his chair. Maybe he should give Anna Belle's things to her mother. After they'd divorced, she was supposed to have changed everything to her mom on all her important documents.

Beneficiary!

Even though he'd been as indifferent as possible during the divorce proceedings, he distinctly remembered the attorneys talking about changing the beneficiaries on their respective life insurance policies. He'd removed her from his after he had checked with Ian, who had assured him that the partnership agreement between he and Colton wouldn't be affected.

Anna Belle had no claim to Game's On You, even though she'd tried her best during the divorce, since he'd established the business while they were married. But the partnership agreement was ironclad: in the event of death, divorce, or imprisonment, the full business and all assets would go to the remaining partner. She hadn't even been able to get alimony because she was the one who committed adultery.

Right now, Grayson could only pray that she'd actually removed him from her life insurance policy as beneficiary and didn't just do a half job like setting up just the new address for the cell phone account. If she hadn't removed him, and Grayson was still listed as beneficiary, the police would really think he had a motive to kill her.

"Now, let's move on to Monday night." Brandon stared at Pam Huron in the hot box. She'd held up under his and Danielle's questions, even managing to refrain from letting her dislike of his partner show too much.

"Okay."

"You said you were the one who spotted the slashed tires on Grayson's truck. Is that correct?" Brandon stared at his notes.

"Yes. I had gone outside to get some cardboard from my car, and I saw it. Then I saw the eggs on his house. I went into the house and told Grayson."

"You just keep cardboard in your car?" Danielle asked.

Pam cut her eyes to his partner. "I belong to an art club and sometimes have to ship supplies or pieces, so I had a couple of flat Priority Rate boxes in my trunk."

Brandon nodded. She looked like the artist type, and not just because of her bright hair. It was more of the vibe she gave off. "Then what happened?"

Pam sighed. "Of course Grayson ran outside to see. He called the police and asked for a report to be taken. He didn't want the eggs to dry on the house and damage the paint, so he decided to wash it off."

"You were in the house when we arrived," Danielle pointed out.

"Yes," Pam grimaced. "I was trying to identify the coat of arms—" Her expression froze with eyes wide and flushed face.

"What coat of arms?" Brandon pinned her with his stare. This was something. . .

"Uh."

He could almost see the wheels turning as she struggled to answer him, but not. He wasn't going to allow that. "What coat of arms?" His tone was harder, his voice louder.

"When Grayson went to turn on the hose, he found something in the hedge. It was a bracelet charm that has a coat of arms on it." Her words tumbled on top of each other as she spoke without taking a breath.

"Where did he find it?" Danielle asked.

"It was caught in the hedge in front of the broken window."

"And no one told us?" Brandon couldn't believe they hadn't reported it—after he'd made himself clear about the suitcase.

"Here." She reached into her jeans pocket and pulled it out. "This is it. I've been trying to find out what coat of arms that is, but I can't even figure out what kind of fish that is."

"Why didn't you tell us that night when we were there?" Brandon asked.

"We didn't know for certain if it had anything to do with anything."

Danielle groaned. "Sure."

Pam sat up straight in the chair. "We didn't. I mean, I thought it was probably from someone throwing the eggs or rock, but that's definitely a charm from a woman's bracelet, which would mean that whoever did that was a woman."

Brandon looked at his partner.

"What?" Pam caught the look that passed between them.

"We're not at liberty to say at this point," Danielle told her.

But maybe Pam knew something she wasn't even aware she knew. "We can tell you that DNA recovered from the paper around the rock has been determined to belong to a female."

Danielle sighed heavily and shook her head. She'd chew him out later, but just having another clue, something tangible, gave him hope.

"Do you have any idea who would want to vandalize Grayson's house and truck?" Brandon asked.

Pam chewed her bottom lip. "I can't think of anyone. Especially not anyone who would do this and take up for Anna Belle at the same time, because the vandalism is definitely connected to her death."

Brandon didn't miss her phrasing. Death, not murder.

"You know Grayson probably better than anyone else at this point. I know you're his assistant and his friend, but is there anything you'd like to tell us? Anything, no matter how insignificant it might seem?" Brandon held his pen over his notebook.

Pam waited a moment before she shook her head. "I know so much points to Grayson, but you have to know, he's innocent. Me? I'd have ripped into Anna Belle after all she did to him and everything we found out, but he didn't. He left town to go hang with his friends and relax and just get away from everything. I respect him for not lashing out." She shook her head. "Do you know what he told me just today?"

"What?" Danielle asked.

"That he had to find a way to truly forgive her in his heart." Pam shook her head again. "I ask you, who does that? A man who has nothing on his conscience, that's who. A man who is good and honest, that's who."

Brandon couldn't agree more.

TWENTY-THREE

He couldn't imagine anything of Anna Belle's he would want at this point.

Grayson stepped into Monique's hotel room anyway, not having the heart to decline when she told him she'd found something of Anna Belle's that she wanted him to have.

"Just a second and I'll get it." Monique disappeared around the corner.

Grayson waited as lightning flashed through the window. Serious storms were forecast for the afternoon.

"Here." Monique handed him a necklace with a round medallion dangling. "It's not too fancy—it's just stainless steel, but it'll hold up forever. I gave this to Anna Belle to celebrate her first communion."

He stared at the medallion that was about two inches in diameter. "Saint Jude?"

Monique nodded. "He is the patron saint of hope and impossible causes. He was also one of Jesus' original twelve apostles. He preached the Gospel passionately, sometimes in very difficult circumstances."

Grayson couldn't speak as he held the necklace. Hope and impossible causes, that seemed to sum up Anna Belle perfectly. He'd been wrong—he *did* want something of Anna Belle's after all.

He slipped it into his front shirt pocket, not wanting to risk tangling the chain by putting it in the pocket of his pants. "Thank you, Monique."

She smiled and rested her warm, worn hand against his face. "She would want you to have it, Grayson."

He nodded. "I'll see you day after tomorrow. Have a safe trip home." Grayson gave Monique a final hug and waited in the Darkwater Inn hall until she'd shut the door before heading back to the elevator.

"Lobby, sir?" The elevator attendant had been courteous to Monique when Grayson had escorted her back to her room. The level of security in the hotel impressed him, considering the bad publicity they'd experienced lately.

Grayson nodded, letting himself get lost in his own thoughts on the ride. He'd finally just come out and asked Monique if Anna Belle had changed her life insurance beneficiary. Anna Belle hadn't informed Monique of any policy, so Grayson had called the agent they'd purchased their policies from years ago. With Monique on speakerphone to verify her information, they confirmed Anna Belle had done as the divorce decree had warranted and changed her life insurance beneficiary to Monique. While Monique had been shocked over hearing she was about to receive two hundred fifty thousand dollars, Grayson was relieved that this would help remove him as a suspect.

The elevator dinged, and he nodded at the attendant before striding across the lobby. Wednesday's earlier spotty clouds had developed into massive thunderheads as the afternoon hours had replaced the morning. What had been a steady breeze when he'd entered the hotel to meet Monique for lunch was now straight-line winds. A storm was definitely coming to New Orleans. Considering the F3 tornado that had been unleashed not too many Februarys ago, residents of the Crescent City were definitely cautious about storm warnings.

He could beat the storm back to Game's On You if he hurried. He and Colton were supposed to meet at four thirty to go over their upcoming schedules as well as the direction of the company. Grayson hated to admit it, but the possibility of him being arrested was very real, and more than a little scary. The partnership papers for Game's On You covered the company in such an event. Everything would automatically default to Colton, but the media attention could hurt the company's reputation.

Anna Belle had said many times that there was no such thing as bad publicity, only bad choices in spinning the publicity. He faced bad publicity because of the death of a PR account representative—the universe sure seemed to have a sick sense of humor.

It was too much for Grayson to compartmentalize at the moment. Shaking his head, he ducked out the front door of the hotel and kept his head down against the wind as he turned the corner and headed into the almost empty parking lot. If he could just figure out who'd really killed Anna Belle, then he—

A woman rammed into him. Or him into her.

"I'm sorry." He spoke at the same time she did as he reached out to steady her. They both froze at the same time as they looked at each other.

Laure Comeau stood before him wearing the familiar blazer of the Darkwater Inn that served as a uniform. The wind shoved a curly tendril that had escaped from the brightly designed head wrap covering her natural hair.

"Get your hands off me." She snatched her arm from him. "Don't touch me."

He jerked his hands back to his side. "I only meant to steady you."

Stormy eyes looked him up and down, then settled on his face. "What are you doing here? Come to stalk me now?"

"Stalk you? What?" She wasn't making any sense. "What're you talking about?"

"You may have everybody else fooled, Grayson Thibodeaux, but not me. Anna Belle told me about the mind games you played." She took a step back from him. "She called me the morning of the day you killed her. She knew what you'd done, what you were doing. She knew you'd put her in a game, you twisted piece of—"

"Whoa. Wait a minute. First off, I didn't kill Anna Belle. I know you want to believe I'm some horrible monster, but that's not true."

"Yes it is. You had her in a game, right?"

Well. . . "Her company had hired—"

"She was in a game you created, right?" She crossed her arms and pinched her lips together, smugness hugging every little curve of her face.

"Yes, but—"

Laure nodded and widened her eyes. "Right. You created a game and didn't even tell her she was playing."

"That's the way her company contracted us." He spoke very fast, determined to be able to at least finish a sentence.

"Whatever. You used things against her like her fear of being stalked."

Now she paused to let him talk, when he couldn't argue with her statement?

She nodded again. "That's right. Just what she thought. You were pretending to stalk her, using the same mask from the guy back in college." Laure wrinkled her nose as if he stunk of dog crap. "That's pretty low, even for you, Grayson."

"I didn't stalk her. Yes, we had someone put on the mask and appear outside her window, but it wasn't mean."

Laure snorted. "You or someone you had do it—either way, that's pretty cruel, don't you think? Oh, wait, don't answer that. Of course you don't think it was. You designed everything to scare her, to torment her, and for what? Just to have fun before you killed her?"

"I didn't kill her, Laure."

"Right. I'm supposed to believe you." She shook her head. "She called you when she figured it out to talk to you, but you wouldn't take her call."

An emptiness settled in his chest. "I haven't lied to you. Yes, she did call me. Twice. She left me a message that we needed to talk. I couldn't take the call because I lost my phone while I was out of town and didn't get a new one until two days ago." He blinked against the driving wind. "She figured out she was in a game?" He'd suspected she would. He'd warned Colton that she'd probably figure it out, but closer to the end. It was a little earlier than he'd guessed. He was pretty sure she'd know as soon as she went into the escape room part.

"Of course she figured out it was a game. She was smart, but then she figured out it was you. And she was scared, Grayson. Terrified. I could hear it in her voice when she called me." Moisture filled her dark brown eyes. "I was so worried about her, I went over to the place on Esplanade Avenue when I finished my shift, but nobody was there. She was already dead."

"I wasn't there, Laure. I know you don't believe me, but I swear, I wasn't there. I had nothing to do with her death." If only he had been there, maybe he could've prevented this from happening. If only he hadn't created the stupid game to begin with. If only he had stood his ground and told Colton no.

If only, if only, if only. But he couldn't turn back time.

"You tormented her with the stalker, then you gave her or sent her that Scheduled Maternity pamphlet. That was the cruelest."

"I didn't have anything to do with that." Although, he could argue that what was cruel was his wife aborting his baby—maybe his, maybe not—and not even telling him she was pregnant.

"Right. That just popped up in her room?" The hardness returned to Laure's face. "The brochure and the mask just appeared there? And that doll? What was with that?"

"That wasn't hers." Wait a minute. . . "How do you know about the doll?"

"It was in her room."

"How do you know that?"

Now it was Laure's turn to clam up, but it made sense now. That's how all of Anna Belle's personal stuff got put back in her suitcase. He glanced at her blazer again. She delivered it to Monique, but why?

"Why give the suitcase to Anna Belle's mother?"

She shrugged, her dislike for him pulling the arrogance back to her attitude. "Someone needed to stand up for Anna Belle. For what you did to her. The police wouldn't listen to me." She broke eye contact to glance at the discarded napkin dancing across the parking lot. "I figured if anybody would stand up for her that the police would listen to, it would be her mother." She shook her head. "Apparently not."

Grayson would normally be annoyed, or at least frustrated by her actions and logic, warped though they were, but he only felt sorry for Laure. She'd loved Anna Belle and had to be grieving.

"Monique and I both want to find out who did this to Anna Belle and see that person brought to justice, but it's not me, Laure. I had nothing to gain from her death."

"Except you had to be furious when you found out what she did. She knew you would be livid, even though it wasn't yours. She knew you'd judge her. She told me your religion wouldn't allow you to condone what she'd done. That was why she couldn't tell you in the first place. She didn't know she wanted a divorce for sure yet, and she knew if she told you, it would be over."

Every muscle in his body had seized. *Not yours.* He couldn't speak. Couldn't move. Couldn't even think in complete sentences.

Laure hugged herself, her animosity battered down. "She said that she was pretty sure you could forgive her for cheating, but if she told you she was pregnant, you'd expect her to have it, whether it was yours or not, and she didn't want a baby. Certainly not if it was Tim's, because if he ever found out, he'd never let her out of his life."

How could someone he loved so much be so shallow? How had he not seen it? Or how had he ignored it? Had he not wanted to believe it so badly that he refused to see the truth?

Laure stared at him. "If you didn't leave that Scheduled Maternity thing for her, then who did?"

"Emmi Dubois."

Shocked marched over her expression. "Emmi? How did she know? Why would she leave it for Anna Belle?"

Grayson shrugged. "I don't know. On video we saw her take it into Anna Belle's room on Thursday morning, then leave immediately after. We have no clue how she knew or why she'd do it. The police have the video, so I'm sure they're following the lead."

"I just don't understand." She shook her head.

"Neither do I. See, I didn't do that, nor did I kill Anna Belle." He studied her for a moment. "I want to know what happened just as badly as anyone."

She nodded. "Um, Grayson, I think I owe you an apology." She paused. "Probably more than just an apology."

"You're going to find this interesting."

Brandon looked up from his desk to his partner who waved a piece of paper in the air. "Do tell?"

"Do you know why Pam Huron couldn't determine the type of fish on the charm?"

He shook his head but grabbed his pen and opened his notebook.

"Because it's not a fish. It's a dolphin."

He scrunched up his face. "Dolphin? That thing doesn't look like a dolphin. I swear that thing looked vicious and not like a dolphin." He'd got to pet a dolphin the last time he'd gone to Sea World, and that one looked friendly. The image on the charm looked fierce.

"Well, it's a white dolphin intertwined with a gold anchor on a blue background." She glanced at the paper to read. "Its original is unknown as coats of arms weren't given to last names but to individuals to be passed down. They were property."

"Huh. I didn't know that."

Danielle grinned. "Me either. But this particular coat of arms is mentioned in twelfth-century France and is referenced to *commeaux* lands."

"Commeaux lands?"

She held out the paper to him and widened her smile. "Used to represent the last names of Commeaux or Comeau."

He snatched the paper. "Like Laure Comeau."

She nodded. "The same Laure Comeau who claims to have been Anna Belle's best friend. The same Laure Comeau who told us Grayson had to have murdered Anna Belle because he was, and I believe I'm directly quoting here: 'a real jerk,' end quote."

Brandon flipped through the file on his desk. "She said Anna Belle called her Thursday and said Grayson was wearing the Mardi Gras mask to scare her."

Danielle perched on the edge of his desk. "But we know it was part of the game and not Grayson."

"But she didn't." He stared at his notes. "She would blame Grayson for Anna Belle's death. Probably enough to threaten to expose him."

"And slashing tires and throwing eggs and rocks with messages is the kind of thing someone missing their best friend would do."

He stood. "She works at the Darkwater Inn, doesn't she?"

Danielle pushed off his desk. "Ready for a ride?"

"Let's go." Brandon followed her to the car.

The wind nearly took his breath away as they broke free of the station and stepped onto the asphalt parking lot behind the building. "Wow, we'd better batten down the hatches. Looks like it's gonna get messy this afternoon." He slipped into the passenger's seat since it was her turn to drive.

"We've got a couple of weather alerts open for the area. Man, I hope the crazies stay home." She clicked her seat belt in its latch.

"Lovely." He latched his own seat belt. "Anyway, I don't know what Laure Comeau thought she'd accomplish, unless it was just to make herself feel better, like she'd done something. At least we'll have something to put on the report for Grayson's insurance company, if nothing else."

Danielle started the car and backed it out of its space. "And we get to chalk one up for solving that part of the whodunit."

"Now if we could just figure out who killed Anna Belle. . ."

"If we remove Grayson from the list of suspects—"

He grinned.

She shook her head as she turned onto the main road. "I'm going to allow, for the sake of argument, he's not at the top of the suspect list. So, if I take him from the top, who does that leave?"

"I still say Emmi Dubois." He pushed the visor back into place. With the weather kicking up, he didn't want Danielle's view out of the windshield to be obstructed in any way.

"I've heard your argument, and I guess I can see where you're coming from." Danielle pulled up to the stop sign and snuck a glance at Brandon. "Sell me."

"We know that the top motives for murder are money, revenge, love, and anger. In this case, no one benefited financially from Anna Belle's death except her mother, who is not a suspect. We've verified that Grayson didn't have any life insurance policies on her or anything."

"Right."

"So if we remove money as motive, that leaves revenge and anger." Brandon shook his head as they turned onto the street of the Darkwater Inn. "We know Emmi had every reason to be angry with Anna Belle, and we can certainly understand her wanting revenge, and there's no question she loves Tim."

Danielle shook her head and made a face as she pulled up behind the car in front of her and stopped. "I know. The logic is there, but man, I just don't feel it. I don't get the vibe from her."

He understood vibes and gut instincts. "Okay, keeping Grayson off the top of the list of suspects, who else is there with motive, means, and opportunity?"

"I'm wondering about Tim Dubois."

"Tim? He was in love with Anna Belle. Why on earth would he kill her?"

She turned into the parking lot and eased along to the side of the building to park. "Because she broke it off with him. Not only did she break his heart—love—but she humiliated him because everybody in the office knew about the affair and that Anna Belle had ended it—revenge."

"Yeah, but I just can't see it."

"He's the one who made the initial contact with Game's On You. What better revenge than to kill your ex-lover and frame her ex-husband?" She parked the car and turned off the engine.

Now that made sense. "Yeah, I can see that." Maybe they should take another look at Tim. He pulled out his notebook and jotted a note.

Together they jogged into the hotel. The first fat raindrops pelted against the glass door as they made their way across the lobby. Brandon smiled at the young lady standing behind the front desk. "Hello. We need to see Laure Comeau, please. She works here."

"And you are?"

Danielle pulled out her shield and flashed it. "Here to see Laure Comeau."

The smile slid off the young lady's face. "Just a moment."

"Thank you." Brandon smiled at the lady before he turned his partner away, moving her toward one of the groupings of chairs.

"You know what's crazy though," Danielle offered.

"Just about every day on our job?"

"Well, yeah." She grinned. "I guess what's crazy to me though is that the complexity of the crime doesn't really fit Tim. I mean, you met him. No offense, but he's not the brightest crayon in the box. Not like someone who could create such a complex game. Maybe that's why I liked Grayson for it so much."

"Logically, I understand."

"You wanted to see me?"

They both turned to face Laure Comeau. Brandon took a step toward her. "Can we sit and talk here?" Several clumps of people stood in the lobby, closer to the large windows than them, but there were a few close enough to eavesdrop. "Or would somewhere else be better?"

Laure's eyes darted about. "I only have a few minutes, but we can talk over there." She led them to the chairs a little farther down. "What can I help you with?"

"We have some questions regarding some vandalism at the home of Grayson Thibodeaux." Danielle whipped out her notebook.

"Wow, he called you already? That was fast." She shook her head. "I guess I wasn't wrong about him after all."

"What do you mean? Have you spoken to Grayson?"

Laure crossed her arms over her chest. "Please don't insult me. You know we talked, otherwise you wouldn't be here."

Brandon was confused. "Wait a minute. You and Grayson talked?"

A cloud of confusion washed over her face. "He *didn't* call and tell you what I did?"

"What, exactly, did you tell him that you did?" Danielle asked.

Laure cocked her head. "If he didn't tell you, why are you here?"

"Vandalism at his house."

Her face flushed and her gaze dropped to the floor. "Yes, I slashed his tires and egged his house and threw a rock through his window, but he's not mad. I mean, he is, but it's okay."

"You told him you did all that and *it's okay*?" Danielle asked.

Laure nodded. "I mean, I told him I'd pay for the window and I'd reimburse him for the new tires of course, but he said he wouldn't press charges. That's why I was upset when I saw y'all. I thought he'd lied and called you." She paused. "Since he didn't, how did you know?"

Danielle pulled the bag with the charm out of her pocket and held it up in front of Laure's face. "You dropped this."

"Oh my gosh! I didn't even realize that'd come off my bracelet." She reached for it, but Danielle snatched it out of reach.

"Did you know you can be charged with criminal property damage?" Danielle asked.

Laure's eyes grew even bigger. "Even though he's not pressing charges?"

"It's up to us whether to charge someone with a crime or not."

Laure jutted out her chin. "I've already confessed to doing the vandalism, and for taking Anna Belle's things and giving them to her mom. Are you going to charge me?"

"Wait, you're the one who went and got Anna Belle's things?"

Laure explained how she'd come to get the belongings and get them to Monique.

"You went into the house unauthorized?" Danielle asked.

"It was unlocked."

That was one of the problems Brandon had had with the whole crime scene: it hadn't been secured. The ambulance had left the scene around four forty-five. The CSI unit hadn't arrived at the Esplanade Avenue address until eleven the next morning. That was almost nineteen hours that anybody could have, and apparently did, go into the house and breach the crime scene. No telling who else had gone in there and removed anything.

"You realize you can be charged with evidence tampering and obstruction of justice?" Danielle could look very intimidating when she tried.

This was one of those times.

Laure's face scrunched as tears pooled in her eyes. "I didn't mean to do any of that. I just wanted to get Anna Belle's stuff for her. I don't know why. I just couldn't bear to have her stuff just left there. I mean, I didn't know she'd been killed then. I thought she'd just died from an allergic reaction. I didn't know it was a crime scene or anything."

None of them did at that time. Brandon offered the young woman a smile. "We'll be in touch if we have any additional questions for you." He steered Danielle away from Laure. "Well, that's one question answered."

Danielle nodded. "Now if we could just answer the most baffling question: Who killed Anna Belle?"

"True that, partner."

Minutes later, Brandon and Danielle stood under the awning of the Darkwater Inn. Rain came down in sheets, driving at an angle.

"I don't think it's going to let up," Brandon volunteered after several minutes.

Danielle sighed. "Want to make a run for it?"

"Might as well. Let's go." Brandon ducked and took off. Rain pelted him, plowing down the collar of his shirt to soak his back. He jumped into the driver's seat. His shirt clung against his back.

"Oh, this is awful." Danielle shook her hair and sent water flying everywhere.

"Hey!" Brandon reached for the stack of paper napkins they kept in the back of the console. He handed some to Danielle before wiping his face and hands and dabbing over his hair. "This is crazy."

"Yeah, I bet patrol's gonna be busy tonight. Poor souls." Danielle chuckled and passed the car keys to Brandon. They'd all done their time on patrol in the rain during Mardi Gras season. When the weather went sideways, police, first responders, and hospitals were on high alert with people just acting out. That and when the moon was full.

"Better them than us." Brandon started the car and flipped on the defroster. He stared out the windshield, waiting for it to clear. He spied movement off the side of the hotel's lot. Two men were under an umbrella. Everything about their body language said they were having an argument: their stance, their gestures, even their posture. "Check them out." He nodded toward them.

Danielle wiped her window with her sleeve. "Hey, isn't that Big Al?"

Alfonse "Big Al" Marcello, rumored to be from *that* Marcello family, ran high-end loan-sharking, gambling, and a little drug and guns running. Nothing to compare to the history of the Marcello crime family, but enough that most every detective knew Big Al by sight. And what he was up to at any given time.

"Pull up there, Brando. It looks like this might get heated, and I'd rather head it off before it starts so I don't have to get out in the rain to stop something."

Brandon nodded and moved the car in that direction. He turned on his lights as he approached the men.

They turned as the car inched to them. Big Al took one look, turned his back to Brandon and Danielle to face the man, then strode off, carrying the umbrella with him.

The other man stood for a moment, then turned and rushed into the alley behind the Darkwater Inn.

Brandon stared after him, then looked at his partner. "Was that Colton York?"

TWENTY-FOUR

"Well, you said it had to be someone who cared about Anna Belle and what happened to her and who thought you were responsible for her death. Laure Comeau fits the bill." Pam leaned back on the couch in Grayson's office at Game's On You, curling her feet underneath her like a young schoolgirl.

"She was very apologetic for slashing my tires. She said as soon as she got paid, she'd reimburse me for my tires." Grayson wrestled with making her pay him. On one hand, she was struggling to make ends meet and he easily afforded the grand the four new tires for his truck cost, but on the other hand, it would be a lesson learned the hard way that actions have consequences, and sometimes those consequences can be very expensive. Still, he understood Laure's feelings of helplessness over Anna Belle's death and wanting to do something—anything to see justice served. He was torn.

Pam pulled her hair into one of those ball-looking bun things on the top of her head. "You're too nice for your own good, Grayson. That woman's unstable. Throwing rocks through windows. Slashing tires. Egging."

He propped his feet up on the leather ottoman between the couch and love seat. "I'm just relieved she's not gunning for the police to arrest me for Anna Belle's murder anymore."

"She should be extremely thankful that she chose not to mess with *my* car that night. I've never claimed to be nearly as nice as you."

Grayson ducked his head to hide his grin, imagining only too well what Pam's reaction would've been if Laure had slashed the tires on Pam's car. It wouldn't have been pretty.

"Too bad she didn't tell you she'd pay for the tires before you spent the money on buying new ones. Or filing a claim."

He snapped his fingers. "I'll have to call and cancel the claim. I certainly don't want to be accused of filing a false claim." Grayson could well imagine how Danielle and Brandon would make something out of it. He'd probably be accused of insurance fraud.

"Look at your policy. You might be able to cancel the claim online or something," Pam suggested. "Those chat options are pretty cool, and then you have the discussion in writing, just in case you need it."

"Smart thinking." He stood and went to his desk.

"I didn't mean right this second."

"I'll forget if I wait."

Pam chuckled.

Grayson awakened his computer and typed in the site address in the search engine. He found his insurance company's page and logged in. While he waiting for his account to load, he glanced at the stack of papers that somebody had plopped in the center of his desk. A sticky note read:

G, these are the insurance papers we discussed. Sign by arrows.
I'll pick up when we meet. —C

With the rain and talking with Laure, he'd almost forgotten their meeting. He grabbed his pen and poised it over the first blank where the arrow highlighted.

"You're not going to read what you're about to sign?" Pam stood on the other side of the desk, frowning her disapproval.

"Colton and I discussed the insurance papers. We have to renew our corporate liability policy annually." He noted her hands were already on her hips. "But, you're right, I should read everything before I sign."

She nodded and took a seat in one of the chairs facing him.

He smiled and lifted the cover sheet and started scanning the information. Just like Pam to keep him on his toes. She was nothing if not. . . Wait a minute. He went back over the paragraph he'd just skimmed. This had to be wrong.

Grayson lifted the page so he could read the top. This wasn't from the insurance company, but a bank. Not the bank the company held their accounts at either. He started reading from the beginning, his heart quickening as he read. Loan papers. A loan for five hundred thousand dollars that put not only the company up as collateral, but also all the company's assets, which included both Colton and Grayson's vehicles, among other things.

"What's wrong?" Pam was on her feet again, hovering over the desk.

Grayson's stomach turned. There had to be a mistake.

"Grayson?"

He met her stare. "Have you heard anything about Colton needing money? I mean, for the business? Did y'all have a meeting or anything while I was out of town?"

"No. Why?"

His mouth was spitless as he held up the papers. "These are loan papers that put up the business, all of its holdings and assets. My truck." He shook his head. "At one time, mine and Colton's houses were listed. I thought when we paid off the initial loan that was changed, but now. . ." When was the last time he and Colton had sat down and reviewed the company's profit-and-loss statement together? Colton had always sent Grayson the report that he said he'd gotten from their accountant. It was a spreadsheet, easy enough to alter. Grayson couldn't remember ever seeing a paper report.

"I don't understand." Pam slumped back into the chair. "What's going on?"

Little things began to fall into place. "Hang on. I'll be right back."

He walked across the building to Colton's empty office. The whole building seemed to have already left. It was quiet and dark on Colton's side, save the multiple flashes of lightning seen through the windows.

Grayson went to Colton's bookcase, to the display of where his St. Andrews souvenirs usually sat unless Colton was playing golf and using the glove and ball marker.

His blood ran cold as the glove and ball tool sat without the actual ball marker.

"What's going on?" Pam asked from the doorway.

He couldn't say it out loud. His thoughts were so jumbled, falling all over each other. He silently walked back to his office, going over everything.

"Grayson, you're scaring me." Pam followed him.

A clap of thunder made her jump as they entered his office again.

He leaned against the arm of the couch. "Tell me I'm crazy. . .tell me I'm so far off base that I'm lost behind the fence."

"You're crazy, but I have no idea what you're talking about." She sat on the arm of the love seat, her feet dangling. "Fill me in."

"Colton brought the Deets deal to me. He fought hard for me to agree to the game. Fought really hard."

"Right." Pam nodded, that ball on the top of her head bopping. "I remember, and I agreed with you, even after you told Colton you'd do it."

"Even though Colton should've taken lead, he insisted I be the creator."

Pam nodded again. "I'm with you so far."

His mind raced. "He went over every detail with me multiple times before he took it to Tim. He said he wanted to get it all set in his mind because he'd be the one on-site. He knew every little secret I knew, including Anna Belle's allergies. He also knew I was angry with her and hurt to the point of desperation."

Pam shot to her feet. "You can't think. . . No, Grayson. Colton's your friend. No way—"

"Would he kill my ex-wife and set me up?" he finished. His tongue burned even as he said the words, but his gut. . .his gut balled into a tight knot.

"He wouldn't. He's your friend. Your business partner. He wouldn't do it." But she didn't sound as sure as a minute ago.

"He's taking out loans on the company and tricking me into signing them without telling me what they really are. His St. Andrews ball marker is gone from the case, and I found it in Anna Belle's room at the rental house on Esplanade Avenue. He was there, not just on-site, but apparently in her room sometime. He knew about her allergy well in advance of her death. He knew about her addiction to those stupid energy drinks."

"He's not on the video at any time even slowing down by her room," Pam argued.

"We're missing eighteen minutes, right? That could've been of him going in her room, then out again." Grayson shook his head. "And if you think about it, well, he knows how to manipulate the video to delete sections and would know just what to tell the police to put suspicion on me and you."

Lightning flashed, followed by a loud clap of thunder.

Boom!

All the lights in the office went out. The hum faded as the computer went down.

Great. Just wonderful. The power had gone out. That loud boom usually meant the local transformer had blown. With the storm, no telling how long it would be before an electric company crew could get out to repair it.

Grayson went to his cabinet, pulled out a battery lantern, and turned it on. New Orleans *was* below sea level and got its fair share of storms and flooding, usually knocking out power for several hours or even days.

The shine from the lantern illuminated his office just fine, but the constant flashing of lightning lent an eerie glow to the room. He sent a text to the power company outage reporting system. An automated response text sent back to him confirmed that the outage had been recorded and would be placed in the queue.

He slipped his phone into his jacket pocket and sat back down on the arm of the couch, facing the love seat with his back to his office door. "I hate to say it, but it makes perfect sense. It's the only thing that does." More than he or Tim or even Emmi, Colton made the perfect suspect.

"But why? Why would he kill her?"

"The business. Game's On You."

"What? How does killing Anna Belle have anything to do with the company?"

It was all so obvious now. . . . How could he have not even thought about it before? "In the event that either of us dies or is incapacitated, the company reverts to the remaining partner. That incapacitation clause includes incarceration."

"Oh Grayson." She plopped down onto the love seat.

"And for whatever reason, he needs money, as apparent by those loan papers." He shook his head, remembering all the little remarks Colton had made over the last year or so about the price of things. He hadn't acquired any frivolous items like a yacht or anything over the last year. He hadn't even purchased a new car for two years, so what did he need the money for?

Pam interrupted his train of thought. "If he's getting a loan, then doesn't that say he didn't do anything in order to get control of the company? I mean, why get the loan if he planned to get the whole company? It doesn't make sense."

"I don't know, but what if he thought the police would arrest me immediately? He seemed surprised to see me actually show up here at the office Tuesday. And maybe that's why he asked you so many times if I was coming in. Maybe he thought I'd have been arrested as soon as I got back into town on Sunday night. Or maybe before then, because he probably thought I'd have been called as soon as Anna Belle died, but he didn't know I'd lose my phone."

"I tried to call you to tell you." Pam's voice held no more argument.

"And he called too. Remember my call log?" Grayson could see it all clearly now. "If he needs the money now and the police seem to be dragging their feet in arresting me and taking me out of the picture, that could be why the loan. Short term. Just until I was incarcerated so he could take total ownership of the company."

Colton had talked so many times about taking the company public, but Grayson had refused. When he'd come back from his last trip to Vegas, he'd started talking that up to Grayson immediately. He said he'd met a financial adviser at the blackjack tables who made the recommendation. Grayson hadn't taken the talk seriously, because who took advice from someone at a card table in Vegas?

"I just find it so hard to believe." Pam shook her head. "I'm not doubting anything you've told me—it's all logical and cohesive. It's just. . .wow. I mean, you two go back to, what, college or med school days?"

He nodded, remembering the first time he'd met Colton York. Grayson had been in his last year at LSU med school in Baton Rouge and had been introduced to Colton by a frat brother. Colton had finished med school the year before and passed his boards. He came back to campus to give an inspirational talk to the nearly burned-outs, and Grayson found him to be charismatic and engaging. They'd bonded over discussion of the best golf courses around, made a vow to play St. Andrews together one day, and became friends who actually kept in touch as the years passed. Colton never lost his ability to draw people in, one of his personality traits that made him extremely good at bringing in business.

"So what now?" Pam asked.

"I don't know." He closed his eyes against the flashes of lightning and sent up a silent prayer for wisdom.

Thunder rolled across the sky, rattling the windows in the office building.

"Should we call the police?"

"I want to be positive before I do that. If I'm wrong, I don't want him to have to answer to the police for something he didn't do." He shook his head. "I've been having to do that every day lately and wouldn't wish it on my worst enemy."

"So you're saying you want to confront him yourself? That might not be the best idea, Grayson."

Lightning flashed across her face, highlighting the concern and worry in her eyes.

"Not confront. I just want to ask him. I think he'll tell me the truth."

Pam snorted. "Are you serious? Do you hear yourself?"

"What?"

"Grayson, sometimes you can be a Pollyanna, wanting to see the best in people all the time." She shook her head. "If you're right and he did kill Anna Belle and set you up to be blamed, why on earth would you think he'd admit it to you? He'd be stupid to do that, and we've already established he's not stupid."

"I think he'd be honest with me." He might not want to admit it, but if Grayson stood right in front of him, looking him in the eye, Grayson figured Colton would 'fess up.

Pam shook her head and pulled out her cell phone. "I think you should at least talk to Brandon first."

Another boom of thunder rattled the building.

"He'll just tell me to let him and Danielle do their job. I'd prefer to talk to Colton myself and see what he has to say for himself."

"What I have to say for myself about what?"

Pam's eyes widened as she looked over Grayson's head. Grayson jumped to his feet and turned.

Colton stood in the doorway, dripping water into a puddle on the floor. "Say for myself about what?"

TWENTY-FIVE

"Man, it's not letting up at all." Danielle stated the obvious as she fell into step beside Brandon, making their way into the precinct.

Water rolled off Brandon's back, and his shoes squished against the worn floor of the hallway. "It's pretty miserable, that's for sure." They rounded the corner and headed to their work space.

The phone on Danielle's desk rang, causing her to rush to grab it. "Witz."

She wedged the phone between her chin and shoulder as she opened her drawer and pulled out an old T-shirt that she used to dab herself. "Uh-huh."

Brandon grabbed his old gym bag from under his desk and pulled out a towel. Thank goodness he hadn't been able to work out in a week or more so the towel was clean. He wiped as much of the rain off as he could.

"I'm impressed. Thanks." Danielle finally sat down but still wiped at her upper arms.

He took a seat as well, the towel now very damp.

"Of course. Just put him in whatever interrogation room is open when they get here and let me know. Thanks again." She hung up the phone and smiled across the desk at him.

"Good news apparently?" It was nice to see her smiling real smiles again. Funny that he hadn't realized until they talked that she'd been wearing stress and strain on her like a favorite sweater.

"Patrol picked up Big Al and are on their way with him to the station right now." She grinned wider. "How's that for good news?"

"That's great news. Fast too. You put out the call, what, fifteen minutes ago?"

"About that. Apparently he was already on the schedule to pick up in relation to an open narcotics investigation. Since our questioning is just to try and pull some information, we get him first before narcs."

Brandon leaned back in his chair. "And it's not even my birthday." He sat up straight. "I'm requesting a background on Colton York."

Danielle stood. "I'm going to update the commander. You know how he likes to be updated when we've got witnesses or suspects across department divisions." She grabbed the folder from her desk. "Be back in a jiffy."

Brandon nodded as she took off. He accessed the system, logged into one of several databases, and looked up Colton York.

Two parking tickets, paid in full. Three moving vehicle violations, all paid without traffic court appearances. Interesting that he didn't have a vehicle registered in his name—Brandon knew he had a car. Nothing really fancy, but a nice car. Might be in the business name though. More and more small-business owners seemed to be doing that lately.

He closed out that system, opened the next database, and typed in Colton's information. No record of any outstanding warrants or charges. No past convictions either.

Moving on to the next system, Brandon did a search on legal documents filed regarding Game's On You. Maybe there was something connected to the business. That might also include Grayson, although Brandon couldn't imagine Grayson Thibodeaux having a thing in common with Big Al. Well, except for knowing Colton York. It was worth looking into anyway.

He typed in the information and sent in the request.

"Hey." Danielle tapped him on the shoulder. "Come on, we've

got a date, and I don't think we should keep Big Al waiting."

Brandon stood, grabbing his notebook. He made sure his side-arm was locked in his desk drawer before following his partner down the hall to the hot box.

"You take lead, since you know Big Al," Danielle said outside interview room three.

He nodded and squared his shoulders. Brandon had served in vice for a couple of years before moving to homicide. During that stint, he'd had the opportunity to speak with Big Al on numerous occasions regarding his involvement in various prostitution rings. He'd always found the man to be cordial if not downright likable, considering their respective positions.

Brandon opened the door and walked into the room. "Hello, Big Al." He was never sure if the moniker had been given to him as a child, a parent hoping he'd grow up to be big in his field, or if it had been bestowed on him in adulthood as a joke. Alfonse Marcello stood maybe five feet nine or ten inches tall and weighed in at no more than a buck seventy-five, soaking wet. He was forty-nine years old but already had a growing, round bald spot in the back of his crown. What remained of his once dark hair was now peppered with harsh gray.

"Why, hello, Detective Gibbons. How nice to see you again." Big Al smiled as Brandon took a seat across the table from him. Danielle sat beside Brandon. "I don't believe I've had the pleasure of meeting this fellow detective." He nodded to her.

"This is my partner, Detective Witz."

Big Al zapped a wheelbarrow load of charm into one smile. "It's a pleasure to meet you, Detective Witz. How may I assist you two good detectives today?"

Danielle cut her eyes at Brandon, who swallowed his grin. Al could be the most pleasant of criminals, but then again, if rumors were true and he was part of the original Marcello crime family of

New Orleans, then the politeness and charm were ingrained.

Since Big Al was so focused on her, it would be better for her to start asking the questions in the interview. Brandon nudged his knee against hers under the table.

She got the point, being very congenial toward Big Al. "It's a pleasure to meet you as well. I believe my partner and I saw you not too long ago. Outside the Darkwater Inn."

He smiled, not saying anything.

Brandon could feel Danielle's frustration. He eased into taking over the questioning. "With the rain coming down so hard, I'm sure you understand why I didn't get out and say hello when I drove up to you."

"Oh. That was you?" Big Al's smile lost a fraction of its wattage. "I completely understand. This weather is just horrid. I do hope my cleaners can do something with my suit, because even with an umbrella, it got drenched." He brushed the fine material. "It's Armani of course."

"Of course." Brandon smiled. "What on earth would have you having a discussion under an umbrella in such weather?"

Big Al stopped smiling. "You aren't going to make me ask for my lawyer now are you?"

"Hey, we're just sitting here having a conversation about a conversation. I don't see anything wrong with that, do you?"

Big Al glanced at Danielle, then back to Brandon. He pushed his chair out from under the table and turned ever so slightly in his seat. He picked at his fingernails as he spoke. "I was merely stressing to an associate the importance of keeping one's word."

Brandon nodded. "Certainly people should keep their word." He studied Big Al. What was Colton's connection to him? Had to be something pretty big for Big Al to contact Colton directly. And, as he'd already pointed out, in this miserable weather. "Especially when money is involved, yes?"

"Most definitely." Big Al sized him up as well. "Debts can pile up quickly, you know."

"Oh, I do." Okay, Colton owed Big Al money. How much? Had to be enough to get Big Al out in an alley during a storm. "I can think of tens of thousands of reasons why."

Big Al raised a single eyebrow. "I could think of half a million reasons why it would be important."

Half a million dollars in debt to Big Al? What was Colton into?

Danielle shot him a quizzical look. He gave a slight shake of his head before staring back at Big Al. "That would buy an awful lot of medication."

Big Al kept his head down, his focus on cleaning his fingernails. "I wouldn't know."

Not drugs. What else could put him that much in debt? "Or make some of the NRA folks very happy."

"I wouldn't know." Big Al shook his head, still looking at his fingernails.

Okay, not drugs or weapons. Half a million dollars.

Big Al looked at Brandon. "But that's nothing but a drop in the bucket compared to what some of those professional athletes who play in big games every week are paid."

Ah. Gambling. Brandon gave a brief nod to Big Al. "I would've said hello to the man you were speaking with, Colton York, but the rain, you know."

"I'm sure Mr. York would've enjoyed speaking to you had it not been storming."

Confirmation. Brandon smiled. "I wonder if I would have time to speak to Colton sometime next week." He lifted his voice and his brows on the last word.

Big Al gave a slight shake of his head. "I would try closer to the end of this week. By this weekend at the latest, I would imagine."

"I see." Colton had to pay Big Al half a million dollars by the weekend. Wow. That was a lot of money to rack up in a gambling debt.

"You know what a nice, congenial sort I am, right, Detective Gibbons?"

"Of course, Big Al. It's one of the reasons I enjoy speaking with you."

"So you know that I sometimes give people a second chance. In rare cases, a third."

Extensions. Brandon nodded. "I've heard that. Very generous of you, Big Al."

"Oh, it is very generous indeed. Our mutual acquaintance, Mr. York?"

Brandon nodded.

"He's a rare case."

Big Al had extended Colton's half-million-dollar deadline three times. That was serious enough for him to be out in a storm, making sure Colton knew the deadline and understood the consequences.

"I see." What was Colton doing? Surely he understood Big Al wasn't one to mince words, but was one to have your face minced if you didn't pay.

Especially to the tune of a half million dollars.

Did Grayson know? What would happen if Colton was taken out?

The room's intercom buzzed. Ah, narcotics was ready to interrogate Big Al. Danielle pushed to her feet, and Brandon followed suit. He smiled at Big Al and extended his hand. "Thank you for talking with me, Big Al. As always, it's been enlightening."

Big Al shook his hand. "Perhaps, if the opportunity arises in the near future, you could speak to someone on my behalf?"

"I'll certainly see what I can do." He opened the door for his partner as they left.

"Okay," Danielle said as soon as they were in the hall, "I followed that Colton owes Big Al half a million dollars, and it's due this weekend."

"For a gambling debt, and his deadline has been extended three times. There's no way Big Al will let it go unanswered. If Colton doesn't have the money by this weekend, he's in serious trouble." While no evidence could be traced back to Big Al and his organization, a couple of homicides had taken place in the city's recent past, for which everyone in the precinct believed Big Al was responsible.

Danielle let out a low whistle as they made a straight line to their desks.

"Exactly." Why would Colton take such a chance? How did he even know Big Al? Brandon shook his head. Gamblers just knew. They usually started out with a local, small-time bookie. They'd win sometimes, usually just enough to pay off their debt, then get in for even more. When they lost, they'd have to go to another bookie to pay the first one. And the cycle would repeat until someone like Colton York ended up owing someone like Big Al Marcello a half million dollars. It was insane.

Brandon dropped into his seat and checked his email. The initial report he'd requested on Game's On You filed papers was there.

"I'm going to talk to Commander Ellender. He asked to be updated after we spoke with Big Al." She grabbed a sip of water from the bottle she kept on the edge of her desk. "I'm not sure how this connects to Anna Belle Thibodeaux's murder yet."

"This might be an answer." Brandon read from the attachment, his gut instinct going into overdrive. "I'm looking at parts of the partnership papers between Colton York and Grayson Thibodeaux that they signed and filed."

Danielle sat on the edge of her desk and took another swig of water.

"In the event that either owner dies or is incapacitated, the company and all of its assets automatically default to the remaining owner." This was it. Brandon's gut was rarely wrong when it wound tightly into a knot like it was right now.

Danielle pressed her lips together and shook her head. "I'm sorry. I'm not following what that has to do with anything. Was Anna Belle one of the owners?"

Brandon shook his head. "No, she wasn't, but if Grayson is convicted and sent to jail for her murder, that's considered incapacitated, and Game's On You and all of its assets would divert solely to Colton." He locked stares with Danielle. "And Colton needs at least half a million dollars to pay Big Al, not counting any other bookies he might owe."

"Is Game's On You worth half a million dollars?"

Brandon tapped the monitor. "According to this report, the business and its assets are valued at two point six million."

"You think Colton set this all up—killed Anna Belle and framed Grayson so his partner would go to jail and he'd get the company?"

He hadn't really thought it through, but. . . "Yeah. It could be. We know Colton and Tim took the deal to Grayson. Colton pushed Grayson to actually create the game, but he was the one who was on-site."

"The time's pushing it. I mean, it's Wednesday evening and he has to pay Big Al by this weekend."

Brandon nodded. "But as you said many times, that energy drink with the cherry juice could've been put in Anna Belle's room from the beginning. She drank at least one, sometimes two a day. It was just a matter of time before she got the one with the cherry juice. Could've been Wednesday when she got there or any time after." He shrugged. "And nobody could have known that Grayson would lose his cell phone. No way to call him back early to start the accusations and questioning."

Danielle shook her head. "And I played right into it, suspecting Grayson from the start and pulling every scrap of evidence to make it fit my scenario."

"Hey, natural tendency. And I don't know it's Colton, but. . ."

"Your gut instinct tells you it is, right?"

He grinned. "Yeah. I'd at least like to ask him some questions."

"Okay. Let me update the commander, and then we'll get in a little OT and go talk to Colton York." She set down her water bottle and grabbed her folder.

Brandon stared at his computer screen again.

Poor Grayson. If they were right, his partner and friend had not only stabbed him in the back in the worst way, but he was a murderer to boot. A murderer who owed a gangster a whole lot of money. That could make someone more than a little desperate.

Desperate people panicked and made bad choices worse.

TWENTY-SIX

"I didn't even hear you come in." Grayson stared at his partner, wondering if he knew the man in front of him. Had he ever known him?

"I came in the back. It's really messed up out there." Colton looked from Pam to Grayson, then checked his watch. "Sorry I'm late. The rain. Traffic was almost at a standstill."

Grayson nodded. "Yeah, it's really coming down out there. Electricity went out about twenty or so minutes ago." He needed to think. There was something different in Colton's eyes.

"I guess everybody else has already gone?"

"Yes. Pam was just leaving too." Grayson stared at his assistant. Hard.

She stood, a death grip on her cell phone.

"You don't have to leave on my account." Colton took off his jacket and laid it over the back of the chair in front of Grayson's desk.

"No, it's okay." She turned to Grayson. "I'm just going to make that call I was telling you about, then I'll head out."

Good. She'd call Brandon. While he'd been against it when she'd suggested it, something about Colton's demeanor right now. . . It was. . .off? Different? Somehow, he seemed threatening, which wasn't usually the case at all.

"Okay. I'll talk to you later." He nodded at her, hoping she'd leave the building and call Brandon from her car.

She started to leave, but Colton blocked her exit from Grayson's office. "You know what, maybe you should stay for our meeting.

Like take notes or something." His eyes were wilder than Grayson had ever seen.

He needed to think, and fast. Something was definitely wrong here. Grayson forced a laugh. "Pam take notes? Seriously?" He laughed again. "Since the weather's so bad and the power's out, why don't you and I just meet in the morning?" He caught Pam's expression—she was scared, and Pam Huron didn't scare easily. "Pam, go on and head on out. I'll talk to you later."

She took a step to move around Colton, but he sidestepped and blocked her path again. His grin at her reminded Grayson of the Cheshire cat.

It unnerved him and chilled him more than the dropping temperatures.

Pam put her hands on her hips and widened her stance. "Colton York, what's going on with you? Move out of my way."

Colton's sardonic smile spread even wider as he reached behind him and pulled the door to the office closed.

In that moment, Grayson knew he was right about his partner. About what he'd done to Anna Belle. About what he'd tried to do to Grayson himself. He took a step toward the two of them. "Colton, I think it's about time you and I had our meeting, don't you?"

Quicker than Grayson would have ever thought possible, Colton grabbed Pam and spun her around facing Grayson. He tugged her back against his chest and pressed a gun against Pam's head.

"Whoa!" Grayson held up his hands. "What are you doing?"

"I think you know." Colton pushed the gun against Pam's head. "Sit down. Now."

"Fine. Just put the gun down. Let Pam go. This has nothing to do with her." He stumbled backward until he sat on the love seat.

Colton laughed, the tone blending eerily with another rolling clap of thunder. "I don't think so, buddy. I think a lot of this has to do with Pammy here." He let her go and pushed her forward.

Grayson caught her before she fell over the ottoman. He steadied her until she got her balance, then helped her move over to sit on the other side of him on the love seat, keeping himself between her and Colton. "Have you lost your mind?"

"Lost my mind? Lost my mind?" Colton tapped his chin with his left hand. The one not holding the gun. "Hmm. Maybe I have." He laughed again. It came out much higher pitched than his natural laugh. He sat on the arm of the couch. "Maybe I have."

Grayson sat forward, blocking Colton's direct line to Pam. "Colton, talk to me. What's wrong with you?"

Colton's laugh died. He glared at Grayson. "What's wrong with me? What's wrong with me?" His voice shook. "*You're* what's wrong with me."

"Me? What did I do?" Just keep him talking. That was the only thing on Grayson's mind. Keep him talking and not shooting.

"What didn't you do? You, always with your perfect life. You had the perfect parents in the perfect house in the perfect part of town. You went to the right high school, were an athlete hero, got into the right college—on scholarship of course—and fast-tracked into the right frat house."

"You were in that same fraternity. That's how we met, remember?" Keep him talking.

"Oh, I remember. What you didn't know was that I had to scrimp and save to attend college. I had fourteen scholarships—fourteen, and all of them combined only paid for half of my tuition. Half. I had to work to pay the other half, and forget about living on campus—I had to live at home until I could move into the frat house."

Keep him talking. "But you graduated and excelled. Really surpassed many others in our med school."

"That's because I had to. I couldn't waste all that money." He shook his head. "That's not the point. I had to work to get what I got while you were able just to float on by in your little perfect world."

"My life was far from perfect, Colton. You know that."

"Really? 'Cause it looked pretty perfect. You graduated with honors, skated through med school, passed your boards without really having to cram like the rest of us. And then right out of the shute, you join a private practice with your buddy's and his father's head shop."

Keep him talking. "Those were a lot of long hours. I wasn't just the low man on that totem pole, but I was also the outsider, which meant I got all the nights and weekends on call. I got all the cases that had state insurance. I got all the hopeless cases that nobody else wanted."

Colton waved the gun in the air, tracing an invisible line up and down Grayson's torso. "Yeah, my heart's bleeding for you. I was out there trying to beat the odds to make enough money for my next meal, and you're out there making money listening to some rich brat whine about how Daddy doesn't spend enough time with him and just buys him new cars. Wah wah wah." Colton shook his head. "And you just walked away from that. Walked away from making all that money, while I was making my rounds with the local bookies."

"You know that's not what happened." The back of Grayson's neck went hot, much like it always did whenever the subject came up. He would never forget his involvement in the matter of the twelve-year-old boy who took his own life. It didn't matter that the boy hadn't been Grayson's own patient, that he'd only been filling in for his friend who was on his honeymoon. It only mattered that the young man had taken his own life the night after a therapy session with Grayson. The guilt nearly killed him then. The memory tightened around his heart right now.

"Whatever. A kid offed himself, and you felt guilty. You'd have gotten over it, but no, Saint Grayson had to take a stand and quit his job." Colton waved the gun toward Grayson's head. "That made Anna Belle furious, you know."

Grayson remembered all too well how angry Anna Belle had been. Furious was quite the understatement. She hadn't spoken to Grayson for days, and when she finally did, it was to tell him to go back to the practice and get his job back. She told him that losing patients was something he had to expect in the medical field and to think otherwise was just plain delusional. It was the first time in their marriage that he had refused her, and as a result, it changed the dynamics of their relationship forever.

"She knew, just like I know, that only someone who is used to their privilege can afford to throw away such opportunities." Colton nodded at Pam, cowering behind Grayson. "Come on, Pammy. Did you know that about golden boy here? I've read your file—you know what I'm talking about. You know what it's like to actually have to work for what you've got."

"Yeah, I do know, Colton. That's why I don't understand what you're doing. You've worked hard to build up Game's On You. Both you and Grayson. The company is doing well, and we've had a steady flow of business."

Colton waved the gun at her again. Grayson twisted to push her behind him. "Yeah, I've worked hard to build up the company. I'm the one out there drumming up business. I'm the one out there bringing us clients. Mr. Perfect here just does the design work."

Keep him talking. "Colton, we both work hard—that's why the business is successful."

He snorted. "You wouldn't even be here if it wasn't for me and Anna Belle. You'd still be working with the New Orleans Police Department." Colton wiped his forehead with the arm of his sleeve. "Isn't that a kick in the head? You worked for the people who are trying to lock you up. Although, maybe you were more vital to them than they'd realized since they seem to be taking forever to make the arrest."

Anna Belle had certainly hated his working for the police, had from the minute he'd told her. But under their new relationship dynamic, he listened to her concerns, then had to make his own decision. None were made lightly. He'd spent much time in prayer before leaving the practice, before going to work for the police, and before going into business with Colton.

"What happened, Colton? We've built this company from the ground up. We've—"

"No! I've built this company." Colton's eyes still had the newness of crazy shimmering in the flashes of lightning. "You had the perfect wife to attend to." He laughed that creepy laugh again. "But Mr. Perfect couldn't do that right, now could you? She went out and had an affair with a middle-class, wormy little fellow. Bet that made you feel really emasculated, huh? Her cheating on you with ole Timbo."

Grayson balled his hands into fists in his lap. He wouldn't rise up in anger, which is probably what Colton wanted. That Anna Belle had cheated on him had devastated him. It didn't matter who she'd cheated with, just that she'd cheated.

"Why are you doing this?" Pam asked.

"For money of course. You wouldn't understand, Grayson, but, Pammy, I would expect you to get it. You see, I haven't been quite as lucky as I might have made it seem. I've been losing. A lot. And now I owe some very insistent people a lot of money."

"Why, Colton?" Grayson shook his head. "If you had come to me, we could've worked something out."

Lightning flashed, highlighting the lunacy in Colton's eyes. "Come to you? Like a beggar needing a handout? Oh, no siree, Bob. No way. I don't need to ask your permission." He straightened, but the gun wobbled. "I had to take matters into my own hands. Take care of myself, just like always."

Keep him talking. "Why kill Anna Belle? Why not just kill me? Would've been easier, I'd think." Grayson never in a million years thought he'd be having such a conversation. Never with Colton. It was insanity.

"What would be the fun in that?" Colton let out that laugh of his again.

"Are you high?" Pam blurted out.

Colton narrowed his eyes, the smile disappearing. "No, Pammy, I'm not high. I'm stone-cold sober, as a matter of fact." He pointed the gun at her. "Here's something I've wanted to know for some time now. I know Saint Grayson here would never have cheated on his wife, even though she was cheating on him, but tell me, since that divorce came through, have you and ole Grayboy here been doing the nasty?"

"Don't be crude, Colton." Grayson shifted on the love seat, trying to push Pam farther behind him. Keep. Him. Talking. "So why kill Anna Belle and not me?"

Colton focused back on Grayson. "Because if you were killed, I could be a suspect. I mean, I'm your business partner, and since your divorce, I'd be the one to gain the most financially. I did consider it, gave it a lot of thought. I even fantasized about what it would feel like to stab you." He shrugged. "Or shoot you. Whatever. But in the end, I knew I'd have a tougher time getting away with it, and time's not really on my side right now."

The panicked look was back.

No, he had to distract him. Had to keep Colton talking about Anna Belle, him, anything but the gun in his hand. "It was pretty smart to lace her energy drink with cherry juice."

Colton smiled, the tension in his posture easing. "Oh, you have no idea the planning I put into this. You thought creating the game was intensive? That was nothing compared to what all I had to do."

"How's that?" Grayson made sure to keep his voice more conversational than confrontational.

"An old friend of mine is a bowling buddy of one of the board members at Deets. When I realized I was going to have to get my hands on the business, and decided the easiest and most efficient way would be to get rid of Anna Belle, then I needed to figure out a way to do it so you would be the natural suspect."

Grayson swallowed the bile burning the back of his throat as he nodded.

"I called up my old friend and asked him to put in a good word for me to the board. Then I made it a point to send flyers over to Deets. Sent one to every board member too, but not to their home. That would be too obvious. I sent them to places I knew they'd see them: their work, their dentist office because they happened to have an appointment the day I did—things like that." He smiled. "I am a sociologist, and a pretty good one. I knew the markers to throw out to get that call. I have to admit, though, I got worried when a week went by and nothing happened. I had to set up a loan as a backup plan, but then Tim finally called."

Oh, he *had* planned. He always touted Grayson as the master game creator. The attention to detail and planning he was showing could prove otherwise.

"Once they called, I knew I could sell them on the deal, and I did. Then I had to sell you." Colton's stare hit Grayson hard. "It was actually easier than I'd expected. For a minute, I thought maybe you would really help me out and kill her yourself. That would've been too easy though. Didn't you ever wonder how she found out about that hunting lease that caused her to come over and leave her five-finger signature on your cheek?" Colton laughed.

Cackled was actually a better description. "You can't imagine what a turn-on that was, man. She smacked the snot out of you in front of everyone. That couldn't have turned out better if I'd written the script myself." He paused. "Well, actually, it could've if you had hit her back. Talk about some great motive for the detectives to play with there."

Keep him talking. "So once you had me hooked and I created the game for you. . ."

"It was almost too easy. When those records came over, I about did handsprings. She had an abortion? Man, I knew right then and there that anybody who knew you would know that was primo motivation to kill her in a fit of rage. It was perfect. And her addiction to energy drinks? Her allergy to cherry juice? It was almost too easy."

"How did you get the cherry juice in her energy drinks without being seen on video?" Pam blurted out.

"Pammy, Pammy, Pammy. . .once I found out what brand she drank, I bought two and filled them half with cherry juice. I had switched my two out with two she had brought on Thursday morning during breakfast when I made a trip to the restroom. Deets people were in the dining room eating, and our crew was eating as well. I came in the control room to check on our crew, being the courteous boss of course, and turned off the camera. In minutes I made the switcheroo. The only glitch was she'd taken her purse to breakfast with her, so I would have to come back. No biggie because I knew I'd have plenty of opportunities. I came back to the control room to let the crew know what time to be finished and was able to just turn the camera on again. Simple. You think you're the only one who can manipulate a video file?"

It was actually more clever of Colton than Grayson would have initially given him credit for. "The ball marker?"

Colton grinned, and Grayson could catch a glimmer of his friend. Then the crazy returned to Colton's eyes. "Genius, right? I knew yours was here in the office, so I planted mine in Anna Belle's room when I switched the energy drinks. I intended to take yours as mine so yours would be missing, but then I realized they hadn't found it."

"How could you be sure Anna Belle wouldn't have seen it? She would have recognized it."

Colton shook his head but relaxed his hand holding the gun down onto the couch. "She would've recognized it as yours, not mine, which would have worked just as well in my favor, especially if she told anyone. But I didn't have to worry. As I'd figured, she never noticed." He frowned at Grayson. "That was some winner you were married to there, buddy. So self-centered that she didn't bother with anything that didn't affect her personally. You should probably thank me for putting everyone who knew her out of their misery." He snorted. "Maybe she should've paid better attention."

Keep him talking. Keep him talking. He remembered the call to Anna Belle's phone from the office. "Did you call Anna Belle on Tuesday afternoon?"

"Found out about that, did you?" Colton nodded. "I knew I needed to have some sort of paper trail that would lead back to you just before you left town, so I called her. Told her that I just wanted to tell her how sorry I was it didn't work out between you two. She tried to get off the phone really quick, but I needed the call to last more than a minute or two, so I told her that I thought you were dating someone."

Colton laughed as he let his gaze shoot between Grayson and Pam. "Guess who I led her to believe it was?" He waved the gun at Pam. "You, Pammy. Oh, her reaction was rich. She said if you wanted to play around with little girls, far be it from her to care." He laughed again. "But you could tell it bothered her. Bothered her but good. So I knew she still cared at least a little for you, Grayson. Which made this even better. If I played my cards right, she'd think you were responsible."

"So how did you know when she would drink one of the energy drinks you put in her room?"

"That's part of the beauty of my plan. I wouldn't know exactly, so I would genuinely be shocked when she had her allergic reaction. It would look good on video, and everyone would later tell the police how shocked I was and worried and how I went to the hospital to see how she was. I had a part to play, and I was going to play it." He crossed his legs at the ankles. "I will admit that I'd hoped she would've drank one of my drinks early that morning, but it worked out just as well as it did." He smiled at Grayson. "You losing your phone on Thursday morning was a godsend."

"What did you do with her EpiPens?" Grayson had to know. The police said the one was in her purse, untouched and untampered with. The one in her toiletry bag had been returned to her suitcase after Laure retrieved it from the house.

"So very simple. Remember those missing minutes on the video?" Colton shook his head. "I forgot to turn off the cameras before I went in there. I needed to just take the EpiPens out of her room. Just three to five minutes."

"Eighteen minutes are missing," Pam said.

Colton nodded and jabbed the gun in the air at her. "You are a smart one, Pammy. And when I realized I'd forgotten and would have to delete some of the footage, I knew that you, on behalf of Superboy here, or the police, would find time missing. I thought per-haps if I deleted more than I needed, it would look like something more was hidden, and I wouldn't be suspect, because if it'd been me, I would've known to just turn off the camera, duh." He laughed, the sardonic sound in cadence with the clap of thunder that shook the windows of the building.

Distract him from Pam. "How did you get the pen back in her purse and toiletry bag? Neither were missing, not from her makeup bag in her purse, nor in her toiletry case."

Colton tapped his skull. "I'm smart, remember? After the ambu-lance left and the Deets crew began to dissipate, I instructed our crew to break it down and leave. I knew there wasn't a camera in the room, so I just slipped the pen inside as we were all in and out of there before I left to go to the hospital."

He stared at Grayson, his eyes cold and cruel. "Want to know what's really insane? I had her Epi in my pocket while I called 911. While Tim performed CPR. All I had to do was take it out and inject it in her thigh."

Pam's hand went to his shoulder and squeezed.

"You can't imagine what having that power feels like. Knowing I could save her if I wanted to, or that I could do nothing and just let her die. It's such a rush. Exhilarating."

Sickening.

TWENTY-SEVEN

"Commander Ellender said we're good for overtime." Danielle stood at the corner of their desks.

Brandon nodded. "Guess what else I found out?" He tapped his pen against his Field Notes notebook.

She sat on the top of the filing cabinet. "What's that?"

"Guess who bought a gun last week?"

"Colton York?"

"You got it." He turned to read the notes he'd made. "He bought a Smith & Wesson HMR model 647, .17 caliber."

"Seventeen? You mean twenty-two?"

He shook his head. "No, a seventeen."

"I've never shot one."

"Me either, but from what the gun seller said and the information I pulled from our team, the thing with this caliber is that the bullet's trajectory is very flat. That's why it's so popular right now. It's easy to be accurate. However, its design also means that the second it encounters an obstacle, that flat trajectory goes haywire. So it's accurate, but it's also prone to deflect if you miss your target."

"And he just bought this last week?"

Brandon nodded. "Picked it up a week ago Monday."

"Like maybe he was planning to need a gun soon? Like in case some cherry juice didn't work?"

"Or he was caught being somewhere he wasn't supposed to be, doing something he wasn't supposed to be doing."

The phone on Danielle's desk rang. She leaned backward to grab it. "Witz."

Brandon pulled his search engine back up and stared at the Smith & Wesson. Sa-weet revolver. The only odd thing was this revolver had an internal locking device with a key receptacle above the thumb piece for the cylinder latch that Brandon considered could be a serious liability in the event that the gun was needed in a hurry.

"Yeah. I hear you." Danielle had stood and moved back to her desk, scribbling as she listened. "This is great. Yeah."

Brandon glanced back at the computer screen. Another nice thing about the Smith & Wesson was its price tag: easily less than a grand. Used or through one of the many gun brokers, five or six hundred.

"Thanks. Just what we needed." Danielle plopped the phone back in its cradle. "That was Kara."

"Oh?" Brandon automatically reached for his pen.

"They found the missing time from the video Game's On You took at the Esplanade Avenue house." She clicked on her computer keyboard.

"And?"

"I'll give you three guesses who it shows going into Anna Belle's room, then right back out, and the first two don't count."

Brandon snapped his fingers and pointed at his partner. "Colton York."

She nodded. "And here are the missing minutes now."

Brandon jumped up and went around to look over her shoulder.

Danielle pressed PLAY. The screen flickered, then Colton crept up the stairs. He looked over his shoulder toward the stairs he'd just come up, then walked past Anna Belle's door and stopped. He looked over his shoulder again to the stairs. Paused. Then unlocked her door, looked over his shoulder to the stairs, then down the hall, before ducking into her room and shutting the door.

The screen went dark, then popped back into action as Colton stuck his head out the door. The time stamp showed only three minutes and twenty-nine seconds had passed since he'd entered the room. Colton looked right, then left, and then he stepped out into the hallway, pulling Anna Belle's door closed behind him. He straightened, then made a straight line to the stairs. The video ended.

"Well, what do you think he was doing then?" Danielle spun in her chair to face Brandon.

Brandon took a seat on the edge of her desk. "Putting the laced energy drink in there?"

"Maybe. But let's look again. I think I noticed something." She turned back to the video and started it again.

When it got to the part where Colton stepped out of Anna Belle's room, just after he shut the door behind him but just before he turned to the stairs, Danielle paused the playback. She tapped the screen, frozen on Colton. "Look, he's got something in his pocket. It's pretty long, because the pocket's not lying flat like it should."

Brandon leaned forward. "Can you blow it up or something?"

"That's beyond my capabilities."

He squinted. "Can you forward it frame by frame?"

"That I think I can handle." She moved the arrow, and Colton moved in slow motion away from Anna Belle's door.

"There!" Brandon tapped the screen. "That's yellow."

"Please tell me that EpiPen lids are yellow." Danielle made a grimace.

"I don't know about all of them, but Anna Belle's are." He looked back at the screen. "So he went in there to remove her EpiPen."

"He could've put the bad energy drink in there at the same time. We don't know."

Brandon nodded, setting his jaw. "But we know what happened to the pen. And sometime after she died but before CSI got there, he put it back in her purse."

"Which was why it wasn't tampered with."

Brandon turned back to the video. "We still have the contents of her purse in evidence. And he's not wearing gloves."

"Do you think he might have left prints?"

"It's worth checking. Those pens would be good to grab and hold a print or two."

She lifted the phone and pressed buttons. "Hey, Kara? It's Danielle."

Brandon headed back to his desk. If only he could call Grayson and let him know they were making progress on clearing him and finding out the truth of what happened with Anna Belle. Everything seemed to be falling into place. If they could get Colton's prints on Anna Belle's EpiPen, then they'd be able to get a warrant. Maybe he'd left something around his house with the cherry juice. Sure, that might be wishful thinking, but overconfident criminals had made far worse mistakes before.

Danielle hung up the phone. "She just came on an hour or so ago and says right now, with the weather, it's slower than usual in the lab, so she'd get someone to go ahead to try and grab a print. If so, she'll run it against the ones we had on file for Colton. If it's a match, no matter what time, she'll text." She clapped her hands and rubbed them together, glancing up at the clock. "I wonder if Colton's had time to make it home. I love this part of the job."

Brandon chuckled. "Me too." He glanced at the clock as well. "With the weather, you know traffic is all kinds of messed up, so I bet he hasn't gotten home."

Danielle stood and paced. "I hate waiting."

"I couldn't tell." He laughed.

She playfully punched him. "Hey, I just wanted to thank you. For the other day. What you said about my whole sister thing."

"No problem."

She took on her serious look. "No, you were exceptionally kind, and I really appreciate it. And you."

He smiled and batted her hand. "That's what partners are for, right? That and getting each other coffee. Ahem."

She laughed. "Fine. I get your hint. But if it's old and burnt, don't blame me."

Once she'd left, he checked his email again, not sure why. He wasn't really waiting on anything, but he just had this sense of. . .expectation? Anticipation? Something. Maybe just excitement because they were getting close to wrapping up the case.

His desk phone rang. "Gibbons."

"Detective Gibbons, this is Nellie in dispatch. We just had the strangest call come in to 911. I can't make heads or tails of it, and we're trained to remain silent and listen in case the caller can't let someone know they're on the phone."

"Right." Brandon didn't know where this one was going.

"Well this call is confusing, but I was able to hear two men and one of them said your name."

"Mine? They said Brandon Gibbons?"

"No, sir. Detective Gibbons."

"What else did they say?"

"Like I said, it's hard to make out."

"Do you have the number they called from? Did you call it back?"

"It's a cell phone, and that's just it, sir, the line is still open."

"What?" Brandon caught sight of Danielle heading across the room toward him, carrying two cups. He motioned for her to hurry.

"Yes, sir. The call is still connected. Would you like me to patch it through? You won't be able to be heard if you speak, but you can hear the call."

"Yes, yes, yes! Patch it through."

"Okay, sir. It'll take me just a couple of minutes. Stay on the line."

Danielle set down the cups and held up her hand in question.

"Cell call came through 911 and can't talk to the dispatcher. Said my name, so 911 is patching it through here. We won't be able to be heard." He put the call on speaker just as the connection sounded.

Laughter sounded, but not happy laughter. Maniacal sounding. "So what do you think I should do with the golden boy here, Pammy?"

"Is that. . .Colton?" Danielle asked.

"I think you should let us go. I don't know what you hope to achieve here." Pam Huron's voice held a wide range of emotions, but Brandon had been trained well enough to recognize fear as the primary one in her words.

" *Let us go*? Are they being held somewhere?" Danielle's eyes were wide.

"I don't know. Listen."

"Let him go?" Colton's voice was nothing short of chilling. "I don't think so, Pammy. I have plans for you and Grayson both."

Brandon stood, opening the lockbox that held his gun. Danielle moved to her desk to do the same.

"What's your endgame, Colton?" Grayson's voice held a hint of fear, but more. . .loathing. "Kinda messes up your whole plan if you off me and Pam both. All your careful planning and plotting just goes out the window if you kill us."

"Where are they? Colton's? Grayson's? Game's On Us?" Danielle asked.

"I don't know. The call is on a cell. When Pam talks, it's loudest, so I'm going to guess her cell phone." Brandon holstered his gun, but his hand automatically stayed on its butt. "They could be anywhere."

"No, I have it all worked out. Figured it out on my drive over."

"Come on, tell us where you drove over to," Danielle spoke to the phone.

"Of course, I originally didn't plan for Pam, but it actually works better with her here."

Rustling sounded over the phone, like Pam had moved or put the phone farther out of view. Brandon knew he liked her.

"So what's your big plan?" Grayson asked.

"With the power out, you and Pam decided to wait out the weather here. I mean, you're comfortable, right?" Colton snickered.

Brandon couldn't help but envision them tied up and trapped somewhere.

"Anyway," Colton continued, "someone broke in to rob the place, not expecting you here. So naturally, they shoot you both dead."

Shoot. He had his gun with him!

"They robbed the place, trashed it good, and ran off. It's so beautiful because I'll get to file an insurance claim on the damage I do to my own building."

"Game's On You!" Danielle and Brandon said in unison.

Brandon lifted Danielle's cell and dialed for the main dispatch. "This is Detective Gibbons, and I have a 911 call patched through to my desk."

"Yes, sir. We're also monitoring."

"Good." He rattled off the address to Game's On You. "Send a patrol car to that address. Tell them not to use the lights or sirens. Warn them detectives are on the way."

"Yes, sir."

"Is there any way you can patch that 911 call into my cell phone?"

"Yes, sir. I just need the number to open the connection."

He rattled it off, and seconds later it rang. "Is it connected?"

"Give me just a moment, sir. And you'll still not be able to reply."

"That's fine." He hung up Danielle's phone and nodded at his partner. "Let's go."

She grabbed the keys off the desk and led the way down the hall. They hustled to the car, being pelted on all sides by driving rain and sideline winds. Danielle slid behind the steering wheel while Brandon got in the passenger's seat. He set the phone on the console as he reached for a stack of napkins from their stash. They got off as much water as they could while they listened to the crackle of the connection come through over the speaker of his cell. Danielle started the car and flipped the defroster on high.

Colton's laugh filled the cabin of the police car. "I know how much you treasure all the golf memorabilia, so I'll take it to my office. I'll think of you every time I use it."

Brandon slapped the dashboard. "Let's go."

"Well, I appreciate that." Grayson's voice wasn't as strong as before. "You don't have to do this, you know."

Danielle whipped the car out of the precinct's lot. Water sluiced up the sides of the cruiser. Flooding was already starting. Headlights and brake lights inched along the street. She turned on the car's lights and siren. "At least until we get closer. We've got to get through all this traffic."

Over the speaker, Grayson's voice rose above the siren's wails. "I see you've thought of everything."

Danielle's cell phone buzzed. She tossed it to Colton. "It's from Kara." He read the text aloud: "Prints recovered on pen. Ran against sample as requested. Match."

"Proof it's Colton!" Danielle's voice rose in excitement.

"Of course I've thought of everything." Colton's voice vibrated Brandon's cell. "You always did think you were the smarter one, but you were wrong. So wrong. I've always been smarter. I let you think you were so you'd do most of the work on the games."

"Gambling is an addiction, Colton. Even after you kill us and get control of the company's assets, it won't be enough because you'll just keep gambling and getting back in debt again. It's a cycle that won't be broken unless, and until, you do something to break it." Grayson's tone sounded firm.

Two cars were stalled on the side of the road. Danielle groaned as she had to maneuver almost into a full ditch to get around them.

A black-and-white waved her through, easing her back onto the road so she wouldn't get stuck.

"Are you going to go all psychological on me now, Grayson?" Colton laughed again. "Oh, please do. This is rich. I can't wait to hear your spiel."

"Okay, here's my analysis. Right now you've reached what is referred to as the final stage of gambling addiction, the desperation stage. You have debts mounting up, your health is showing signs that the stress is eating away at you—you've lost, what, a good twenty or so pounds in the last several months? I'm betting you're suffering from insomnia as well. Your relationships have deteriorated, and I can attest to that. You have no friends anymore, and you can't even talk to your coworkers and employees anymore. Your financial problems have reached critical proportions. I bet you've even gotten a foreclosure notice, because I bet you've taken out a second, possibly a third mortgage to cover previous debts."

"Textbook psycho talk, but please do go on. You're nothing if not entertaining with your own self-inflating ego."

Danielle swerved to miss a car that skidded through a stop sign. The phone shot to the floorboards. Brandon bent to pick it up. Danielle had to brake suddenly to get into the other lane. Brandon's head collided with the dash. "Sorry," she said.

"It's okay." Brandon put the phone back on the console as Grayson's voice continued.

"It's obvious you've reached the end of the line. You feel hopeless, powerless, depressed, filled with guilt, shame, and remorse."

Colton laughed again. "Powerless? Who's the one holding the gun and the power right now, huh?" He snorted. "I'm not depressed. As a matter of fact, I'm happier now than I've been for quite some time. And as for feeling guilty or shameful? Are you kidding me?"

"But the problem gambler, you, in this desperation stage needs to do anything to escape the intolerable reality your life has become."

Grayson's voice grew louder and firmer as he continued. "Some problem gamblers leave their family at this point, preferring to run away rather than face what they've done. Others attempt suicide. Still others make the decision to finally get help."

Colton snickered. "Now you can shut up, buddy. I'm tired of listening to you drone on."

Brandon lifted the mic to the police radio and requested an ambulance be sent to Game's On You. "Better safe than sorry," he told Danielle.

"But Colton, you have to—" Grayson started.

Colton's voice cut him off. "Pammy, what do you think—what are you doing? Are you recording? Are you on a call? Let me see." His voice went deeper. "Show me! Turn that phone over."

Rustling sounded, muffled grunts and groans.

"Nine-one-one? You've been on the phone with them for eleven minutes? They record every call!" The desperation and rage in Colton's voice made the hairs on the back of Brandon's neck stand up and take attention.

Pam's scream and Grayson's frantic *"No!"* sounded simultaneously, just as a gunshot rang over the phone.

The connection went dead.

TWENTY-EIGHT

"Stop!" Grayson jumped to his feet.

Pam's cellphone lay dead on the floor, and the bullet Colton had shot it with was embedded into the back of the love seat they sat on. Pam curled up on the love seat behind Grayson.

Lightning flashed across Colton's face. Rage lined every feature.

Colton pointed the gun at Grayson. "You have no idea how long I've been waiting to shoot you. Every time you beat me on the golf course, every time you went on one of your vacations, every time you made a condescending comment, I wanted to shoot you in the face."

Keep him talking. Distract him. The police were on the way—Grayson just had to keep Colton from shooting them for a few more minutes, at most. "There is a fourth stage in gambling addiction, Colton. It's known as the hopeless stage. In the hopeless stage, suicide is often the only option the problem gambler sees at this point."

"Suicide?" Colton shook his head. "Do I look suicidal to you? I think you're delusional, buddy. I'm the one holding a gun on you, not on myself."

Boom!

Pam flinched at the thunder.

"But after you kill us, you pay off your debts, you lose the company, then what? You'll have nothing. No source of income because you know you won't be able to hold down a job working for someone else. With no money and the need, oh, that desperate *have-to* desire to bet on something, anything, will demand you gamble. And then what? No money. Nobody to get money from. Not able to gamble. You'll hit the hopeless stage in no time."

"Shut up." Colton's eyes were as lifeless as glass staring back at him. "You just shut up. I'm not hopeless. That's just psychobabble crap."

"Is it, Colton?" Grayson took a step toward him, just a little, barely noticeable step. "I think deep down in places of your heart you don't want to even acknowledge you know you have an addiction. You and I both know that addictions are signs of weakness."

Another boom of thunder shook the building.

"I am not weak!" Colton's hand wobbled as he pointed the gun at Grayson's head. "Not that I'm a gambling addict, but if I were, addiction is a disease, not a weakness."

Keep him talking. Grayson forced a laugh. "Seriously? Let's just compare addiction with true diseases, why don't we? With addiction, there's no infectious agent, no pathological biological process, nor a biologically degenerative condition. The only *disease-like* part of addiction is that if people don't seek help with it, their lives will get worse."

"Shut up!"

But Grayson had to keep Colton talking, even to the point of making him angry. Anything to give the police time to get there. "It's been proven that addictive acts occur when precipitated by emotionally significant events. All addictions can be prevented if we understand what makes these events so emotionally important. The start of addiction can be stopped if that desire can be replaced by other emotionally meaningful actions. It's been proven that addictive behavior is a symptom but not a disease."

"I said, shut up already!"

Colton wasn't laughing anymore, but the crazy haze once again clouded his eyes.

Lightning strobed the room.

"But that's good news, because unlike many diseases, addiction can be cured." Grayson took another baby step toward Colton. "You can be cured. Let me help you."

Rage took over the crazy in Colton. "Help me? Help me? You? Help *me*?" He pointed the gun right at Grayson's head. "Sit down. Now. Or I pull this trigger." He moved the gun's trajectory to Pam.

Grayson dropped back onto the love seat, almost on top of Pam, but he shielded her from Colton. He'd pushed his partner too far.

"I don't need to be cured from anything. I just need to do what I need to do and move on. And since Pammy's little phone call, I don't have as much time nor can I carry out my original plan." He pointed the gun back at Grayson. "So you see, now I have to change my plans. You know how disruptive that is, right? How frustrating it is to have your beautifully detailed plan derailed by someone else's inability to do as they're told."

Grayson lifted his chin. "Like you're doing to me?"

"Oh, still so smug, aren't you, golden boy? We'll see how smug you are when you're lying dead and cold on the floor." He lifted the gun.

Grayson closed his eyes and silently prayed.

"How smug will you be, Colton, when the police come and arrest you?" Pam's voice trembled, but she kept going, moving out from behind Grayson. "When they put you on death row for three murders, if they don't just kill you, you'll be in a cell all by yourself. No one to bully. No one to listen to your rants. No one to care. Who would even come visit you, Colton?"

"Aren't you the sassy one now, Pammy?"

How long would it take the police to get there? The weather would delay traffic, understandably, but this was ridiculous. "She's got a point, Colton." Grayson admired his assistant for standing up, but right now he knew Colton was at that unstable point that made him capable of anything. "Think about this. What kind of legacy are you going to leave? What will people think of when they hear your name?" Play to the ego.

"What do you mean?"

"Most people have children to carry on their name. You, Pam, and I don't have that." Put them in the same category. Make Colton relate to them personally again. "So our reputations will be all that remains from us. What are we leaving behind that people will remember us by?"

"I'm not dying here. You two are." Colton's eyes narrowed.

Another boom of thunder sounded.

"But you'll be in jail. No way will you walk away from this free and clear. You have to know that."

"Yes I will." Colton's words were as hard as his stare. "And I'm tired of dragging it out." He waved the gun at Grayson. "Come on, get up."

Grayson struggled back to his feet. "You don't have to do this."

"Yes I do. You made this much harder than it had to be." Colton motioned to Pam. "You too, Pammy."

She stood, visibly trembling.

Colton must have noticed that too. "Sorry you got caught up in this. You shouldn't have stayed late with him. If you'd gone with all the rest, you would just have to deal with losing your boss in the morning. Now, well. . ."

Was that remorse creeping into his voice? Grayson took a step away from Pam, drawing Colton's attention.

Quick bursts of lightning sizzled across the sky, a rolling boom of thunder almost on top of it echoing in the night.

"Look, if you take off now, leave, you'll save yourself two more murders being on you. With just Anna Belle's, you might not get the death sentence. You could have hope of actually getting out of prison before you die." Grayson took another step away from Pam. "You could just run. I have some cash in my safe here. I'll give it to you." He took another step away.

"It's too late for that. The police will be here soon."

"Then go. Take the cash and run. Get away. Go where they'll never find you. Start over somewhere. You're a great sociologist, remember? You can do it."

"Stop psyching me, Grayson."

"I'm not. You can get away."

A clap of thunder vibrated the windows.

Colton pointed the gun at Pam. "Time's up, Pammy." He leveled the gun at her. Closed one eye and tilted his head slightly.

Boom!

As fast as the lightning streaked, Grayson shoved Pam to the floor. It felt like a fist hit his chest, spinning him to the left. His left bicep burned immediately as he fell onto the love seat. He struggled to catch the breath that had been knocked out of him.

Pop! Pop! Pop!

"Grayson!" Pam's scream pierced the storm that suddenly sounded louder than before. She knelt beside him. "Oh my gosh. You're shot!"

He glanced at his left arm. Sure enough, blood oozed across his shirt sleeve. Grayson felt dizzy, off-kilter.

Brandon was beside them, pressing his jacket, somebody's jacket, into Grayson's arm where he'd been shot. "An ambulance is already on the way. Just be still. Hang on." To Pam, he gave orders. "Keep this tight against the wound. We radioed for an ambulance."

"Brandon?" How did Brandon get inside the office? He struggled to sit up, braced against the love seat.

Brandon gently pushed him into place. "It's okay. You and Pam are safe. Danielle shot Colton."

"Good." Pam helped hold the jacket on his arm, applying enough pressure that it started to sting.

"He's not dead." Brandon offered.

"Better." Grayson tried to smile at Brandon, but his chest hurt. He winced and let out a little whimper. If he was shot in the arm, why did his chest hurt like blue blazes?

"You jerk, had to be the hero, didn't you?" Pam had tears in her eyes.

"What, exactly, happened?" Brandon asked Pam. "Nine-one-one had patched the call through to my cell so we could keep up with what was going on, but in the last minutes, all we heard was a gunshot and your scream."

"Colton was going to shoot me, pointed the gun at me and pulled the trigger. I thought I was done for." Pam cut her tear-filled eyes to Grayson. "But when the gun went off—and let me tell you, it sounded like a cannon—anyway, when it went off, Grayson pushed me out of the way. I fell to the ground, but somehow or another, he got shot in the arm."

"My. Chest." He might've been shot in the arm, but his chest hurt worse. Grayson reached to place his hand over the area that hurt, his pocket area. A long, narrow rip was there, but in the bottom of the pocket sat the necklace of Anna Belle's that Monique had given him. He gave a shaky smile as he pulled it out.

It had a bullet-sized indentation in it, but it wasn't a hole.

"What's that?" Pam asked.

"The bullet must have hit that and deflected into your arm. That's probably why your chest stings like the dickens." Brandon turned to speak with Danielle.

"What is it?" Pam asked again.

"It's a Saint Jude medallion. Monique gave it to me this afternoon."

"Saint Jude?"

"The patron saint of hope and impossible causes." He smiled as he ran his thumb over the stainless steel. "It's Anna Belle's."

In her own, crazy, do-it-her-own-way manner, Anna Belle had just saved his life.

TWENTY-NINE

"He was lucky." Dr. Shannon spoke in soothing tones to Brandon and Danielle in the hall of the University Medical Center New Orleans. "As you suspected, Detective, the bullet hit him in the upper left quadrant of his torso. The stainless steel medallion he had in his pocket deflected the bullet, and it tore through his left bicep, exiting straight through." She shook her head. "If the bullet hadn't been deflected, it would've hit his heart and most likely killed him."

Brandon nodded. Grayson had been right—Anna Belle had saved his life in a way.

"Thank you, Doctor," Danielle said.

"He'll need rest. We have him on antibiotics, just to make sure the wound doesn't get infected. If he does well tonight, he should be able to be released tomorrow. Midmorning or so."

"Will he suffer any permanent damage to his arm?" Brandon asked.

"I don't anticipate any." She gripped the chart to her chest. "He might feel stiffness when there's a storm like the one we had earlier tonight hits, and if he's left handed, he won't be pitching in the majors, but he should have full range of motion. I don't even expect him to need any physical therapy."

"Thank you. Is it okay for us to see him now?"

The doctor nodded. "His friend is still in there with him, but she should probably go home to clean up and get some rest. A lot of rest. She looks like she needs it pretty badly."

"It's been a long evening for them. I'll see if we can get her sent home."

"That would be great, and you don't stay too long either. He needs his rest too. I've signed off on giving him some mild pain medication to help him sleep tonight and have instructed the night nurse to encourage him to agree to take it." The doctor turned and strode toward the nurses' station.

Brandon looked at his partner. "So, I'm thinking it's probably best if I, instead of you, ask Pam to go home." The last time the two of them had interacted, it was clear they weren't fans of each other.

Danielle smirked. "Well, I did just shoot Colton, so that might've bought me a few good points, but yeah, you go ahead and ask." She shrugged but continued to grin. "Just know I'm willing to force her to go if need be."

"I have no doubts." He laughed, hoping she was only kidding, then sobered as he rapped on the hospital door room with his knuckles before walking in. "Grayson?" He did a gut check when he saw his friend lying in the bed, a big bandage around his left arm and an IV dripping into his right hand. Grayson looked almost as pale as the white sheets he laid on.

"Hey, Brandon." Grayson looked at Brandon's partner. "Danielle."

Brandon nodded at Pam, not quite ready to see Grayson looking so unusually pale. Then again, considering what he'd been through, maybe he didn't look quite so bad after all. "How're you feeling?" he asked.

"Like I've been shot." Grayson tried to laugh but winced and grabbed his chest.

Pam shook her head and thumped Grayson's uninjured arm. "Millions of people out of work in the United States, and you want to be a comedian on top of everything else."

Brandon looked at Pam, really looked at her. Dr. Shannon was right—the young woman definitely needed to clean up and get some rest. She had dark circles spreading under her eyes. Her normally shiny hair had become clumpy in the weather and laid limp on her shoulders. "Pam, I'm supposed to tell you, straight from the doctor, that you need to go home and get some rest. We're even postponing taking your statement until tomorrow."

Pam opened her mouth, to protest, he was sure, but Grayson interrupted. "See, I told you. Go. Home. Take a shower, get some sleep, and eat something already."

"I'm fine." But she looked anything but.

"You definitely need a shower," Grayson said. "I know I would give my left arm—pun intended—to be able to take a hot shower right now."

"There's that attempt at humor again," Pam said.

"I don't think going home was a suggestion," Brandon said. "Not from the doctor anyway. I'm officially here to kick you out until tomorrow."

"You can't make me—"

Danielle straightened beside him. "Yes, we can. It's doctor's orders that Grayson gets rest so that he can heal. The patient needs sleep, which means you have to go."

"Like you care what Grayson needs?" Fire blazed in Pam's eyes as she stared down Danielle.

Thankfully, his partner didn't become confrontational in the moment. She actually softened her voice, although her tone was just as firm. "We have to take Grayson's statement. We'll have to take yours as well, but we can't take them together." Danielle crossed her arms over her chest and shifted her weight from one foot to the other. "If you'd rather give your statement now, I'm happy to take it. We can go to the waiting room or cafeteria right now. Your choice."

"Or," Brandon interjected, "we can take it tomorrow morning

after you've rested and eaten and feel a little better. You can come into the station, say about nine, and give your statement." He softened his tone. "I'll even buy you one of the nastiest cups of coffee you'll ever taste."

Danielle snickered. "Only if he makes it." She winked at Pam. "He makes the most horrible coffee."

Pam stood, her gaze darting between Brandon and Danielle, as if she was not only confused by Danielle's obvious attempt at camaraderie but also torn as to whether she should leave Grayson alone with them.

Grayson solved the dilemma. "I'm fine. Go. I'm going to tell them what they need to know, then I'm going to buzz a nurse to kick them out, give me that pain medicine that Dr. Shannon was kind enough to order, and get some shut-eye."

"Okay. But I'll see you in the morning. I can come before I go to the police station."

"Don't you dare wake me up that early." Grayson winked at her. "I need my beauty rest, you know."

She nodded, hesitated, then bent down and planted a peck on his forehead. "But I'm leaving my phone number with the nurses' station in case you need anything and instructing the nurses to call if there's any change whatsoever with your condition." She looked at Brandon. "I'll see you at nine."

Grayson chuckled, then groaned and pushed his hand against his chest after she left. "Just wait until she remembers she can't give her number to the nurses because her phone got shot." He winced. "It's been a bad week for cell phones for Pam and me. Must be some kind of record."

"Yeah." Brandon sat in the chair Pam had just left, pushing it a little farther from the bed. "We can wait to take your statement tomorrow too."

"I'm fine. Really." Grayson let out a slow breath as Danielle pulled up the chair from the corner. "I owe both of you a big thanks for saving my skin tonight. We both would've been burnt toast if you hadn't shown up when you did. Talk about perfect timing."

Brandon shook his head. "Perfect timing? We were about five minutes later than we should have been because of the storm." He nodded at his partner. "It's amazing we made it at all, what with this one driving like a crazy woman."

She rolled her eyes at Grayson. "Don't listen to him. He knows not what he's talking about. I drove better than he could have."

"Speaking of crazy, how's Colton?"

"The doctor says his surgery went fine and he'll be able to walk," Danielle told him. "The bullets hit him in the knee, shattering the kneecap. They did a replacement and repaired most of the damage, but he'll always walk with a limp."

"Heard you'll be okay but not eligible for pitching." Brandon nodded at his arm. "Does this mean you won't have to give me strokes the next time we play golf?"

"Not hardly." Grayson looked at Danielle. "Thank you. All kidding aside, I'm very grateful to you."

"It's my job." But the tips of her ears reddened.

"You could've hesitated, but you didn't. Your quick thinking and reaction saved two lives tonight, and I will forever be grateful to you."

"You're welcome." Her voice wobbled, and Brandon recognized the emotional lump she tried to swallow down.

They stared at each other for a moment, Grayson and Danielle, before he looked over at Brandon. "Now, what do you need to know?"

On to business. Brandon pulled out his Field Notes notebook and flipped to the next blank page. "We heard a lot on the call. Pretty clever of Pam to dial in to 911."

Grayson nodded. "I didn't even know she'd done it. She's pretty clever."

"What tipped you off that it was Colton?" Danielle asked.

"Loan papers he tried to trick me into signing by making me believe they were our insurance policy renewal forms. From there, it was the St. Andrews ball marker that—"

"A what?" Brandon asked.

"Colton and I went to play St. Andrews golf course in Scotland together a couple of years ago. We bought matching ball marker tools with magnetic ball markers. I found one stuck to the lamp in Anna Belle's room at the rental house. I wondered at first if it was mine and she took it for sentimental reasons." Grayson paused. "I was obviously wrong."

Brandon ached for what still had to be hurting his friend.

Grayson let out a breath. "Anyway, when I got back to the office, I realized that my marker was still there but Colton's was missing."

"You found a clue and didn't tell us?" Danielle asked.

"Yeah. About that. I'm sorry."

Brandon nodded. "So between the loan and the ball marker, you figured it out?"

"That and knowing that Colton was a gambler. I mean, we all knew he liked to go to Vegas, and he always bet on every game. I didn't realize how bad he'd gotten. I didn't realize it was an addiction until now. But when I started piecing everything together. . . He was the one who got the Deets contract but had been so adamant that I create the game, despite mine and Anna Belle's relationship. . . . All the little things started falling into place, I guess."

Brandon nodded. Much like they had for him and Danielle as the evidence came in. "I have to admit, it seems a little strange that you'd confront him with Pam there and all."

"Oh, I tried to get her to leave, but as you just saw, she kind of has a mind of her own." Grayson shook his head. "When Colton showed up, I think both of us realized something was off with him. Something bad. She tried to leave, but he wouldn't let her. That's when he pulled the gun."

Grayson shifted in the bed, then frowned and readjusted. "I don't mind telling you, that was one of the scariest moments in my life, to look down the barrel of a gun and know the person holding it had totally taken leave of his senses."

"Is that your professional opinion?" Danielle winked.

Grayson grinned back. "Yep." He sobered. "Addicts are a little crazy. They're desperate, and the worse off they are, the crazier they become. They'll let nothing stand in the way of feeding their addiction, whether that's alcohol or drugs or, like in this case, gambling. Colton wouldn't let reason and logic stop him. All that mattered was getting the high from gambling. He needed money to pay off prior gambling debts, not because that's what is logical but because that would allow him more credit so he could gamble again. It's never about the debts or consequences, only about being able to feed the high."

"He was running out of time too." Brandon remembered the seriousness of Big Al's threats. "His desperation would have been at an all-time high."

Grayson nodded. "Which would have forced him not to wait for the loan or for me to be arrested, despite his best efforts. He needed to get enough to pay that debt so he could gamble again. He probably already had a reservation to Vegas made."

Brandon shook his head. "We'll check. That's just crazy."

"That's addiction. It's all-consuming, and as you know all too well, life threatening."

"Once he had the gun on you, then what?" Danielle asked.

"I tried to reason with him. That's when I knew he was an addict. There was no chance in that. So I did the only thing I could think of—I kept him talking. There was always the chance I could play on his emotions and get him to let us go, although very unlikely. But really, the only thing I was trying to do was buy us more time. I figured if I could wear him down enough, maybe I could tackle him, take him down."

"Play the hero?" Brandon asked.

"Yeah. Don't we all want to play the hero?"

"I think you succeeded in that tonight." Danielle's smile was genuine.

THIRTY

"I didn't expect him to plead guilty to first-degree murder." Brandon tucked his notebook into his pocket. "Now that you've completed giving your statement, I can tell you that."

Grayson stared at Brandon. "I'm not real sure what that means."

"It means that there won't be a trial, you and Pam won't have to testify, and the judge has set the date for the sentencing." Brandon pushed his chair closer to Grayson's hospital bed. "That means you should have no problem with filing the paperwork to enforce the partnership agreement and take full control of Game's On You and all its assets."

"That is a relief." Grayson leaned back against the hospital bed's pillows. "I have to make a couple of new hires. Any suggestions?"

"To be the other team leader?"

Grayson shook his head. "No, I've decided to promote Keely Masterson, Colton's assistant, to be team captain on that side, and I promoted Pam to take over my team."

"What are you going to do then?"

Grayson rubbed his still-bandaged arm. "Create games and work on my golf game."

Brandon laughed. "I've seen you play. You need the practice."

"At least now I'll have an excuse." Grayson rubbed his shoulder. "I was shot, you know."

"Oh, you're gonna milk that one forever, aren't you?"

"You bet I am." Grayson stopped smiling as he considered the word he'd just used. He swallowed. "What does that mean for Colton?"

"It means he'll spend the rest of his life behind bars."

"Parole?"

Brandon shook his head. "Not likely."

On one hand, Grayson was glad that the person who took Anna Belle's life was going to pay for the heinous crime. On the other hand, it was Colton, so Grayson was torn in his emotions. He understood the parameters of what addiction did to someone, the way it robbed the person of the ability to care about right from wrong. Colton knew what he was doing was wrong, but he'd justified every action. . .in his mind.

That didn't make it right to kill an innocent person.

Grayson swallowed again. Anna Belle was by no means innocent, but that didn't mean someone else had the right to end her life.

Complicated thoughts.

"I thought Pam would be here. We finished taking her statement before I headed over here."

"She came by, but I sent her to the office. Someone needed to tell everyone what was going on with Colton and assure them everyone still had their jobs."

"Yeah. That would be a fear."

Grayson nodded. "Pam told me she and the rest of my team had been worried when I was the only suspect for killing Anna Belle."

"Hey, you weren't the only suspect. I never believed you capable of killing anyone, let alone Anna Belle."

Grayson held out his fist, and they did a fist bump.

Brandon straightened. "Anyway, about hiring. . . You pay decent?"

Grayson laughed. "I don't think you're suited. You'd be bored."

Brandon snorted. "Not me. I'm trying to think of someone. I know one of the dispatchers is looking for something with less stress. She's had a kid and is looking for something that isn't as emotionally draining." He stopped grinning. "On second thought, I've seen how intense your planning is."

Grayson nodded. "In all seriousness, it is pretty intensive, but it's usually all in fun and everyone leaves together with a new, positive bond."

"I have to say, I was surprised at how much detail and planning goes into one of those things. Every turn seemed like a big mind meld type of thing."

"It is." Grayson gave a little half smile. "I'll share a little secret with you. About the time my tires were slashed, I actually wondered if I was in a game."

"What?"

"Yeah. I mean, if I were creating a game for me, and I really wanted it to rock my reality, I'd have orchestrated it like this. Ex-wife dies in something I created. All the circumstantial evidence seems to point to me, not enough to actually arrest me, but building up that I believed I would be arrested. Learning what Anna Belle did would definitely be a trigger for me. Throw in the added stress of someone vandalizing my house and vehicle. . .well. . ."

Brandon nodded. "I see what you mean, after knowing what exactly it is your company does. That would be really messed up though, man, for your partner to have orchestrated all that against you."

"More messed up than him killing Anna Belle for real and trying to set me up for it?" Grayson raised his eyebrows.

"Well, no. Point taken."

A silence filled the space of the hospital room. Not awkward, just. . .silence.

"Speaking of. . ." Grayson had a thought this morning. He hadn't mentioned it to Pam yet because he was pretty sure that he already knew her reaction. He trusted Brandon's gut instincts. After all, his friend had been the one person on the force who had fought to prove him innocent. "I want to ask your opinion about something."

"Sure, lay it on me."

"I'm thinking of offering one of the positions to Laure."

Brandon sat up straight in the chair. "Comeau? As in the woman who slit your tires and egged your house?"

Grayson nodded. Brandon's initial reaction was exactly why he hadn't mentioned his idea to Pam. "Hear me out. She's very loyal and dedicated."

"I'll say."

"She seems like a hard worker."

"She's creative, I'll give her that."

That's what Grayson thought. "I think given the right outlet for that creativity, she'd be a real asset to the company."

Brandon slowly nodded. "Yeah. I can see that."

"Well, if I can sell *you* on the idea. . ."

"Who do you need to sell the idea to?"

Grayson widened his eyes. "Pam."

Brandon let out a roar of laughter. "Yeah, good luck with that one, my friend."

"Excuse me, am I interrupting?" Monique stepped into the hospital room.

"Of course not." Grayson waved her over. "What are you doing here? I thought you were supposed to head back to Breaux Bridge this morning."

"Well, once the fine New Orleans police detectives called me to tell me about Colton's arrest and guilty plea, and about what happened to you. . .well, I couldn't leave without checking in on you."

Brandon stood and held out the chair for Monique. "I was just about to leave, Mrs. Fredericks. I'll leave you two." He gave Grayson another fist bump. "I promised Danielle I'd get your statement and get back so we could close the case. I think she's ready to wash her hands of you."

"Yeah, tell her I said hello. And I mean that sincerely."

"I know, and I will." Brandon nodded at Monique, who had taken the seat, then headed out of the hospital room.

"Now, tell me the truth—are you okay?" Monique asked Grayson.

"Yes, ma'am. The bullet went straight through my arm without hitting anything major. I should actually be released after the doctor makes her rounds this morning."

"When Detective Gibbons told me that you'd been shot. . . Mercy, Grayson, I was so worried about you." She reached and grabbed his hand.

He gently squeezed her hand. "I'm okay. Really."

Her dimming eyes filled with moisture. "Well, I'm very glad. I feel like we just reconnected, and I'm not ready to lose you all over again."

Grayson rubbed his thumb over her knuckles. "You're stuck with me." He sat up in the bed. "Did they tell you what happened when I was shot?"

"No. Just that you were shot in the arm but were recovering in the hospital."

Oh, she was going to love this. "Remember how you had given me Anna Belle's Saint Jude necklace after lunch?"

Monique nodded.

"Well, I still had it in my pocket. When the bullet hit me, it hit the Saint Jude medallion. That deflected the bullet from entering my chest, where the doctor said it would've most likely hit my heart and killed me. Instead, it ricocheted and went through my arm."

Monique covered her mouth with her hand and tears escaped her eyes, silently rolling down her gaunt cheeks. *Mon doux Jesus!*

He reached over to the bedside table where he'd put the necklace after he'd shown Dr. Shannon. He held it up, the indentation almost dead center on the two-inch medallion. "And if it had been more expensive, like made out of gold or silver, it might not have deflected the bullet. That it was stainless steel helped save my life." He smiled. "The gift you gave me saved my life, Monique. Thank you."

"It was Anna Belle's. Even in death, her love for you shines."

He didn't know about that, but her necklace had for certain saved his life. He laid the necklace on the covers in his lap.

"I wanted to let you know that I've come to a decision," Monique announced.

"What?"

"With the money in Anna Belle's account and the value of her life insurance, that's way more than I could ever need." She stared at him. "Do you need any of it? I don't mean to pry or get in your business. I just want you to be taken care of. Anna Belle would want that."

He pressed his lips together to stop the grin. Monique probably didn't realize that most all of the money in Anna Belle's account was from the divorce settlement. "No, ma'am. Now that I have full ownership of Game's On You, I'm good."

"I didn't think you needed any money, but I wanted to make sure." She straightened. "Since it's more money than I need and you don't need any, I talked to a financial adviser at length about my options. After talking with him and reading all the information he provided, I decided I'm going to set up a scholarship fund in Anna Belle's name. Specifically for girls who show a strong financial need."

Grayson nodded. "Oh, Anna Belle would love that." As many times as she had complained over the years about having to renew her multiple scholarships to afford to stay at Louisiana State University in Baton Rouge, scholarships were important to her.

Monique sat on the edge of the chair. "The adviser said that if I set up the principal not to be touched, only the interest, on this investment, we should be able to award the first scholarship in three years. One that would cover tuition and room and board."

"I think that's perfect, Monique. It will honor Anne Belle's memory forever."

"I'm glad you feel that way, because I also have to set up a foundation to oversee the administration of the scholarship, and I need at least three people to sit on the board of the foundation. Of course I will, and I'll probably ask Laure Comeau, unless you object."

He shook his head. "No. She knew Anna Belle very well. She should be on the foundation." Grayson already knew what was coming next.

"And I'd like you to consider serving on the board." She held up a hand to ward off the argument he already was forming in his mind. "Just consider it. You and Anna Belle might've been divorced, but you knew her best back in her college days, when she was happy and living on a scholarship. You knew the fire for life she had."

Anna Belle always did have the burning to live life to the fullest. Right, wrong, or indifferent, she was always vibrant. Always moving toward the next thing.

"Just consider it. Pray on it before you make up your mind. That's all I ask."

He hesitated and then nodded. He would pray on it. He had several things he needed to pray about and would, as soon as he had more than a minute alone. "I will."

"Thank you." Monique stood. "I have to get back home now. So many final touches for the service tomorrow morning." She nodded at his arm. "You'll still be able to make it, yes?"

"Yes, ma'am. As soon as the doctor makes her rounds, I should be released."

"Good. Then I'll see you tomorrow."

"Drive safe, Monique."

She pressed a feathery kiss on his brow, then left.

For a moment, he was alone. It was quiet. Comfortable. Nice to be alone with his thoughts. Grayson grabbed the necklace, running his finger over the indentation. Had he not had this in his pocket, he most likely would have died. He wouldn't have had it in his pocket had Anna Belle not been killed. She wouldn't have been killed, wouldn't even have known Colton, had he never fell in love and married her.

The *wouldn't haves* and *what ifs* weren't random—he'd never believed that. Everything happened for a reason. There were no coincidences. That is where his faith came in—God could take any situation, no matter how awful it seemed, and turn it around for the good. Anna Belle's death, in a way, saved his life. That might make him feel guilty, but it also saved Pam's. Who was he to say what God's purpose was in all the pain and grief?

EPILOGUE

Sitting on the back pew, Grayson fixed his eyes on one of the stained glass windows. A dancing spear flickered across the sky, then the earth trembled—positives and negatives of nature colliding. St. Paul's sanctuary rattled.

The priest chanted in Latin, swinging a canister of incense over the casket. The service drew to an end. A tidal wave of grief engulfed him. He swallowed hard, then took a deep breath, fighting the bile rising in the back of his throat. Looking around the sanctuary again, he knew many weren't here to actually pay their last respects. Many were here just to be seen, friends of Monique's who had learned of her bequeath. They were in for a surprise when they learned she was using almost all of the life insurance money to start the scholarship fund in Anna Belle's name.

During the final prayer, Grayson made his way to the marble foyer and pushed open the ornately carved door. Stumbling to lean against the outside railing, he gulped fresh air, trying to clear the dizziness from his head—the tightness from his lungs. Looking back toward the church, he forced himself to breathe through his nose—taking slow, deliberate breaths. It was so hard to imagine Anna Belle lying in that deep-stained, mahogany box in the front of the sanctuary. He shook his head and took another long breath. The clean, fresh scent of rain wafted into his senses, clearing his mind.

He should've stayed inside the church, to be there for Monique, but there was something too personal about Anna Belle's funeral. His pain was too raw to share the emotions with the people there, most who wanted a handout from Monique. He smiled as he considered his mother-in-law. Anyone would be hard-pressed to pull the wool over her eyes. She was one smart cookie.

Grayson walked ahead to the adjacent cemetery, where the funeral home had already set up the tent, five rows of folding chairs, and stands of flowers. The open grave sat waiting, like a big mouth ready to devour.

No, he wouldn't allow those thoughts to hold him.

He stood behind the chairs, looking at the multiple arrangements of pink roses. They were beautiful, all ten stands, just as he'd ordered. Anna Belle would've loved them. There was so much left for her to love.

The tears he'd not shed for her choked him. The priest's words had been seared upon his heart, but no more than the scar he'd carry on his chest from her Saint Jude medallion that had saved his life. He was alive because of her. Not because of what she did or didn't do, but because of who she was, as the young woman he fell in love with.

Tears escaped the confines of his eyes, but he didn't care. He was alone—out by where Anna Belle's body would finally be at peace. He believed with all his heart that in her final frightening moments, she'd had Jesus as her Forgiver, her Comforter, her Savior.

He moved to pluck a pink rose from one of the arrangements and held it over the empty grave. As Jesus would forgive her, he needed to as well. Grayson pulled petals off the rose and let the wind drift them into the open grave. He whispered prayers and granted Anna Belle his forgiveness, not because she deserved it but because he needed to.

Grayson tossed the lonely stem into the open hole in the ground as well. Thorns with the beauty—good with the bad. He reached up and wrapped his hand around the warped and dented Saint Jude medallion he wore around his neck. He closed his eyes and pictured Anna Belle as she'd been when they'd met: young, beautiful, vivacious. . .alive. He opened his eyes, smiling. "Goodbye, Anna Belle. Thank you."

In that moment, he let go of all anger, animosity, and pain.

And it let go of him.

Sweet surrender.

Dear Reader,

Thank you for journeying to New Orleans in a web of deceit and confusion with me. Sharing a place that has such connection for me was a pure joy. South Louisiana offers such a laid-back attitude that I often miss "home." I hope you enjoyed sampling a taste of the flavor of Louisiana.

Years ago I watched the movie *The Game* with Michael Douglas and Sean Penn and was enthralled. There's just something grabbing about messing with a person's mind and life by using their own feelings and instincts against them. When this story first began forming, I wanted to use all that intrigue to mess up the *game master's* life. The end result is quite the ride!

As the characters came alive to me, I found the theme of forgiveness and acceptance coming out in the story. Some of the emotions within this story are very personal to me, and I'm honored I was able to share them with you. It is my wish that you may be touched by Grayson's faith journey as well.

I love hearing from other readers, so please connect with me. Visit my website—www.robincaroll.com—to sign up for my newsletters, contact me, and follow me on various social media sites.

Until next time. . .

Robin

DISCUSSION QUESTIONS

1. Anna Belle came from humble beginnings and hated it, doing everything she could to overcome. Have you ever had to overcome something in your past that was out of your control? How did you handle rising above it?

2. Although a Christian, Grayson struggled with forgiveness and acceptance. How do you handle forgiveness? Discuss some practical ways you can move into a forgiving mind-set.

3. Danielle allowed feelings and events in her personal life to creep into her work life. Discuss your thoughts about that. If we are the sum of our experiences and education, is it wrong to bring our personal bias into our workplaces?

4. Anna Belle was unliked by many for her actions and attitudes. Discuss the difficulties in looking past someone's unlikable qualities to see them as God does. From that perspective, is it easier to like someone?

5. Monique had no delusions of her daughter's behavior but loved her in spite of that. Discuss ways someone can reconcile affection without condoning destructive behavior.

6. Although she was Anna Belle's mother, Monique refused to allow guilt over Anna Belle's own bad choices and decisions. Have you ever felt guilty over someone else's issues? How did you handle the feeling?

7. Even though Grayson was angry with what Anna Belle had done to their marriage, he grieved for her. Do you think this is common? Why or why not?

ABOUT THE AUTHOR

"I love boxing. I love Hallmark movies. I love fishing. I love scrapbooking. Nope, I've never fit into the boxes people have wanted to put me in." **Robin Caroll** is definitely a contradiction, but one that beckons you to get to know her better. Robin's passion has always been to tell stories to entertain others and come alongside them on their faith journeys—aspects Robin weaves into each of her twenty-five-plus published novels. When she isn't writing, Robin spends quality time with her husband of nearly three decades, her three beautiful daughters and two handsome grandsons, and their character-filled pets at home. Robin gives back to the writing community by serving as executive director/conference director for American Christian Fiction Writers. Her books have been recognized in such contests as the Carol Award, Holt Medallion, Daphne du Maurier, Romantic Times Reviewer's Choice Award, Bookseller's Best, and Book of the Year. You can find out more about Robin by visiting www.robincaroll.com.